The Reader studied the upturned cards in silence. "In your past," she finally said, "The Princess of Flames—a woman, perhaps . . ."

"Woman? What sort?" Sedry demanded, grinning. The Reader tapped the card.

"The Princess of Flames, as you see, holds a naked sword. She is not like other women, content with a household, small pets, her needlework. She has her own strengths . . ."

"The Bastard, by all that's holy!" Sedry exclaimed.

Behind him, Elfrid held her breath, her sword ready at hand . . .

THE PRINCESS OF FLAMES . . .
" . . . held my interest from start to finish! Full of revenge, action, and intrigue . . . I'm looking forward to seeing more of Ru Emerson!"
—Patricia C. Wrede

THE PRINCESS OF FLAMES

RU EMERSON

ACE FANTASY BOOKS
NEW YORK

This book is an Ace Fantasy
original edition, and has never
been previously published.

THE PRINCESS OF FLAMES

An Ace Fantasy Book/published by arrangement with
the author

PRINTING HISTORY
Ace Fantasy edition / January 1986

ISBN: 0-441-67919-6

Ace Fantasy Books are published by The Berkley Publishing Group,
200 Madison Avenue, New York, New York 10016.
PRINTED IN THE UNITED STATES OF AMERICA

For Mom and Dad, who always encouraged;
For Doug, who lived to tell about it;
And for Bill Spahr, for the push that got it going again.

• PART ONE •
• THE BASTARD •

1

GENTLY. ELFRID LET the held breath out slowly as the third sphere took solidity and hung with the other two—iridescent, luminous—in the shadow of the minstrel's gallery. One of her legs was going to sleep; she shifted, warily, eyes and concentration given fully to the fitful illusion that floated at arm's length over Alster's grand ballroom. *Good. Now, then*—

Her brow furrowed. It was courting a headache, attempting defined vision, but maybe this time—

The left globe, the right one, suddenly, faintly, both held images: man, woman. A smile curved her lips, was quickly stifled as the holos dimmed. *Mother. Father.* Rolend had had the right of it, after all, and her tutor was wrong: Start with familiar images for any defined vision, *then* work back to the school exercises, once you had the feel of it.

In the central globe, a tiny flame illuminated the flanking images, the girl casting them: perhaps sixteen though thin enough to be years younger. The grey eyes, with their grave, solemn gaze, alone belied this.

An hour at this particular skill would bring on headache, too. The so-called Royal Gifts did, worked hard enough, honed as she honed hers. True, she'd probably never be called on to make official use of them. But she'd made liars of those who'd held full Royal blood, both sides, to be a requisite to the Gifts. Compared to this advanced form of the Moss-Light, Aura took no training, no effort at all, the Flame (seldom more than a weak spark, even in the strongest of Alster's line)

3

was mere child's play, and Truthing just a rather boring exercise.

The rare Healing Touch—now *that* would be a thing to develop, wouldn't it? That would show Sedry! Of course, one would have to find someone willing to suffer a bastard's touch to work it. Not impossible.

The vision was wavering again; impatiently, she pushed aside the busy mental chatter, the well-worn thoughts. Her eyes went proudly from one smiling face to the other.

"Elfrid! You—girl! Elfrid, I say!" The holos vanished, the globes that had held them gone as though pin-pricked. The central one flared briefly as the Flame bloomed, winked out. *Damn.* Elfrid sighed as Panderic's voice, age-shrilled and edged with peevish anger, echoed down the narrow hall; then she untangled her long legs and slipped from the high ledge. No good ignoring the old woman; as Nurse to all of Alster's brood from Sedry up, Panderic knew most of the hiding places in this end of the castle, would know if she were being evaded. Would be, for days, even more difficult to live with. She dragged her loose daygown, tucked for comfort into the wide, plain girdle, circumspectly down around her ankles.

"Panderic?" Elfrid's voice was low, rather husky, and she had to repeat herself as the old woman hove into sight: Panderic was more than half deaf.

"So there you are! Wearing my feet out, looking for you!" She brushed irritably at the grey hair that had slipped from her coif and was clinging damply to her ruddy forehead. "The King has asked for you, at once—though why ever he should," she added under her breath, and scowled at her square, wrinkled hands. Elfrid's hearing was excellent, but her thin, impassive face gave no notice of having caught the comment, any more than she took note of the insult of Panderic's manner, her addressing a Princess, even a nominal one, as "girl." None of the King's other children had ever been addressed so casually: It was "my Lord," "my Lady" from infancy, from Crown Prince Sedry and Princess Sigron right down through Prince Rolend. Of course, Alster had married the Lady Sigurdy, and Elfrid, as the first and only child of the King's young Margan mistress, had learned at an extremely early age to ignore Panderic's cutting, half-heard remarks, the jibes of the Crown Prince and of Prince Ascendant Hyrcan, the snubs of her half-sisters.

It was not only her siblings, and her nurse, that looked upon her so: Elfrid was keenly aware that most of those within Arolet's high walls, indeed most of Darion's nobility, regarded the King's bastard daughter with strong disapproval. Had she been a weaker person, this would have left her with a deep sense of inferiority. Somehow, Elfrid had emerged from childhood with her self-esteem reasonably intact.

This was due largely to Alster himself, for he treated this youngest child as he treated the rest of his children, though by custom, he should have removed her from court at the least—more properly, exiled her, *and* her mother. But Alster had done neither, had imperviously weathered the rumble of disapproval that circulated through the Court.

It was an action totally in character for the Peasant King, as his baronry (privately) called him. Alster openly preferred the company of his weapons-masters and grooms to that of his peers or even his legitimate children; and young Elfrid, only child of his beloved Miriellas, was the solace of his age. Like him in looks, though thin for one of his line, her eyes darker, she was like him in thought also, and it had become his habit in this last year to spend afternoon hours with her whenever possible. Together they rode, visited the kennels or the stables, fished or hunted; Elfrid held these precious hours as a shield against the unpleasantness of the household.

Moments after the old Nurse had found her, Elfrid, the dayrobe again tucked to mid-calf for ease of movement, sped down the narrow, circling staircase that led from the nurseries to the King's personal apartments. It wasn't much of a day for fishing, but they might ride. Or her father might, perhaps, take her to the barracks again: Alster, in the face of custom as applied to both females and illegitimate offspring, had permitted the Armsmaster to lesson her in the use of a bow. Gontry, fortunately, had cared no more than Alster for custom, merely for skill which he claimed to see in her, and he had praised her novice attempts at the mark, even suggesting to the King that she might do well with the sword.

Elfrid slowed so as not to slip on the smooth stone of the stairs and a rare smile touched her lips. Her fingers flexed. Of course, she wouldn't dare. Her father wouldn't, and Gontry wouldn't. But a sword, Alayya, Elorra, a sword—

She stopped abruptly before reaching the King's hall, still

hidden by a last turn in the stairs as angry voices reached her. Her father's basso rumbling, the words unclear. Another, high and threatening to crack like a boy's under stress or fury: Sedry. Darion's Crown Prince, her eldest half-brother.

". . . and I am sick of it, Father!"

"Who gave you the right to be sick of anything?" Elfrid pressed back into the cool, rough wall, frightened. Alster's quick temper was renowned, but she had never heard him in such a fury. "A fine son, a wonderful son—a tick against my bosom! No, worse, a damned young fool!"

"It is my holding, Father, you granted it to me on my twentieth birthday!"

"Your holding, Prince, yes. Under a degree of supervision you clearly still need! By the Two, what would you? To take full control of the Marches, untutored and untested? You have learned *nothing* these past years, Sedry! I cannot trust you to rule one province sensibly, let alone all of Darion after me! Young idiot, planning with the sons of my barons to our complete ruin—"

"We did no harm, Father! We did more good anyway than your carping advisors and their never-ending diplomacies would have had me do. Old men, waving their truce flags with palsied hands—bah!" He spat. "It makes me sick! The barghests have been edging into Darion since I was a boy—do you think bits of cloth on sticks will stop them?"

"A Prince of Darion," Alster snapped, "does *not* refer to the Fegez as barghests! That is for the untutored and ill becomes you, Sedry!"

Elfrid edged down a step, another; the stone dragged at the plaits she still wore despite Panderic's insistence they were childish and improper for a near-grown girl. Sedry spat again.

"They will soon have all of Darion, thanks to you and your boot-licking old cowards. Is that what you want, Father? What we did, my men and I—"

"Men?" Alster laughed harshly. "You and your 'men' may have brought war upon us, fool of a boy, carrying a raid into their mountains as you did. The Fegez are not taking that lightly and the Two only know what it will take to appease them."

"Appease? Appease the barghests?"

"Appease, I said and meant," the King overrode Sedry's wild laugh sternly. "Would you rather wipe them entirely from the lands, Prince? Go then, you and your band of puppy followers, if that is your choice! Only do not blame me for your deaths, Sedry."

"Oh, bravely spoken, Father," Sedry threw at him wildly. "You would like that, wouldn't you? To be rid of me—"

"Sedry!" Alster's bellow echoed in the narrow staircase. Elfrid dropped down abruptly, clamping her hands between her knees to stop them from shaking. Quarrels were something she knew well, particularly between her father and his volatile, high-strung eldest son and heir. But never so fierce as this! And she hated scenes, hated shouting, *hated* it! "If I wished to disinherit you—*if*, mind!—I should do so. Though I find no pleasure in a choice between you and Hyrcan. He is even more his mother's brat than you. Pah. All of you, *all* Sigurdy's spawn: sly, glib, self-serving, just as she was. I was never happier than the day I sent her to Elenes."

There was a nasty little silence, broken again by the King. Gone the rage; he spoke clearly, incisively, each word carrying the weight of a blood vow. "Watch you, first child of my loins, and heed what I say. This is the last time ever you will disobey me, or those advisors I sent to the Marches with you to aid in your education. Another incident such as this last, and you will find yourself an exile, asking sanctuary of the Beldenians—you *and* your young rowdies. A Prince is not a law unto himself, even you know that much. There is the Barons' Council, there is the Witan, both of which must be taken into consideration. I say nothing of common good, and less of common sense, for you doubtless would not understand."

"How you can say this to me!" Sedry exclaimed, clearly striving to contain his own fury. "*You*, who have bent the laws more than once to your own choosing, your whim! You shrug off the advice of your precious Council, you gainsay the Witan at will—"

"Do I? Never to Darion's harm, as you have, Sedry. And do not you dare to judge me!"

"You ask this—of Queen Sigurdy's eldest?"

"I do ask it—of the *Lady* Sigurdy's eldest, Prince! She has not been Queen since I exercised sense and sent her to serve the Two, as you very well know. Name me once that I set aside discretion and imperiled Darion." Silence. "You cannot, can you?"

"You twist my words, Father!" Sedry's voice rose, cracking with fury. "I can name once when you went against Council and Witan both, to say nothing of custom and honor; so can my Lady Mother!"

"You were a child of few years and less discretion than you have now—were that possible—when your mother left my household for the convent at Elenes—"

"Left by your order, Father—"

"Do not interrupt me! You know nothing of that matter, Sedry. You know nothing of anything!"

"I know to take her word before yours, at the least!" Sedry burst out, his speech scarcely intelligible. "To set aside your wife, to nullify that union in the face of convention and all the teachings of the Two! You—you, who openly flaunt the spawn of your last plaything to shame the sight of your honest children!"

"Silence!" the King roared. His echoing cry was cut across by the scree of metal against metal: One of them had drawn a blade. Elfrid hurled herself down the steps, halting with her heels against the last of them. Sedry stood so near she could touch him, his back to her. His tall, lean body was taut, arms stiffly before him, shieldlike. His cloak lay in a dark blue pool at his heels where it had fallen; his head was turned as though he looked sidelong, warily at the King, who faced him from mere inches away. The old man's usually pale face was suffused, his short white beard quivering with the fury that glared from light grey eyes. It needed nothing of the Aura that cast a greenish nimbus about his shoulders and hands to show how very angry he was. His dagger—an ornate, jeweled toy, touched against his son's belly.

A clatter of booted feet came down the hall as three of the King's household guard, alerted as she had been, careened full tilt into the corridor. Elfrid withdrew up the stairs, silently, unwilling to be seen. Sedry's last words burned in her ears.

"I am not armed, Father. See you that." The Crown Prince's voice was pitched to include the guard.

"I see it. Olfan!"

"Sire?" One of the guards ran forward.

"The Prince is unwell, overwrought. Escort him to his apartments, see that he remains within."

"But, Father—"

"Do as I say, Olfan." The King cut firmly across his son's

plea. "The Prince's meals will be taken to him, until further notice."

"Father—!"

"As you wish, Sire." There was sound of a brief scuffle. Footsteps receded down hall, were gone.

Silence.

"Elfrid?" Alster's voice. The girl moved down the last few steps once again. The King stood where she had last seen him, dagger hanging forgotten from his right hand. "You heard that, didn't you, child?" Elfrid nodded. "I am sorry."

"I don't care, Father." Not entirely a lie—not enough, anyway, to trigger the King's extraordinarily sharp Truthing-sense. Repetition over the past sixteen years had taken the edge from the words—a little, anyway. "Sedry always knows what to say to hurt most." The King laughed shortly, and with little humor.

"He does, doesn't he? Impatient, Sedry. He was always impatient, even as a boy. Always wanting more than he could take on." Alster made to wrap an arm around his daughter's thin shoulders, frowned at the dagger as though uncertain where he had gotten it and why, returned it with a shrug to its gemmed forearm sheath. He drew the girl close to him. "He was impatient for a bow when he should have been content with wrestling, playing with his dogs, with the other boys. When he got his bow, he wanted a sword. When he was learning control of the Moss-Light, he wanted to perfect distant sight and full Flame. Of course, he didn't want to *work* for them. Now, he should be learning statecraft, and he wants to rule all Darion." Alster sighed heavily as they started down hall. "What do you think, Elfrid—should he?"

"No." They played this game often lately: he asking questions of her as though she were his most trusted councilor, she pondering, replying with grave care.

"And why not?"

"He is too hot-tempered. He does not really care for Darion, only as another thing to be his, a possession. And—and he can only rule after you are dead, Father." The King chuckled, his good humor rapidly returning.

"Clever lass, you know your Sedry all too well, don't you? You really do mean that last, though, I hope?"

Elfrid glanced up at him. "You mean, do I speak the way Merasma does? No, Father." The King laughed aloud this

time, throwing back his head as they strode into the warm,
sunlit courtyard.

"Clever lass, indeed! I daresay Merasma has never spoken
her true mind in her entire life. Just what she thinks you want
to hear. Tiring young woman." He spat. "They're all tiring,
all Sigurdy's brats. Just like she was, nice to me for what they
can get. And they wonder why I divorced her and sent her
away. *They* thought 'women', every one of 'em, Sedry right
on down to Sigron. Well—it wasn't, damn them all! I'd like to
see any of 'em married to a creature like Sigurdy as long as I
was! They'd have found reasons for divorce soon enough—
sooner!" His arm tightened around Elfrid's shoulders. "They
aren't any of them like you, baby."

Elfrid scowled at him, exasperated. "I'm not a baby,
Father!" The King chuckled, delighted.

"There now—you see? No, no," he soothed, "of course
you're not a baby. But you're younger than Rolend by four
years. You're my youngest and last."

"I've sixteen years, nearly seventeen," Elfrid said flatly.

"Shhh, I know it, lass, I know it. Come. We have only
an hour today. What shall we do with it? Want to fish?
Hmmm?" He smiled at her, tugged at one of her long, dark
plaits. She was still scowling as she looked up, but grinned
abashedly as he winked.

"Not really, Father. The river is too low, and it's hot. There
are new puppies at the stables, and—well—and perhaps if
Gontry is about—"

"He might give you another lesson with that old bow of
Rolend's, mightn't he? Said he would, I know. Keep it to
yourself, girl, we'll avoid fuss while we can. But, we'll see.
New puppies, hmmm?" They moved across the courtyard.
High above, Prince Sedry glared out of his window; narrowed
eyes followed them tightly until they disappeared beyond the
Princess Tower.

2

THE CROWN PRINCE'S "illness" lasted for six months, and Sedry never forgave Alster for it—though he did learn the wisdom of prudence of speech and, perhaps, to keep a tighter rein on his temper. Ever brooding, he added another grudge to his walletful. Had Alster given him more than token ruling of the Eastern Marches, the Crown Prince reasoned sourly, the matter would never have arisen. But to spend half a year imprisoned for an insult to the King's last mistress and her wretched child—*that* was beyond bearing.

Elfrid, well aware of Sedry's hatred, became adept at avoiding him when he was released from his apartments, which only added fuel to his dislike: a sneaky child, what business had she in hiding from him? What was she up to, other than ingratiating herself in the King's favor?

Sedry's rancor would have greatly surprised Alster, who never held onto an anger once the reason for it was past. It never occurred to him that in this, as in so many other things, his children were very unlike him: It would never have occurred to him to have Sedry watched after his release, would have horrified him had anyone suggest he use the Truthing to invade his son's mind. After all, the boy'd been punished, he'd learned his lesson. Hadn't he?

Twelve days after the Crown Prince's "recovery," and only three before he was to return to the Marches, it fell out that Hyrcan rode in from the North to petition the King for books for his mother; Rolend, still underage for his Southern holdings, had come from Castle Orkry, twenty leagues south and

11

west, where he was completing his studies and arms training. The King had gone on an overnight hunt, taking Elfrid with him. That evening, a meeting was held in the upper chambers of the long-deserted Princess Tower.

The last rays of sunset were fading from the stone sill, and far below noises of men and animals were dimmed. A table and stools, hastily brushed free of several years' dust, stood against the opposite wall, near the door. Candles, a blackened lantern, a pitcher of wine and several cups littered the rough wooden surface. Sedry leaned back against the bare stone wall, stool balancing precariously on two legs. His eyes idly followed the movement as he swirled dark red wine in his cup; a faint ball of Moss-Light set the ripples alight. Rolend, cheek pressed against a soft, faded hanging, stared out the window across Lertondale's roofs and the northern forests beyond. Hyrcan was an immobile shadow near the closed door.

"If we're only waiting for the ladies, brother—"

"Then we shall wait, Hyrcan. They cannot go as they please, the way we can." The Moss-Light, forgotten, extinguished itself; Sedry drained his cup, dropping the stool back to four feet as he rose. His body, lean and hard despite six months indoors, displayed a fighter's easy grace as though the wearer was well aware of its beauty. His face stood out clearly in the flaring candle flame as he leaned forward, revealing sharp shadows laid by prominent cheekbones, a firm chin, clean-shaven but for the thin point of pristine, reddish beard. Pale, silvery grey eyes lay deep under dark lashes and straight brows. Dark golden hair, touched with red, falling thickly to his shoulders, was pulled back from the high, smooth brow by a severely thin band of silver. A fine-drawn, handsome face— nearly beautiful, save for the slightly petulant mouth.

"Why do we need them anyway, Sedry? Another year, they will both be wed and gone. Morelis likely to Embersy." Hyrcan's voice was rather high, a little nasal. "This does not concern them."

"It may. And if not them, then their lords, whoever they may be. Besides, Hyrcan," Sedry continued winningly, "we have had this out before, you and I. When I first confided in you. Remember?" Hyrcan smiled: He remembered. Sedry had spoken to him first. Sedry knew how to make you feel like someone. Partly his Trait, of course—Sedry's Charisma, if of a different nature and otherwise directed, was no less strong than Alster's—and no less effective even when you knew. Like his own Trait, the only part of his share of the Gifts he ever worked: Even when you *knew* that stomach-wrenching Fear was enhanced, it didn't matter.

"Merasma and Morelis are of our blood," Sedry went on. "They are as—call it greedy, if you like—for power, for wealth, as we are."

"I know all this," Hyrcan growled as he stepped away from the wall and into the wavering light. His heavy, close-set brows nearly touched. "Refill mine as well, Sedry," he added, thrusting his cup forward. Sedry poured wine for both of them, adding a dipper of water to Hyrcan's cup. Hyrcan seldom drank, and then only the weakest of wines.

Seen with the rest of his family, even with only these two brothers, Hyrcan might have been, as his mother teasingly called him, a changeling. Shorter than either brother by fully a head, though three years older than Rolend, Hyrcan had only the pale grey eyes to mark him as Alster's. Dark haired, pale skinned and freckled, his features were even more delicate than those of any of his sisters.

Hyrcan was possessed of lashes and lips the pale Morelis might well envy. Something, however, glimpsed through his almost effeminate face, kept him from being judged handsome or even pretty. Trait, yes. But also, Hyrcan was one of Darion's most skilled swordsmen, muscled superbly, though he tended already, at twenty-three, to fat. More than this, he was a dangerous man, one who would kill often, for amusement or for no great cause, without qualm.

"Attend me, brother Hyrcan," Sedry continued, raising his cup in a salute before he drank. "You know, but you do not properly piece together your knowledge. Merasma and Morelis are like us, as I have already said. Also, they are women: curious, rather bored by the household routine they follow, and not above snooping, shall we say? Enhanced by the Truthing, which they both have in full strength. If we do not include them in our plans and they learn or suspect—which they would, I have no doubt—well! I would wager you that all would be in their pale little fingers within two days of today, and they would trip over their beautifully embroidered hems to reach Father's ear with the tale."

"Oh." Hyrcan considered this, blankly. "I see." He made a wry face, drew a deep breath and drained his cup at a swallow.

"We must cater to them, flatter them," Sedry continued earnestly. He hadn't pressed his Trait so hard in months. "We must convince them that *our* course can only work to their benefit, that tale-bearing would cause them irreparable harm —though of course, we will scarcely mention this as a point when we seek their aid tonight!—that Father can serve their ends less well than we can. You see?"

Hyrcan grinned suddenly. "Once they have sided with us, they cannot tell Father what we mean to do without muddying themselves, can they?" Sedry raised one fine, dark gold brow.

"How astute of you, Hyrcan! One forgets that behind the master sword-arm there is also a noble mind." Hyrcan appeared greatly pleased by this remark. "What have *you* to say, Rolend?" Sedry turned towards the window. "You are uncommonly quiet this evening."

"Am I?" Rolend moved abruptly away from the hanging, empty cup dangling forgotten between his long fingers. "My apologies, then." Sedry laughed genially.

"Accepted, certainly, little brother. Though your silence hardly calls for pardon; it is a relief from the noise of the rest of us. But—you seem uncertain, Rolend. Have you still doubts? Give them to me, I will dispose of them for you." The young Prince of Gennen's eyes were warm as they met his oldest brother's: Sedry was still Rolend's hero, his protector, someone to look up to, though no longer the untarnished idol of his childhood.

There was a certain resemblance between these two brothers, more so than any other of Alster's children. And like Sedry, like Alster, Rolend's Individual Trait drew men and women alike to him. But unlike his father (who used his Charisma to get away with flying in the face of convention) or his brother (who used his mainly to wheedle or to bed village girls and the young wives of his March companions), the youngest Prince of Darion's Trait was leavened with a compassion rare in the present Royal line, and Rolend felt the responsibility of such a sense most keenly.

At twenty Rolend was thin for his height, showing no tendency to either Hyrcan's fat or Sedry's incipient softness. His face was angular, eyes deep-set under straight brows. The

beginnings of a moustache, palest gold like his hair, touched
his upper lip.

"No—you have convinced me, Sedry." Rolend turned
away again, eyes on the early moon that hung framed in the
window against a ruddy, cloudless sky. "It is my own conscience I must wrestle."

"Conscience?" Hyrcan laughed harshly. "Where was
Father's conscience when he divorced our mother and sent her
to Elenes? Because he was bored with her? What has conscience—?" He subsided as Sedry dropped a hand to his forearm and threw him a warning look.

"I know all that, Hyrcan," Rolend replied impatiently. "It
is different for you. I'm sorry for Mother, of course—a divorce, with all that implies; retirement in a convent—but she
left when I was still a baby, and I have never seen her since.
How could I feel the way you do? And I cannot believe that
is worth the deposing of a King—no, Hyrcan, do not try to
frighten me in silence!" he snapped, meeting the Prince
Ascendant's glare with a level, cold look of his own. Hyrcan's
Aura flared a fitful muddy red and died. "I cannot believe
anything grants the worth of our actions!"

"If Mother were all—and I agree with you, Hyrcan, that it
is sufficient reason—you know that is not my only reason,"
Sedry put in quietly. His hand tightened briefly on his
brother's arm, and as Hyrcan showed no signs of renewed
anger, let it drop.

"I know," Rolend sighed. He raised his cup, scowled
briefly into its dry interior and stepped to the table. "You
have told me, often enough, Sedry. No," he added, filling his
cup and drinking it off, "I mean no criticism. Perhaps you are
even right," he went on somberly, more to himself than his
brothers. "Perhaps it *is* wrong for the Baronry to be stripped
of rights they have long had, particularly when we must count
on them for armsmen against Marga or against the Fegez. Or
Genneldry, though the truces should keep Genneldry from our
necks. I know, I know; the lands Father returned to them are
another reason." He sighed again, shrugging as an embarrassed smile tugged at his lips. He bit it back. "And—and
Elfrid. Truly, Sedry, you make too much of the child. What
can Father do, save enjoy her company? She's—cradle curst."

"How daintily you phrase it!" Sedry mocked. Rolend
slammed his cup to the table.

"All right, then, she's bastard! And female, brother! And of Darion! Under such a treble burden, there is nothing Father can do to elevate her! Were Father King of Marga instead of Darion, she might have full rights, Father might have had the woman declared morganatic, the child legitimate. Here, she continues to *live* solely because of Father's good graces. He cannot give her the throne, what do you want?"

"One would almost think you liked the creature, Rolend," Sedry remarked dryly. He scowled. "I have no idea what Father intends, but you know full well what he thinks of custom! Is it not enough that he keeps her in the household? He might have sent her back to her mother's kin in Marga. He might, better yet, have consigned her to the coif of the Two, as he did Sigron when she refused to marry the man he chose for her. By the Two, a sensible man would have had her smothered in her cradle!"

"He is right, Rolend." Morelis's sharp voice carried across the chamber, even though she pitched it low. She and her twin, Merasma, had entered unnoticed. "I am sorry to be late, Sedry. Even with Panderic's aid, we had to actually walk all the way to chapel and slip out the back during services. Some of our women are not to be trusted."

"And old Panderic is?" Hyrcan demanded.

Morelis fastened her slightly protruding, pale-lashed eyes on her younger brother. "Of all people, you ask this? Panderic protects all of us, but she would martyr herself for you, Hyrcan. I would trust her before you, certainly!" Her chin came belligerently up. Merasma moved away from them in her unobtrusive, effacing way.

"Sedry is right," Morelis continued flatly. "It is an insult to all of us here—to *me*!—that Father's mistresses should have been housed with us here! When this last woman finally died—"

"—for which the Two and all the saints be honored—"

"Very amusing, Sedry," Merasma snorted. "They might have let her die barren. Thereafter, not only must he keep that wretched child in the apartments, he must make a favorite of her." She flung her hands wide. "I cannot bear it!"

"You need not, much longer," Hyrcan grumbled. "What of the rest of us?"

"And how often, *dear* brother," Morelis demanded on a

rising note, "have you been constrained to the household apartments with the creature? You are a man, free to come and go as you please. To ride to the hunt—to return, for that matter, to your own holdings, while Meras and I—"

"Call them holdings, if you will," Hyrcan replied stiffly. He and the outspoken Morelis—she and Merasma were barely a year his senior—had never liked each other. "It is Father's poor joke, that. You merely add to it. Ersonbol of South Embersy will probably claim you within the year, anyway. So what does it matter to you?"

"If he is not instead offered Elfrid," Morelis snapped. Sedry and Hyrcan both stared at her. "He looks upon the unmarried royalty these days," she continued, enunciating distinctly and carefully, as though to the halt-brained, "with an eye to making them contenders for three instead of two. Or so he has told *us*."

"He dare not!"

"No, Sedry?" Morelis laughed sourly. "Would Ersonbol care greatly that his bride was bastard, provided she was Alster's and therefore a link with the throne of Darion?"

"A link separated from Sedry so far as to be worthless," Roland protested unhappily. He found Hyrcan easier to stand against than the twins. "There are six of us, counting Sigron as we must, even though she's female and under vows, between Elfrid and any right to the throne. All he can give her is a dower—"

"Which comes from my portion and Merasma's, little brother. But it is the *idea* of the thing," Morelis went on angrily. "To be set in competition with—with—"

"Enough!" Sedry slammed both hands flat on the table. The women jumped; Hyrcan laughed uncertainly. "We dare not stay here long, even though Father is away. And the Two know when we may all be together again, without chance of suspicion. Time is short. I do not wish to stare for months on end at my apartment walls again. Meras—Morelis—are you for me?"

Morelis took the seat Roland held for her before bringing her chin up to gaze long and hard at her brother. "You must have believed I would be," she said finally, "or I would not have learned of this meeting at all, would I, Sedry? You would never have taken the chance."

"Perhaps not. You, sister, must in turn trust to what I have offered you, or, again, you would not be here—looking, as you do, to the main chance."

"As Alster's child, I see no other way to forward myself, do you? No. The risks are properly balanced, Sedry. Or I would not be here. Nor, at this moment," she added with deadly sweetness, "would you, brother." Sedry smiled genially.

"How well we understand each other, Morelis. The snake in the hawk's claw—but the snake still has fangs." He turned in his chair. "Merasma, my dear. Are you of Morelis's mind in this?"

Merasma shrugged; Aura flickered bluishly across her shoulders in her discomfort at the sudden attention. As quiet as her twin was outspoken, Merasma seldom voiced her own mind, preferring to reply with what the questioner wished to hear. Here: "I do not care for what Father has done of recent. I dislike the girl."

"As definite," Sedry replied sourly, "as one might hope for from you." But he smiled engagingly as Merasma met his eyes expressionlessly.

"Was that a joke, Sedry? Your humor has ever eluded me." She turned away. "It does not matter. We are here, both of us. What plans have you, and how do we aid them? Remember that Morelis and I cannot stay long, we are expected soon after chapel."

"You are right, of course. My apologies, sister." Sedry hitched up one handsomely trousered leg to sit on the edge of the table. Rolend moved back into the shadows by the window as Hyrcan snaked a stool under him. "Hyrcan and I have reached our majority, and Rolend is not far behind. But Father still guides our least move as though we were still children. He tolerates no initiative of any sort—well, look what happened when my men and I drove the Fegez back over the eastern border! We might have had them at our throats next, you all know how well we dare trust the barghests!"

"We know. Time," Morelis reminded him sharply, "is short. Father does not delegate, though he should. Continue."

"He has done *nothing*," Sedry continued, "save to maintain Darion as our grandfather gave her to him." A movement near the window brought his head up. "All right, Rolend. The merchant fleet was Father's idea, and a good one. I grant you that. Lertondale is a larger trade center than any city in Marga or Genneldry, and Carlsport has trebled in size the past thirty years.

"But that Darion remains intact at all is not due to Father. He could have held the Mantran provinces in the South, particularly if he had brought in mercenaries from Belden, as I advised. The barghests will come down upon us in numbers, next winter if not this, but he will not allow arms against them. He wants peaceful neighbors, he says. He prefers," Sedry added nastily, "to play at tig with his newest toy."

"Or the hunt," Merasma put in, loudly and unexpectedly. She stared at her elder brother defiantly. "I suppose you are all aware that the creature has a bow? And uses it?" Sedry stared at her blankly.

"He would never dare—no, of course he would! He flaunts the very traditions, the laws! It is a wonder to me the commons cling to him so, to say nothing of the merchants. One would think a divorce, followed by a flock of mistresses—"

"It was only three mistresses, to be fair about it," Rolend reminded him mildly. "And the commons and merchants are unlikely to desert him: Father has made the latter wonderfully rich and has taken the weight of the baronry from the necks of the former. Of course they adore him. Even without the Trait, they would adore him."

"But a bow!" Sedry continued softly, almost to himself. "Weapons are forbidden women—"

"A custom seldom adhered to, Sedry, as you well know," Rolend cut in. "Half your Marcher Barons' wives can wield bow as well as their husbands. And what of the Lady Aldion, leading the charge against the Fegez two years ago, horseback and in full mail?"

Sedry waved the Lady Aldion aside impatiently. "Her bastardy would in any event prohibit weapons," he said flatly. "Show me the exception anywhere in Darion to *that*, brother!" Rolend shrugged, turned back to the window.

"The Barons grumble, and with cause," Hyrcan put in abruptly.

"Of course they do," the Crown Prince said, bringing himself resolutely back to the matter at hand. "Who would have a man with the manner and mien of a common peasant for his King? If that were all—but it is not all, it is far from all; last year Father and his precious Witan took their right of setting the taxes on their own fiefs. And that is only the most recent of the insults heaped upon them. The King openly supports the serfs against their rightful lords! A Baron can no longer compel his peasants to work the fields, to remain tied to their natal villages, cannot command their herds—''

"*Their* herds, by the Two," Hyrcan mumbled to himself.

"Gods, the peasants adore him, but what of that?" Sedry finished.

"That is their business," Merasma said primly. "It is in poor taste for a Prince to seek the adulation of the commons, it lowers him."

"We are of your mind, Sister, remember?" Morelis replied dryly. "It is *Father* we need convince." Merasma flashed her a dark look.

"He is too old for lessoning." Sedry leaped to his feet, prowled the chamber restlessly. "It is not as though our Grandsire did not attempt the task. No—no, he is hopeless. For Darion's sake, he must step aside."

"He will not, Sedry." Hyrcan stared gloomily at his hands.

"Of course he will not! I never had hope of that—at least, I lost hope when he gave me the Marches to rule and then gave me five old men to see that I made no move, no law, that might not have been his own." Sedry turned neatly on one heel to stride back to the table and leaned on it to gaze at his siblings in turn. "Darion will be nothing at all, do I wait for him to die and leave her to me. She will be part of Genneldry or Marga, or overrun by barghests. That is, if he does not disown me in one of his increasingly frequent peevish rages." His eyes went again from one to another of them. "He is capable of that, you know. Readily. In which case, Hyrcan, he might disown you as well, and drop the mantle on young Rolend's shoulders." He smiled over his arm at the youngest, who glanced uneasily away from the window. "As the lesser of all possible evils," Sedry added, with a disarming grin, which brought a brief smile to Rolend's lips.

"He does not care for any of us, does he?" Morelis's lips were set in a thin line. "Meras and I—he leaves us to our own devices for months at a time, occasionally deigning to see us brought to some state meal, to put us on display for visiting princes. Sigron—buried alive like Mother within Elenes, and for what? For refusing to wed old Creav of Genneldry—sixty years old and half mad! And—''

"That was not such a poor bargain," Sedry remarked pointedly. "Had Sigron swallowed her temper and married the old pig, she'd be Queen and Regent for a young prince. Just like Queen Tevella is now. However," he continued blandly, "my apologies. You were saying?" Morelis glared at him, a corner of her mouth twitching.

"He scarcely likes you, either, Sedry," she snapped finally. "And as for you, Brother," she added, glancing only briefly at the Prince Ascendant.

"Yes?" Hyrcan demanded, his voice dangerously, deceptively soft. Morelis offered him a nasty little smile.

"Court tales have it Father has himself purified by the priests whenever your shadow touches him . . ."

"Sister—"

"Enough, damn it!" Sedry snapped. Morelis directed another evil smile at her younger brother and turned away. "No. Father does not like us much. Rolend, a little. He cares enough for the one who hunts with him tonight, though. Her own bow, you say, Meras? The Baronry will be furious indeed when they hear of it! Ah, well.

"Notwithstanding. Father must deal with *us*, for the Bastard alone is of no practical value to him, and he is practical when he must be. Our two fair sisters are excellent trading tokens for Darion—"

"How kind of you to say so!" Merasma burst out in a rare show of anger. Sedry turned a hand, raising his shoulder in the merest of shrugs.

"Nevertheless, true. The same as it is for Belladessa of North Embersy, who may become my Lady if Father and his old men seal the bargain. It is a fact of life for our kind, and you know it full well, Merasma. A Princess is traded for gold, prestige, peace—or she brings them with her. That you are of Darion, the prestige is yours. Belladessa, unlike you, will give thanks daily if she is given to wed the heir to Darion's throne, instead of the fourth son of Marga's Jochim." Merasma bit back a further outburst behind thinned lips, moved away to stare out the window.

"No," Sedry continued, "Father may not like any of us, but he must deal with us. He cannot disown all of us. A son, and a legitimate one, must succeed him. But this is beside the point. In another year, two at most, Father will be unable to disown anyone. I would only add," Sedry continued, with a fine show of diffidence, "that neither of you, my sisters, will lose by siding with me if my plans bear fruit before you are—ah—bestowed.''

"Of course not," Morelis replied sharply, cutting off with a look whatever reply Merasma intended. "We are also your pawns, Sedry, to be well set on the gaming board. How certain are you of your strength?"

Sedry shrugged. "How certain is anything? The Marcher Barons will surely be one and all for me, since Father does nothing to protect them from the barghests. Many of the younger Barons and younger sons number themselves mine already. The Southerners still see the border mountains as theirs. And Father has never cared overmuch for what any of his lords think. He rides over them as our Grandsire rode over the peasants. Unlike the commons, however, the Baronry may snap at the hand that chastises it, and may draw blood." Rolend stirred uneasily. Merasma moved away from the window.

"We should—not talk of blood," she said. Sedry laughed.

"Gods but you *are* delicate, dear Merasma! And yet—if you could slide a dagger between Elfrid's small ribs, undetected, would you be so dainty, I wonder? No," he forestalled her angry reply with a raised hand, "that would never be your way, would it, Meras? Poison, perhaps? An accident—"

"What do you take me for?" Merasma hissed, gazing up at him with cold fury in her pale eyes.

"Why, one such as myself, dearest Merasma," Sedry murmured. The two of them might have been alone in the darkened chamber. "One who knows the value of a calculated risk. One whose Trait is a sensible one: How useful, dear sister, to be unseen, unnoticed, merely because you wish to! One skilled in the Fire, as much as any of us are, an opportunist, one who believes in chance—in, perhaps, the form of a young woman standing alone at the top of the curved inner stairs. Or sitting alone on a narrow ledge above the minstrels' loft. Think: A sudden appearance could startle a young girl lost in thought, and coupled with a spark of—"

"No!" Rolend's voice was deep, harsh. "We have had this out before, you and I, Sedry. There will be no accident to Elfrid, now *or* when you succeed. No spilling of Father's blood, and that includes that girl's!" He drew level with his eldest brother, met his gaze levelly and unafraid. "I will not tolerate it."

"*You* will not tolerate—?"

"I have said so, Brother!" Rolend overrode him furiously. Hyrcan stared at his youngest brother in slack-mouthed astonishment. "It is not right, to begin with—no, hear me out! All of you! It is wrong, and against all the teachings of the Two. But more to the point, Sedry, do you really think you could harm Elfrid now without Father knowing you behind it? He has never, ever, used Truthing against any of us—you know that, all of you! Do you doubt he'd use it under such circumstances?" Silence. "And he'd know, with or without it, no matter how carefully you planned."

Silence.

"Think! You know Father's affection for her! If Elfrid fell from the nursery window tonight, one of us would be blamed for it! If she ate poorly cooked fish and fell ill, you would be halfway to Genneldry this time tomorrow, Sedry, for having poisoned her." Rolend paused. The silence had become uncomfortable. "Put aside all thought of accident, Sedry. I would guard that child's life more lovingly than I cared for my own, were I you."

Sedry stared at the gathering dark for several long minutes. The only sound was the rustle of Merasma's robes against the bare floor. Finally, he nodded, slowly. "You are right, of course. And I see why Father thinks so highly of you, Rolend." The boy smiled briefly; his eyes, hidden in shadow, were still hard. "You think, when the rest of us act. You reason, and I see the patterns of my actions often only later. Besides," he continued thoughtfully, "*I* will need do nothing to the girl, if she continues this unnatural interest in arms. The commons might stand for it, the nobles never will."

"Whatever they do will come to your accounting, Sedry," Rolend said quietly, "even if Father allowed her a sword." Hyrcan laughed.

"He'd never dare!"

"No? If she wished it, he might well. And Elfrid is capable of such a thing, Hyrcan."

"Well, it would not surprise me," Morelis remarked spitefully. "The child is positively mannish in most respects."

"Not all," Merasma put in. Her eyes were bright with malice. "*You* saw her making sheep's eyes at that young Marcher last Harvest Fest—"

"Oh, well," Morelis said. "That."

"Well, she did,"

"Yes, but *you* saw him as well as I did, sister." Morelis laughed briefly. "All bone and March-cut hair—" She sobered. "Unimportant, in any event. Continue, Brother, we're nearly out of time."

"Well—" Sedry paused, put his sisters' gossip firmly aside. *Gods*, but women led petty lives! "It will not matter what Father intends, unless he moves quickly. Which he will not, knowing Father. And consider, Sisters, that a marriage to Embersy's heir would take his precious Bastard from his side for good. He wouldn't want that, would he?"

"Keep in mind what I have said," Rolend put in. "Any harm to Elfrid will be traced back to us. And I will withdraw, here and now, any aid I can obtain from the South if there is to be harm to Father—or Elfrid—later. I swear that."

"I will keep it most firmly in mind," Sedry assured him. "No, I mean that, Rolend. But it is growing late, we had better not test the Gods' patience this night."

"Morelis and I must return through the chapel, that means an additional distance for us," Merasma said. "And I think we know enough for one night." She rose abruptly. "Come, Sister." Sedry bowed gravely, prettily, over the outstretched hands in turn, held the door for them as Merasma summoned a faint ball of Moss-Light and they silently followed it down the darkened, deserted hallway.

"How much longer?" Hyrcan demanded abruptly. "Mother has not been well this past year, another winter in Elenes may kill her."

"Mmmm? Oh—Hyrcan, you know I will strike as soon as the Baronry is behind me." Sedry pushed the door partway closed and moved back to the table. "You have begun to sound out your own friends, haven't you? Good. Very good. But the signs are not yet favorable—"

"Hah." Hyrcan eyed his older brother sourly. "Superstition, Sedry! You put faith in things forbidden! Cards, bowls of water, old women to read meaning into the ripples—this is all against the ways of the Two," he finished, somewhat priggishly.

Sedry laughed quietly. "Now, Hyrcan. I grant you the priests prate against fortune tellers. But it is not as though I used diviners, such as the barghests do, reading the future from the guts of a dead sheep!'' He gazed dreamily out the window. ''But the paths of the stars—there is something to what they say of that, Hyrcan! I have found that out more than once. You know, it is truly amazing what this woman told me recently, and with no more knowledge than the hour of my birthing! She—'' he glanced at his brother, sighed. ''Well, never mind.''

''You do intend to free Mother at once?'' Hyrcan had followed his own laborious thought, ignoring Sedry's passion with ease of long practice. ''I know you, Sedry. It does not bother you that Mother is a prisoner in that place, does it? I mean,'' he amended, embarrassed, ''it is a house of the Two, of course, and holy. But so poor! The chambers are drafty, the food poorly cooked, there are no diversions—That she should be there, that she should—''

''I know, Hyrcan.'' Sedry wrapped an arm around the Prince Ascendant's heavy shoulders. ''I feel as you do, believe me, Brother. I cannot show it as you do, that is all. You know that. Trust me, my brother. My first act as King will be to send you to Elenes, to bring her home.'' He smiled. ''There. Are you satisfied?'' Hyrcan nodded slowly.

Sedry raised his voice. ''Prince of Gennen, have I your pledge?'' Roland sighed faintly, closed his eyes. Nodded.

''My word on it, Sedry.''

''I will not forget this, Roland. Leave now, youngling. Take the back stairs.'' Roland moved silently across the chamber, slipped through the door and was gone. Sedry's hands remained lightly on Hyrcan's shoulders. ''I vow to you, Brother, that Mother is high in my thoughts. A day never goes by but I feel the insult to our blood.''

''But it is the insult to you, not to her, that you feel,'' Hyrcan replied with the sudden, rare shrewdness that on disconcerting occasion reminded family and companions he was not quite as blank of thought as he appeared. He shrugged then, grinning foolishly. Like Roland, Hyrcan had never wholly lost his hero worship of this dashing elder brother, even though he knew Sedry's flaws as well as his own. Better, since Hyrcan was not given to introspection. ''The result is all that matters, Sedry.''

''Good. I need your aid, Hyrcan. Father is a dangerous foe, we must be cautious, you and I.'' His hands dropped away, conjured up a ball of Moss-Light, which he tossed back and forth. "I return East within the week. We will not dare use the post, since we never have before. Nothing unusual, nothing unexpected; remember that!"

"But if I need to send you a message, Sedry."

"Message birds, perhaps. I have played at them, this past year, several are trained between my holdings and those of Eavon and Gorst. It would be simple to train others between Eavon's lands and the southernmost of yours, Hyrcan."

"You trust old Eavon? He is a close friend of Father's, Sedry!"

"I know it. But he has five sons, and his youngest, Baldy-ron, eats from my hand." His sisters' gossip struck him: all bone and March-cut hair—Gods, could it be? His idealistic young follower and the Bastard? He banished the thought hastily, lest he laugh aloud and Hyrcan take offense. "I have promised him lands of his own, he would never get them otherwise. I will see that a present of birds and a trainer for them are sent to you in the near future; you must remember, should any ask, that we spoke of them, and I promised them to you."

"I will."

"Good. Come, Brother." He and Hyrcan clasped arms and the Prince Ascendant moved into the dark hall with the cat's grace that sat so oddly on his short-legged bulk. Sedry stared after him somberly for some time, finally roused himself to pinch out the guttering candles and seek his own chambers.

3

NINE DAYS AFTER the clandestine meeting, Sedry departed for his Eastern holdings and, to all appearances, thereafter settled down. There were no more wild parties or hunts, no raids on neighboring Fegez villages or the herds and fields of the commons. The Prince spent a good deal of his time lessoning—statescraft as much as training in his personal Gifts—and he listened with grave and correct attendance to his father's marshals, taking advice, counsel and even outright orders with a show of quiet good grace.

A year went by—a second. Even Sedry's strongest detractors were forced to admit that a wondrous change had come over him, and Alster, only too pleased to believe that his eldest had finally come to his senses, was delighted. During the Crown Prince's visit to Castle Arolet for MidWinter—where he gave both Witan and Barons' Council the same solemn attention—Alster once again publicly named him heir.

Hyrcan remained, for the most part, alone in the North with Alster's advisors (his personal tutor in the Royal Gifts, intimidated by Hyrcan's all-too-exceptional grasp of his Trait and his indifference to the rest of the family Magic, had long since given up and returned to his monastery). The Prince Ascendant rode frequently to visit his mother, as he always had, in open defiance of his father's dictum that the Lady Sigurdy remain in strict confinement, but otherwise contrived to keep in the King's favor.

Hyrcan's new hobby of message birds was deemed by his advisors to take more of his time than seemly, but since Sedry had been reinstituted in Alster's favor, he was not rebuked for it. Such hobbies likely would have to satisfy Hyrcan, unless Sedry found other tasks for him.

Rolend attained his majority and was given both the Southern holding of Gennen and a flock of advisors to aid him in its maintenance. The youngest Prince spent nearly as much time at Arolet as at Mergriv, but he was otherwise acquiescent to his father's wishes, and Alster was heard to remark on frequent occasion that Sigurdy had not marked them all.

Two years wrought a great change in the King's youngest: from a thin, overly solemn child, Elfrid had grown at eighteen into a tall, slender woman, her body hard-muscled, nearly lacking in feminine curve. She topped her half-brothers, even the King, by several fingers. Her face, though scarcely beautiful, was striking: Dark grey eyes were deep set in a long, fine-boned oval as deeply tanned as any armsman's. A spray of freckles crossed the bridge of her nose. The somewhat wide mouth seldom creased in a smile, and she had become, if possible, even more retiring. Elfrid took little pleasure in the pursuits of the women's chambers, preferring riding, fishing and hunting. She had become, in two years, deadly with a bow, swift and skilled with sword.

She no longer attempted to hide her interests, as she had at the beginning. Impossible in any event: her first crossings with the lads Gontry lined up against her were the subject of conversation in every ale-house and market stall across Lertondale within the hour. Had the girl in question been other than Elfrid, the reaction would have been shock and strong disapproval. She, however, was looked upon tolerantly by the town folk as somewhat of an oddity and—like her father—not held to convention. Since it was Elfrid, it was merely another facet of her singularity, and the commons and merchants rather admired her for it.

The nobility was scandalized, as much for the trousers she wore on the fighting floor as for her sex and birth. Sedry, virtuously aware that *he* had not spilled the tale, lost no time in playing upon offended sensibilities; continuing, in fact, as he had since first riding from Arolet, to build support against the time he would take Darion for his own.

The actual force that rode with him needed be no more than five hundred since he planned to attack Arolet. A calculated gamble, this: The King's second home, Orkry, stood well to the South, in the field of the greatest discontent. Lertondale was, as it always had been, the King's city. But Arolet was riddled with ancient escape tunnels and back passages, most of which were known to very few. By means of these, Sedry intended to take the King and his household by surprise. Orkry could be fortified against him, and Sedry intended to waste no time, no advantage, in a siege. Let the folk of Darion see him as firmly settled on the throne, and the surprise would disarm any support the old man might otherwise be able to muster. As for the City—let the merchants and commons dare attack him on Alster's behalf, and they would see at once what sort of man ruled them!

The main body of Sedry's following would have to be scattered, ensuring that no aid would come to the King. Under Hyrcan's picked man, two thousand would stay in the North, where Sedry was uncertain of the quality of his support. The release of the Queen Mother should aid him there, but still—

To the East—an inordinate number of the elder Marcher Barons showed no sign of loss of loyalty to the old King. Surprising, really, since he lacked nothing of following among the younger Marchers and the scores of unlanded sons. The commons in the Marches had been restless of late, but that was of no consequence: War with the barghests would keep them occupied.

Lertondale would have to be heavily invested, of course: Sedry intended to take no chances there. The South: Strange, how the peasantry there loved his father, the nobles certainly did not! Sedry had already arranged for Beldenian mercenaries, for in the South there might be real fighting. And Genneldry might see the civil strife as its chance to annex more of Darion's borders.

Hyrcan and Rolend, of course, would be with him when he took Arolet: A show of family solidarity would be an additional sword on his side. Hyrcan had refused to be left in the North in any event, and Sedry thought Rolend—still suffering misgivings, though he had sworn a large company to his banner—would be invaluable in keeping the Prince Ascendant in line. Rolend, in any event, was one of the few men in Sedry's camp who genuinely was unafraid of Hyrcan, unaffected (or so it seemed) by Hyrcan's Trait. Hyrcan, carried away, could ruin everything. Rolend could control him, if anyone could.

Three days before the Threshing Fest, two years after

Sedry's six-month "illness," five hundred mail-clad, armed men gathered in the Hunter's Glade four leagues southwest of Lertondale, from there moving through the dusk in bands of ten or twelve working silently towards the ancient bolt-hole that led to the banquet hall deep within Alster's ancient home.

4

THE CRASH ECHOED down the halls, shaking the floor. It brought the girl instantly awake but it took several moments for her to realize what must have caused it: The inner gates had been torn from their old hinges, had fallen into the tiled entry directly below her windows. Harsh cries from without seemed to confirm this. She leaped from her bed, flinging the light nightrobe across the room. A wisp of Moss-Light to locate the precious new shirt and breeches she had dropped only a few hours before—there. She left the greenish light hovering overhead as she dressed, one ear attuned to the shouts in the courtyard. The mail shirt: no, leave it. Too recent a thing for familiarity—moreso than the breeches and shirt the King had finally, reluctantly permitted her for arms-training—it would slow her, hinder more than it helped. She snatched the serviceable sword belt, the loose dagger from the table and sped barefoot to the King's apartments.

Sedry has done this: She knew beyond doubt, even before the men appeared at the end of the hall, racing towards the King's personal guard. All of them wore the Crown Prince's pale blue and white. Elfrid threw herself forward, crying out encouragement, rousing the guard to action. One of Sedry's following flung himself at her, laughing, and died with the mocking smile on his lips.

Footsteps echoing in an enclosed space brought her sharply around: more men, coming down the inner spiral. Some were clad in the colors of the Crown Prince, some in the red and yellow of the Prince Ascendant. The arms of all three brothers fluttered from the staff borne in their midst. *Rolend, in league with Sedry? Gods, no*. Rolend? It didn't bear thinking about.

She tore her mind free as the invaders bore down on the King, who had emerged from his bedchamber and stood, bewildered and in his nightrobes, sword in hand.

Alster was not so fuddled as to drop his guard, however, and two of his opponents were badly blooded before he himself fell, struck on the head with the standard. The standard bearer died a breath later as Elfrid's blade sank into his throat. The King's guard came to her aid, then, and those who were able fled towards the main gate. The guard followed. The girl was left with the fallen King, the dead and the dying.

For a moment she gazed expressionlessly down at the dead standard bearer; she bent, then, dragged him across the hall, let him fall onto one of his fellows. The standard clattered after. She moved back, then, swiftly, to kneel by the King, a hand against his brow, the other resting against the hurried pulse in his throat. *I've killed*. The thought was a vague wonder but at the moment meant nothing. The old man's eyes opened then, claiming her full attention. He did not seem, at first, to see her.

"Father?"

"Elfrid. My—my sons." His voice was unsteady. He pulled away from her with an effort, to gaze at the bodies sprawled against the opposite wall, at the standard, tilted at a crazy angle, its colors clearly visible. "I believed Sedry, I trusted, I—." His eyes closed. "Not all my sons!" he cried out wildly and fell back against his daughter. She steadied herself, drew a deep breath. Not dead, he'd fainted. A little blood trickled down his brow, matting his white hair. Violence against an old man, but that was not his real hurt.

Smoke drifted down the corridor. A woman's shriek rose above the noise of battle, was abruptly cut off.

Surely they had not fired the castle! But the smoke lessened, was gone. *No. No, they will not burn us out, they need not*. She sat back on her heels: fighting all around, but none of it coming nearer. *No simple assassination, this. Sedry has come upon us with full strength, to wrest Darion from the King*. And: *Poor Father. He thought the boar had drawn its tusks*.

She considered moving the old man to his bedchamber, defending him from the door. No, no good. He was heavy, she might drag him inside but would never be able, alone, to get him into bed. And Sedry knew the back ways of Arolet as well as she did herself. There were two passages in that room besides the normal one. Sedry would know of them. To move him elsewhere? Where? To that—no, also. Too late. All right, then.

She set her lips, let a held breath out slowly, brought the long, thin dagger from her belt and laid it on the floor next to her sword, near to her knee. She pressed the King as close against the wall as possible, partially under the heavy hangings, and turned back to wait.

It could not have been as long as it seemed. More smoke, gone as quickly as it came. Cries and the clash of weapons, close but fading towards the apartments where Merasma and Morelis—still unwed, still unpromised—yet lived. From the other direction, then, heavy fighting. Drawing close.

Elfrid reluctantly put her father's fingers aside, scooped her blades into long, steady hands. Figures cut through the gloom, materializing as they came into the light. They stopped as one man when they saw her standing alone in the midst of the corridor, still men and the fallen standard behind her.

"You!" Hyrcan stepped forward, a chopping motion of his hand ordering the seven with him to stay put. His teeth gleamed in a wolfish grin as he took in the spill of pale robes behind her and to her right. "You and Father in one place. I have the luck!" Elfrid brought her sword up.

"Have you, Hyrcan? Touch him on your peril!"

Hyrcan laughed, but his eyes remained ugly. His Aura, still a seldom thing, cast a dark ruddy glow about his shoulders, and hands; his Trait radiated Fear about him on all sides. "Sedry told me the old fool had done it. A knight's arms for a bastard!" There was a faint, protesting movement behind him. He spoke over his shoulder. "The first of ye to move is a dead man!" He spat. "Speak to *me* of dares, bastard, having dared that!" He closed the distance between them with a cat's bound, tapping at her long blade with his own. "Protect him, then—if you can!"

Elfrid swallowed fear. Her face, long since trained to lack expression, remained impassive. She stepped lightly back and to the side, remaining between her half brother and their fallen father, sword at the ready. Her left hand, clutching the dagger, dropped away to the side.

Gesture: hopeless, fool's gesture. She knew it. A year and a half of sword under old Gontry was nothing, not against Hyrcan's ten or more years. Her blade, forged for her weight and her arm, was too narrow, too light, to beat his down. Her arms, strong from constant workout, were still nothing compared to his. And he had killed before, for pleasure, in need—and she?

Fatalist, she chided herself grimly, undercutting a slashing attack and almost breaking through his guard. *He lumbers like an old bear, he is no longer fresh—and he is drunk on his treachery.* She brought her chin up, then, forcing a cool smile to counter Hyrcan's grin.

So intense was her concentration that she was barely aware of the laughter among Hyrcan's following as two of the men set wagers against her. The sudden, uncomfortable, silence as another of their number—the twined serpents of his arms dark shadows against the pale green tabard—harshly shut them up.

Baldyron? She would have known him anywhere, under any circumstances (*Fool!*) let alone these. Eavon's son, and at bloody Hyrcan's back?

Fear wrenched her stomach, threatened to drown her. "Damn you, Hyrcan," she hissed. "Do you think you can use that on *me*?" Hyrcan grinned evily. "Do you really want," she added, her voice a low, gentle sound at strong variance with the cold hate in her dark eyes, "to bring the family skills into this?" The tip of her blade crackled; sparks flew. Hyrcan paled. Shook his head. "Afraid," she could not refrain from adding, maliciously, "you cannot beat me otherwise?"

The Prince Ascendant leaped forward with a wild cry; somehow, she clung to her sword, parried his furious blows.

That she held out at all was as much a tribute to her skill and courage as to Gontry's teaching, but she dared not move from the King and that worked against her. Her sword arm was beginning to ache, hand and shoulder were both numb from the interception of an overhand blow that would have separated head from shoulders. Her legs felt leaden. An echoing cry filtered through to her dazed mind: Sedry. Sedry comes!

Hyrcan feinted, lunged suddenly, his point slicing through her shirt, across her ribs. She cried out, stumbled, but as the Prince Ascendant moved forward, sword upraised to kill, she thrust with her left hand, sheathing her dagger in his belly. He stared at her, dumbly, tottered back a step, fell. Elfrid, dizzy and ill with the pain that flared from her side, dropped heavily

to one knee, managing by sheer will to hold her position between Hyrcan's men and the King. Grey eyes moved from one
to another of them, avoiding the dark figure clad in the arms
of the House of Eavon. *Gods, how could he? Hyrcan!*
"Touch the King if you dare. Any of you." No one moved.

Hyrcan groaned then. One of those in his red and yellow
moved forward, probed the Prince's wound with gentle
fingers, brought the large, shaggy head up to rest on his knee.
"If he dies, King's pet," he spat.

"If he dies, Hyrcan's minion, Rolend is Prince Ascendant,"
Elfrid broke in coldly. Dark hair clung to her brow. "You
can do nothing to me worse than what Sedry has already
planned." There was no answer to that. One or two of the
men seemed distinctly uncomfortable.

Another silence, broken by a clatter of swift footsteps down
the circular staircase leading to the nurseries. Sedry and
Rolend, accompanied by perhaps forty men, burst into view.
Behind her, the King stirred and muttered something, but
when she risked a glance, he had fainted again.

"Move from him." A glance had sufficed to apprise Sedry
of events and he stood before her, lips compressed against a
rising fury. His Aura cast a ruddy glow across the fallen standard.

"No."

"Will my brother live?" Sedry's narrowed eyes did not
leave the drooping figure before him. Hyrcan's follower,
joined by Rolend, nodded, realized the Prince could not see
him, and spoke.

"Aye—likely. With care. It's an ugly wound and deep, but
he should live."

"Rolend. Send a man to fetch Panderic. And go yourself—"

"No, Brother. I am needed here." Rolend gestured to one
of his following who turned and sped back the way they had
come, but he himself moved to Sedry's side. The Crown
Prince spared him a black look which Rolend met levelly.
Damn the boy, I should have known he'd be trouble. Sedry
finally shrugged, turned back to Elfrid.

"Move, I said. *Now!*" A spark leaped from his hand,
struck her shoulder. She shuddered as it struck, but made no
other move.

"So you can kill him, Sedry? Where Hyrcan failed? No."

Her blade wavered, steadied. Sedry laughed, briefly and without humor.

"Hyrcan is a fool. I do not intend to slay my father."

"No? There is little you would not do, Sedry. But I have nothing to lose in any case. I was dead when you breached the walls tonight, you know it and I know it." Rolend started forward, checked himself.

"No." Sedry matched his voice to hers: expressionless, flat. "Darion is mine, mine as she should have been long since. I have it all."

"All?" *Poor Father.*

"All. I can afford mercy." A cold smile moved across his face. A corner of her mouth twitched, the dark eyes, narrowed with pain, briefly sought Rolend's. "I will not harm Father. You, Bastard, are of his blood. It saves you."

"A lie." *Doesn't he realize I can tell? Does he think my half-blood denies me the Truthing? Or does he simply not care that I know he means our deaths?*

"No lie. I need not lie, I have won. I cannot afford to drive the Baronry from me. Or Rolend. I promised him, long since." Sedry spoke over his shoulder. "Tell her, Brother. Perhaps she will believe you."

Rolend moved forward to kneel beside her, wrapping gentle hands around her shoulders. Compassion radiated from him, threatened to overwhelm her. "He speaks the truth, I swear it, Elfrid. By the Two, I swear it, kinswoman. I would not have joined with him otherwise." *He believes this. Sedry lies, Rolend tells the truth—and Baldyron of Eavon, oh, Gods, Bal, at Hyrcan's back, aiding my bloody brother in this lowest of all deeds, you of all men!* She swayed in Rolend's grasp.

"I have no wish to injure you further, Bastard," Sedry continued coldly. "I am no Hyrcan, to be baited into a fight and to lose to overconfidence. You are bleeding, you can barely sit upright. I need only wait." Silence. "Move aside. You are of no use to him, no use at all."

It was a bitter truth. Elfrid bit her lip as Rolend pressed the torn hems of her shirt against her side, setting her hand over them. "Your word I will trust, kinsman," she said finally. Rolend bowed his head. The sword fell from her fingers to clatter against the tiles as, with Rolend's aid, she pushed to her feet. Sedry pressed past her to kneel before the tapestry, his attention on the old King. *If Hyrcan has ruined this for me—he must not die in Arolet*! He drew a deep, relieved breath: The pulse was slow but strong. "One of those struck him with the standard," Elfrid said, her voice so low he scarcely caught the words. "I killed him for it."

"Blast Hyrcan," Sedry gritted out. "He should never have—well, it cannot be undone. Praise the Two, he is not badly hurt, I think." He rose, gestured to his men. "See to them. When the King is again conscious, the Bastard tended to, bring them to the Reception. Rolend, remain with Hyrcan. If Panderic thinks it safe to move him, put him in his old rooms. Otherwise, use Alster's bedroom."

"Brother." Rolend inclined his head submissively but closed the distance between them with one long-legged stride. His fingers bit into Sedry's arm. "You *swear* to me—"

"As I have ten times before, at least," Sedry replied impatiently. "I will lay no hand to the creature, and no harm to Father." He turned and strode rapidly away. Elfrid leaned back against the cool wall, eyes closed. She opened them as a blade touched lightly against her arm. Fighting to remain upright, to stay on her feet, she moved down the hall, following the men—strangers, all—who carried the King.

5

IT WAS NOT until two days later that the King was able to stand before his eldest son, however, and it was immediately clear to all who saw that audience that the old man had taken terrible harm. Alster had shrunk visibly since the storming of Arolet, had become a man much older than his sixty years and he did not seem to see well, for he stumbled often and frequently passed a hand over his eyes. He was muttering to himself as Elfrid brought him into the great Reception Hall, her strong right arm keeping him upright as they walked towards the dais. Elfrid, still in the torn and bloodied boy's clothing she had worn the night of the invasion, her hair roughly plaited as though she had done the work without comb or mirror, set a pace to match Alster's. It was several long, silent minutes before they reached the base of the three broad stairs which led to the throne.

Sedry stood to the right of the carven seat and a step below it, since he was not yet crowned; Aura cast a self-satisfied, greenish gold shimmer over his hair, picking out the jewels set in the dark velvet tunic, the emerald ring on his right forefinger. "As one of full kindred, we exempt the Prince Alster, late King of Darion, from show of homage. *You*, we do not." Elfrid met his cold gaze squarely, bending her knee only when two of his men moved forward with grim purpose. Another silence, which Sedry finally broke. "You do not ask of your fate."

"Why? It is mine, whether I know of it beforehand or not. You will tell me, when you decide to."

Sedry's eyes narrowed. "How cold a creature it is! I cannot decide whether you are brave, as some of these insist," he waved a hand to take in the hall, "or merely incapable of honest emotion." He dropped down to sit on the top step. "Nay," he went on levelly, "I spoke the truth when we last met. It would negate all I have planned, should I kill Father. Or you. I would not wish to, of course." *Lies.* So strong a lie as to set the Truthing ringing through her mind like a cracked bell. "But more importantly, the Baronry would never trust me again, and I need their support.

"However, I cannot imprison you within Darion's borders. The Prince Alster would be a constant danger to the peace and security of the lands."

"Exile, then."

Sedry nodded. "A clever creature. Precisely how I have chosen. You and he are thorns in my side, therefore in Darion's." He paused a moment, as though to consider. "You know the law. However. I take into account his age and infirmity. You and he shall have ten days, instead of the three given by law."

Elfrid sprang to her feet. "Kill us and have done, then! He will never survive such a journey!" Her voice filled the hall, silencing the buzz of disconcerted conversation around them. "Look upon your father, Prince! He is unwell, and the shock of your deeds has unseated his reason! He cannot walk half the length of Darion, it may snow within the week, and there are lion and boar within Arlonia's forests. The cold alone would kill him, the first night!" She paused for breath; when she spoke again, her voice was flat, expressionless. "Even I might not survive the journey afoot to Carlsport this late in the year. Nor might many of your armsmen. This is murder at one remove."

"You know the law—"

Elfrid laughed sourly. "The law! You are the law in Darion now. Such as that is. I tell you, and all these who serve you," she went on, pitching her voice once again to fill the hall, "that it is murder if you send this mad old man afoot into exile!"

Sedry glared at her, glared around the chamber for silence. He sighed finally, ostentatiously. "Very well. A mount for the old man—yes, I must allow that." Elfrid opened her mouth to speak, shut it again as Sedry held up a warning hand. "A mount. Food and drink for ten days. A bag of coin to gain passage for both of you to Embersy or Belden."

"My weapons—"

"You have none. No exile may bear weapons, and you are twice over denied arms, whatever my father may have given you. However," Sedry continued as he rose to pace the narrow top step, "I am aware that there are dangers between here and the sea, dangers Darion's previous King failed to deal with. I deny them to be as great as your girlish hysteria would make them. But the Prince Alster may retain his dagger. You shall have a staff, such as any maiden might use for walking."

"And do we reach Carlsport," Elfrid replied evenly, "it will be by the grace of the Two, Sedry, not your doing." The Prince turned sharply on one heel, his normally pale face flushed.

"You will address me as Prince, Bastard! You have been granted more than most who have traveled that road, do not deliberately seek to anger me. The fate of the old man rides on your viper's tongue—will you send him to the coast alone?" Elfrid held silent with tight-lipped, visible effort. Alster's fingers scrabbled at her arm, drawing her concerned attention.

"Were all my babies slain when the barghests came upon us? It were the Fegez, truly, I know it. None else are so fierce in their attack." He peered at her, blinking, but appeared to hear none of the soothing words she whispered against his ear. "I should know thee, lad, that brought me from the halls where the barghests feast. Art my Hyrcan? Nay—nor brave Sedry." Trembling fingers ran along her jaw, dropped away. "Thou'rt beardless like my young Rolend, but not he." His face collapsed, tears ran down his seamed, greyed cheeks. "Have no sons, lad. No, nor daughters, either. It brings only pain." He turned, pulled away from her, arms outstretched. For one brief moment, his Aura was a terrible, golden splendor that lit his entire body. "Dead, all dead!" he cried out in a terrible voice and then, coughing, he staggered against his daughter who winced, set her teeth against her lip, and lowered him gently to the floor.

There he sat, suddenly still, gravely contemplating his hands and murmuring to himself.

When Elfrid rose, her face was white. "This you have done, Prince Sedry!" Her outcry tore the air between them. "The

Two will call you to reckon for it, how will you answer Them?"

"It was not my fault!" Sedry flared. "I warned Hyrcan! I warned all of them, all those with us! The old man was *never* to be harmed, but he chose to fight, damn him! Would you have ordered those men to die like sheep? He fought, they had no choice!"

"He would not have done otherwise!" Elfrid shouted. Two of the Prince's men moved to stand between her and Sedry, blades drawn. "This is Alster! A greater swordsman than you, Prince! Even in his age, he would never have stood tamely to be taken like an old serving dame by such as you!"

"Silence!" Sedry bellowed. Elfrid bit her lips. Her face was pale, her breath came fast and deep. "Remove them! Give them a mount suitable for the Prince, give them food and drink. You, Bastard—choose clothing for you both, I will have no one say I sent you ill-clad into the cold. And I would have your word—such as it is—that you intend to head for Carlsport, and will make no attempt to stray from that road."

"It is a better word than yours," Elfrid replied evenly, "and you have it. I will not chance Father's life for hope of present vengeance against such as you." Without further word, she turned, aided the old man to his feet, and led him slowly back through the door.

When they were gone, Sedry motioned to his new Steward, heir of a minor Eastern baron and his closest friend.

"What of my brother, Nolse?"

"He mends, Sire." Nolse smiled, a mere, secretive turning of the corners of his thin mouth. "He was awake a short while since, and the old woman was feeding him broth. He—ah—." The smile widened a little, bringing a malicious light to his cold black eyes. "He does not approve of your plan to exile the King."

"Prince," Sedry reminded him, one hand stroking his narrow beard absently. "Damn Hyrcan, anyway, he nearly ruined everything, he and those fools with him. Seven of them, Nolse, and not one willing to drag him aside!"

"Mmmm." Nolse could imagine that all too well; he walked in constant dread of the Prince Ascendant.

"Fortunate the girl was able to hold him off."

Nolse laughed. "What? Grateful to the Bastard?"

Sedry shrugged. "You know what I mean." He eyed his Steward sidelong. "Did you see her? I never have. But they say she has a talent."

"I was with you," Nolse reminded him. "But I spoke to Baldyron and Jessack afterwards, they were both there. Jes said it wasn't luck held your brother off so long, and Bal says she could become his equal. If," he added, the corners of his mouth tipping up, "of course, she lives so long." Sedry raised his brows: Eavon's youngest had undeniable talent with his blades. "But you are right, of course, Sire," Nolse went on. "The Northern Lords would never have accepted Prince Alster's death, not even in clean battle."

"Nor would most of the Marchers. Even in the South, there are more dainty men like Rolend than you would believe, Nolse. Genneldry does not appear to sit with them so poorly as all that! And we need their support. I still need Rolend." Sedry dropped back to the top step, leaning back on his elbows to gaze dreamily at the high ceiling. "Exile, then. An excellent means beyond a dilemma that has confounded men since the first throne was usurped, I daresay. But—it is a long journey to the sea from Arolet. And they say Arlonia is rapidly returning to the wild."

"They say," Nolse replied neutrally.

"Boar have been seen near the road, and there are rumors of bandits. I should have that seen to."

"Of course," Nolse agreed gravely. He and Sedry looked at each other then; the Steward inclined his head and left the chamber. Sedry went back to his contemplation of the ceiling. No need to speak aloud thoughts better kept quiet: Nolse thought as he did, knew what he wanted. How he wanted it. He could trust Nolse to see to matters. He smiled, widely and unpleasantly.

Nolse stopped near the door to pick several men out, sending a few to the stables to relieve the guard, to the outer walls to keep watch, ordering the remainder to take afternoon meal. In the hall, he found young Baldyron of Eavon.

It helped Nolse, a little, to think of him that way. True, Baldyron was youngest of Fresgkel's brood save for the child Elyessa, and six years younger than the new King's Steward. But face to face with him—Bal had the confidence, the inner strength of an eldest son; he kept his own counsel for the most part, and Nolse, normally outgoing and able to chat with any-one, found himself extremely uncomfortable around the young Eavon.

Not that Bal was rude, no. He didn't need to be. He just *stood* there, his dark face blandly polite, his deep brown eyes expressionless.

What irritated Nolse the most, he decided as he approached the younger man, was that Bal positively towered over him. "The King sends his regards, Bal, and asks that you locate Alster's councilers. They are to come to him at once. He suggests that you seek food thereafter, as he will need to see you during fourth watch."

The Marcher inclined his upper body gracefully, turned and took the stairs at a rapid pace. Nolse stared after him, frowned briefly. Something wrong—Bal looked pale around the mouth, haggard and rather ill.

Nolse shrugged. As long as it wasn't the sweating sickness, it was nothing to do with him; Baldyron wouldn't welcome solicitous questions about his health—nor, come to think of it, about much else.

Nolse turned and started back towards the main hall. Things to accomplish, and quickly; Sedry was depending on him. Who, then, to send? Who could be spared for the ride to Carlsport, who could choose the best (and cheapest) ambush, and set it safely within the Forest? The malicious little smile curled his lip as he descended the main stairs and started for the temporary barracks: the only drawback to his plan, so far as he could see, was that he wouldn't see the look on *her* face when it happened.

Baldyron halted abruptly at the head of the stairs. Councilers, Gods, where did a man find them, and of all the times for Wodeg's slimy heir to hit upon him for Sedry's chores! He glanced, rather wildly, at the long hall with its numerous, closed doors. The third door to his right opened into the apartments of the Twin Princesses; two elderly servants were gossiping just inside. He dispatched the women on his errand and moved further down the hall.

His face was set, grim. Fortune grant that he recalled his way from the night before, and more, that he recalled what he knew of Arolet's pattern of rooms and halls! There was much to be done and—fourth watch, bless Sedry, well could it have been worse—little enough time for it.

He slipped, light-footed, down a darkened corridor, to the right, into the room he shared with the fifteen men he had brought to Sedry's service. Out then, cloaked, a tightly bound bundle under his arm, his free hand brushing the wall. Down and to the—right?—and right again—

His sense of direction held true; he brought up in the banquet hall, now dark and deserted. The floor was still littered with the debris of battle, and there was a smell of burned, wet wood. No guard watched the bolt hole. He hastened inside, gradually increasing his pace, until he was nearly running towards the Hunter's Glade.

6

ELFRID SLOWED HER pace. The King might be asleep; he had spoken less and less frequently over the past hour. And there was no point in rushing the horse: a sorry old beast, years beyond its prime and lame besides. But as long as it was not forced above a plod, its pace was smooth and it seemed unlikely to fall in its tracks. The King—*no, the Prince. Prince Alster*—lay with his face against the knotted black mane. A tear ran unnoted, silently, down her cheek.

They were two hours beyond Lertondale, beyond the last outlying farms, approaching the first trees of the Forest where the King and his daughter had often hunted. Past the last of the silent, staring folk. Elfrid had spared herself the sight of so many frightened, shocked faces, had held her eyes to the road as much as possible, glancing up only to make certain that the old man was holding to the saddle, ignoring the guard that had accompanied them for the first league.

It was over, done. Whatever support Alster might have counted upon would vanish like spring snow when word spread from the City. For the old King was mad: The whisper of it had gone like a cold wind through the merchants lining the road as Alster smiled at them, waving and laughing, breaking occasionally into garbled senseless speech. Elfrid had urged the horse to what speed it could manage, had breathed a prayer of thanks when Lertondale was left behind.

Her fingers brushed the long, jeweled ceremonial dagger that had been her father's. At least Sedry's stooge, Nolse, had not held to Sedry's charade when the first league was gone;

45

he had handed the gaudy toy to her before all five armsmen turned back to Arolet.

The near useless dagger and a staff, shod in brass and of her height, were their only weapons. Their provisions were bundled and tied to the horse's thin withers: a heavy winter cloak, waterproofed without, furred within; two hard sausages and several small loaves; a lump of butter; two skins of wine. Flint and tinder. The narrow leather pouch that clinked as it struck against her leg contained a generous handful of silver coin. Sedry had permitted her a change from the filthy shirt and breeches. He had derived a good deal of malicious pleasure from prohibiting her similar garb. The walking cloak, the slightly shorter skirt in a dark, serviceable wool, were probably warmer than breeches would have been, but they were awkward, tended to wrap around her legs and slow her down.

Sedry had not offered her the mail, the leather underjerkin that had been Gontry's gift to her the previous summer, and she had not asked for them.

She glanced up, shivering, as the sun dropped behind a high cloud bank. It would be cold and dark early. It might even rain.

A prickling along that inner sense that controlled the Gifts: Three grey and white birds flew low overhead, were lost against the trees westwards. Sedry's, beyond doubt. She gripped the dagger hilts. Alster's cause was lost, he himself was. She was, though at the moment, she hardly felt it. There was no room: Guilt/anger/frustration swept through her. "A wounded, novice fledgling of a swordswoman to protect him with a nail tool," she murmured bitterly, her mouth twisting in sudden pain as an awkward step jarred her body, setting her side to throbbing again. No, not her fault, that she *could* tell herself and believe. That her father had trusted Sedry—not his fault, either, that was merely Alster. Sedry's fault, that he was so like his grasping, shallow mother? No one's fault, everyone's.

It didn't matter. Sedry left nothing to chance, it was not his way: they would never reach Carlsport alive.

Alster stirred, mumbled to himself and sat upright. "I am cold, lad; cold." She pulled the horse to a halt, bracing him as he slid to the ground. The old man squinted at her, one hand clinging to the mane. "I should know thee, lad. I know all my

pages. Art new to my service?'' The archaic, March-accented
Ordinate of his youth was strong in his speech, though he had
suppressed it most of the years of his manhood. He turned
away, still bracing himself against the horse, walked a few
paces to peer down the road. ''Where is my Elfrid? Does she
come with us?'' The aged gelding stood with its head down,
ears twitching.

''I am Elfrid, Father. Hold, I have you a cloak.'' The old
King gazed around him blankly.

''Did you say she comes—my Elfrid? She is a good child,
boy. All my others—all dead, all dead.'' He tilted his head
back to stare, unblinking, into the pale grey sky. ''Sweet
blossoms, look you at their dark beauty. The groves flower
heavily, the harvest will be bountiful.'' He took another step
back the way they had come. Elfrid watched him anxiously,
but as he made no step beyond the support of his mount, she
reached for the pack.

Awkward, having only one arm to reach with, but finally it
was done, the cloak drawn around the old man's shoulders,
the bundle retied and returned to the horse. Her own cloak
was thin, the fur lining worn, and it was all she had.

An even greater effort was required to persuade Alster to
mount again, and to aid him in that task. Her knees were
shaking by the time they started out again.

The King sat upright for a while, gazing about and carrying
on a voluble conversation with himself, speaking now and
again loudly enough for his companion to hear.

''A bird there—'ware, lad. They spy upon a man, 'tis said.
A handful of corn, that's to settle them.'' He closed his eyes,
sang snatches of Fest songs. Silence a while. ''All gone, my
sweet boys, my pretty girls. And how shall a man of old loins
get more? Miriellas?'' Elfrid started. It had been long since
anyone had spoken her mother's name. ''Miriellas, my beloved, give an old man his kiss, say again how glad thou art to
see me. Nay, thou'rt never Sigurdy! I sent her,'' he giggled,
''to the stables, to forage among the mice!'' Silence again.
''All dead.'' There were tears in his voice. ''The great halls of
Arolet, the broad halls of Orkry, shivered. Not one stone, they
say, remains upon another.'' He laughed, a thin, tearing
sound. Elfrid shuddered. ''Is it not dark, lad? Then we must
stop the night.''

''It is not yet dark, Father. A ways further.''

"I am no Father," Alster replied sternly. "My children are dead. A butterfly!" he cried out joyously, staring up the dusty road towards the autumn-dulled trees, leaning perilously forward. Moss-Light whirred briefly around the horse's head. "Alayya, Elorra, by the Two, it is a sign! Halt, lad! My Elfrid comes, and we must await her!"

"I am Elfrid, Father."

"Do not call me Father, my children are dead. I—cannot see my hands before my eyes, surely it is time we stopped for the night?" A small silence. "My Elfrid could see in the dark, they say, but she is gone."

"Father—"

"She flew away," the King continued dreamily, "like an owl. The barghests were confounded."

"My father—"

"I am no Father, I tell thee! My children are dead." Silence, save for the soft plod of the horse's hooves on the dusty, narrow road. The forest was thickening around them, clouds covered what was visible of the sky, and a chill wind touched them now and again, ruffling Elfrid's dark hair where it had escaped its long, rough plait, tossling the King's already wild white locks. "We must stop," the old man said fretfully. "They travel by night, the beasts, the Fegez. My Elfrid could stay the beasts, but she is not here. The Fegez—who can stay them, now that brave Sedry is dead?" He muttered to himself a little longer, at length leaned forward to wrap his arms around the horse's neck, closing his eyes. His daughter wiped her cheeks with cold fingers.

She dared not go much further: It would take time to gather wood and build a fire, and she must do this while there was still daylight. Fire would be needed against the cold, if nothing worse. Even though it might draw things to them—no, enough.

She halted suddenly, biting back a cry as the horse bumped her side. Echo? No. Another horse, coming from behind at a furious pace. *So. He would not even give us a full day. I had thought the dark of Arlonia better suited to the assassination of a King, but Sedry was ever impatient.* She glanced swiftly to both sides, drew the dagger and moved back down the road to stand between the horse and the approaching rider. Impossible to hide here: no rocks, no brush. No time.

Early dusk and a rise hid the horseman from her until the

last moment, though the noise of his approach seemed to echo
in the silence of the Forest. Then a broad-chested bay, a
knight's mount but plainly, severely trapped, burst into sight.

The animal stopped several paces distant, pranced away
nervously, came back as a strong hand dragged at the reins,
was still. Elfrid stood motionless, Aura playing about her
hands, bringing the dagger clearly into sight. For several
moments, the rider sat silent. Then, with a sudden, violent
movement, he thrust back his hood to reveal a long, dark face,
broad across the cheeks, a neatly trimmed beard following his
rather wide jawline, accenting it. Beneath the cloak, Elfrid
could barely make out the device on his tabard: vert, twined
serpents.

Gods, Gods—of all those Sedry might have sent to kill
them, of all his boot-kissing following who might have taken
the deed to him! She felt slightly sick, now that the moment
had come and old Fresgkel's favorite son sat before her. A
wash of anger buried nausea. *And you blamed Father for putting trust in Sedry! What of yourself?*

"Does the House of Eavon seek to secure itself with
Darion's new King?" she demanded harshly as he made no
sound, no movement. "Come then, do not let honor stay your
hand!" Dark eyes met hers, but instead of reaching for his
sword, his hand went back to loosen and bring forth a bundle.
This he dropped to the ground before her.

"For the aid of Alster, King of Darion. And—," he hesitated. "And for thine own, Lady."

"No more Lady than he is King," Elfrid replied evenly.
"What trick is this?"

"No trick."

No; unlike Sedry, he spoke the truth. "Then—why? What
you have done is worth your death."

"Dost think I do not know it?" His Ordinate was heavily
Marcher. "Do not misunderstand me, Lady. I cast my lot with
Sedry, I will take up and bear the results. But I will not see
such a wrong done to this man who was King and carries
Kings' blood in his veins." He hesitated. "Nor to thee, who
art his kind."

She swallowed, hard. "And yet you stood with Hyrcan—"

"I already pay for that. Sedry put me with him," he
laughed sourly, "to hold him back. Hold back Hyrcan! As if
any man could!" He sobered, gazed at her in silence for some

moments. "No. Thee saved his life. Hast earned arms, whatever is said." He glanced briefly at the sky. "Thy wound—
how bad?"

"Painful, nothing more." A lie; pride forbade any other
answer.

"Hast use of thy arms?" he pursued. She shrugged.

"Sufficient."

"Perhaps." He seemed unsatisfied but dropped the matter.
He cast another glance at the sky, pulled at the reins, set the
horse to dancing backwards. "Beware Arlonia, Lady Elfrid."

"Beware—why?"

"I know nothing else, save that. Beware Arlonia, watch
every shadow."

"Why do you tell me this? Why do you—?" Baldyron
pulled the horse around and touched its flanks lightly with his
heels. The animal surged forward. Elfrid watched blankly as
he vanished back the way he had come.

She blinked, knelt to inspect the bundle, calling up a ball of
Moss-Light to hover over the darkening road. A woven cloak
for wrapping: extra warmth for the old man. Within—her eyes
went wide, her fingers groped across the rough cloth. A sword
—*her* sword, by the Two! How had he got it? And, Gods!
breeches and shirt: not hers, possibly large for her, but clothing she could fight in, when the need came.

More: She pushed the pants aside, uncovering a bow, two
spare strings, a handful of long, black-fletched arrows. The
flights, the pattern on the shaft were unfamiliar; the aged
leather belt quiver she knew as an old one of Gontry's. She
wiped tears aside roughly.

More still: bandages and ointment in a wicker jar; a flat
cloth of herbs. She held them to her nose, sniffed gingerly.
Brother-love, to numb the pain in her side, treyfoil, to prevent
infection. Gods, he had thought of everything!

She fingered the arrows: old, but still true by the look of
them. The sword was a reassuring weight against her knee: By
the Two, they had a chance where there had been nothing. She
spared one brief, warm glance back down the deserted road.
And for thine own, Lady. "No man ever called me Lady before," she whispered.

She shook her mind free, busied herself with the bundle,
fastening sword and quiver to her waist, tying the bow to the

saddle, pulling the warmth of the cloak across her chilled shoulders.

Something less than a league and they could stop, but haste was needed; Moss-Light was near useless in a search for firewood. The King sighed in his sleep as the old horse moved reluctantly down the road.

7

"DO NOT *FUSS*, Panderic!" Hyrcan grumbled, pushing his old nurse aside as he wrestled himself higher in the bedding. The pale grey eyes were narrowed, the delicate mouth thinned with pain and displeasure. "You should not have let them go, Sedry."

"Have a care how you speak to me, Hyrcan," Sedry replied evenly. "I am quite put out with you. You and your hasty little sortie nearly cost me this . . ." He ran a finger lightly over the circlet that bound his brow: gold, this one, its dark red stones nearly hidden in the fine tracery of vines and leaves.

"It was stupid of you to let them live—"

"It would have been more stupid of me to kill them," Sedry's voice overrode Hyrcan's with finality. Hyrcan scowled, but fell back against the cushions, plucking at the covers with fretful fingers. Ten days had brought little color back to the Prince's face, and he had yet to rise from bed. "Think, Hyrcan!" Sedry urged. "To kill any King, no matter how poor a ruler! Worse, to kill my own father! The nobles would one and all be thinking to themselves: 'He has done this, which of us is safe with such a man?' No, brother. I showed mercy instead. By exiling them—"

Hyrcan snickered. "I know you, Sedry. You sent them, but they were never to reach Carlsport alive. Were they?" And, as Sedry's glance strayed from him, "You know you can speak before Panderic!" Sedry shrugged.

"So?"

"Then one knows why four men were waiting at the

crossroads in Arlonia, though not why they are dead.''

"How did you hear of that?" Sedry demanded. Hyrcan shrugged, gasped and closed his eyes briefly as he settled his shoulders.

"I heard. Well?"

Sedry pulled to his feet, began to pace the chamber in long strides. "Who knows? I do not! Not yet, at any rate. Between them, they had that pretty dagger of Father's that he wore to fests and a plain staff." He stopped to scowl out the window. "Those four were not trained armsmen—"

"Common thugs," Hyrcan cut in. Sedry shot him a dark look.

"Still capable, any one of them, of dealing with what they had to face: a mad old man, a wounded girl. They tell me," he went on, "that three of them were shot with arrows: black-fletched arrows." He turned back to meet his brother's eyes. "I know the fletchings of every noble in Darion, Hyrcan. No one uses black."

"No. The Bastard," he added flatly, "is capable with bow. They say." He closed his eyes again, allowed his old nurse to rearrange the pillows.

"She is, I have seen her. Better with bow than with sword, for which you had better daily thank the Two, Hyrcan. But she had no bow!" Sedry slammed a fist into his open palm. "And even if she had—you marked her, remember? To pull a bow with a half-treated slash across her ribs? I think not! The fourth man," he went on, only his eyes betraying how very angry he was, "wore the dagger in his breast."

"A pretty puzzle," Hyrcan mumbled, feeling comment expected of him.

"Aye. One which may remain unsolved, though I sent young Eavon and five of his men to see first-hand for me."

"Against four, the Bastard—"

"Stop carping on her, brother Hyrcan! What could she do? She had no weapons, and who in Darion would have dared give them to her? The burghers of Lertondale? How would she have used them? But," he added, more to himself than his brother, "who would have fought—for them?" He scowled at the carpets, finally roused himself. "It is over, beyond my grasp, and I have done as I said, though scarcely as I intended. They boarded the Gyrfalcon, our mad father and his pet, four days ago. They will reach North Embersy three days hence."

"You could send word," Hyrcan said, after a long silence. Sedry, who had resumed his pacing, shook his head. "Your birds," Hyrcan insisted, "could—"

"No messenger could wing across the Sea. Let it be, Hyrcan."

"It was me nearly died, not you, Sedry!" Hyrcan flared. Sedry leaned against the wall, tilting his head back to contemplate his brother dispassionately from half-closed eyes.

"Yes. I know that. Because you were a fool, Hyrcan." He formed a wraith-ball of Moss-Light, tossed it lightly from hand to hand. "You let your hatred of the child overwhelm your talent with a sword. And your sense. Worse, your promises to me! If you had died—think of it! Slain in combat by a barefoot wench who still scarcely knows which end of a blade to point!" He smiled briefly at the black expression on his brother's face.

"Morelis will be Queen in South Embersy before the year is out," Hyrcan said stubbornly.

"Perhaps. But of no matter. Morelis is much too practical to embroil herself in such a notion." Hyrcan closed his eyes, suffering Panderic to brush bits of damp hair from his broad cheeks with a moistened cloth. "But you are unwell, brother," Sedry went on smoothly, "and I should not upset you." To the nurse he added, "Shall I send the healers?" The Queen Mother's personal monk-physicians were already in residence at Arolet, having covered the distance between Elenes and Arolet in record time.

"No need, Sire," Panderic replied with quiet deference.

"You know best, I am sure. But I will alert the guard; do you need anything for him at all, send." Panderic made a deep courtesy as Sedry turned and strode from the chamber.

The King moved slowly back down the hall towards the great staircase that would bring him to the main floor and so to the Reception. Another meeting with Alster's stubborn old councilers within the hour—Gods, they were difficult! But they were learning, rapidly.

A bad thing, he reflected, if Hyrcan were to die. Not for his precious self, of course. Sedry held no one particularly dear, least of all this dangerously homicidal brother. But their mother's faction was loyal first to the Prince Ascendant (Crown Prince now, until Sedry got an heir of his own) since

Hyrcan alone had remained openly devoted to Sigurdy in open defiance of Alster's orders. And Sigurdy herself had always loved the Changeling Prince more than the rest of them. Her kin, her family's supporters, would have to be given time to transfer their full loyalties to the new King. In the meantime, the Queen Mother's support would be crucial, and while Sedry was confident she would support him for himself, it would be much easier with Hyrcan at his side. No. Everything must be done to see that Hyrcan recovered. He was necessary.

Sedry came down the broad stairs rapidly, halting in the hallway as the outer doors opened to admit men: six of them. Mud-splattered, dirty, wet, they looked as though they had ridden through the night's rains. The dark blue and pale green of the leader's colors could scarcely be made out for the travel stains.

The King moved forward then, bringing a welcoming, winning smile to his face as he gestured a servant to his side. The six knelt stiffly. Sedry dropped a hand to the leader's shoulder.

"Baldyron, my good friend Bal, I had not thought to see you until tomorrow at the earliest! You rode hard." And, to the servant, "Bring a mulled wine and toast for these men. No, not here, we will be in the closet yonder." Wrapping an arm around the tall, lean Baldyron, he drew him towards the small room that had been, until recently, Alster's private accounts room. The other five followed wearily.

Within, lanterns cast a cheery glow on whitewashed walls, a fire burned low. Another servant slipped in behind them, scurried around to toss more wood into the grate, to turn up the lamps. "Shed your outer garb, lest you catch a chill, be at ease," Sedry urged. A tired smile crossed Baldyron's face, was answered by a warm one from the King. By the time the six were seated, cloaks removed, mail unlaced at the throat, wine and cups had been brought. Baldyron raised his steaming cup in silent salute, drank deeply.

"My thanks, Sire, and that of my men." His voice was deep, flatly tired. "We spent little time at our ease, knowing thou wouldst wish word at once." He tilted back his head, drained the cup.

At a gesture, one of his men fumbled at his belt quiver and brought forth a long, exceedingly slender shaft, tipped with a dartlike point, feathered in a curious pattern with raven's plumage. The shaft itself was overlong as compared with a standard Darion arrow, and was unpainted, save for the tiny red marking at the upper edge of the fletch: a harpy, displayed. Sedry squinted at the device, along the shaft, turned the weapon over with deft hands. He let it fall with a faint clatter to the polished table. The point and the first several inches of shaft were dark with dried blood.

"I do not recognize the cut of it at all," the King muttered. Baldyron watched him steadily. "Who in all Darion uses raven's feathers?"

"None," the young Marcher replied promptly, the carefully rehearsed speech falling easily from his lips. "They are considered ill fortune among the commons, common by the nobles. The cut of the shaft itself is more Beldenian than Darion, I would say, and yet—not quite so. I have never seen their like in Darion before." Save, he added to himself, those five I carried for so many years, those odd darts that caught my eye in Carlsport.

Worry drifted through his mind: Who had noted them in his gear? His father would know them, as would the Rhamsean who had claimed their origin to be the Western deserts beyond the sea. What would that little trader have thought, he wondered, had he known his exotic shafts would save the life of a King—and a Lady?

Another worry—how strong, really, was the new King's Truthing? Less than Alster's, certainly: Sedry had ducked tutoring most of his youth and avoided exercises whenever he could. Even Royal Gifts had to be worked. Caution, he reminded himself, and tamped the mental chatter that might give him away. Sedry was speaking; with an effort, he roused himself, brought his wandering thoughts back to his companions.

"It makes no sense!" Sedry poured himself more wine, ladling the warm beverage into Baldyron's cup over his protest. "No, you have earned this, my young friend, as well as my love for your deed. We," Sedry went on, self-consciously formal, "shall not forget the haste you used, satisfying our curiosity as to this attack against our poor father. Even though we still do not know what chanced, beyond the report of it in Carlsport. "Could you—could you discover who they were?"

Baldyron shrugged. "They were not known to any of us,

nor were they clad in any household colors." Sedry only just restrained any outward show of relief. "They looked to me, frankly, like riffraff from Carlsport, rather than honest swordsmen." *By the Two*, he added grimly to himself, *how you can hold so virtuous a mien!* And, tiredly, *What have I done, what harm to myself, my men, my family, in following this man?* His face showed nothing of his mind and once again he pushed such unsafe thoughts firmly aside.

"Well, I suppose it does not matter," Sedry remarked finally, sighing heavily. "A strange puzzle, but he is safe and I suppose that is all that matters, is it not? But for you—," he smiled brilliantly at his companion, "youngest son of Eavon you may be, but there will be no lack of honors for you, my friend!"

"I did not do it for that!" Bal protested uncomfortably, but the King merely laughed, effectively silencing him.

"I know it—and all the more do we love you! There are few men a King dare trust, Lord Baldyron. Art one such. The house of Eavon is denied thee, I know," Sedry went on, lapsing, as he occasionally did, into the archaic second person used in the Marches, where he had lived so long, "but shalt be another after the barghests are driven back, if thou'lt have it." Baldyron met his eyes, and with a faint sigh bowed his head to the inevitable.

"I—am honored, Sire, and truly grateful. Though it is little enough I did for thee—"

Sedry pushed away from the table to smile down on him. "Nay. Retain your seats, all of you. Do not stand on ceremony this once, my friends. My council awaits me, but stay and finish the wine. Food will be brought to you shortly. Bal, please do not leave yet, I would speak with you further before you return to the Marches."

"As thou dost choose, Sire." The Marcher inclined his head again as the King strode from the chamber, a sudden spring in his step. *And why not?* Baldyron wondered sourly. *No one will dare trace the deed to him, he is clean of it.* He turned back, pressed his back into the chair. Gods, but he was tired!

"We learned nothing, nothing at all," one of his armsmen muttered, staring gloomily into his empty cup.

"At no cost to ourselves, and at some reward," the man next to him replied. "Isn't that enough for thee? As to why those four were in Arlonia, or who sent them—now, I would

make no guess to that, in any case, nor wilt thou, if art wise!''
He threw a glance at his young lord, but Baldyron was staring
gloomily into the fire with half-closed eyes and did not appear
to hear them. "As to who killed *them*, now—"

"She—"

"Do not dare speak of her within these walls, if thou'd'st
keep thy tongue," a third urged sharply. "Drink what the
King has provided and do not think on any of it!" He drank
deeply of his own, grinning as he reached to replenish his cup.
"We are not made to think, that is why we have lords, to think
for us!"

"Mmmm. May be." The first man shook himself, glanced
at Baldyron again, drank. Then, after a contented silence:
"They say the old King and the Bastard have reached North
Embersy."

"Not yet. But at least the King can not blame us that they
live," the first man muttered. His companions shushed him
violently. Baldyron turned away from them, gazed down at his
hands with dark, troubled eyes. *Can he not?*

• PART TWO •
• THE ARCHBISHOP •

8

THE LEAD HORSEMAN peered at the swinging sign in the early dusk: The paint was faded, but his keen eyes could make out —just—the griffin and the banner behind it which might once have been properly red. He raised a hand, waved it back and forth in signal before dismounting. Several horses drew up behind him as he pressed against the heavy door and entered the building.

It was nearly as dark within as it was without: A low fire burned in the heavy stone fireplace, a lantern hung from a beam near the center of the large central room. Candle flames fluttered in the sudden breeze, straightened again as he pushed the door to behind him. Three of the tapers marked the length of a rough counter, where a man and a woman stood, watching him warily, he with his arms folded across a broad chest, she polishing a tankard with the corner of her apron. Three men in rough cloaks sat near the fire drinking; they gazed with open suspicion at the newcomer who strode, apparently unnoticing of them, across the room to front the barman.

"The Red Griffin?" The barman eyed him a moment longer, then nodded once, sharply. "Fengel Cormric?" Another nod. The tension in the ale-house was thick enough to stumble over. "I am Fidric Hamansson of Rhames. I was told in Carlsport we might find lodging here for the night. And food."

"Who said?" The woman spoke in a low voice that might once have been sweet but was harsh with years and privation.

"The portmaster. One Venpar Hesk. Old man, game leg. Mismatched eyes."

61

"Venpar Hesk? I know 'im." The barman might have relaxed, a little.

"He said to remind you of a bet," Fidric went on, "a quartered flag, and a ship named *Joyous—*"

"Say no more." The big man smiled suddenly, held out a capable, square hand. "Ven sent ye, all right. How many in your party?" The woman set her tankard aside, picked up another and shook water from it, resumed her slow polishing.

"Six. Two are women, and we'd like a room for them, if there is none for the rest of us." The barman seemed to find this grimly amusing.

"Somehow, sir, I doubt we'll have trouble."

"In that case, sir, we will take three. My Lord Archbishop needs the solitude, when he can have it." The tankard clattered to the floor.

"Archbishop?" the woman breathed. Her eyes were round, awed. "By the Two, sir, not Gespry!" The barman touched her arm.

"Shhh. It does not do to ask questions, wife." Fidric smiled, leaned forward to plant an elbow on the counter.

"What possible harm? It is indeed Gespry, goodwife. We ride to aid your King Alster against the eastern barbarian. But—I tell you what you know already, I am certain."

"Nay, not Alster." The woman spoke nervously. "Sedry, Sedry is our King. Has been these eight years past."

"My pardon. A slip of the tongue." Fidric replied smoothly. He turned to the man. "Come now, do tell me, can you set a round of ale for us? I shall go aid my friends."

"That I can," Cormric responded, quickly "Go wife, more cups! Or, perhaps a wine would suit better, good sir?"

"Whatever will not short you, my good landlord," Fidric replied. Several long strides took him back to the door; candle flames bent again as he slipped back outside. Cormric moved to the back door, bellowed into the darkness beyond. A thin boy of perhaps ten—by his features the barman's son—scrambled after Fidric to aid with the horses.

Moments later, the company sat at a table near the fire: The landlord had built this back up, had lit sufficient candles to give both the air and actuality of warmth to the room. The three local men had moved into a corner, the better to observe the newcomers and to discuss them without having to whisper.

One of the women leaned forward, forehead resting on slender, extremely white hands. The deep hood completely covered her face. The other, however, had thrown cloak aside and was holding small, delicate hands to the fire. Beyond doubt, this was Fialla, the Archbishop's Lady, as famous, some would say infamous, as he. Blue-black hair, twisted back simply for traveling, escaped around her face in wispy curls. Her eyes were hooded by thick lashes, but now and again glanced around the room: They were wonderfully large, dark blue. Even the heavy, loose garments she wore for riding could not totally conceal form. Jewels gleamed at her ears and on her fingers.

Two of the men were clad like Fidric—professional arms-men, these, their clothing alone showed it. The sky blue tabards, edged in brightest yellow, marked them as being in service to some lord who could bear the cost of covering his following in proper fashion. The token in gold upon each breast was Gespry's: two swords crossed, upholding a mitre. They were windburned, keen-eyed and even as tired as they must be, sat with that tensile ease which marks a man of skill. They were openly armed.

One of the two was so like Fidric as to surely be his brother: similar in height and build, his dark hair worn long, dark brown eyes in a freckled face that kept him, like Fidric, from looking his age. They could have been anywhere from twenty-five to forty.

The third man was shorter, his hair a near-black mass of grey-streaked short curls. His nose was crooked; a long, drooping moustache—shot, unexpectedly, with as much red as grey—covered his upper lip.

The remaining man sat between the two women, one long, narrow hand resting on the table, the other on Fialla's shoulder. Firelight glittered on his ring of office, touched red on the mail shirt, the forearm dagger sheath. The Archbishop leaned forward to speak quietly against his mistress's ear, oblivious to the watching folk. She smiled back, reached up to squeeze his fingers before holding her hands out to the fire again. The Archbishop leaned back in his chair, drained his tankard and closed his eyes. The barman and his wife exchanged glances.

Surely this could not be Gespry, Archbishop of Rhames! The renegade monk—so the Darion priests called him—the

Sword of the Two, righter of wrongs. The best and most well-known fighting man in all the lands! Everyone knew the tales: how Gespry had fallen on the besiegers of Neldwy in South Embersy with only fifteen hand-picked men and freed the city; how, cornered, he had fought his way alone through ten mounted Arlesians and come out only mildly scratched. How he had eradicated so many of the southern pirates, there had been no raids on the coastal lords, on *either* side of the sea, for three years.

Of course, they had also heard of Megen Cove, the great sea battle there; there had been rumors, of recent, that Gespry had died of the wounds suffered during that battle.

Well, he had not died, clearly, for this was a man and no ghost; but he was thin, cheekbones pressed tightly against wind burned skin, the bones in hands and wrists indecently visible. And his hair—that was purest white, though the man had not passed his thirty-fifth summer. There was a shadow in the brief smile he gave the beautiful Fialla, as though he still held pain in check by sheer will. The man nudged his wife— empty cups. Go. She cast him a glance, suddenly shy, but moved to the table. At her approach, the Archbishop opened his eyes, then stood and bowed with such swift grace she was taken aback.

"For your courtesy and your roof, goodwife, my thanks and that of these my friends."

"I—by your leave, Lord, I mean, your Grace." His manner confused her; the barman's wife had never received such courtesies. With a visible effort, she recovered. "There will be food shortly. Plain, I fear—"

"To which we are one and all used," he assured her. The smile he gave her was warm and brought a timid one in reply. "Plain food, well cooked, is always welcome," Gespry went on. "And your ale is splendid." She smiled again, more confidently this time, bowed and went back to her kitchen, a warmth under her ribs where she hugged the Archbishop's words close.

The atmosphere in the tavern slowly returned to normal. Though the Archbishop's company was exotic in appearance and large for the Griffin, they sat quietly, ate what was brought, and conversed in low voices over ale thereafter, like any other travelers might. Two of the three men in the far corner left after a time, several more came in. It was late when the last of the locals left and the barman closed the door, setting a stout pole across it.

"There! That should hold—"

"You expect trouble?" Fidric moved to the landlord's side.

"No. But as one does in Darion these days, I prepare against it and hope it does not come," Cormric replied grimly. He glanced at the table where the Archbishop and his lady sat, heads close together, and seemed to come to some decision. "By your leave, if I might speak with you a moment—"

"Certainly. Gespry hoped to do so in any case. He wishes to learn something of the road to the King's city, if you can tell us."

"Oh," the barman's face set even more grimly, "I can that. Yes, indeed."

He went back to his counter, fetched a draught of ale for himself and bowed to the Archbishop before he sat. "Your man tells me you want knowledge of the Lertondale Road."

"So we do, sir. We got little before we came, and little again in Carlsport. Folk seemed—unwilling, I think—to speak of it when we asked. To speak of anything, really."

"Little wonder, sir. I put my life, and that of the woman and the boy in your hands, so to say, speaking myself. A man never knows, anymore, what thing will be taken in offense, or what ears it will reach." His eyes wandered around the common room as he drank. "This is a good place, this inn. Been mine since I gave up the sea, more than ten years ago. Used to be a decent living, until recently." He brought his gaze back to the Archbishop. "How many did ye pass, from the port to here? I'll wager it was none."

"You'd win," Gespry replied. "We met no one in a full day's travel. Is that usual?"

"Wasn't. Folk're afraid, have been for some years. Oh— Arlonia was always a little wild, but four-footed dangers only. But there are more thieves in Arlonia than boar now."

"Odd," put in the short, dark man who had given his name as Gelc. "We met no trouble." The barman grinned crookedly.

"Not so odd. They attack those unable to protect themselves. A band such as yours—well! But they are the least of our worries here." He fixed his eyes on his empty cup. "Those sent to bring the outlaws to justice—those sent to protect us— well, a man says all he dares, and no more."

"King's men?" inquired Fidric's brother Boresin, "You warn us against the King's men?" The landlord paled, swallowed hard.

"By the Two—no man would dare—!"

Gespry touched his arm reassuringly. "Never mind. You have taken care of us, the least we can offer in return is courtesy and—shall we say—silence? I will study your words, sir, and hold them to myself, my word on it. Now," he added suddenly, "they tell me there was revolt in Lertondale a while since, what of the City?"

"If you travel there," the landlord replied flatly, "you will see. It's not for me speak such things before ladies."

"Ah. Then you have said enough, and again, my thanks."

"The road between here and the City is fair enough traveling, though it's gone rough in the past two years. Used to be, a wagon could make good time straight across the land, Carlsport to the Eastern Marches. If ye've only horses, ye'll have no difficulties, but ye'll not wish to travel at any speed. Horse broke both forelegs, not two leagues from here, a month ago. No, less. Holes," the landlord added tersely. "And mud, where it's gone into the creek. That should have been diverted, but it's not been."

"Then we'll need extra time for travel, and a close eye to the road itself. Are there diversions between the Griffin and Lertondale, or do they hold together in the Forest?"

The landlord shook his head. "The worst of that's behind ye, but if ye met no danger between here and Carlsport, ye'll meet none further on. Your arms, your very numbers protect ye."

"Well, then." Gespry looked around the table. "What say you, my friends? An early start and we may reach Castle Arolet before dark tomorrow."

"May," the landlord agreed, "if the weather holds. Shall I call you at first light?"

"Do so," Gespry replied. "And breakfast, if you have it."

"You'll have breakfast, sir. Your rooms are the open ones at the head of the stairs. A good night to you all." The armsmen rose, one of them aiding the still hooded woman to her feet. As she stood, the covering fell away from her hair, and the landlord bit his tongue to stop an exclamation. For her hair was as white as the Archbishop's, her skin so pale, so translucent, the veins stood out clearly against her temples.

Eyes of the lightest possible blue met his briefly before she turned away to let the armsman lead her to the stairs. A silver star glittered on her right cheek.

Tarots Reader! He'd heard of them, a man did, traveling the Seas as he had. A few men, a few women, born with that lack of color to skin and hair had the ability to read futures—usually with the Tarots, often without. Some, it was said, could actually control events, some read your thought or press their own upon you. Not that *he* believed such rubbish. But—

He'd known of the Archbishop's Reader, of course, he'd just forgotten about her until now. He hadn't forgotten the other woman, though: no man would. The Archbishop of Rhames never strayed from his monastery without the Lady Fialla. Or perhaps it was the other way about, that she would not permit him to travel without her. He glanced at her. The tales had understated her mien, he thought. Just to look at such a woman, you could see why the Archbishop wouldn't leave her behind. But what would cause a woman like that to dare sea battles, cold, and privation as she had? A man would be honored beyond right!

Suddenly aware of his gaze, she turned, smiled warmly at him before starting up to the room she and the Reader were to share. The innkeeper felt the blood in his face, as though he were a green boy caught staring. It was good of the Archbishop, he thought confusedly, watching as Fialla vanished into the gloom at the head of the stairs, not to force the matter on a Darion household. Not that I would care, that she is mistress and not wife, that he is a servant of the Two and so forbidden any woman. Many of Darion would care indeed.

He blew out the candles, banked the fire, extinguished the lantern, and checked the doors once again. They'd had no troubles this year, but he built no hopes against that. A man wouldn't live long in times like these, building hopes where he had no right, and he had the woman and his boy to look after.

"Gespry!" A soft whisper stopped the Archbishop in mid-stride.

"Fialla?" A small hand reached for his, held it briefly.

"It goes well, my Lord. You must relax somewhat!" The Archbishop's smile was a brief flash of white in the near-complete darkness.

"Think you? Yes, of course it does. I know. Speak softly,

Fialla my own. The walls have ears, remember that!''

''So you have told me: the King's Steward has spies every-where. I shall not forget.'' A pause. She reached then, to take Gespry's shoulders between her hands. He stood still briefly, then closed the distance between them, leaning down to rest his head against her shoulder. ''You *must* relax. My Lord the Archbishop is a most untense man—are you not?'' Small, deft fingers worked at the muscles at the base of the neck, brushing lightly at the white hair that curved into the hooded cloak.

''Of course.'' The voice was, momentarily, mocking, and as tight as the shoulders. It returned to normal: Warm, low, a slightly dry flavor, as though each word was unimportant.

''Is it worth this?'' she asked suddenly. The other drew away from her.

''You ask now?'' A dry chuckle. ''A trifle late, dear Lady.''

''Well played,'' she replied, her own tone dry. ''But yes, I do ask now. For tomorrow at this hour, it will be too late. Tonight, it is not. Is it worth this?'' Her hands brushed the tight shoulder and neck muscles, dropped to trail across his back: Below the shoulder blades, she could feel the wide, snug bandage that covered most of the Archbishop's chest.

One long, narrow hand found hers, and he led her to the end of the hall, away from the occupied rooms. The light from a nearly full moon broke through heavy clouds to fall across their shoulders: Her hair gleamed more blue than black, his shone like new snow.

''It *is* too late. It was too late before the Reader cast the Pattern for us.''

''All this? Is anything worth it?''

''Perhaps.'' The dark eyes that met hers were unreadable. ''The Two know my thoughts, Fialla.''

''As do I,'' she murmured. Her companion laughed, quietly, briefly.

''Do you, I wonder? Perhaps.''

''Perhaps,'' she mocked him softly. She turned away. ''I am going back to my chamber. The Reader is already asleep, I should be if we are to ride so far tomorrow. You had better also. Tomorrow evening—''

''Yes. Tomorrow evening. Luck may have as much to do with it as skill and long practice.'' He gazed broodingly out across the moonlit trees. Shook himself slightly, and kissed her fingers. ''Pray me good luck, if you will aid me most.'' Inwardly Fialla sighed. *No use. At least I know I tried.* "Good night to you, my Lady. Pleasant dreaming."

"And to you, my Gespry." She glanced back from the door of her room; he still stood in the patch of moonlight, gazing once again across the Forest. What she could see of the dark face under the silver-lit hair was expressionless but remote. *There is nothing you can do or say*, she told herself sternly. *Go to bed.*

9

"YOUR EAR, BROTHER." Sedry started at the unexpected voice against his left ear; wine slopped over the edge of his cup and pooled on the edge of the table, dripping with muted "plops" onto the floor. "I did not mean to startle you," Hyrcan continued as he dropped into the seat next to the King's. He did not sound particularly sorry. "You must have been deep in thought."

Sedry gazed at him somberly, if not soberly. His eyes were red-shot, blurry. Was Hyrcan making mock of him? Difficult to tell in any event. And wine, as much as lack of use these past years, had dulled his Truthing—ah, by the Two, who cared, anyway? "I have reason enough," he said finally, "with revolt spreading across Darion like the sweating fever—"

"Not in the North," Hyrcan cut in flatly. Sedry could barely make out his brother's face, his chair was just outside the light cast by the single lantern; what he could see was not pleasant. Hyrcan might have been smiling to himself, there in the shadows. "As I told you by means of my birds, it is unlikely the North will revolt again for some time. With a son from every major household being held in Castle Kellich as surety for the behavior of the Baronry, with fully half the armed commons dead or prisoner—"

"They might feel they have nothing left to lose," Sedry muttered. He emptied the contents of the decanter—his second since dinner—into his cup. He did not bother to offer any to the Crown Prince: Hyrcan still did not drink.

"No. I think not. There is a very fine line, Sedry, in such matters, which you do not really understand. Lack of practice, I expect."

Sedry laughed. "As against you, brother, most certainly. The Scourge of the North will be remembered when Darion herself is only a myth." Hyrcan shot him a glance which Sedry returned as levelly as he could. No easy task, drunk or sober: He increasingly feared this younger brother, though Hyrcan raised no threat, overt or otherwise, against him, never held his Trait over Sedry. In truth, of course, he had no need to, and they both knew it.

It was a wonder that the lands around Kellich, where the Crown Prince made his home, were not complete wasteland, surely a miracle that any folk lived within ten leagues. The last three revolts Hyrcan had put down so savagely that the whole country reverberated with the horror tales even yet. Women would slay themselves, it was said, and their children, rather than be taken prisoner by Hyrcan. Word had it that he put those he took in cells, without food, by twos and threes. The cell door would close, not to be opened again until those within were dead.

Few knew whether there was any truth to this, since Hyrcan did not speak, nor did the dead. The King knew it for fact, which only added to his fear of his brother.

When the Crown Prince's wife and young son had died of sweating fever earlier in the year, rumor spread (in the most hushed of whispers) that Hyrcan had suspected Evrieh's baby to be not his, that he had killed them as he did his prisoners. Of this tale, even Sedry knew nothing: There had been a recurrence of sweating fever at about that time. That no one had seen the Duchess, the young Prince, for weeks before their announced deaths—again, a thing not uncommon with so contagious a disease. The bodies had lain in state, as though the Prince had had nothing to hide; they had been wasted in appearance, but sweating fever did that. Hyrcan's behavior throughout had been exemplary. But—

"I came South," Hyrcan said into the silence, "to tell you of my successes, and to offer my aid in the Mountains, if you need me." Sedry brought his attention back to the moment.

"No. With Rolend imprisoned, the South is helpless."

"His captors remain firmly yours?" Hyrcan demanded. He had been for Rolend's death, when their younger brother led

the Marchers in revolt. But Sedry had chosen the dungeon for
Rolend instead, his life forfeit to his followers' behavior. Hyrcan resented it, still.

Sedry laughed loosely. "Now, brother! Merasma looks to
the main chance, always has! A choice between her idealistic
little brother and Darion's King?" Hyrcan shrugged. "No.
And the old Earl eats from her fingers. In the East, though—"

"Aye, the barghests."

"My Beldenians arrive within the week." Hyrcan stopped
in the act of untying his mail; his dark brows went up. "Do
not seek," Sedry went on impatiently, "to lesson me, brother.
They do not come to Lertondale this time."

Hyrcan chuckled. "It is your business, Sedry. If you recall,
I fully approved of your dealings with the City. These merchants grew fat under our father, it was more than time you
taught them their true importance in the scheme of things.
No," he went on as Sedry drained his cup, "I merely wondered that you had the nerve to recall the mercenaries."

"My nerve is where it should be," Sedry snapped. Hyrcan
chuckled again. "I own that it has been quiet enough across
the River since I had the bridge and trees decorated—" Hyrcan slapped a broad thigh, laughing loudly.

"I like that! 'Decorated.' Mind, brother, to keep close
watch on them, these commons still remember the lax days
under Alster."

"They will forget." Sedry stared into his empty cup. There
was a long silence.

"What is this," Hyrcan demanded abruptly, "about the
warrior Archbishop of Rhames?" Sedry, eyes still blankly ab-
sorbed in the interior of his cup, shrugged.

"I sent to ask his aid, he agreed to give it. He will lead the
Beldenians against the barghests. He arrives in a day or so,
depending on how the road from Carlsport holds."

"Why?" Hyrcan's face was set, his expression forbidding.
Sedry looked up at him in mild astonishment.

"Why? Why not?" He fumbled with his disorganized
thoughts. "Since when has Rhames needed reason? One year
he aided Genneldry against South Embersy, the year before
that North Embersy against Arlesia—that is how he serves the
Two. Ask him, if you are so curious."

"I would not get an answer worth having." Hyrcan's scowl

had deepened. "What do you know of the man, Sedry?"

Sedry shrugged. What had gotten into his brother? "He is Rhames' Archbishop, and that of North and South Embersy both—when they are at peace sufficiently to accept him, that is. He is an excellent swordsman, a brilliant tactician, a strong fighter. He has the strengths of the Two, the Holy Gifts, such as the Darion priests—all priests—wield. He throws in his lot as a mercenary, though he takes no pay save for his keep—"

"He travels," Hyrcan cut in flatly, "with a whore and a fortune teller."

Sedry tilted back his head and laughed loudly. "I might have known! I feared a swordsman's jealousy, but it is the monkish strain our mother set in you that is offended!" Hyrcan's expression was black indeed, but Sedry laughed again. "If his company offends you, brother Hyrcan, you had better leave before he arrives."

"Why?" Hyrcan demanded.

"Because," Sedry sobered, set his cup aside with a thud, "I know you, Brother. You will find an excuse to fight him, and I will not have that. I need him to lead the Beldenians against the barghests. Much depends on his aid. I cannot trust you to leave him alone."

There was a cold little silence. "No, I will not leave," Hyrcan said softly. "But I warn you, Sedry. Beware this priest!"

"What—foreseeing?" Sedry laughed, ignoring the look Hyrcan gave him. The Crown Prince had never shown any real ability with the Royal Gifts—save, of course, his dreaded personal Trait—and he had come of recent years to disclaim them as bastardized versions of the Gifts rightly belonging only to monks and other dedicated servants of the Two. Whether Hyrcan felt his own lack or not, no one knew; the Crown Prince was not given to such confidences.

"Sense," Hyrcan said finally. "One of us needs it, brother."

Sedry laughed again, undismayed. "I shall indeed beware Rhames. Since he is a greater swordsman than I shall ever be, I shall take care not to annoy him. But from all I have heard of the man, I shall like him."

Hyrcan studied him. "No doubt you will, brother." He yawned suddenly, cavernously. "It has been a long day for me, and a long ride; I am going to bed. Shall I aid you to yours, or will you have your tame monkey?''

Sedry scowled. "That is another thing. Leave Nolse alone, you bait him."

Hyrcan sneered. "What—does he weep on your shoulder?"

"Must everyone fear you, brother?" Sedry countered in exasperation. "He is my Steward, not yours. Leave him alone."

Hyrcan stood, bowing deeply, with a strong suggestion of irony in the movement. "Of a certainty—Sire." Sedry held out an arm and Hyrcan moved forward to take it, coming into the light for the first time since entering the room. The long, near-black lashes cast shadows upon his cheeks: broad cheeks in an obese face, surrounded by long, oiled curls. The body on which this head sat was no less grotesque. Hyrcan, though he kept his fighting skills at an awe-inspiringly high level, had long since given up the fight against encroaching fat.

The feminine, deceptively delicate lips curved into a slight smile; a broad hand reached, steadied the drunken King as he pushed up and away from the table. Firelight glittered on the Crown Prince's well-worn hilts as he wrapped an arm around Sedry's shoulders and led him into the darkened halls, waving the guard away when they would have aided him, leading him up the broad stairs and finally into Alster's old apartments. Sedry collapsed onto the bed, watching through half-closed eyes as Hyrcan spoke to Ogdred, the King's chief gentleman of chamber.

"Hyrcan?" Dread swirled around his throat; the words fought their way past. He had to know. The room swayed, steadied.

"My liege?" Hyrcan's behavior was exemplary around the King's household.

"What—truly happened to your wife and son?" Compulsive words: He was afraid, terrified, as soon as they forced themselves out. Hyrcan turned slowly, his eyes mere slits, his expression, briefly, at once bland and terrifying because of it. *This*, Sedry knew, *is the face Hyrcan wears when he kills*.

He swallowed hard against rising bile, but as suddenly as Hyrcan had turned to face the King, he relaxed. The broad face assumed an almost grotesque expression of grief, and his eyes closed briefly.

"My liege, you know they—died of fever, this last spring." Bowing then, he strode swiftly from the chamber. *Lies*. Sedry needed no Truthing to tell him as much, more than he needed anything beyond his eyes to tell him how near death he had been.

He started convulsively, a strangled cry catching in his throat, as Ogdred touched his arm gently, began aiding him from his clothing. *Aye, brother. I will not trust. But it is not the worldly priest I fear!*

It was nearly dark when the outlanders approached Lertondale, but not dark enough to cover the sad remains of the City's brief, savagely fought revolt. Fialla and the Reader bent forward, hoods pulled low, eyes held to the saddle-bows. Even the armsmen were unnaturally quiet and tended not to look too closely at objects around them. The air was still and fetid. Gespry alone sat upright, gazing about as though he would call the City into his memory for all time. His face, dark under pale hair, was grim.

There were no folk on the streets at all, save an occasional clutch of King's Guards. These seemed one and all nervous, though they walked in groups of at least four, weapons at the ready.

The water in the River was low and turbid, lantern light from the bridge casting sullen patches of yellow on its surface. Severed heads stared vacantly from the lamp pillars. After a moment, even the Archbishop looked away and urged his horse forward at some speed. The rest of the company clattered after him. Across the River and up a short winding road, Arolet beckoned.

The moon was rising when the Archbishop pressed aside the hangings to lean across the wide stone sill. Sedry had granted them a set of apartments that had once been a part of the nursery. A room was set aside as a reception, leaving the other three as sleeping chambers. The largest of these, with its eastern balcony and long row of windows over the courtyard, had been taken by the Archbishop and his lady. To their left was the small chamber allotted the Reader, while to the south, across the corridor, was the room shared by the armsmen.

A small hand brushed across the Archbishop's ear; he turned to take it between both of his. Dark blue eyes asked a question; he nodded once, gathered her close to him.

"As well to believe we are spied on," he murmured against her hair. "Safer for us." Aloud he added, "Fialla, my own, you must be as tired as I, and I am dead. The King will not

send for us until tomorrow, surely; it is late and he knows the
ride we have made.'' He bent forward to kiss her brow.
''There are no spy holes,'' he breathed, ''directed towards the
bed. You may be grateful for that.'' She ruffled his hair,
laughing gently.

''I am furious,'' she whispered back. ''In the very sleeping
rooms! I shall not undress until the last candle is out!''

Gespry laughed again. ''Here,'' he said aloud, wrapping an
arm around her shoulders. ''Perhaps another log on the fire—
A much nicer room, you'll admit, than what we had in South
Embersy four years ago.''

''Much,'' Fialla admitted. ''For one thing, it has windows—''

''And look—it is so clear tonight, I warrant you can see the
Eastern Mountains.''

Fialla leaned against him. ''I would rather not talk of them,
Gespry.''

''No. You are not pleased that I fight the Fegez, are you?''
She shook her head. Black hair, loosened for the night but not
yet plaited, flew across her shoulders. ''An enemy like any
other,'' the Archbishop continued.

''Not so,'' Fialla countered. ''But I will not argue the matter with you, Gespry.''

''No, let us not argue. The air is pleasant, let us step onto
the balconies a moment, shall we?'' He drew her with him,
leaving the heavy draperies pushed aside. Dim light from the
chamber caught his scabbard, the dagger sheathed on his left
forearm. Once against the balustrade, Fialla turned, wrapping her arms around his neck and drawing his head down to
her shoulder. ''There are three spy holes that I can readily
see,'' he whispered, and tersely gave her the locations.
''Another thing. There is a panel—no, do not look!—a panel
five paces from the fireplace. When we return, I will place the
screen against it. I hope you will have no need for it, but if you
do—''

''If I do,'' Fialla replied steadily.

''Brave Lady. Count the third brick from the floor, five out
from the mantle. You will need to press quite hard, the
passage will doubtless not have been used in many years. Once
within the passage . . . '' He paused.

''Within . . . '' Fialla prompted.

''Straight ahead until you come to stairs. Left at the foot.

Always left. Tell the Reader, alert the men when you have a chance. There are others, many others, but I doubt you will need any but this. *If* you need it. I do not foresee any danger to any of us.''

Fialla's fingers rubbed lightly at his neck. "No, you are no longer tense. The wager marks are cast, the coins upon the table, and we now play out the game." Aloud, she added, "I agree with you, the view is wonderful, my Gespry. But I do not have your swordsman's blood, and I am freezing. Come within, and draw the hangings." Gespry made her a slight bow.

"As you wish. Shall I build up the fire for you?"

"No. I am tired, I would rather sleep, I think." She moved towards the bed, gathering her hair to one side for plaiting as she did so, pressing aside the bed hangings with her shoulder. Gespry picked up a low folding screen and set it between bed and fire, precisely against the wall. Their eyes met.

"That should shield you, my dear." He started around the screen towards the fire.

"No. The candles also." Fialla's voice was firm. Gespry laughed as he strode to pinch out the nearest of them.

"It has been so long, I forgot your custom in a strange hall! Total darkness for my Lady." Two more candles followed the first, plunging the bed into gloom.

Gespry moved back towards the fire then, slightly favoring his left leg, frowning as he put weight upon it. He pulled off his cloak with an impatient gesture, undid the ties that held his mail in place, stripped down rapidly to underjerkin and breeches before leaning towards the fire. He yawned, stifled it with the back of one long hand, fished into his jerkin to bring forth the long string of prayer beads. These he drew over his head, kissing the two bound pieces of polished amber that hung from the ends. He dropped to one knee, winced, then to both, faced the fire, closed his eyes.

The priestly night-ritual of the Two followed: The Archbishop was swift but thorough, intoning the prayers with not only correctness but a proper sense of worship.

To the left of the mantle, the Steward's spy was impressed in spite of himself: The Archbishop might scorn the true way of priests as far as foresaking women was concerned—but what a woman this Fialla was!—yet there was no doubting his piety. A little self-consciously, the man followed the sign of the blessing, watched the Archbishop finish his prayers and rise to his feet with a swordsman's grace, though he seemed to bite back a cry as the weight went onto his left leg. The spy remained where he was until Gespry vanished beyond the screen, out of his sight in the darkness, and various faint noises assured him that the man had completed his undressing and gone to bed.

10

DARION'S KING AND the Archbishop of Rhames met formally for the first time the next morning: Sedry was subdued, his Aura, his charismatic smile in abeyance, but there was reason for that. The King's head ached with the early hour and the previous night's indulgences. Otherwise, his manner was exemplary, his greeting cordial enough as he stepped down to kiss the Archbishop's hand and receive his blessing. For his part, Gespry was correct, precise in his movements, in the bow he made the King, yet wonderfully charming in manner. It was with great reluctance, and only with the knowledge that they would dine together that evening, that Sedry dismissed him and went on with the morning's business.

The Archbishop strode from the receiving hall, briefly closing his eyes as the doors shut behind him. *One more barrier crossed, Darion's King has taken to me.* There remained few now, and only one Gespry was concerned with: Crown Prince Hyrcan. A man to fear, that one.

As the Two would have it (Alayya, Elorra, how a man's luck ran!) the Crown Prince was said to have ridden in the night before. *A wonder,* Gespry thought sourly as he walked back to his apartments, *that we did not bump into each other at the gates.* He dismissed Hyrcan from his thoughts, then, smiled graciously at the hall guards and at the two maid servants who gazed at him in awe-struck astonishment, only belatedly remembering to curtsy as he passed.

Fialla sat on a low stool just inside the balcony, the early sun lighting her needlework: She was mending a dark brown shirt. As he entered she glanced up, smiling briefly, warmly. "You are as hard on your clothing as a green lad, Gespry." He laughed, wandered out past her onto the balcony, stretching hard.

"The King has not grudged you women, Fialla. You need not do such work—"

"Bah. I want it mended properly. And I need things to occupy my hands."

"Poor my Lady. We shall bring a cart next time, rather than a baggage horse, you never have sufficient needlework, have you? Belden," he added, stretching again and leaning out to gaze down into the courtyard, "is late. We remain here another seven days, perhaps ten. But the King has an extensive library for his young Queen and her tutors, he has already granted you its use." Sedry's bride—a child of twelve—had come to Arolet the year before, from North Embersy. It would be four years before she was crowned, and she was presently engaged in finishing a rather extensive education.

"How very kind of him," Fialla exclaimed. Gespry nodded.

"Most kind. You and I are to dine with them tonight."

"She is said to be a lovely child."

"Fair, they say," Gespry agreed. "Pale for my tastes, of course," he went on, touching her black curls. "They say she is intelligent as well, and well versed. Odd," he continued dryly, "for a Northern, where it is often difficult to tell the men from the sheep by their brains—"

"Gespry!" Fialla laughed, horrified.

"No, I promise to behave. Come, set aside that wretched shirt. I have no need of it until we ride against the Fegez." Fialla shivered, briefly closing her eyes, but smiled reassuringly as a hand touched her shoulder. "Very well, no more of them either. Come with me; the King has given us free run of Arolet, and I would walk outdoors while it is warm."

"Well, Brother?" Sedry sat on the top step of the dais in the nearly deserted reception. Hyrcan moved from the shadows behind the throne to stand beside him. "Well?" Sedry repeated testily. "You have seen him, what have you to say?"

Hyrcan shrugged. "From a formal meeting?"

"You saw him." Sedry glanced up, wincing at the sudden pounding between his temples.

"All right. I still do not like him, brother."

Sedry scowled across the chamber. At its far end, Nolse was pressing the tall double doors closed behind the last of the council and, at a gesture from the King, went out himself. The brothers were alone.

"A reason, Hyrcan? A genuine reason? I found Gespry pleasant company. I liked him enough at first meeting, and I am certain now I shall like him better the more I know of him." A faint tickle at the inner senses, which Sedry pressed aside. Why should the Archbishop trigger a faint sense of—something—what?—in him? Nothing. Hyrcan's presence, perhaps. Meetings long awaited were never what you expected, anyway.

Hyrcan laughed briefly. His expression was sour. "He gives himself airs, Sedry. I daresay he writes poetry, or plays the viol or the gambra." Sedry leaned back on his elbows, gazing up.

"Hyrcan—I believe you are jealous." The Crown Prince snorted derisively. "Looks: He has them. A fair woman, who gives up her comfort to travel with him—"

"A whore," Hyrcan snapped.

"If you prefer—but a highborn and exceedingly beautiful one, from what I hear. Intelligence, piety, wealth—legendary skill with his blades and with a bow—"

"Huh." These last rankled with Hyrcan, badly. "He was nearly killed at Megen Cove."

"A mast fell on him," Sedry remarked pointedly. "No, Hyrcan, it is clear to me that you do not like the man for his very attributes. And heed me, brother! There will be no trying of Gespry! Grant that you are of his class with sword—"

"Better," Hyrcan cut in flatly. Sedry waved an impatient hand.

"As you choose, I do not care greatly. Darion needs Gespry. If only because the Beldenians will follow no one else. Cross me in this, brother, and you will cross me in no other thing. Ever." There was a tight, nasty silence. Hyrcan moved then, jumping neatly down three stairs so that he and the King were eye to eye.

"Surely you are not threatening me, Sedry?"

"No. I vow that." Sedry held his gaze steady with terrible effort: His sudden recall of his question to Hyrcan the night before did not help his nerve. Alayya, Elorra, had he been as drunk as that? "I rule Darion, Hyrcan. Remember that! You are of great aid to me, brother, and I do not forget what I owe you. But no man is irreplaceable, remember that also.''

Another silence, even tighter than the last. Then Hyrcan suddenly smiled, a movement of his mouth that went nowhere near his eyes, and he bowed formally, backing down two more steps as he did so.

"Your pardon—my liege. Gespry of Rhames is a thorn in my side, but I will leave him alone, if you say.''

"I do say.''

"As you wish. Now, if you have no more need for me, I had better go see that your stable hands took proper care of my horse last night.''

"Certainly.'' Sedry rose as his brother moved swiftly, lightly from the hall, the catlike grace of his step even more of an anomaly than it had been when he was barely of age and still in trim.

As the doors closed behind the Crown Prince, Sedry slumped back onto his elbows, rousing himself from a dark study with effort. Nearly the noon hour; a brief meeting with Nolse and messengers from Orkry. Then it would be time to eat, and today Juseppa had only history and language lessoning, and so would eat with him. The King smiled briefly as he thought of his young Lady.

She was exactly right, he mused. An excellent move from a political standpoint—North Embersy was a good ally to have, if only for the increase in trade. More: though pretty enough to please even Sedry, who had a certain discrimination in such matters, Juseppa was still young enough not to interfere in his indulgences with other women. And there were many, many of these.

Most of them, conscious of the honor involved, had bestowed themselves freely upon the King: The Mayor of Lertondale's wife was one of these, the Chatelaine of Orkry another. Many others had yielded with only the slightest touch of persuasion, as had Nolse's golden-haired lady, and several of Juseppa's honor maidens.

Of course, Sedry was not above actual threat, blackmail, or straight force followed by threat of discovery when necessary: the daughter of his chief counciler, Maldiss, with her pale braids tucked demurely around her head, the form no man would eye twice in Arolet's halls, clad as she clad herself. Or Eavon's daughter Elyessa, with the deep red hair hanging in heavy ripples to her knees, the spray of freckles that crossed a slender straight nose—Gods, those wide, green eyes, so helpless! Before long, unfortunately, he would have to start giving up such pleasures, or at least he would have to become much more circumspect in their pursuit. Then again, Juseppa was such an innocent, so devoted to him: Maybe she'd believe what he told her. In any event, she was still four years from his bed.

Sedry sighed, his good mood fully restored: Counting his women did that for him.

And then, tonight: Gespry and the Lady Fialla would take evening meal with him. Nolse had brought in the reports from his men; every one of them had been outspoken in their praise of the Lady. And, once again he irritatedly repressed that nervous *something* that crossed his mind—Hyrcan be damned. He *liked* this Archbishop!

11

TEN DAYS LATER and forty leagues to the East: Gespry pulled
his horse up short and leaned perilously sideways to gaze into
the valley, eight fathoms distance straight down. Some four
leagues in length, it was at least five furlongs wide. Here and
there were stands of pine, ash, or willow, but most of the
gently rolling ground was open meadow. A river undulated in
a shining, shallow ribbon its entire length, heavily edged in
bush and thicket.

On the north side of this river stood the Darion camp. The
Beldenians, a force at least half again as great as the Marcher
army, held the south bank, stretching out along the water.
Throughout both camps, all brush and tall grasses had been
cleared. In the midst of the mercenary camp, set apart in a
clearing of its own, stood the Archbishop's blue and gold
pavilion, Gespry's banner flying from the pole set in the turf
before it.

Gespry's eyes took this in rapidly, moved on. The far wall
rose, like the one he sat on, in sharp granite cliffs, innocent of
tree or bush, overhung in many places. It was even higher than
the south wall.

"By the Two," Gespry exclaimed testily. "What was the
King thinking of! Or was it those fool Marchers? This place
has trap written all across its grassy belly!" His white hair
streamed back away from his thin face in a sharp breeze that
brought the tang of rain with it. The Reader and the Lady
Fialla, holding well away from the steep ledge with the pack
animals, exchanged resigned glances. The Archbishop had

been in a temper since they'd set out, his mood as black as the sky. Boresin urged his own horse forward.

"I had understood," he began apologetically, "that it was for shelter from the wind—"

"Thrice blast the wind," Gespry snapped sourly. "I had a damned sight rather wake up tossled than with a barghest knife in my belly!" He smiled, suddenly sheepish. "Boresin, your pardon, it is not your fault. I am more than uncommonly saddlebroke today, though, and I do not like the look of this cut!"

Gelc dismounted, limping forward to peer uneasily down into the valley. "They must come across that plain at us; a watch could see far enough to give warning. There is nowhere for them to hide to sneak up on us, and I do not see how anyone, armed or not, could climb down those walls."

"Ah," the Archbishop said moodily, his dark gaze sweeping the valley again, "but you are not a b—a Fegez. Perhaps no one human could—"

"No. They are men. They can be slain as men." Fialla spoke from the depth of her thick woolen hood. The tremor in her voice was only noticeable to one who knew her well. The Archbishop stirred at her words, turned back to her side. The dark eyes were worried as they sought hers, relaxed a little as she smiled.

"As the Lady says." Gelc's face was impassive.

Gespry raised up in his stirrups. "Come. If it is a trap, it is too late to worry the matter. At least tonight. I would reach shelter from this wind before the rain begins as well." So saying, he turned his horse and started down the narrow track that would take them almost a league back the direction they had just come, through a deeply folded, mountainous pine forest, and so through a wide, heavily guarded cut and into the valley itself. Boresin and Fidric, leading the two pack animals, followed, leaving Gelc to bring up the rear. With a sudden motion, the Tarots Reader spurred forward to catch the brothers. Fialla spared one final glance for the valley far below, one worried look after the blue-cloaked rider now several lengths down the trail. She pulled cloak and hood more tightly around her and urged her tired horse forward. At least under the trees, the wind would not be as stiff.

A great cheer went up as they entered the Darion camp, men

rushing from the picket lines, from the messes, half-washed and still wet from the river, to see the legendary Archbishop of Rhames and his small following: the same five, the least young archer among them knew, that had followed him the past ten years. Even the Tarots Reader threw back her hood and the Lady Fialla waved and smiled from her place at her Lord's side. Gespry himself, in an abrupt change of mood, reached down to touch hands and shoulders, a warm smile transforming his face.

The cheer was redoubled as the company forded the shallow water and entered the Beldenian camp: Many of these men had fought with the Archbishop before, many of them had participated in the battle of Megen Cove, when the Genneldrean Navy was effectively removed from the Seas. A sergeant of the archers pushed to the fore, dragging a companion with him: his nephew, a boy only this past summer taken to service.

"Look there, Zormerian!" he demanded, his seamed face breaking into a joyous smile as the Archbishop rode nearer. "Now that is a man to serve under, laddie! Not like Darion's King, who commands from safety a hundred miles away!"

"But Uncle Zorec, they say King Sedry rides to join the army within the week." The old sergeant glared at the boy. Listening to gossip again, was he? "Well, they do say as much!"

"*They*," Zorec replied sourly but recaptured his good mood all of an instant as the Archbishop leaned down to grip his arm and murmur: "Good man, sergeant!"

"As to the King," Zorec went on, but in a much milder voice, "I'll believe that when I see it, not before. But that," he reiterated with warmth, "is a man to serve under. Although," he added, staring after the horses, "he is so thin, I barely know him! And his hair was golden!" It troubled him: Gespry'd changed so little, compared to what a man might have expected, and yet—

"They say he was badly hurt," the boy remarked, leaning around the older man to gaze after the riders. "They say he nearly died."

Zorec blinked, pulled his thoughts back together. "And so he did," he said somberly. "I was there, wasn't I? Aided the Lady Fialla from the *Wave Cleaver* onto the *Storm Rider* with these very hands—though she'd only leave after her Gespry was taken across." Zormerian, who had gazed at the beautiful

Fialla of Rhames with his young heart in his eyes only moments before, turned to stare at his uncle in speechless awe.

The interior of the Archbishop's tent was pleasantly warm, particularly after the biting wind they'd faced much of the afternoon. It was a large shelter, a gift from certain Beldenian nobles in gratitude for Gespry's assistance against the southern pirates. Silver lanterns hung from the inner frame, while still unlit candles in wide-footed brass bases held down the corners of an enormous map of eastern Darion that covered most of the long table. A number of chairs and three-footed stools were grouped around this table, which would serve as a war council for Gespry and his Beldenian Captains—and such of the Marchers as would consort with the mercenaries. Fine carpets of South Embersean weave covered the thick meadow grasses, save the two places where the sod had been cut away for fire pits. To the rear were sleeping places for the armsmen and an alcove for the Reader. Beyond these, a curtained chamber for the Archbishop and his Lady.

"Another trial," Gelc muttered. "Always another." The Archbishop, who had doffed his boots as soon as they had reached shelter and was now prowling the carpets barefoot, laughed briefly.

"As you say, my good friend. And to my mind, nearly the last of them. But caution, cloth walls hold few secrets!" And he nodded towards the flap, where one of their three Beldenian door warders and honor guards could be seen pacing about.

"Folk see what they wish to see," Fidric remarked. He was leaning against the table, studying the map. "What would any of these wish to see, save Gespry, alive and well? Things go well, Gelc, stop worrying." Gelc scowled at him. Fidric briefly met Gelc's eyes, turned to the Reader, who had settled down under one of the lanterns and was already engaged in laying out a complex pattern of cards in the pool of light: Nine points, a wide space, an enclosing circle. As he watched she turned up a card, laid it by itself in the enclosed area, canted to the left: Three of Blades, open battle. "We are safe as we ever are before a fight, arms-brother," Fidric went on. "The Reader has seen nothing—"

"Nothing," the Reader agreed calmly, leaving the others to wonder, as they frequently did, how she could concentrate so completely on her cards and still follow the conversations around her. She looked up, gazing from one of them to another, her eyes holding Gelc's at the last. "Nothing yet."

"Yet?" The little armsman pounced on that. She shrugged.

"You know me, Gelc Garnacsson. What I see. What I cannot see. I see as yet nothing that creates a major deviation from the Pattern set back in Rhames, when this journey was decided upon." She turned over another card, setting the Archer beside the 3 of Blades, canting it to the right. "There are conflicting patterns, brought about by the manipulation of so many individuals, so many different people. Can you sort out the individual crossings of a battle while you participate therein, swordsman? Or predict its outcome by the first crossings?"

"No," Gelc admitted. "But *you—*"

The Reader sighed gently. "I know." It was a heavy burden, building a Master Pattern. On occasion, such as this one, she felt it keenly. "There are variables," she said finally. "As you well know, Gelc. Enough of them, concerted, could destroy the Pattern, no matter what I predict."

"But—"

"But I see no such disturbance now. Or in the near future."

"My apology, Reader."

"Accepted, Gelc." Tranquilly, she turned back to her cards, adding another three with slow deliberation to the uppermost stack, neatly squaring the edges with deft fingers before setting another in the center of the design. The Madman, upright, stared back at her with his mismatched blue/brown eyes.

Gelc turned around to face the Archbishop, who had abandoned his pacing to sit on a low-backed, cushioned chair; Fialla stood behind him, absently rubbing at his neck muscles. "One would think," Gespry said suddenly, "that you did not trust Gelc."

"Trust?"

"To my sword. Among other things." Gespry twitched as Fialla's fingers dug deeply into muscle at either side of his neck. Boresin, who had been lying flat on the far side of the Reader, eyes closed, now propped himself up onto one elbow.

"Not so, Gespry. Pay no heed to Gelc. You know what he is like before battle."

Gelc snorted; Fidric shifted. "You were not much better

aboard the Wave Cleaver, brother,'' he said, placatingly. One of the Beldenians came in with heavy pewter mugs, several leather flasks.

"That was different!'' Boresin protested. He waved his brother aside, sorted out cups, sniffed cautiously at the various containers and with a shrug began pouring from what he seemed to consider the best of several bad bargains. "I was never a sailor,'' he added, passing cups down for Gespry and Fialla—the Reader never drank anything but her herb teas. Fialla leaned across to grip the armsman's hand.

"If you love me, you will not mention Megen Cove again.''

"Of course. I am sorry, Fialla.''

"Drink,'' Gespry advised mildly, following his own advice. "We are all tired and overwrought. That was too long a ride, and with this trap at the end—ah!'' The last a sharp intake of breath as Fialla's fingers dug into his shoulders.

"Now, I swear,'' she said humorously, but in a tone which brooked no argument, "that do any of you say 'trap' again—!''

Gespry's hands came up to cover hers. "Not while my neck is in your grasp, my dear! Yes?'' The bell outside the tent clanged and the young guard entered, rather apologetically, to advise the Archbishop that the captains of both forces, together with ten of the Marcher Barons, would be pleased to meet with him after the dinner hour.

12

IT WAS A long and hard meeting, lasting well into middle night. Fialla, who had retreated into the curtained bedchamber with the Reader as soon as the first Beldenian Captains arrived, had reason more than once to be proud of her companion: There, Gespry speaking with Woldeg, the Marcher responsible for the choice of this camp, and in just the flat, inflectionless voice that was Gespry at his most furious. There, again, the somewhat dry but not unkind response to an obvious remark on someone's part and there, the warm reply to an intelligent suggestion.

So Gespry won men to his side, and so he had always dominated tactical meetings, whether at his monastery, at the King's council in North Embersy, or anywhere else. A sudden, intense wave of misery washed through her. The Reader's hand came away from her cards, touched her forearm.

"He is well, Fialla. Do not fear for him."

Fialla smiled: A poor effort, she knew, one which would fool no one. *I must not allow this sort of thing*, she chided herself angrily. *It is unfair to him and to me, and dangerous to all of us!*

"Trust," the Reader went on somberly. "All goes well with him." There was reassurance in the light blue eyes, warning as well.

A sudden sharp argument in the main chamber of the pavilion: Gespry and Nevered, the most conservative of the Darion nobles, as easily identified by his loudly voiced thoughts as by his carrying, treble voice.

90

With a light touch, the Reader drew her companion's attention, indicated the Tarots with a wave of her hand. Fialla, welcoming the diversion, moved nearer and bent her head to the pattern spread across the rugs.

From association with the Reader, she knew the kinds of them, a little about them. Major arcana, twenty-five of them, often poorly executed upon the cards. Finely done in the case of this Reader, whose patron stinted her in nothing. Thirty-five minor arcana, blue and gold, in five suits: Blades, Sheaves, Water, Fire, Earth.

The Reader had begun the simplest pattern this time: a reading for an individual. Four thin piles of cards guarded the corners, surrounded a double Indicator: Princess of Flames covered by, crossed by the Priest. Out from the four stacks, centered between their corners and parallel with the flat sides of the Princess, she was now placing other cards. Five of Blades: skirmish, either in words or actual fighting. Upright, and therefore no threat. Seven of Blades: ambush, challenge. Also upright. Fog.

The Reader hesitated, one slender finger tapping this last card. Finally, she shrugged. Fog, deceit. The journey had reeked of it from the start, it appeared in all their readings. No point to attempting a further clarification, certainly not in this reading. She spared a glance towards the main room, where Gespry was arguing persuasively with the elderly Beldenian, who was determined to send individual scouts both eastward and into the upper edges of the valley.

"You can send men, sir, they are yours to use as you see fit. You will have no argument from me, if that is your final word. Now, whether you will get any of them back again, that is another matter, and I for one doubt that you will." He allowed sufficient room for the other to speak, went on as he did not. "We are not woodcrafty, sir. Not as a Fegez understands it."

Another voice, the heavily accented and archaic Ordinate marking the speaker as Marcher as much as the low rasp placed him as elderly: "Barghests are Two-benighted foxes. Or ghosts. Thou'lt see nothing of them until they choose it, and then—well, 'tis too late for thee then."

Gespry again: "Now, my Lord of Marchham, none of this about ghosts, you'll scare me and my men here with that kind of talk!" A roar of laughter; the conversation was, for a while, more relaxed. There was a clink of cups: someone passing wine again.

The Reader turned a final card, laid it below the center of her pattern. His dark face lit by the fire he bore in his cupped hands, the Prince of Flames gazed upwards, as though he offered what he held to the Princess. The Reader sat back on her heels, and a rare frown crossed her brow. "Odd," she murmured.

"Odd?" Fialla had listened to the arguments with half an ear; now she brought her attention back to the Reader.

"The Princess." The Reader looked up, went back to her cards.

"Yes." A pale figure, the Princess, under her crown of flames, the sword in her hand touched with blue fire, her face stern, unafraid.

"These," the Reader went on, gesturing towards the first three cards, "indicate battle, confusion, deception. No danger."

Fialla nodded. Indicated the last card, looked a question.

"The Prince," the Reader murmured. "Placed as he is—he should be of the Pattern, in it already. And I have not yet seen him."

"Perhaps kin—"

"No." The Reader paused, her fingers brushing the cards lightly. "Not kin. And yet—"

"Yet?" Fialla prompted. The Reader gazed at her blankly for a long moment. "Odd." She shrugged. "The Prince of Flames and the Princess are much alike; of the major arcana, these two are more closely tied than any of the others." She shrugged again. "It poses no threat to the Pattern, I will understand it soon enough."

She reached for the topmost card in the packet to the right of the Prince, held it lightly for a moment before she turned it over, set its corners to touch both Prince and Princess. The Madman.

"Surprise," Fialla whispered. "But—good or bad?"

The Reader frowned. Something seemed to upset her, but it was gone from her face a moment later as she swept the cards together and began sorting them into a face down pile. "It was a murky reading." She squared the edges and returned them to the silk-lined, jeweled case Gespry had given her for their safety. "They will not require my services tonight." Not a question.

"No," Fialla agreed. "Their talk is all war and battle tonight. Another night, certainly. The Beldenians, at least."

"Good," the Reader said simply. "I am tired, and need sleep."

"They will not be much longer," Fialla smiled at her. The Reader smiled back, rather shyly.

"No?"

"Unlikely. Fidric has been plying them with dark Beldenian wine since they arrived." She hesitated, reached to lay a small hand on the little case. "Does it never—never upset you?"

"Upset me. My Gift?" The Reader settled her back against the Archbishop's low bed, considered the question gravely for some moments. "No." She met her companion's eyes. "It's not as you see it, you know."

"Not—how?"

"The Patterning." She lay her own hand on the jeweled box. "We don't play God, we usurp none of the rights and powers of the Two. Though most, who see beyond the simple fortune-tellers we all are, think that."

"Not—"

"Not you, of course," the Reader went on as Fialla hesitated. "You've seen more of the Patterning than most, you and the armsmen. Gespry. But it's still other than what you think." She paused to marshal her thoughts. "It would be right to say that you know Gespry well, and that, under many circumstances, you know what he would do or say."

"Under most, I think," Fialla replied. She tucked her feet under her skirts; the night was beginning to cool.

"A—training in the Tarots, such as I have had, gives you such a sense with people you do not know. And the Patterning—that is merely the making of a form involving many people, the way they will react. It is partly the cards, partly the Gift, now and again something that is both of these and something more.

"Here—," she hesitated momentarily. "Here, I can say that—because Darion's King is a certain kind of man, because he thinks certain ways and does certain things, because his brother the Crown Prince is a certain kind of man—all of them, you know as well as I—because of these things, because of the way they have come together, a certain outcome will ensue.''

"If we hold to our own paths," Fialla added. The Reader nodded gravely.

"Moreso in this case than in any other I have ever sought to control; there are more variable ends to weave into the Pattern than sense would attempt. But that, too," she added with a deprecating smile, "is also a part of the Pattern: *that*, perhaps, only Gespry of Rhames and I would be such fools as to try.''

"Gespry—," Fialla began. The Reader's eyes caught hers again in that look which held both understanding and warning. "Have care to your own part," she said finally. "Remember it well, and do not fail it, even for the least moment! That is one of the weakest threads in our weaving, that we might forget one simple thing, and speak aloud the wrong word at the wrong time.''

"I shall not forget," Fialla reassured her somberly.

"Yours is truly the hardest, I know," the Reader said. "Could it have been another way—"

"I know. Never mind." Her attention was drawn to the outer portion of the pavilion: The meeting was breaking up. The Darion men—still arguing as they left over the numbers of armed men who should be left at the various keeps, the numbers of additional men to be brought here—left a very short time later. The Beldenians were not long behind.

Gespry was alone, slouched in a high-backed chair at the far end of the table, a half-emptied wine cup within easy reach, legs splayed out before him. He opened his eyes as Fialla drew a seat near, taking one of his hands in both of hers. The Beldenian warder who had earlier announced the arrivals studiously averted his eyes as he cleared cups and bottles away. Gespry smiled tiredly.

"How well you dealt with them," Fialla murmured.

"Do you think so?" The face so near hers was perilously near exhaustion. Fialla nodded.

"Or I would never have said it. But you are tired, you need sleep.''

Gespry shrugged, a rueful smile tugging at his wide mouth.

"I could sleep a week. But I must tell Fidric to replenish my cup less often, I have no head for that dark stuff." The young

Beldenian came back for the last of the bottles, tugged the
map straight in the middle of the table, and bowed his way
out.

"All the more reason to sleep," Fialla replied gently. She
pushed away from the table, blew out the nearest of the
candles and lowered the wick on two of the lanterns. A third
had guttered moments before, the fourth they would leave
burning the night. "Come—now, I say, my Lord!" Gespry
groaned but allowed himself to be led away.

"What was decided?" Fialla asked as she pulled the curtain
into place behind them. Gespry rolled onto the soft bedding
with a little sigh and closed his eyes. "No good sleeping in
those pants," she added tartly, "half the trail from Lertondale
is on them. If you want under the covers tonight, you'll have
to shed them." Another groan, but the Archbishop, eyes still
closed, sat up with her help and began pulling off the heavy
overshirt, tugged at the laces of his underjerkin as Fialla
worked his boots off. Thick woolen pants followed: Gespry
sat on the edge of the bedding as Fialla pulled the covers
down, unaware of the chill, though he now wore only lightweight, knee-length drawers and a wide, snug bandage wound
tightly about his chest from just under the armpits to nearly
the last of his ribs. He was more asleep than awake as his
mistress bundled him into a loose, long-sleeved nightshirt,
snuggled under the soft linen and furs gratefully as she tucked
them about his neck before extinguishing the main lantern and
undressing herself.

"Nothing much was settled this evening." A drone of voice
came from the bed; Gespry had heard her earlier question
after all. "What ever is? And the Marcher Barons are prouder
than most men, displeased in the bargain that they must beg
aid from the Beldenian mercenaries."

"Who are themselves proud," Fialla said, reducing herself,
with a shiver, to the thin underdress, barely remembering to
lay her cloak to hand to serve later as a robe before hastening
under the covers herself.

"Who are indeed proud," Gespry agreed drowsily. "But
they speak to each other, even if only to shout, so there is yet
hope. Odd, though—"

"Odd," Fialla prompted, after a rather long silence.

"Mmmm? Oh. Odd how little they know of the Fegez, these

Marchers. They have lived among them most of their lives, and they are many of them older, men given their lands by Alster fifty years ago. And still none of them have fought barghests hand to hand—"

"Gespry! For shame!"

"Their choice of words, Lady, I but quote." He sighed. "And so one cannot even get a decent description, let alone a straight story on this shape-changing business. Which they all seem to believe in without reservation. They will say nothing beyond that, however.

"I could not part them from this maledictable valley, them *or* the mercenaries, though I think I persuaded them to send no more small scouting parties, and to post extra guards about the camp." Another sigh. "Tomorrow may give us more. They have sent for one of their younger men, he is supposed to know—"

"To know?"

"Mmmm. Lord of Korent." Gespry was more than half asleep. "I think that was the name, I had to separate Grolpet from his brother's throat just then, and had no chance to ask again."

"Lord of Korent," she prompted. "Why are they sending him to you?"

"He is the easternmost of the Barons, he knows the Fegez better than any of the rest of them. But I gathered that he was not pleased to receive the summons. I may need you to soften the boy for me, Fialla."

"Boy? Come, Gespry!" Fialla raised onto one elbow. Gespry rolled over to face her, settling the covers around his shoulders. Dark eyes met hers briefly, closed again.

"I gather he is young. Young for a landholder, anyway. He was barely of age when he received Korent from King Sedry—as a favor for his aid against the old King, for his aid in Alster's deposing and exile." Fialla closed her eyes briefly. Gods. She thought she had detected an uncommon hostility in her companion's voice. "I must say," Gespry added blandly, "I look forward to meeting this young Marcher lord."

13

IT WAS BARELY daylight when Fialla awoke, but Gespry was already gone. So were all three swordsmen: the Archbishop, still far from satisfied with their safety, was taking an early circuit of the valley. The heavy trousers, muddy boots, and woolen shirt he'd worn the day before were missing, as was the distinctive sky-blue cloak, lined and edged with pale yellow.

Fialla hastened into her own clothes in the early chill and hurried into the main portion of the tent.

There were low fires burning in both firepits, and the air was noticeably warmer. A note, confirming Gespry's whereabouts, had been left on the table with her breakfast: fresh fruit, warm bread not long from the fire. Several strips of lightly spiced, dried meat, a pot of apple butter. Near the fire was a steaming open pot of the drink called coffee Gespry had discovered during one of his commissions in the deserts west of Rhames, and upon which he had become thoroughly dependent. Ordinarily, she would not have given the pot a second glance, but this morning anything hot looked good to her and she filled the Archbishop's thick mug, carried it gingerly back to the table and sat as close to the fire as she could, stocking'd feet thrust towards the warmth.

It took several swallows—horrible stuff, but it certainly warmed your belly!—before she looked on the food with any interest. Something to eat, first, then she would ride herself, around the Beldenian camp. Most of the men out there knew her from one or another of the Archbishop's campaigns, and it would be a good time to become acquainted with as many of the rest as possible. Fialla was well aware of her effect on these men, knew her worth to Gespry in that respect, but more, she could sometimes learn things, solve petty grievances, deal with the matters for which the overly busy Archbishop and his armsmen had no time.

Her feet were a little swollen from the long hours of riding the day before and her boots were tight, soft as the leather was. A scarf then: silvery stuff, an ornament against the plain dark wool of shirt and divided riding skirt that brushed the tips of the boots. A tabard over that, padded for protection against cold and wind, bearing both Gespry's arms and those of her own family: a hound at the alert before a tower, underneath the motto "Iyo gepartes": *I serve.* Over all, the heavy cloak of dark grey that matched shirt and skirt but was lined, unexpectedly, in a rich, deep blue.

The cold hit her like a blow as she stepped outside, making her gasp. She drew gloves from her belt, sent one of the guard for her horse.

It was a pleasant ride, for all the cold. For well over an hour she rode about the camp, stopping frequently as an armsman would drop his tasks to call her name, to speak of the last time he had seen her or to ask of the Archbishop's health. This last with some anxiety, for the Mercenaries looked upon Gespry as one of their own. Fialla dredged up names—ranks when she could not recall names, other times, situations from the past—from her capacious memory, and was amply repaid by the warmth of response from those she spoke with.

Several times she dismounted for greater ease in speaking to a number of men at once. Word preceded her, and those who had not already ridden out flocked to her side.

It was with greatly restored confidence that she rode back to the pavilion, and the smile she gave the guard who handed her down from her mount was more than perfunctory this time. The boy stared after her dazedly as she dropped the flap into place behind her.

Another mug of Gespry's coffee for the chill—ugh. She must take the time this very afternoon to look out her small supply of teas. They were not where they should be, must be simply buried where they did not belong. In the meantime— perhaps Grolpet had sufficient to share, though Beldenian tea was scarcely better than Gespry's coffee. King Sedry had offered her something he called "chocolate"; imported, he said, from a far distant land, warming, if a trifle sweet for her taste. Fool, she thought, to have refused his offer of more.

The tiny bell rang outside, and one of the guard raised his voice: "One to see the Archbishop."

"Let him enter," she called out, pushing the mug away. The flap moved aside, a tall, lean man entered, approaching the long table with a ground-eating stride.

Young was her first thought; but the dark brown hair falling across his temples was lightly frosted, as was the well-trimmed beard that followed a rather wide jaw, emphasizing both that and the somewhat prominent mouth under the thick moustache. A nice mouth, perhaps; at the moment it was thinned with displeasure. His hair was as long as Gespry's but worn all of a length, falling from a center parting to his shoulders, Marcher-fashion. The narrowed eyes could have been black.

Is this another of them? she wondered with a brief impatience; certain of the Darion nobles—though few of the Marchers, she had to admit—had been outspoken on the subject of a vowed servant of the Two traveling with a woman in any fashion, let alone one who was mistress. Displeasure—exhaustion also, she suddenly realized. The man was practically swaying on his feet. She gestured towards empty chairs, pulled one with padded back and arms away from the table. "Sit, sir."

"After thee, Lady," he replied, and waited until she had taken a seat of her own before sliding into the one she had offered him. *Mannered for a Marcher, if abrupt.* "I am Baldyron—Korent. They tell me his Grace is not in camp, I must see him at once." Ahhh. Then the displeasure was nothing to do with her.

"He is riding the parameters of the valley, seeking to increase our safety here. I look to his return at any moment. But as to yourself—have you eaten yet, Baron?" A silence. He ran a sun- and wind-darkened hand through his hair, scowled blankly at the table. "I doubt you have," Fialla went on. "You have the look of a man moments away from a long ride. Here is bread and fruit, a little dried meat. And coffee, which is at least hot, though you may not care for its taste."

"I have tasted it before, once. My thanks, Lady." He raised his chin and looked at her, seemed to see her for the first time: His eyes widened. Aware that he was staring, he colored, brought his gaze down to the food she was setting before him.

"In truth," he went on, flatly, though the antagonism was gone from his voice, "I do not believe I have eaten since noon-meal yesterday. For a time, it was unlikely I would get away."

"Duties?" Fialla inquired. She set a mug of coffee before him. He chewed, swallowed, shook his head.

"Barghests—thy pardon, Lady. Fegez." He bent over the steaming cup. "They have surrounded Korent. A sortie at the north walls allowed me to slip away by the south."

"What danger to your hold?" Fialla asked. She made a face at the cup she had absently taken up, pushed it away.

"None, at present. I constructed it well, against the possibility of such war." Troubled eyes met hers. "I am needed there, however. I had no business leaving."

"Of course." No point to arguing with him. There was no arrogance in his last words: he felt his responsibilities keenly.

Unaware of her scrutiny, he leaned back in his chair, drained his cup. "My thanks, Lady Fialla. At least, I—." For the first time, he seemed embarrassed, at a loss for words, "I presume—"

"I am Fialla," she assured him. "No thanks necessary, sir."

"I was more hungry than I thought." A genuine smile briefly erased care from his brow and fully ten years from his aspect; he could not yet have been thirty. "Hast saved my life, Lady Fialla."

Fialla smiled back. "A pleasure, Lord Korent."

A shadow crossed his face, was gone so quickly she might have imagined it, and he smiled again, shook his head. "No. Korent is my house name, but Baldyron—Bal—is how I am called."

"Lord Baldyron, then. If you wish more coffee—"

"No." He shook his head again. "I look upon it as medicine. One drinks it in need, never otherwise." A jingle of harness, the soft thud of shod hooves drew his attention. Fialla moved lightly to her feet as the flap was pressed aside and Fidric stood with his back against it, admitting first Gelc, then Boresin, finally Gespry himself, the distinctive blue cape, his white hair flaring in a last gust of wind before the flap fell into place behind him.

The Marcher, in any event, had no doubt as to his identity, for he rose to his feet, closed the distance between them and dropped to one knee before the Archbishop, his head bowed.

Fialla stared. Gespry had gone a dead white under his tan and a brief, terrible fear gazed out of his eyes. He closed them, bought his hands up in the Blessing. Light briefly filled the chamber, haloed the Marcher's dark hair. Gespry was himself again as he clasped the Marcher's hand, but Fialla was still shaken. *Alayya, Elorra, what did he see?*

"My Lord of Korent?" Gespry inquired, smiling pleasantly at the man before him. "No? Lord Baldyron—Bal, then. My deepest appreciation, sir, you have ridden swiftly, and they tell me the woods between Korent and this valley are thick with barbarians." He stepped across to the fire, then back to the table and his accustomed seat, bringing the open pot with him. At a gesture, the young Baron took the seat at his right hand.

Fialla moved back into the bed-chamber, shed cloak, tabard, and boots. A moment's rummaging in her pack brought out both soft, high slippers and a packet of fine-work which she carried back to the fire with her. Gespry had pushed aside his coffee and was studying a four-cornered dart, a tiny caltrap, in the light of one of the lanterns.

"Use care, your Grace. The points are poisoned." Gespry nodded. The entirety of the tiny object was an ugly dark green in color.

"With what?"

"Nightshade, most likely. They use it most often, so that a man die in hellish dreams." Fialla shuddered. "Though it is not the only poison they use: In battle, they prefer monk's hood or nicotine. A man might yet kill a Fegez or two with nightshade in his veins. I found that one at first light—here." He spread the upper edge of his cloak, fingering a rent there, a roughened point between two rings on his mail.

"The Two were with you," Gespry murmured, handing the dart back. "They use these—how?"

"They are blown from pipes, occasionally fitted to shafts. The creatures use knives also, and a short bow similar to our own. Swords, but seldom. Spears, now and again; the points are soft metal but treated as the caltraps are." Baldyron's eyes held, unfocused, to his hands. "They are one with wood and tree, a handful of mounted men are no match for three Fegez. I do hope," he added, rousing himself with a visible effort, "that thou hast allowed thy shepherd mercenaries no sorties in search of enemy. They will find more than they bargain for." Gespry shook his head.

"That much I already knew."

"Good. I have no sympathy with thy hired swords, sir. But we need them."

"The Beldenians and your Barons," Gespry responded mildly, and in a clear change of subject, "call me Gespry, my friend. You had better do so as well." A pause. Baldyron nodded then, and behind the expressionless face, he seemed pleased.

"As thou dost wish. Now, then." A long, dark finger stabbed at the map, indicating a position something less than ten leagues from the valley and northwest of it. "Showest a Fegez camp here, but it has not been for some days. That clan has Korent surrounded, backed by reinforcements from—." His hand moved again, brushing another red-marked circle.

"And you know this—?" Gespry asked. Baldryon shrugged.

"Clan markings; this area is inhabited only by the Grey Stalkers. I counted forty-five men with the body paint and the tattoo of the Grey Stalkers among those beyond my walls. No more than sixty men are allowed the markings of one clan at any time, so it follows that if any men of that clan are left in the camp thou hast marked on this map, there are not enough of them to constitute a fighting force. An ambushing force—that is another matter, as I have told thee."

"I—see." Gespry was eyeing the map: Korent was set in a narrow valley surrounded by foothills, well to the fore of Darion's borders. The young Baron was in a tight placing indeed.

"Now, as I see it," Baldyron went on, "thy forces here constitute a threat they must deal with, between thy location in their territory and the size of the camps. Those with doubts that the Fegez will engage this army are fools. And if my father's friends have suggested to thee the safety of thy numbers here—"

"Frequently," Gespry cut in dryly.

"Pay them no heed. The Fegez are not fools, for all they are not civilized. They know what sort of threat is posed to them here. Do not trust to the guard posted by our men or thy own; double what thou hast. Treble it nearest the river, the barghests will use the water and thy men will never see them until too late. Send no small sorties, no individual guards, but do send out companies to patrol the parameters. Concentrate thy forces here"—his finger indicated the easterly-most end of the valley,—"and here"—a point halfway along the northern cliffs. "I know well how that wall looks, but a barghest would see it as a stairs and no barrier at all."

"I see."

"Your horses?"

Gespry nodded. "Already thought upon, my friend. The mercenaries have brought them within the camp, away from river and outer boundaries alike."

"Good." A silence as the two men studied the map.

"Since you know the Fegez so well," Gespry ventured finally, "perhaps you can tell me more of this—changing of shapes they are said to do."

Baldyron smiled, faintly, briefly. "How shall I answer such a thing? If I say it is true, thou'lt doubt anyway."

"Men seldom really believe in magics until confronted with them. I bear," the priestly Fire played across his fingertips, "certain of them in my service of the Two, and so am more open-minded, perhaps, than many." Silence. "It is true, then?"

Baldyron shrugged. The smile was gone as though it had never been. "I have never touched a beast clad in men's clothing, armed with men's weapons. I have never touched a Fegez warrior in night battle. And I carry in full Darion's gift, that I believe in little I cannot touch. What I have seen, though—." He shrugged again. "What a man sees under light of moon and star, perhaps each must decide himself."

"What you yourself believe, though," Gespry pressed, after another little silence.

"Oh—." Dark, shadowed eyes met his briefly. "—they change, sir. But take no word of mine for it, thou'lt see soon enough." Fialla, unnoted near the fire, clenched her hands around the embroidered cloth to stop them shaking, fastened her teeth against her lower lip. Such fear filled her with disgust, but there was no controlling it. Baldyron cleared his throat. "I return to Korent this evening." Gespry's head came up.

"Impossible."

"Not so. I must."

The Archbishop frowned, got to his feet. "Scarcely safe for you."

Expressionless eyes followed him. "Little in my life has

been safe: My childhood was spent in these Marches, I grew up with barghest raids. Or dost thou think," he added sharply, as Gespry made no move, "that I worry for the safety of my lands and title? That I cling foolishly to King Sedry's chance gift, to the point that I would die to remain Baron of Korent?"

"I said nothing—," Gespry began mildly, but Baldyron went on unheeding.

"There are two hundred armed men there, protecting another three hundred folk. Herdsmen and farmers, Archbishop. They depend upon me, they took shelter in my walls when the Fegez came upon us some days ago. I owe them—"

"What?" Gespry overrode him sharply. "Your life as a sacrifice? If you left Korent so well guarded, do you think you will aid them by dying halfway between here and there?" Fialla cast him a surprised glance: unlike him, such an emotional response. The Marcher Baron shook his head slowly, unwillingly, but his expression remained stubborn.

"I will not die. I am no Fegez, but I know the ways between this camp and my home." A silence. "I am of more use there than here, I know this. Thou hast men enough without another minor landholder."

"You intend, I hope," Gespry inquired finally, "to rest yourself and your horse first?"

"I have already arranged with my father—Fresgkel of Eavon—for another horse. And I will not leave until dusk. For all the rumors, the Fegez see in the dark no better than we."

Gespry sighed. "Well, it is your choice, sir."

"It is. My father has a place for me to sleep, I wished to give thee what information I had for thee first. If would'st have further speech with me," he added diffidently, "send to Eavon's tent, I will come before I leave tonight."

"Please," Gespry said. He smiled warmly; the tension in the pavilion vanished. "I see I shall need to revise what few plans were made last night. Let me take in what you have given me thus far. Return here, if you will, for evening meal. I will have more questions and since I was responsible for your dangerous journey, at least allow me to feel that I have sent you on your way properly fed." The Marcher Baron's smile was brief but it reached all the way to his tired eyes.

"My Lord—"

"Gespry—"

"Gespry, then. I will. Lady Fialla," he added, bowing over her hand and placing a kiss on her fingers. "My thanks for sharing thy breakfast with a cold and hungry man. I will see thee later, the Two willing." Once again he knelt before the Archbishop, rose to clasp hands with him, and was quickly gone.

Fialla hastened to Gespry's side; as the Marcher Baron disappeared in the direction of the Darion camp, he slipped back into his chair. Wide eyes stared dazedly towards the flap. "Gespry," she said firmly. Small hands gripped his shoulders, shook him. "Gespry! What is it?"

"Nothing, Fialla." But the eyes that met hers were black-pupilled.

"Gespry, what? What did you see in him that I did not?"

Gespry laughed; for some reason, this was grimly amusing. "I'm all right, Fialla. Never mind. Just—an odd twitch. The Gods laying out my grave, perhaps."

"Hush, Gespry!" Fialla knelt at his side, took both his hands in hers. They were cold and at first unresponsive.

"I—all right, Fialla. Truly." He freed one hand, tipped her chin up so that her eyes met his. "Nothing to worry about. Not now."

"No?" She was still anxious, unable to find the reason and so all the more upset. Why would he not tell her what was wrong? Something was, still, however well he concealed it.

"Nothing. A—." He smiled briefly. "Nothing." And with that, she had, for the moment, to be satisfied.

14

THREE COLD, RAINY days went slowly by. The nightly meetings in the Archbishop's tent grew steadily more tense. The Archbishop himself was subdued, and seldom contributed to the planning. The waiting was telling on him; the constant quarreling was not improving matters.

Nor did the return of the young Baron of Korent the second morning, white-faced, delirious and afoot. He had staggered into the Archbishop's pavilion, interrupting a stiff and non-productive session between Gespry and old Eavon; had collapsed into his father's arms, muttering, "No use, no use, too many of 'em," before he went off into a dead faint. There was a deep cut across his cheek, running into his hairline, right to the bone. The old man had found the caltrap in his son's belt pouch. The cut, fortunately, was clean and had bled freely, or Baldyron likely would never have reached the camp at all.

He had put in an appearance that evening, pale as a ghost and silent, offered no word of his own, and left early. A night's sleep seemed to put him in better shape—he looked less likely, to Fialla's concerned eyes, to fall over if he stood too rapidly—but his eyes were dead, dark blots in a pale face, as though he already counted friends, comrades in arms, serfs—all Korent—against his soul.

What he had gone through on that attempted return to his lands, he firmly refused to discuss, even with his father, remarking only, "I am here. Enough!" But his face had aged visibly.

So had Gespry's.

On the fourth morning, however, there was a change. Two
separate pieces of news were brought in: The Fegez were on
the move, a large band of them moving east and south through
populous lands. At the rate they moved, and by the direction,
they would intersect the eastern end of the valley, just as
Baldyron had indicated they might. And other message birds
had come from Arolet: the Crown Prince had already left for
the battlefield, the King would follow in a day or so.

Hyrcan, in fact, arrived the next evening but went directly
to the King's pavilion, curtly refusing Gespry's offer that he
attend the planning sessions across the River.

The Crown Prince's presence, Fialla knew, weighed heavily
on all of them, particularly on the mood-sensitive Gespry. But
at least outwardly he threw himself enthusiastically into battle
plans. Though these were of necessity few, and dependent on
the Fegez.

Gespry argued long and hard over this first battle, turning
aside both the suggestions of the Marchers to throw all they
had against the barbarians and the thought of the Beldenians
to remain where they sat, drawing the Fegez into the open.
"We cannot send a full force of armed against them, sirs, it
would be foolhardy. They would break and flee, and then what
would we do? Pursue them? And on the other hand, which of
us truly believes they will attack us straightly if we wait upon
them? No," he went on, cutting off loud argument with a
chopping motion of his hand, "a small sortie to begin with.
We do not wish to frighten them away on the first day; we
have come here to engage them, have we not?"

"A small force can draw upon reinforcements. This is no
all-or-none single throw." Baldyron spoke up unexpectedly,
came around the table to the Archbishop's side. "Gespry's
decision was reached with my aid. Perhaps you think him innocent as regards the barghests? Do you think me also
unknowledgeable?" Gespry frowned briefly, his lips formed
the word "Fegez." "Gespry of Rhames came to our aid, at
our asking. I suggest we follow his advice, since we sought it,"
he finished forcefully.

Gespry glanced up, met dark dead eyes briefly. "As my
friend Bal says, I am an innocent in the ways of these Fegez.
However, I have listened to him, and to you all, and I know a
little of battle." He pushed to his feet suddenly, leaned on the
table. "Those of you from Belden know me well, I hope you

do not doubt that. And you who are Darion—well, have we not spent enough long, weary hours together? I have begun to assess you, surely, you have begun to assess me?'' No reply. Several of those nearest him found items of intense interest beyond the Archbishop's shoulder or on the carpets. ''We have, still, the choice of battle time and place, if we move swiftly. We can lose that, due to stupidity or this failure to agree we seem infected with. Now, a sortie still seems to me the best way to deal with the barbarians. A testing of strengths, a testing that will enable us to learn more of their manner of fighting, enable us to plan better and more carefully for the battles to follow. And do we need aid tomorrow, a second force can be ready—''

'' 'We'?'' Gespry sought out the speaker: Cretony, Earl of Marchham, a short, heavy-set and rather dour man of middle years.

''Of course. I am a fighting man, sir. I earn my bread honestly.'' Nervous laughter from the other side of the table. Cretony eyed him dubiously.

''An injured man,'' he began, ''however skilled—''

Gespry cut him off in a voice which brooked no answer. ''Who has long since healed, my Lord. Now. To give the Fegez a false sense of security, I say we need no more than a hundred men, and it is to my mind to seek volunteers. Perhaps another two hundred at the ready.''

''You will lack no volunteers,'' Gelc remarked blandly, his voice cutting through the babble. ''We three,'' he added in the ensuing silence, a wave of his hand including the brothers, ''head your list, of course.'' There was a sudden change in the pavilion; almost a sense of release, as though the point had passed for argument. Gespry inclined his head.

''Of course.''

''My name below theirs.''

''Friend Bal.'' Gespry nodded without turning; he could not bear to meet those eyes again, turned back to Gelc, who had jumped to his feet. ''Make the choosing, arms-brother. But not just mercenaries, do you think—?''

Another babble from the commanders behind him.

''I think,'' Gelc remarked, already halfway to the flap, ''that I will gather some companions for a short ride in the morning. A mixed party, I think.'' He tipped Gespry a wink, turned neatly on one heel, was gone. The brothers followed.

Cretony of Marchham scowled openly after them; one of the younger Marchers laughed uncertainly.

Gespry turned back to the company. Baldyron was sprawled back in his chair again, eyes closed, but he opened them as the Archbishop resumed his own seat. "Hadst better reckon the Crown Prince among thy party," he said. Gespry nodded.

"I had planned for it."

"Good. He will be there."

"He took no part in the planning," Eavon grumbled. Baldyron sent him a sidelong, warning look.

"Thy tongue, Father. Thy grey hairs are of no account to Prince Hyrcan, and would not save thy skin, did the Crown Prince wish it from thee. No," he added thoughtfully, "he did not, and would not. Hyrcan cares only for the killing, not how it is arranged for him."

"Thine own tongue," Eavon tapped him on the arm, "is somewhat overlong."

Baldyron smiled tiredly. "Perhaps. Perhaps." He shook himself and got heavily to his feet. Without further word to any of them, he pushed the flap aside, was gone. Eavon stared after him anxiously, rose to his own feet.

"Thy pardons, all," he murmured, sidling towards the exit. "The boy is not yet well, I had better see to him."

The rest of the council left not long after, most of them grim faced but resigned: Matters had been taken from their hands, and whether they wanted the Archbishop's small sortie or not, it was now a fact. There was nothing to do now but prepare, if not for the battle in the morning, then for those which would surely follow.

Gespry had not moved from his chair, had barely managed civil and proper responses as Marchers and mercenary captains trooped out. Fialla came to join him as the tent emptied, combing her fingers through the fine white hair. "You need sleep. As much as young Bal does," she urged quietly. Gespry transferred his blank gaze to her face.

"Not so much as that, and pray do not mention that name to me again! I shall have nightmares tonight, I would as soon he did not figure in them." A faint smile took the sting from his words.

"It goes well, Gespry. You have done everything that could be done. Even the Reader—," she glanced across his shoulder to where the Reader sat, cross-legged, several paces away. Once again she was working the smallest personal pattern, setting cards to the four corners of the Prime of Swords. She paused, a final card in her hand, set it down before replying.

"No danger."

"None?" Gespry laughed, without amusement.

"To you, no. In a battle there is always danger. But no harm to you, little loss of life. No damage to the Pattern." Gespry closed his eyes. Fialla took one of the long hands between hers and held it tightly.

"There is always danger," she whispered. "Always. Has it ever stopped you?" Dark, troubled eyes met hers.

"Fialla, think on it, *think*!" A muscle twitched in the thin cheek, just below his right eye. "To fight, yes, anyone can fight when the cause is great enough. But to command the lives of others, men who will probably die terribly because *I* sent them out, because I chose them—"

"I know." What could she say? "I thought—only, perhaps—to reassure you." She hesitated again. "Gespry, you have waited the night before a battle just this way, a hundred times, two hundred. And you fear this way every time. I know. Because it is good to live, because you feel an honest concern, a love for those who follow you. Because you understand your responsibility to those who follow you. It has never stopped you, or them, from doing the thing you must."

The tall, thin figure gently detached her fingers. "I cannot—I know what you mean to say, Fialla." He swallowed. "And I thank you. But—." The low voice cracked, his face twisted briefly. "I—I have no right, none! My own life, *that* I could throw away, and who would gainsay—?"

"Shhh," Fialla soothed, one anxious eye on the flap. If any entered now . . . "I would, Gespry, you know I would. So would we all."

He swallowed again, shook his head. "I have no right. I—I cannot—I—." His mouth moved, but no words came. "If I fail you, Fialla. All of you."

"You will not—"

"You cannot say that and *know*. And—if the Two should find me unworthy and the Fire is denied me, what then?" He buried his face in his arms.

Fialla pulled her companion to his feet by main strength, led

him back into the alcove before any of the Beldenian guard
could enter and see the Archbishop in such a state. As they
passed the Reader she spared a glance for the pattern. The
Prime of Swords: battle. Surrounding it, the Princess of
Flames and against this, Ten of Blades, triumphant outcome.
The Lady of the Birds, her own card—the Priest, Gespry's,
and crossed by Fog. As she watched, the Reader turned
another card, another: The Prince of Flames, the Madman.
She moved on, quickly, drawing her companion with her.

"You," she said firmly, pressing her companion back onto
the bed, "have finally proven yourself human, my Gespry.
You are also overtired and badly in need of sleep." A silence.
A tentative smile, then, from the other.

"I am sorry, Fialla. I never meant to—"

"I know you never did. It's not wrong for you to lean on
me, you know."

"I—no. I suspect you are right, I need sleep."

"Then sleep," she replied brusquely, but not unkindly.
"You had better be properly awake tomorrow, I insist upon it
if you are going to fight these barbarians!"

"Certainly, my dear. Point well taken." The frightened
figure in the outer tent might have been dreamed by both of
them. He sat up, began working his way out of shirt and
breeches, finally pulled the underjerkin off. Fialla laid a light
hand on the wide bandage, the nightshirt in her other hand.

"Is it comfortable still?"

Gespry shrugged. "I suppose. It accomplishes its purpose."

"So it does." She ran her fingers across the ends, checking
that her stitching still held. "It makes my breasts ache just to
look at it," she added. Gespry cast an amused eye at her ample
bosom, barely confined by the undershift, and laughed
quietly. "Yes, laugh at me," she mocked gently.

"Not at you, dear Fialla. Never at you." The dark eyes were
warm. "Thank you."

"At your service," she replied lightly. Impulsively, she bent
down to kiss the smooth cheek. "Take care on the morrow. I
will have no other chance to say it, you know." Her companion nodded.

"So I shall. Come. Will you turn down the lantern, or shall
I?" There was silence in the darkened room thereafter. Fialla
lay still, eyes following shadows of men and horses across the

outer canvas walls, until she was certain Gespry was truly asleep. Beyond, in the wide, carpeted chamber, the armsmen slept also, Gelc a little apart so that his gentle snore did not keep the others awake.

The Tarots Reader remained awake most of the night, laying out her cards in the now silent pavilion.

15

FIALLA WOKE IN the grey hour before dawn, her ears picking up the muted clink of harness, the grass-muffled but unmistakable sound of many horses nearby. The right side of the bed was unoccupied but still warm. She raised up onto one elbow, blinking sleepily. Gespry stood near the curtain, gazing into the main chamber, jerkin and breeches already donned, shirt in his hand.

"Not that shirt, Gespry. The brown."

"Mmmm? Oh." With an effort, it seemed, he brought himself back to the moment, came back towards the bed. Fialla was already on her feet, rummaging through one of the packs. One shirt, another—she held out the proper one.

"There. For luck, as always. Though I still think you wear it to battle because it does not show blood so readily, the less to upset me." Gespry grinned engagingly; the prior night's doubts and fears were forgotten.

Beyond the thin curtain, she could hear the armsmen moving around: Gelc's querulous voice, a calm response from Fidric. The Reader and another speaking near the outer flap. People already. Of course. It was always like this.

Fialla's head emerged from a low-necked, heavy saque; deft fingers tucked a pleated and embroidered muslin collar into the dress and fastened it snugly at her throat. Her feet slid into the fur-lined slippers and she wriggled her toes gratefully in their warmth as she pulled the snood-ties tight and dropped the confined bundle of her hair between her shoulder blades.

"Come, let me aid you into the thing, I will have to shave you by the fire."

Gespry sighed but allowed himself to be installed in the dark, plain garment without comment. "Someone has already arrived to speak with you," Fialla went on, "as always. Here," she added, throwing a soft cloth across his chest and pressing a small copper bowl into his hands. She brought the rest of his kit, pushed the Archbishop into his favorite seat and handed him coffee before taking the copper and filling it with hot water.

"As you love me," Gespry implored weakly, "allow me half my coffee before you begin!" Fialla laughed.

"How dare I refuse you?" But the Archbishop's jawline and cheeks were thickly covered with white lather before the first of the Marchers—Eavon, Marchham and three others—gained admittance.

The outer flap was thrown back, admitting air that was cool but no longer chill: The weather had changed during the night, clouds and wind were gone and the day looked to be both hot and clear. Gespry waved a hand, indicating chairs.

"Take your ease while you can, sirs. You all know where the coffee is." He did not seem surprised when no one accepted his offer of refreshment: With the exception of Baldyron and his father, none of the Marchers and few enough of the mercenaries cared for the beverage.

Fialla brushed the razor across the shaving cloth, already damp and soapy, drew it smoothly, deftly over Gespry's jaw. The Earl of Marchham winced and swore softly under his breath. Gespry laughed. "An excellent way to keep a man honest with his lady, sir, do you not agree?" Eavon laughed also, though his eyes moved to and held a spot well above that where Fialla wielded the sharpened blade. "Who rides today?" Gespry went on.

"Ask who'd not, you'd have a shorter list by far," Gelc muttered. Hour and impending battle both worked to edge his temper.

"A round hundred," Eavon said. "Thy man here and I made a list, he said thou'd'st have names."

"So I would. My thanks." The words were almost unintelligible: Fialla had tilted the Archbishop's head back to draw the razor upwards along his throat. Cretony watched with tense, horrified fascination. When she had finished and taken the shaving things away, he shook his head, sighing with relief.

"By the Two, it would be worth my life to let my woman do that! I admire thy nerve, Gespry!"

"She is better at it than I," Gespry smiled. He ran a hand over his chin. "She grew tired of the cuts on my face some years ago, and took the task from me perforce. However. You are quite certain you will take no coffee?" He shrugged at their refusals, filled his own heavy cup to the top and wrapped his hands around its warmth.

"How much time have we?" Eavon demanded suddenly. Cretony shook his head.

"Thy son took a few men at first light, said he would find out—"

"Young fool!"

"Not Bal. Thy eldest, Telborn," Cretony corrected him with a certain sour satisfaction. "Hast more than one, though a man would seldom know it any more, Fresgkel. Telborn said they would go to the southern rim, there are places where they can watch the eastern end of the valley from safety."

"Now," Eavon grumbled, "*that* sounds more like Telborn." He was not overly fond of his eldest: a narrow-minded, harsh creature in his late thirties. Alayya, Elorra, he wondered irritably, as he did on increasingly frequent occasion, why could it not have been Telborn that swore to Sedry, and Bal who was eldest? "Baldyron," Eavon went on, half to himself, "has changed since he gained Korent. More than I would have thought possible." An open, cheerful child who had grown into an open, loving and cheerful young man; had turned, then, and nearly overnight, into one morose, withdrawn, uncommunicative.

What had caused it? The old man still didn't know—still, years later, worried it at odd moments. His support of Sedry against the old King? Gods knew he'd said little enough to his father of the matter, then or since, knowing how Fresgkel felt the matter. The closeness between father and son had faded when Bal had begun to ride with young Sedry. Inevitable, of course. And his disastrous marriage to Woldeg's imperious daughter Kresalla! How Sedry had had the face to call it *reward*! And Bal—he'd taken it like all things of recent years; whatever he thought stayed behind that impassive young face, a secret from his father, from all men.

Well, the Gods still looked out for men, however strange

their ways, though it was perhaps a shame about the child, a definite waste of the good Korent armsmen who'd died protecting Kressala and the baby. Fool woman, insisting on a journey to Court when she had! Well, the Fegez had made short enough work of her.

The old Baron glanced up, suddenly aware he'd been wool-gathering. "He's a good lad, though," he added defensively, somewhat sheepishly. Cretony scowled at him. "Who said otherwise, Fresgkel? The boy's too much on thy mind of late. Why worry him so much?"

Gelc moved forward, interposing himself between the two men neatly, a long piece of heavy paper in his hand. Two columns of names filled it. Gespry turned aside to read it, light from lantern and the opened flap falling across it.

"I know most of these men," he ventured at last. Gelc came around to his side.

"No more'n I expected. Mostly the younger men, since it's to be a hit-and-run fight. I had to include old Zorec, though—you recall him—"

"Of course. The old Sergeant. I should remember *him*, he has a burn ointment that is most excellent."

"I know." Gelc shuddered. He remembered, and damn Gespry for bringing such a thing up at a time like this! Gespry's burns had been terrible indeed, he himself still carried red scars across his ribs from those last desperate moments aboard the *Wave Cleaver*. Sparing one reproachful glance for the Archbishop, he went back to the list, and he and Gespry went through it in fine.

The Marchers exchanged glances. No wonder the man had such a strong following! Those few men he did not know, those few he did not remember, Gelc described for him, reminded him. Those who rode with him for the first time would be remembered the next.

Gespry finally drained his cup, put the list aside and began working his way into his mail. Boresin materialized at his elbow to aid. The tossled white head broke through the neck, and moments later Gespry was adjusting the dagger belt on his left forearm while Bor tightened the neck lacings.

A clattering and splashing of horses fording the river, hurried conversation near the entrance. One of the Beldenian guard entered with a tall, heavy-set Darioner. The latter went briefly onto one knee, was up almost immediately.

"Sir—"

"Gespry, if you will," the Archbishop corrected him mildly. The Darioner moved to Eavon's side, his mouth pursed tightly. "Telborn of Eavon to thy aid, sir." There was insult in his voice, scarcely concealed. "Father," he added, inclining his head towards the old man as an afterthought, "they have reached the valley floor at the upper end. They are perhaps two hours distant."

"So long as that? It is not so far as—"

"They are afoot, a sign of overconfidence," Telborn cut in sharply. Gespry turned aside to clasp his sword into place. "They must have found Korent overly easy," Telborn added with ill-concealed spite. His father laid a hand on his arm.

"I would advise thee, son, to say no such thing in thy brother's presence. He is unbalanced on that subject and likely to do thee harm." Telborn looked at his father impatiently, jerked his arm free.

"Let him dare try, I have had no cause to thrash Bal in some time." Gespry eyed Eavon's eldest sidelong. A pity for the commons when *he* inherits Eavon, the Archbishop thought. He began to draw on his boots, neatly tucking his breeches in as he went, leaving no hand hold for a ground fighter. Fialla returned moments later, ignoring Telborn's sour expression with ease of long practice, and began pulling the white hair back into a plait, fastening its ends with a leather thong.

"Fidric has seen to your horse, Gespry," she murmured as she finished. "You've water in the bottle at the saddle-bows, bread and sausage in the small pouch as usual."

"Good. I should not be gone long enough to need them, but as well to be prepared. My Lords," he continued, turning to take all of them in, "this should be an auspicious beginning."

"One hopes," Eavon replied. One hand, Gespry noted with amusement, was fastened in a murderous grip on his son's forearm, forestalling whatever remark that worthy had been about to make. From the expression on his face, it had not been a friendly one. "Our wishes," Eavon went on, "for thy good health and safety."

"Which I shall take, with thanks, and with the hopes I shall not need them," Gespry replied gravely. "The Two guard you all." Turning away from them, he dropped a light kiss on Fialla's brow before striding swiftly into the open.

A cheer went up. Fialla could make out his voice, but not

the words. Another cheer. Another voice then—whose? Telborn pressed past her and was gone; Fialla, at a gesture from the old Baron, preceded him and the Earl of Marchham but stopped just under the raised flap.

A mounted force filled the open ground before the pavilion; beyond them, a haze of mountains and pale sky, a brilliance where the sun would appear at any moment.

Baldyron—it was he who had followed the Archbishop's words with his own—moved to take the reins of his horse from one of the mounted. The rest of the company sat with bowed heads as the Archbishop raised his hands to offer a brief prayer. Palest gold light flared gently outwards from his fingertips, bathing the company for the least of moments in the Blessing. Without a backwards glance, then, he stepped forward to take hold of his own horse—a restless creature, white as his hair—and vaulted easily, lightly into the saddle. And they were gone, splashing across the river, heading at a gallop across the valley floor, bearing rapidly eastwards. Fialla, eyes shielded against the flat rays of the rising sun, thought she could still see the billowing blue and yellow of Gespry's cloak.

16

NIGHT. THERE WERE victory celebrations across both camps: Gespry's initial sortie had totally routed an army of Fegez three times its own size, with no loss of life and few injuries. The Archbishop's pavilion was almost unbearably crowded by the time full dark set in, and the noise level was such Grolpet's minstrel had long since given up trying to make himself heard.

"Naiver saw anything like um." Sevric, Grolpet's half-brother, had begun his celebrating early and was already beginning to sink into a black study. Lacking audience with his brother or the other mercenary captains, he finally fastened onto Fresgkel, Baron of Eavon, who listened to him with what politeness he could muster—though with minimal comprehension: even when the man was sober, Sevric's Ordinate was so heavily accented, contained so many bastardized words, he was difficult to understand. "Demons," he continued morosely, "at's what 'ee be."

"Demons?" Eavon frowned. He'd heard enough of such talk among his own kind the past twenty years, and was thoroughly bored with it and all its variations. Nor did he, Fresgkel, put stock in it. A man could claim to see anything. "By all accounts, enough of them were slain today. One cannot kill demons." Sevric stared at him through red-shot bleary eyes.

"Demons, I say and mean." He transferred the glassy stare to his wine cup. "A rise out of the grass, where ye'd swear was no one." He ran a square finger over the thin cut just under his hairline. "And then," he went on indignantly, "a shoot *darts* at ye, afore ye can proper run um down!''

"Ugly," Eavon sympathized, inwardly shuddering. There was no doubting the reality of a barghest dart, and the mercenary had had a close call, closer than most lived to tell of.

"Might ha' been poisoned," Sevric continued darkly. His pale blue eyes slid sideways, picking out Gespry, who sat talking earnestly with Grolpet and one of Woldeg's many boys. "Were not for Gespry, I'd ha known for sure, but he warned and I ducked." He grinned, suddenly, bibulously cheerful. Eavon repressed another shudder. This poor young Beldenian sot had obviously not yet held a man in the throes of a barghest poison, or had to aid such a man, out of pity, early from his sufferings. And Bal—enough, he ordered himself sternly, and brought the full of his attention back to the faintly weaving man before him. Sevric was still speaking. "And t' Archbishop run it through before it could gain its feet. At which thing they are uncommon fast."

"I know it," the Marcher replied soothingly. "Did'st well today, all of thee, losing no lives."

"Aye." Sevric sank back, suddenly, into gloom. "None yet," he added grimly, draining his cup. "A say a man dies horribly."

"Do not think on it," Eavon interrupted him roughly. "Hast escaped. And I misdoubt we'd see another such attack for some days. The creatures are cautious." But Sevric refused to be cheered.

"Aye, certain. A'll sneak up on us, or come in force at night. Worse than straight attack, from these."

"Not if thou—prepared as all of thee are. And the barghests are not owls or wolves, whatever is said of them."

"No?" The mercenary gave him a frankly disbelieving look.

"No," Eavon replied firmly. "They must strain to see in the dark, just as we do. Come," he added, clapping the man across the shoulders, "need'st more wine. They tell me," he went on, with the ingenuous air of a man changing the subject of conversation for the better, "that Gespry's pale lady will read her cards among us later. Thou art Beldenian and hast experience in this. Is it worth its while for a man such as myself?" Sevric, distracted and much astonished, appeared to give the matter serious thought. Finally shrugged.

"She speaks truth, whether ye believe her or no. But I thought ye of Darion—"

"Oh, well," Eavon replied easily, filling his cup and his companion's, "I, like most, believe in things tangible, the Lady's cards are scarcely that! But unlike many of my kind, I doubt it will endanger my standing with the Two, and I'm willing, at my age, to try many a thing I might have avoided in my youth. After all, there are odder things in this world than the Lady's Tarots." He raised his cup in toast. "To thy continued well-being." Sevric grinned, good humor fully, if temporarily, restored, and moved off to join his half-brother. The Marcher stared after him, shaking his head.

"What perplexes thee, Fresgkel?" The Earl of Marchham came up behind him. Eavon gestured with his cup, pulled it back cautiously and drained the top inch before it slopped onto the carpets.

"That boy, yonder. The mercenary. Were we so headlong at his age, I wonder?"

"What mean'st?"

"Well—," Eavon considered. "So callous of life, for one thing. That lout missed death by a hair this morning, and such a death—." He shuddered, drank deeply. "And already it has become a matter of brag to him, and another notch in the Archbishop's legend. Nothing more."

"Has it been so long, can'st not remember?" Cretony inquired with dry solicitude. "In a word, yes. As I remember it, worse. More drunken, more often, certainly more reckless."

Eavon laughed. "Daresay we were. But we had cause, then. After all, Cretony, thou and I were the first to take holdings in the Marches—"

"Thanks to old Elgurd. Remember how they said it was to make peace at Court?" Fresgkel grinned; he remembered, all right. And "they" had been right: He and the Earl—then just Cretony, second son of Elgurd's Horsemaster—had been the wildest of Alster's contemporaries. "Odd, how," Cretony went on, dreamily but with that underlying malice that marked his own brand of heavy-handed humor, "that Elgurd should have fathered poor old Alster, and Alster become father to the fair Sedry? One dare count on nothing for one's offspring."

"Shhh!" Eavon hissed, glancing around them frantically. Such a remark within the hearing of any of Sedry's spies—

Nolse's, more correctly—would be paid for in blood. March-ham could not be that drunk!

Nor was he. He tipped his friend a grave wink. "Relax, March-Brother. Our beloved Crown Prince and his are across the River, celebrating Hyrcan's blood bath. And none of Woldeg's slimy brat's ears are about tonight."

"Cretony—by the Two, hast lost all sense?"

"I? No. When do I speak thus, save with thee? And where safer than such a crowd?" He shrugged, drank. "But let it be, if thou dost wish."

"I certainly do!" Eavon replied warmly. "Now then. I need thy advice. Gespry has promised his Tarots Reader tonight, and I thought that I might, perhaps, test her skills. What think'st?"

Cretony eyed him thoughtfully. "Wilt thou really, Fresgkel? Would'st imperil thy standing with the Two for it, even?" More of his heavy humor: The Earl was notoriously agnostic. "Well. Interesting. Tell thee what—if thou'lt do it, so'll I."

"Good. I would not be the only old fool present." Eavon countered Marchham's sharp scowl with a beatific grin. After a moment, the Earl grinned back, and the two began to laugh.

Several paces away, Fialla sat alone at the end of the table, staring absently out the open flap across the numerous fires of the Beldenian camp. A tall figure moved across her line of vision: The Baron of Korent stood before her, bowing with grave courtesy.

"May I join thee, Lady? And," he added as she gestured towards a seat for answer, "is there anything thou'd'st have?" She smiled, was met with an answering smile that warmed his dark eyes and moved him to rare gallantry. "Hast only to name it, and 'tis thine."

"I am well, I thank you," she replied gravely. He pushed his own full cup to one side.

"I—I do not intrude upon thee, do I? Because —"

"No." With a final effort, she shook off the last of her black thoughts and gave him full attention. Again a smile kindled his face but slipped as he turned his head, picking out his father, Marchham and the Archbishop at the table's other end.

"He fights very well, Lady Fialla, for one so badly hurt as they say he was."

She nodded, her own face grave. "He was. Worse, perhaps than you have heard, the Two know we tried to keep it secret, how bad it was. For a time, we thought—," she drew a ragged breath, went on with determination, "thought he would not fight again. Ever. A death sentence for such a man."

"Yes, it would be." Baldyron's dark gaze remained on the Archbishop, who was regaling the two elderly Marchers with some story that left all three roaring with laughter. "That would explain to me why he fights here, however," the young Baron went on. He turned back to her, his mouth sardonic under the heavy moustache. "Well? Why else would such a man as he aid backwards Darion and her more backwards Marches—against such as the barghests?"

"You—believe he uses Darion and your need, young Lord, as a trial of his strengths before he goes in search of wealth and greater glory?" Fialla leaned forward, and one small hand darted out to grip his wrist, hard. Baldyron stared at her in speechless surprise. "Think you," she went on sharply, "that my Gespry has changed so because of a wayward mast? Or perhaps you think he was always such a man, taking only those battle contracts which would earn him the most gold and honor? Have you learned nothing these past days, did you learn nothing of him today, fighting at his side?"

"I—"

"You think because he is mercenary," Fialla swept on unheeding, "that he has no honor! You are a leader of men, and *that* is how you have judged Gespry? I mistook you, Lord Korent, I mistook you indeed, if that is the kind of man—"

"Lady Fialla!" Surprise had turned to distress, and effectively silenced her. "Thy pardon, I beg thee, I meant no such offense as was taken! I know him only as a mercenary, fighting first here, then there, without cause—"

"Save that," Fialla replied, gently mocking, "of the oppressed, the poor, the weak—no, you do not know my Gespry. Listen to me, then." She closed her eyes. *My Gespry, Gods, my beloved*—she shook her mind free with fierce effort. When she opened her eyes again, they were fixed on a distance beyond the Beldenian fires; she did not seem to see the young Marcher Baron at all.

"He was not intended for the priesthood, he is the son of a Rhamsean Earl who was Eyydayyen VII's Lord of the Wardrobe, and should have been Wardrober in his own right. But he made few friends at court, he was reserved, rather shy as a boy, most of those around him thought him conceited, arrogant. He had few friends, and no close ones. And Eyydayyen's heir Benneq hated Gespry. To be fair," she sighed, "Gespry hated Benneq as much as the Prince hated him. There are people like that: They meet, and for no reason would kill each other there and then, without knowing anything further. It was that way with Benneq and Gespry; time and constant forced company only made it worse. There were quarrels, scenes—finally, the two were not permitted to oppose each other at tourneys, since any fight between them might be the last."

She drew a deep breath. "It was during one of the King's hunts the thing finally happened: The chase led into the Forest and they were separated, somehow, from the others. Gespry came from the woods late in the day. They found Eyydayyen's heir later, dead."

"Gespry killed him—"

"In defense of his own life. He told me that much, once long ago. That he regretted the deed almost at once. He still regrets it.

"Being Gespry, he made no attempt to flee, nor to excuse himself or cast blame upon the Prince. He threw himself on Eyydayyen's mercy. And I suppose the King was merciful, though he scarcely intended it. He spared Gespry's life on condition that Gespry enter the monastery and take vows, renouncing forever all claims on his heritage."

"But—would no one speak for him?"

"None of his kindred were permitted to, none of his friends would. His father disowned him publicly at the trial."

Baldyron gazed at his hands. "He has traveled a distance since then."

"He has." Fialla closed her eyes briefly, went back to her study of the dark valley beyond the Beldenian fires. "For over a year he devoted himself to that calling, withdrawing into the life, paying at least a part of what he considered his debt to Benneq. But he was never meant for such a life, though his dedication to the Two is an honest one.

"The next spring, the Govvin, the western desert nomads,

made a pact with South Embersy, and sought to remove
Rhames from the maps. It was good timing on their part:
Most of our army was fighting Genneldry for possession of
the Calabad Islands, and even if they could have been
withdrawn without terrible loss, they would have had to fight
their way to Rhames from the sea. Gespry sought the King's
leave to gather men to him and attack the nomads. He did,
and with such success it was five years before the Govvin
stirred from their tents again. They have since," she smiled
faintly, "given Rhames a wide berth." Another smile touched
her face. "It was the first journey such as this that I made with
him."

"Hast been with him—thy pardon, Lady." Bal's gaze
dropped back to his hands; he reddened. "I did not mean to
pry."

"It's not prying," she assured him, and touched his hand
lightly. "I want you to understand him. I have been with him
the past twelve years. It was not easy, even though the stan-
dards in a house of the Two there are not like those here. But
after the Govvin, Gespry could do no wrong. Eyydayyen and
the Bishop were willing to give him almost anything he wished,
particularly since he made no attempt to break his vows and
resume his family name and status. It worked well for
everyone: The King had an ally who posed no threat to the
throne, the Bishop's son became Wardrober when Gespry's
father died. And Gespry—he would never have been happy at
Court.

"My own family promised me to Gespry before I ever
reached my naming ceremony and he was still fencing with
willow branches. I never saw cause to break that vow, however
my family felt: I felt then—I still feel—that I best fulfill our
honor, our motto, my duty to King and country at Gespry's
side, keeping petty matters, small cares from overwhelming
him and distracting him from what he does best. And," she
added simply, "I love Gespry. I have loved him since I was a
child."

Baldyron raised his cup to her, drank. "It is easy to see that,
Lady."

"I know." She inclined her head. "He acquired the service
of Gelc and the brothers during the ousting of the Govvin."

"He has something," the Marcher admitted, "that binds
men to him. I never gainsaid that."

"He has." She drank, pushed her cup aside. "After the nomads, it was South Embersy herself. Once again, Gespry got leave to take a hand-picked army, again won a victory that was the turning point in the war. He always was a brilliant tactician. When the old King died, seven years ago, Megesic gave him free rein to go where he would, knowing how it spoke for himself as King and for Rhames. The Master named him Archbishop a year after and gave him dispensation to continue as he had begun against the Govvin."

"And—the Reader?"

"She came to him ten years back, when she was still learning her craft. She could go where she chose, Readers hold no national allegiance. She chose to stay with Gespry." Impulsively she leaned across the table, gripped his fingers. "Thank you, my Lord."

He gazed at her in some confusion. "Lady?"

"For listening. Sometimes," she went on simply, "I need to speak of him."

"Whenever you wish," he replied, gravely polite. He smiled abashedly, his ears, his face ruddy. "My thanks, for correcting my misunderstandings."

He turned away from her as movement down table caught his eyes. Gespry had leaped to his feet, laughing and a trifle unsteadily, was holding up both hands for silence.

17

"FRIENDS!" ANOTHER SWELLING of voices. Abrupt silence as Gespry waved them down. The Reader sat at his right hand, her cards spread in a golden-edged fan before her, her head bowed over them. A faint, bluish haze emanated from the Tarots like the least of fogs. "As I promised, the Tarots Reader who rides in my company has kindly offered to lay out and interpret futures tonight for those of you who would have them. Anyone—ah, Lord Eavon, I hear you are interested, perhaps you will be first?" There was much laughter as the old Baron, somewhat red in the face, moved forward.

"Might as well, hmmm? Too old to frighten—what say, lass," he added as he took his place opposite the Reader, "shall I have a fourth wife before I die?" Baldyron smothered a smile. His own mother, Fregkel's third wife, was very much alive, still lovely, and still the adored center of his father's world, but it was an old joke of his.

The Reader met his eyes, smiled. Her slender fingers brought the cards into a pack, squared the corners neatly, fanned them again before him. At her gesture, he chose one, turned it over and set it between them. The Horseman.

"How little we know even those kin-close," Baldyron murmured under his breath. "Of all those here—I never thought my father would do this," he added aloud as Fialla turned to him.

"Will you let her read your cards?"

He shrugged. "Perhaps. I do not believe—but then, it cannot harm me, can it?"

"A wise attitude, Baron." In silence they watched as the Reader riffled the pack, allowed Eavon to separate them into five neat piles, reassembled them and began to lay out the simple four-sided pattern with the Horseman at its center. Total silence from the onlookers: the minstrel, who had begun to play again, broke off and put aside his instrument so that he could peer across Sevric's broad back.

"This," the Reader began quietly after she had put the remaining pack aside, "represents you yourself, Lord. A fighting man, no longer young—see you, his hair is frost colored as your own. Not yet too old to fight, for he holds a bared blade across his knees. Not at the ready, he has learned to temper the hot-headedness of his youth with wisdom. A man who loves life, who has lived it well. This—," the small hand moved on to the card at the upper right, Six of Sheaves, "indicates fruitfulness. You have many sons, have you not?"

"Four living," the old man replied promptly. "And one daughter," he added with no less pride. "What's this one?" he went on, pointing out the reversed Lady of the Birds.

"Ah." The Reader sat back, gazed at him with some amusement. "A woman, sir, as you might guess. Young and fair." A chorus of remarks from the onlookers, which Eavon ignored. "But not a proper one for you. A woman such as this desires only position or wealth. A woman who would wed with you, but bed with any—." Another chorus of hoots. A dark scowl over his shoulder silenced most of them. "But she is not important," the Reader went on, gently malicious amusement still curving her lips, "since by this—the Lady of the Well, against your left shoulder—you are already wed, and that most happily." Eavon looked as abashed as a boy. The Reader actually winked at him before going on to the next card: Nine of Sheaves. "This, of course, portends grandchildren, a continuance thereby of your house and lineage."

"Ah." The old man sat back. His eyes were on the cards; His face was still red. He turned then. "Silence, the lot of thee!" he snapped. "Remember I am not alone at this tonight!" Silence he got. "What else, lass?"

"Five of Blades, in the position of near future. Victory in battle for you." There was more to it, more that she would not tell him, certainly not under such circumstances as these. And—*preventable*? Perhaps. She examined Options, running the various patterns through her mind, matching them to the Patterns she must hold for Gespry's plan to remain intact. No. She held her face serene as the knowledge washed through her: *One of the sons who rode here with him will not leave with him.*

"As to the rest," she said. She dealt out an additional four cards at an angle between the first four, pushing aside pain for that which could not be averted. Eavon leaned forward, interested almost in spite of himself. The remainder of the reading went swiftly; the old Baron pushed to his feet, embarrassed to have been the center of attention, but overall pleased and even impressed. How she'd known half of that—

"Interesting, Lady Reader, I'll grant thee that much. As to the truth of it—well, hast entertained me, and that alone is worth the time of it." She inclined her head gravely, swept up the cards and sorted through them as another of the Marchers —Woldeg's second son—slid into the chair.

Cretony followed, and after him came several of the mercenaries who, unlike the Marchers, put total stock in the Reader's words. Three of the elder Marchers, then. Half a dozen of the younger. A pause.

"Any else?" Gespry inquired.

"Baldyron, hast not had thine!" Ambersody, a Marcher of middle years and low intelligence moved to the younger man's side and dropped a heavy hand to his shoulder. Bal scowled, made no effort to move.

"Aye, Bal!" Keric, Woldeg's middle son—nearly as much a fool as Ambersody—took up the cry. "Come on, Korent," he demanded cheerfully, "Would'st not know what chances at home?" There was a tight silence; Gespry interposed himself neatly and casually between the two men as Bal leaped to his feet, face set and suddenly pale. The Archbishop gripped his arm, spoke quietly against his ear. The Marcher considered, shook his head sharply. Gespry spoke again; Bal shrugged. A smile turned the corners of his mouth.

"Of course. I but waited until the impatient children were out of my way." There was some laughter at his remark. He spared Keric a black glance, moved to the table and dropped neatly into the chair across from the Reader. Gespry, an oddly intent look on his face, moved down the table, hitched one leg up to sit where he could command a view of the cards. Fialla came around to lean against him and he wrapped one long arm around her shoulders, but Gespry's whole attention was fixed on the Tarots.

A riffling, a second. Five cuts. The cards were fanned before him, face down, and Bal chose from them with grave deliberation, turning the Prince of Flames up between them. Fialla caught her breath, her eyes went wide. Gespry stiffened, but his gaze remained on the pack which the Reader was setting out in the now familiar, sparse pattern.

The Reader studied the upturned cards in silence for a few moments. This was going to be a difficult reading, the first genuinely potentially disastrous one she had had all evening, though there had been many about the camp which presaged the deaths of those for whom she read. And there was an intelligence in this man's eyes which boded ill for her abilities to dissemble. Leave aside the worst of it, together with that which could aid no one: the death less than a year since, of the wife who hated him, the daughter she'd been taking from him when Death intervened and took both.

The Reader cleared her mind, laid a slim hand on the Prince of Flames and began to speak, choosing her words with care.

"This is yourself, Lord Marcher. A young man, impulsive and fearless. A right thinker, an honorable man. One who often moves to right what he sees as a wrong, seldom stopping to consider the consequences to himself." It was Baldyron's turn to color, as had most of the men who had held the chair before him.

"To the right, here," the Reader went on, "the Seven of Blades. Surprise attack, an ambush—"

"To me, or to Korent?" he demanded. For answer, she squared the pack, dealt another card across the Seven. The Seneschal, reversed—portent of bad news. Another: Three of Earth.

"To you. On account," she went on, slowly, feeling her way with the cards. "On account of one dear to you. Kindred, perhaps." The young wife, as he'd last seen her; the Reader sensed that much. His thought vanished as though he'd turned it harshly aside. Not one dear to him, no.

She pressed aside Vision, moved to the next card: Alayya, Elorra, disaster on every side! Baldyron was still frowning at the Three of Earth, opened his mouth to begin another ques-

tion, closed it again. "Here," the Reader said, "surprise."
Her fingers tapped the Madman.

"Surprise." Bal considered this gravely. "When? And
what, or canst tell?"

"Soon, by its position. Less than a year, certainly. Likely
much sooner."

"Bad?" His keen gaze had transferred to her face.

"Oh, good, since he is upright. But—even a good surprise
dealt by the Madman brings a degree of adversity with it." She
hesitated as her fingers moved on to the card in the place of
immediate future. Tamped, hard, against the Visual Percep-
tion: She was already exercising great care not to project
anything with these Marchers, though she could not always
avoid catching *their* thoughts. But here—if he *saw* in his mind,
or even sensed a little of his involvement in the Pattern! Caution, care and again caution. There could not be enough of it.

"This may be a person. If you do not know such a person—it must be one already known to you, if a person—then
several who have the attributes of the Princess. That person—or those persons—will aid you against the dangers
represented by the Seven. And, perhaps, in other matters."

"They. Or she? It *is* she, isn't it?" He frowned at the
Princess of Flames. Not that he believed any of this, of course.
But—something, almost as though a face pressed against his
memory. The Reader cleared her throat; the half-formed vision vanished. Of course he didn't believe! But—

"The Princess is usually she," the Reader said finally. She
temporizes, Fialla knew. She will not lie, but she dare not give
full truth, and so hedges it. "A woman with the heart of a
warrior, a woman similar to the Prince of Flames. Impulsive,
honorable. Unwilling to set aside any fight, given to battle
without considering the odds." She smiled. "A lifemate, if
you have the fortune to know her." Bal shook his head, a
faint smile turning his own lips. The Reader dealt her additional cards. "Wealth in your future, though it is of no great
importance to you—"

"No." Her words were touching against some core, and
again he nearly sensed something: his thought? Hers? Or some
influence of the Tarots themselves?

"Fog," the Reader went on. "Very soon, things will
become unclear. You will need to choose between a thing of

unknown future and your straight course. Do not deviate from that, the happiness of many will depend on your choice." Another card. "The Merman. The Archer. A long journey, many battles. Here, the Prime of Swords." She hesitated. "Avoid a confrontation, though it cost you great pain. Avoid it no matter what the cost to you." She made to turn over another card, stopped as his fingers touched her wrist.

"You speak so seriously. I must not provoke—"

"Dare not."

"If I do?" he demanded. She gazed at him unhappily, laid an additional two cards across the Prime. King of Night, Sword, both reversed. "If I do?" he persisted. She shook her head. "Lady, what do you see? Tell me." No avoiding it. Her stricken eyes met, held his.

"Why, then," came the whispered, reluctant reply, "you will die."

18

IN THE SILENCE that followed, the wild cheering, laughter and unsteady singing across the camps and all around the Archbishop's pavilion, drowned earlier by the level of noise within the tent itself, could be clearly heard. Baldyron, suddenly aware of this, glanced swiftly around at the confused Marchers, the bewildered mercenaries, before bringing his gaze back to the somber-faced Reader. "Well then," he said lightly, "I must be truly cautious." His eyes were grave, belying the smile on his lips. *He is unnerved by her words,* Gespry knew, *but he seeks to ease the atmosphere—a quick-witted man, this Marcher.* Baldyron, now on his feet, bowed. "My thanks, Lady, for thy warnings." She smiled up at him, wide blue eyes still troubled.

"It was not all warnings I gave you, Lord Baldyron, remember that. Remember also you have friends and allies, and that good can come of this as easily as—"

"I shall not forget," Baldyron replied, again smiling. He turned aside as she began to gather up her cards and sort them. "Come, Father, that was thirsty work! Get me some wine and we will talk of thy women!" The party began again, louder than ever. Fialla squeezed Gespry's arm affectionately, went to join the Reader.

The Archbishop poured himself a dollop of fresh wine, added a liberal amount of water to it and edged himself further back onto the table to drink it, but as he lowered the cup a commotion at the entrance drew his eye. One of his Beldenian guards was arguing with someone—Darion, by the sound of his unaccented Ordinate, and possessed of a fury, for his speech was loud and abusive, slurred and thick with anger. Even as Gespry slid down and started towards the flap, the young Beldenian backed into view, hands out, palm up, as though he sought to placate the unseen person. A coarse laugh; a sword, moving with deadly precision, flashed in the firelight to touch the guard's throat. Gespry, with a gesture to Gelc, leaped forward. At the flap, however, he halted so suddenly the little armsman slammed into his back.

"My—Lord Prince," he murmured, astonished. Hyrcan, with another ugly, thick laugh, waved his free hand, his narrowed eyes never leaving the guard. Fear spread like oil, became palpable,

"M'lord Archbishop," he replied, mockingly. "Tell this damn fool to move."

"Yes, Brezok," Gespry said gravely, not yet daring to move himself. "Take yourself from the point of the Crown Prince's sword. Not a healthy place for you."

"N-n-no, sir." As cool as the evening had turned, the guard's brow was slick with sweat. Slowly then, he stepped back—again; another cautious step, this time to one side, and then another. Suddenly free of Hyrcan's impaling stare, he turned and melted into the shadows.

"Wonderful guard Grolpet chose ye!" Gelc muttered sourly. He drew his breath in sharply as the Crown Prince's Trait struck him in full force. *Who*, Gespry thought, *can blame the boy? Hyrcan has come to kill.* Hyrcan turned, bringing his full attention to the slender figure at the pavilion's entrance.

"You." The pale eyes, an inner fire burning in their depths, sought and fixed on the Archbishop's.

"Myself," Gespry replied. The Fear, after the first stunning moment, was not as hard to hold as he'd feared. Though Gods knew it was bad enough, even sieved through his own skills.

Hyrcan scowled. "You out-spurred me today."

"I, Prince? Not so." For a wonder, there was a casual grace to his speech at variance with the cold in his stomach. To be the object of so much hatred . . .

Hyrcan spat. "I killed more barghests than you!"

"I do not deny it, Prince." He scrubbed both hands down his breeches, pressed Gelc behind him as unobviously as he could. To his surprise, the armsman did not attempt to force

his way out. In fact, he seemed to be, in turn, urging the rest
of the Archbishop's again totally silent party back inside.
Good. An audience right now might prove exceedingly unwise, given the Crown Prince's unstable temper. But as Gelc
vanished back inside and Gespry risked two steps into the
open, another slipped out: Fialla. Followed by Baldyron.

"You do not deny it." Hyrcan stumbled over his words,
took a step forward. His face was suddenly a deep, furious
red. "Yet whose name is cried tonight from one end of the
Darion camp to the other? Yours!" he shouted.

"Prince, I do not—"

"No. You do not." Vicious edge to the mimicry, his voice
dangerously under control. The sword which had hung forgotten in his hand came back up. "They say you are skilled with a
blade, Archbishop of Rhames. Show me."

"No." Gespry moved another step, cautiously, further into
the open.

"No?"

"No. We have a common enemy, Prince—"

"I have one greater than barghests. *Archbishop*."

"I will not fight you, I say. If you harm me, it will undo my
contract to your brother the King and these Beldenians who
came to Darion's aid. I will not risk that for the sake of your
pride, Prince."

"I will kill you," Hyrcan replied between set teeth.

"Or, perhaps, I might become lucky and injure you,"
Gespry went on, smiling diffidently. "And you are needed,
Prince Hyrcan, to fight Darion's foes."

"You play with words, coward of Rhames," Hyrcan said
flatly. "They mean nothing to me." Fialla moved forward,
stopped as the intense eyes came to rest on her and the Fear hit
her like a blow. "Leave my presence, woman. A prince of
Darion does not consort with whores." Gespry's breath was
an audible hiss as his hand caught his sword free. Fialla cried
out; Baldyron stepped between the Archbishop and Hyrcan,
hand gripping his hilts.

"Do not soil thy hands on him, friend Gespry." He turned
to front the Crown Prince, his face set. "Prince—"

"Shut up, young Eavon," Hyrcan thundered. There was a
tight little silence.

"*Korent*, Prince Hyrcan," Bal said finally. Hyrcan
snickered.

"By my brother's grace only. And for what? I never understood why Sedry chose such weak men for his favors. Perhaps because you all slobber so nicely at his feet. Sedry is fond of bootlickers, at least he rewards you properly." Bal's sword tore free of its scabbard.

Gespry gripped his shoulder and dragged him back. His eyes held Hyrcan's. "He is mine, my friend. The Crown Prince has chosen his way out of this world and into the better he scarcely deserves. Fialla!"

"Gespry?"

"Go inside," the Archbishop ordered. "This is no place for you."

"No!" she shot back at him.

"Gespry," Baldyron began uncertainly. Gespry held up an imperious hand for silence, drew off his short cloak and flung it behind him.

"Stay with my Lady, Bal, since she will not hear me. As for you, Prince of Fiends," he added pointedly, his sword coming smoothly up and out, "there are words between us I will make you eat!"

Hyrcan laughed, not at all dismayed. A cold fear ran through Gespry. *No man fights the Scourge of the North and lives*! None, in recent years, had. To deliberately seek such a battle—the swordsman's reflexes took over then, banishing fear of any sort as Hyrcan leaped eagerly forward, tapping the Archbishop's blade up with his own. Gespry moved to one side, freeing his dagger from its arm sheath and letting it fall into position behind his back as his sword slid up the Crown Prince's with a loud scree. There was a startled, choking sound from somewhere behind him as Hyrcan jeered: "Make me eat them, Archbishop—if you can!"

Hyrcan's sword pressed down, slipped harmlessly away as Gespry executed a swift, circular movement of the wrist. Three crashing blows rang out. Hyrcan pulled his blade back then, began a slow, light-footed stalk to the right, a fierce light in his eyes, teeth clenched in a mirthless grin. Gespry pivoted easily, smoothly on one heel, expressionless eyes fixed on his opponent. Hyrcan's grin widened, became positively evil as his point described a figure in the air between them: the blessing of the Two.

He sprang then, almost without warning, his sword a blurring arc. Gespry, however, had seen the intention in his eyes and parried easily, bounding forward in the same instant, his point slipping past the Prince's guard to touch his earlobe. A drop of blood poised there, fell to his dark shirt, was replaced by another. Hyrcan cursed under his breath, spun, and pounced. The Archbishop, startled, nearly fell. Behind him, Fialla bit off a cry and closed her eyes, but after a moment, opened them again. Better to know what chanced. Baldyron's hands held her, unnoticed by both of them, in a tortured grip.

Hyrcan lunged, pulled back adroitly before Gespry could pierce his guard again, lunged once more. Gespry's ears rang. *We are well matched—I and the Butcher of Kellech!* He deflected a wide, wild swing that reverberated up his arm and set his shoulder throbbing.

The Crown Prince, though possessed of a fury, fought with cold logic behind his sword: Seeing that his broadside strokes did not unnerve his opponent, he made no more of them and began to concentrate on short, swift blows, sudden changes of approach, the unexpectedly swift and graceful footwork for which he was renowned.

For a long time they fought, neither able to gain an upper hand. Gespry danced back suddenly, out of reach, brought his dagger up and began a slow, soft-footed stalk to the right. They were circling now, bent forward, sword and dagger held wide, elbows high. Hyrcan slashed, Gespry parried easily, turned and began a stalk now to the left. Hyrcan matched him, pace for pace, eyes holding his opponent's.

"This is foolish, Prince Hyrcan."

"Do you concede?" Hyrcan grinned wolfishly. "I will kill you anyway, you cannot save your blasphemous skin by cowardice!" The Fear pressed outward from his heavy body.

"Oh, no!" Gespry chuckled. He parried the Fear as coolly as he'd parried sword strokes but prudently countered with no similar thing of his own. "I thought to save your foul hide, for King Sedry to deal with!" It was Hyrcan's turn to laugh and as he did, he lunged. A portion of Gespry's embroidered sleeve came away with his point. "Blind luck!" the Archbishop taunted. He straightened his lean body, brought both blades together with a clash, held them loosely before him. "Listen to you, man! You breathe like the village elder already, and I am still fresh!"

"Shut up."

"Why? I have wind to fight and speak both—and to laugh

at the spectacle you are making of yourself.'' And Gespry chuckled again. Hyrcan gritted his teeth, aimed a ferocious blow at the Archbishop's head which missed by a hand's width. Gespry laughed with delight. "Prince of Fiends? Oh, no! I rather think, Prince of Jesters instead, Hyrcan the Fat and Unwieldy!''

"*Shut up!*'' the Crown Prince bellowed.

"Are you unused to an opponent who can hold against you for more than a few moments?'' Gespry inquired kindly, dodging as Hyrcan brought down an overhand swing at his neck. "Who is it you fight, Prince—old men and green herder lads?'' He stood back, laughing openly, gently shaking his head, sword dangling loose in his fingers. He skipped nimbly to one side as Hyrcan slashed at him again. And again.

"I will gut you!'' Hyrcan swore in a dreadful whisper. His eyes were red-rimmed, sweat ran down his broad cheeks, soaking into his shirt. His Trait was gone; he no longer had the strength to wield it and his blades both.

"Will you! Come on then!'' Gespry invited mockingly, flinging both arms wide. For one long moment he stood totally exposed to any swift, well-dealt stroke, but Hyrcan, now roused to a near insane frenzy, was beyond this. Gespry laughed. "Shall I cower? They say you do best with terrified peasants. Shall I weep? Beg mercy?'' Fialla choked and turned away to bury her head in Baldyron's shoulder. The Marcher's arms wrapped automatically around her. "Come on.'' Gespry deftly switched sword and dagger between his hands, back again. "An easier mark you cannot have had since the last unarmed imbecile child you ran down!''

With a terrible cry, Hyrcan flung himself forward, this time tearing a long rent up the front of the Archbishop's shirt. Blood followed: a red line ran from collar bone to the bandage across his chest. The Crown Prince's triumph was short-lived, however; Gespry brought his dagger up and around, feinted, and laid a long, ugly cut across his opponent's sword hand.

Hyrcan shrieked and nearly dropped his blade, but set his teeth against his lower lip, and somehow forced his fingers to retain their grip on the hilts. He began a slow stalk to the right. Blood ran down onto his blade, dripped from the point onto the ground. Gespry crouched, pivoting on one heel, now and again striking out: mere feelers; now parrying with easy grace as Hyrcan brought his sword down in a broad overhand swing. The hand was bleeding freely and would have hurt him terribly, but the Crown Prince's mind no longer had room for anything but the Archbishop's death.

Voices then, distant, coming nearer: " 'Ware! The King comes!" but neither man heard. There was only here, only now, only the face of the opponent, the cut, the parry and countercut. Hyrcan brought his sword up in an overused maneuver and found himself suddenly disarmed, the Archbishop's sword under his ear.

"And now, my Lord Prince," Gespry said with an ease belied by the grim set of his face. "There are words between us, concerning my Lady—"

"Your whore," Hyrcan spat. The blade pressed closer, breaking the skin. Hyrcan blinked once but neither moved nor spoke.

"Ho! What is this?" Sedry leaned across his saddlebows, scowling down at the scene before him: a circle of excited, babbling men, Darioners mingling with mercenaries. The Lady Fialla moving swiftly forward, Baldyron of Korent's hands falling away from her shoulders as he stumbled back, the two of them pale as death. Two swordsmen at the center of the wide circle—*by the Two, what passes here*?—who upon closer look were his brother Hyrcan and the Archbishop of Rhames. Sedry's scowl deepened. Both men were bleeding, both held blooded weapons. "What is this?" he demanded again, coldly, and slid from his horse before Nolse could move to aid him.

Gespry came back to the moment with a start at the King's words and turned away from Hyrcan, sheathing his blades smartly as he approached Sedry's entourage.

"Your Majesty, what a surprise! We did not expect you so soon! You came swiftly indeed."

"No reason not to," the King replied, and some of the pleasure he felt at Gespry's words was in his voice, but his narrowed gaze stayed on his brother. "Hyrcan?" The Crown Prince's expression was surly, his Aura just muddily visible, a true sign of murderous displeasure. Sedry turned back to the Archbishop, a mildly questioning expression on his face. Gespry smiled, shrugged diffidently.

"A demonstration of sword skills, Sire. For the benefit of these men, and for their entertainment."

"A demonstration?" Sedry spared his brother another

coldly furious glance before bringing his astonished gaze back
to the Archbishop's bloody and ruined shirt. Gespry's own
gaze followed the King's, and he laughed ruefully, pulling the
tatters together over his bleeding skin and the blood-stained
bandages. "Do they carry demonstrations to blood in
Rhames?" Gespry laughed again, shaking his head.

"Certainly not! And it was not so intended, Sire, I promise
you, but I touched the Prince's ear, as you can see and, well,
understandably, it angered him."

"Ah, yes," Sedry replied dryly, his eyes moving from Gespry's shirt to Hyrcan. "And your hand, brother, you cut
yourself by accident on your dagger, of course." Hyrcan met
his brother's eyes sullenly, but said nothing. Without releasing
Hyrcan's gaze, Sedry addressed himself to the Archbishop. "I
thank you for the attempt, your Grace, to cover Hyrcan's in-
discretions, but it is not necessary. I need none of my Gifts to
see the Truth: My brother challenged you."

"By your leave, Sire, not so," Gespry protested, still smiling. "A demonstration—"

"I challenged him," Hyrcan burst out suddenly. His eyes,
dark with hatred, fastened on Gespry. His Aura flared the
dark red of an old, half-healed wound. "I would have killed
him, too, Sedry."

"And made me most unhappy," Sedry replied mildly,
though his face was set. "Come, brother. You have had
enough sport for one night." A silence. Sedry scowled at the
Crown Prince, who in turn scowled at Gespry. The Archbishop blotted at the cut on his breast, to all appearances
unconcerned with the scene of which he was part. "Come
now, Hyrcan," Sedry ordered flatly. A spark of the Royal
Fire—Sedry had no more of it than that, and only when he
was as angry as he now was—crossed the space between them,
crackled at Hyrcan's boots. "Unless you wish assistance from
my armsmen, that is."

"Do not touch me, any of you," Hyrcan snarled. The
Crown Prince turned his back and stalked off towards the
Darion camp. Sedry watched until he had crossed the River and
vanished beyond the first tents, then moved to the Archbishop's side.

"Your Grace, are you badly hurt?" Gespry shook his head,
smiled briefly. "I beg you pardon for my brother—"

"You need not, Sire," Gespry replied. "It was no one's

fault, and, actually, I believe the Prince may have been drunk." Sedry, his eyes straying back towards the Darion camp, shook his head.

"Oddly, that is one of the few failings Hyrcan does not have. No, he did this as he does all things," the King went on, more than half to himself. "In despite of sense or command. A law unto himself, Hyrcan is." He blinked, brought his attention back to the Archbishop. Fialla, a flush touching her unnaturally pale cheeks, was dabbing at the cut on Gespry's breast with the hem of the ruined shirt. *Alayya, Elorra*, a shiver of pleasure ran through his belly, *to have such a woman*! With a tremendous effort, he brought his mind back to the immediate. *The Two rot Hyrcan, if he's cost me this man's aid*! "Your Grace," he began. Gespry waved a hand, silencing him.

"He did no real harm, Sire, as you can see. And we did provide entertainment for those here." Sedry tilted his head back and laughed heartily.

"Entertainment! Elorra's navel, one never knows when you are jesting, your Grace!" He inclined his head, kissed Fialla's hand, remounted. A train of armsmen followed him, a score of pack animals, squires trailing them. A wagon, another. More armsmen. Gespry gazed after them until, like Hyrcan, they vanished behind the first of the Darion tents across the River.

19

"THERE, FIALLA. A scratch, no more. Don't worry." He gently moved her hands away from his shirt, setting a light kiss on her fingers. "I *should* have killed him," he murmured under his breath.

"No!" Fialla protested weakly, a mere breath against his shoulder.

"Thou should'st have." Baldyron had heard Gespry's words as he came up. "Thy man Gelc has broken up the party," he added.

"The Crown Prince did an earlier and better job of it," Gespry remarked, smiling. Baldyron smiled in reply, briefly and with clear effort. He was still deathly pale.

"So he did. I—," he hesitated. Swallowed. "I would speak with thee a while. If I may." Fialla glanced at him, a frown crossing her brow. By the Two, he looked almost ill.

"Certainly, Bal." Gespry winced as her fingers brushed against the cut, which was now bleeding freely, and she brought her full attention back to him. "Gelc!"

"Gespry?" The armsman, in the midst of dismissing the Beldenian guard for the night, came to his side.

"Where are Boresin and Fidric?" Gespry wiped his brow with a grubby sleeve.

"Celebrating, somewhere yonder." Gelc gestured vaguely towards the eastern edge of the camp where fires burned high and an occasional raucous cheer rose above the general babble.

"Well, you had better join them, had you not?" And, as he

hesitated, "Go on, Gelc! You need not nursemaid me any longer tonight. And you'd like to, wouldn't you?" Gelc grinned.

"I—well, yes. Now ye mention it."

"Off with you, then." And, to Baldyron, as he pressed his way through the flap behind Fialla, "Touching, really, how they manage to keep a constant eye on me."

"I can understand it," the Marcher smiled faintly, a meaningless turning of his lips. He shook himself, seemed to come back from a long distance. Except for the three of them, the pavilion was empty, the fire had burned low, and only one lantern cast light upon the table. Gespry dropped into his favorite chair, tilting his chin back to look up at the Marcher. The effect was that of a precocious child deliberately charming its elders, and Bal, in spite of the cold that had settled around his heart, found himself smiling back, matching warmth with warmth. "They protect thee because they love thee."

"Really—d'ye think so?" Gespry appeared to consider this. "Yes, I know they do. Disconcerting in a way, of course. They have all been like old women since we left Rhames this time. Fialla, my dear, can you look me out another shirt? I fear this one will need a wash and some mending."

Fialla sighed. "When do they not? Never mind, Gespry, I need honest work for my hands anyway."

"Even she worries," Gespry smiled absently after her, rousing himself to search out a wine jug with liquid still in its bottom and two clean cups. "I must be better protected than the King himself."

"She should not worry," Bal's voice was a faint, oddly forced sound behind him. Gespry frowned, pushed the bottle aside. The Marcher wasn't drunk, so what was the matter with him? Baldyron closed his eyes briefly, drew a deep breath, plunged on. "Hast beat Hyrcan before, and under less favorable circumstances—or does she not know this? That thou'rt —Alster's daughter, the Lady Elfrid?"

Cups clattered to the table, forgotten, as Elfrid whirled and leaped, dagger already to hand; Bal, stunned, instinctively blocked the weapon with his forearm. There was a brief struggle, a thump as two bodies fell against the table and to the floor. Fialla flew back into the main room.

"Gespry—Gespry, what are you doing?" She ran forward to grip her companion's shoulders, tried vainly to pull her away from where she knelt, knee to the Baron's chest, dagger to his throat. Baldyron lay motionless, his face so white that Fialla, for one terrified moment, thought him already dead. "Have you gone mad?"

"Mad? Not I," Elfrid replied grimly, adding in a terrible whisper to the man beneath her, *"How long have you known?"* Baldyron swallowed. The blade pulled back a little, he could see the point, the hand that held it steady, the set, cold face.

"Known?" Fialla demanded. "Gespry—I do not understand—what you are saying?" But her hands fell slackly to her side.

"This is not Gespry, Lady Fialla. Thou need'st not dissemble to me," Baldyron said flatly. Above him, the white-haired figure set her lips in a tight line. The dagger had not moved so much as a finger's worth.

"Fialla. Leave us."

"No, Gespry. So you can kill him?" Her hands clutched at Elfrid's shoulders again. "No!"

"I will kill him anyway, will you watch? The choice is yours, stay or go!" The dagger lay at the Baron's throat once more, pressing against the hammering pulse. Baldyron closed his eyes and gave himself up for dead.

"Listen to me. *Listen to me!*" With strength born of desperation, Fialla gripped her companion's white hair, forcing the dark grey eyes to meet hers. "He knows! What of it? Did he betray you to the King, to Hyrcan? Wait, that is all I ask, wait! Give him a chance to speak!" There was sudden doubt on the thin face and she pressed on, words tumbling over one another. "Look at him, he is unarmed, unable to defend himself. Can you kill him, so? I cannot believe that of you! And you would not kill a man without allowing him a defense; that is unlike you, unworthy of you!" The dark eyes shifted back to the Marcher Baron, who lay motionless under the knife, his own eyes open again.

"As you choose." Elfrid sat back on her heels, sheathing the dagger as she added flatly, "She has given you your life, young Lord of Korent. I hope for your sake you can say the right things to me." And, in another voice altogether, *"Gods,* why did you not keep silent? Why place yourself in my hands, have you no conscience?" She stumbled to her feet and turned away. "Do you think I want to kill you?"

Fialla looked worriedly from one of them to the other. Baldyron sat up, rubbing his throat, and signed her with a jerk of his head to leave. This time, reluctantly, she did, sparing them one last unhappy glance before the curtain to the bed chamber dropped into place behind her.

There was a long, uncomfortable silence. Elfrid squatted by the fire, feeding it small sticks with what seemed to be total concentration. "They all know—thy following?" Baldyron asked suddenly. She nodded.

"They are not mine, however. They are Rhames'."

"Thou—art not Rhames, then."

"No, no of course not. There was a Gespry of Rhames when I was still living in Arolet. But he was injured, badly at Megen Cove, worse than even his mercenaries suspected. I rode here in his place, lest they think him dead or invalid. As well as—," she hesitated, "—for reasons of my own." She turned, pushed to her feet. "There is a strong resemblance between us; we are cousins at some distance—"

"There must be resemblance, to so fool thy Beldenians."

"Enhanced, of course." The Archbishop's Fire played briefly across her fingers.

"I—of course." Baldyron moved away on legs that were beginning to shake, dropped into a chair. *I thought only to aid her, and I nearly died for it. I only thought to aid her—*He was recalled from these stunned thoughts by a bitter, humorless laugh.

"It worked well enough, until now. How long have you known?"

"Only—," Bal swallowed against a tight, dry throat, "—only no time at all. Since I saw thee move to fight Hyrcan. It—it was as though it had come back, the night the King—the night Sedry took Arolet."

Another humorless chuckle. "Somehow, I always knew Hyrcan would prove my undoing. But I feared the creature itself, never suspecting there was another possibility to the thing." The dark eyes met his like a blow.

"And now," Baldyron said bitterly, "fearest I shall go straight to Sedry, laying forth the tale. Better, that I shall hold it to me, choosing my own time, letting thee live in fear for thyself and those with thee." A silence. His mouth tightened. "Is this how you see *me*, or how you see all men? Perhaps it is thy present companions, or perhaps art without honor thyself, reading all men in thy mold! Or, is it that I serve a base King and am so cut of his cloth?'' He turned away. ''Do you know nothing of me?''

''I—I see. You would have me trust you. Trust!'' She laughed faintly. ''Consider my placing! One false step, one only, and I am dead, Fialla is dead—Gelc and Bor and Fid, the Reader. Would *you* trust anyone, in my place? I scarcely dare trust myself! My life is worth less than the shirt that covers it, but it is not just my life that rides on my decisions.''

''And yet,'' Baldyron cut in flatly, ''hast brought them with thee, knowing the cost if thou wast discovered.''

''Do not throw that into my face,'' came the bitter reply. ''I do so often enough, I assure you!''

''To assume a man honorless, to give him no benefit of the doubt—by the Two, I would have sworn thou didst know me better than that! We have fought together, drank together, you and—I . . .'' He groped for a wine bottle, poured with a hand held steady only by firmest determination and tossed off the contents of the cup at a swallow. ''I thought better of thee than that.''

''Which of me?'' she demanded. With a dry little laugh.

''Why—either of thee,'' Baldyron replied, matching her tone. ''I have met both the Lady Elfrid and the Archbishop of Rhames, and both have the born honor of a knight. Or—so I thought,'' he finished bitterly.

''How can you say this, how can you know?'' Her cold anger was suddenly gone, replaced by bewilderment, an agitation that cut through his own antagonism. He moved to her side, taking the hard swordsman's shoulders in his hands to shake her gently. ''I do. I know, Lady. I am sorry for my harsh words, this is not the time for them, and thou'rt right, I have no right to judge thee. I was unthinking when I spoke, but—I thought to offer my aid to thee. I still offer it, but— here, sit. Hast had a grave shock, and that after hard battle this morning and a duel against one I would never cross.''

''And yet you did, not an hour ago.'' A faint smile, not quite reaching the troubled eyes. In the same moment, it was gone.

Baldyron grimaced. ''I did, didn't I? More fool I, but not yet a dead one, for which my thanks.'' He filled his cup, pushed it into her hands and pressed them upwards. ''Which thou wilt repay by drinking this—all of it.''

Another silence. Baldyron let his hands fall away, but continued to gaze at her, trying to catch her eyes with his own, to somehow reassure her. No response; her own gaze was blankly beyond him. Bitter, hopeless anger surged in him: He impulsively freed his dagger then, holding it out to her. "Take it, kill me now. While thy intention is still strong. I would not cause thee such fear, nor would I distract thee from this part thou play'st, for whatever reason." He pressed the blade against her hand. She started, gazed at it and then at him, pushed it aside.

"No. Put it away, I will not harm thee." A mere whisper, and it shook, like the hands that twisted in her lap. Baldyron dropped the blade and, greatly daring, took her shoulders gently between his hands, held her so. As soon as she became aware of his touch, tensed against it, he released her.

"I am glad, however it falls out," he replied. "Like most men, I would as soon live as not. But remember that I must perforce trust thee, who carries my best hid secret." And, as a frown crossed her face, added, "It has been fully eight years, but he has a long memory for wrongs, has Sedry. It is not good to think about, the death he wants for the one who armed the old King and his youngest daughter."

"Ahhhh. But you are safe—even if I would, I could not dare use that knowledge without being first betrayed."

Baldyron laughed quietly, but his eyes were hard. "Sedry's court is not Alster's—they say none this side of the Sea can match it for intrigue, and Nolse's spies are everywhere. Hast no need to do more than give word of my guilt to any of Sedry's household, that thou hadst it from another. Less: wouldst need only begin a general rumor, attaching blame to me. Once word reaches Sedry, I am a dead man, and Korent again King's lands." Elfrid shuddered. "Think'st thou he would stay his hand for so small a thing as proof?" Silence. "So you see—we are evenly matched, you and I."

The silence stretched uncomfortably. "Why do you tell me this?" she asked in a small voice. Baldyron shrugged.

"A substitute for trust: Mutual fear. Though I own," he went on simply, "I would rather have had the first." Elfrid laid her fingers on his shoulder.

"I am sorry, Bal. I cannot. I dare not, however much I owe to you—"

He shook free from her grasp. "Thou owest me *nothing*."

"Don't speak so, you know I do! Dared I trust any man," she went on hesitantly, "It would be you, for the aid you gave Father—and me. But there is no trust in me, I have never dared to it before for myself, I do not know how, and I cannot now, when other lives depend upon me." And, in a whisper as she turned away: "I am sorry."

"Who," he demanded suddenly, "will replace Sedry?" Elfrid started. "There is motive beyond thy aid to Gespry here, what else might a man think?"

She gazed at him, searchingly. Shrugged finally. "Not I, did you fear it. A woman and bastard both, upon Darion's throne? No. Rolend, of course."

"Sedry holds him—"

"I know—I—" she studied his face again. "All right. Sedry sent to Gespry for aid, a time since, as you know. Rolend—also sent, asking that Gespry aid him and Darion—"

"I had heard," Bal said tentatively, "he never interfered with internal matters."

"No. There were circumstances, this time." She smiled briefly. "Myself. To prevent me coming alone to remove Sedry from Darion—and Hyrcan, of course—he—well—," she fumbled to a stop. There was sudden color in the pale face. "I doubt he would have interfered, save to physically restrain me, had matters in Darion been less serious. As it is, of course—"

"I know," Bal put in hastily as she paused. "The North—Lertondale—"

"All of it," Elfrid finished, rather grimly. She fetched a sigh, closed her eyes briefly, continued. "In any event, the Reader cast the matter into cards after Rolend's messages arrived, and a Pattern came clear. And so—here I am, here we all are."

"You intend to kill Sedry—"

"I? No." And, as he eyed her dubiously, "Understand me, I would, five times over for what he did to Father. But Rolend does not want his blood shed, nor does Gespry. What *I* want scarcely matters. And," she added flatly, "it would cause Sedry pain to lose Darion. Death would cause him no pain at all."

"Rolend," Bal reminded her gently, "is Ascendant at present. Behind Hyrcan—"

"Then," she replied with a smile, suddenly and unnervingly

regaining Gespry's facile speech, "we had better remove Hyrcan first, had we not?"

Alayya, Elorra, worse by the moment! His face showed
none of his dismay, however, as he refilled her winecup, again
pressing it towards her lips, wrapping her hands around it.
This time she raised it in a brief salute before drinking. He inclined his head, reached to lay a tentative hand on the white
hair.

"How came you by this? It was dark as mine—"

She closed her eyes. "By all the old tales, it should have
been white when we came before Sedry in the Reception, the
afternoon he exiled us. Gespry's is, has been since Megen
Cove. Mine—." A deprecating smile crossed her lips. "It's
still as dark as yours; Fialla puts a thick mess on it when she
washes it that bleaches the color."

The voice subtly altered. Was, he realized with a faint
shock, Elfrid's as he remembered it: low for a woman's, resonant, lacking that charming lilt that was Gespry's, but
somehow no less pleasant. She sighed. "In a way, it is a relief.
That you know. That someone does. To play such a role, con-
stantly—"

"Which I discovered only by merest chance," he urged.
"Tell me what has chanced with thee these years. Me, you
know of."

"No. I barely know who you are. Little enough about you. I
still do not understand what drove you to aid a sick, mad old
man and his bastard daughter—"

"Enough," Baldyron cut in roughly. "I told thee then. I
swore to Sedry when I first came of age, more than a year
before Arolet. I was young for my age, I suppose. Craving action of any sort: against the barghests, against the old and settled way of things under Alster—Sedry appealed to that. He
can still be appealing, when he chooses."

"I know Sedry." Flatly.

"I—of course. Most of us were displeased that day, when it
became clear he would not allow the King to live out his last
days in comfort—exile for such an old man was not necessary,
particularly after he—lost his wit." His gaze dropped to his
upturned hands. "And for thee—"

"I was there," Baldyron went on quietly, "when thee
fought Hyrcan in the King's halls. And I saw thee in contrast
to Hyrcan and Sedry; more honorable than they, protecting

thy father's very life with thy own." Elfrid, embarrassed, looked away.

"I was also in the Reception," Baldyron went on after a moment's silence, "when Sedry exiled Alster and thee. There was muttering, but already we knew better than to brace the King for it. And then, so short a time later, I heard him and Nolse laughing as they plotted thy deaths. And thee, with only a staff and an old, worthless dagger—I could not bear it." He stared across her bent head with unseeing eyes, as though the things he spoke of held a misty life of their own against the darkened wall of the tent. "The luck was mine," he went on diffidently, "that I was not missed. And then Sedry sent me to Arlonia, to find why his ambush failed." He laughed. "And rewarded me with Korent."

"I never thanked you," Elfrid began tentatively. Baldyron shook his head.

"Hast, by living. And I own," he went on with a faint smile, "that I did not encourage thanks that night. I was furious with Sedry, moreso with myself. Afraid, I can admit that now, that the deed would be traced back to me, and fall upon not only my shoulders but those of my following, perhaps even my parents, my brothers and sister. Sedry is a vindictive man, as I was beginning only then to see. But tell me of thyself. Please." She turned away from him to stare at the faded and misused map on the table before her.

"We reached North Embersy on a Genneldrean ship from Carlsport. I was nearly crazed myself by the end of that first year: little money, nowhere safe to go." The corners of her mouth turned up in a dry, humorless smile. "North Embersy had permitted us to land, offered us sanctuary, allowed us to go where we would, vowing us safety—but I killed three assassins before winter set in. We left in secret, me afoot, him horsed on an aged, lame nag as we had left Lertondale."

"Where did you go—how did you live?"

"I cut wood. Or herded goats at villages or farms in exchange for bread and meat, shelter for the night. It did not take long before I realized the hazard of my position." Again that faint, deprecating smile. "Well? A lone woman, no matter how thin and plain, traveling with a mad old man? I cut my hair, named myself Cyrel, and journeyed thereafter as a boy, Father's page as he—as he thought me after—." She swallowed, shook her head impatiently. "I fought as a blank shield when I could, so keeping what weapon skill I had, adding to it, a little, now and then. It was a long time before we worked our way across North Embersy and into Rhames.''

"And sought sanctuary from the Archbishop."

"It was odd," she replied obliquely. "I had known of the relationship, though few folk do. It's in the old family records, they're not often read. Sedry does not know, or did not. And even I was not aware that when I brought Father to the monastery, *he* would be there."

A silence. Elfrid began tracing one of the lines on the map with one long finger. "Father died a year later. He never regained his senses; to the very last, he thought of me as one of his pages, and wept for his lost Elfrid." Silence. "Gespry was good to me, he took me in as one of his armed. I grew out my hair and again became swordswoman. It was of no import to Gespry whether folk talked of the amazon that rode with him or not. What people think is not of great importance to Gespry, he only cared that my sword arm was as useful as that of any of his other armed.''

"An unusual man."

"An unusual man," she agreed gravely. "I was with him," she went on, "when he broke through the siege at Newldwy, I was at his side when he flattened the pirates off the coast of Belden and so gained this pavilion, as a gift. I was aboard the *Wave Cleaver* at Megen Cove." She sighed, faintly, closed her eyes.

"My—my friend." Baldyron spoke up finally, hesitantly, compelled by the very lack of expression on the thin face before him. "Please give this up. It is madness, and can only end in thy death."

"No. If Sedry dies, if Hyrcan dies, why should I care? It is worth the cost to me."

"You cannot—"

"Cannot what?" Her voice was suddenly cold and harsh. She shoved his hand aside and pushed to her feet, though she still leaned heavily against the table. "Well? Are you so much Sedry's man after all? Do you think to dissuade me and so save him?"

"Hast not listened to me, or to anything I have said to thee?" he snapped. "I think to save *thee*!" He scrambled to his feet, pushed her into her chair. "No, sit still and listen to me a moment!" She glared at him but made no effort to rise. "Ten Sedry's are not worth one of thee, canst not see that?" He knelt before her and clasped his hands. Elfrid gazed at him in astonishment. "There is no way to convince thee, save to swear to thy service."

He cleared his throat, and slowly spoke the words that would bind him as liegeman. "I, Baldyron, Baron of Korent, son of Eavon, vow from this day forward faith to Gespry, most honored." Grey eyes met, held his as he continued "and Elfrid, Lady Princess of Darion. This do I swear, by Alayya, by Elorra, with sincerity, without ill intent, with fealty. By the Two do I consecrate myself to this end, forsaking all other swearings, for all my life, from this day onward." And, before she could move or speak, rose to his feet. He gazed down at her momentarily. "Do not rise, friend Gespry. I know my way out."

Fialla hurried back from the alcove, dropping into the seat the Marcher Baron had just vacated. The hands she took in her own tightened.

"Gespry?"

"Fialla. Did you hear him? He—swore vassalage to me. To Gespry. I—I—why?" The thin face turned towards hers was still pale with shock.

"Tell me."

"I—." Elfrid drew a deep, shuddering breath, let it out slowly. Some of the bruised, frightened look left her face. "Did I never tell you," she whispered, "of the man who brought me my sword—and hope—on the Carlsport Road eight years ago?"

"Oh, Gods," Fialla's eyes went wide. Elfrid nodded.

"I had—not forgotten him, I could not. He—it was so cold that night," her voice dropped to a whisper again. "So cold that when I touched my face with my fingers, it hurt. And Father, laughing, talking, seeing things not there . . ." Silence. "When he rode into sight, I knew we were dead, both of us. It would have been so easy for him to kill us." The long hands tightened convulsively on Fialla's.

"No, I hadn't forgotten him. Just—I suppose I hoped he was dead, or elsewhere, anywhere. Not here." She shook her head. "I didn't understand him then, I don't yet. Why he should have risked *everything* to save us."

"And yet," Fialla prompted gently. Elfrid shook her head again.

"And yet he did. 'For thine aid, Lady.' No man ever called me Lady—but he did. And he brought my sword."

"And you don't understand him?" Fialla smiled. "He has honor, your young Marcher—"

"Not mine," Elfrid protested faintly. Her cheeks burned.

Fialla smiled again, let the matter ride. "And now, what?"

"I don't know." Elfrid pulled her hands free, ran them over the turned-up corners of the map. "I—that he knows, Fialla, it terrifies me, and yet—"

"And yet . . ." Fialla paused, went on when Elfrid only shook her head. "You think him untrustworthy?" Pale hair flew as she shook her head. "Well, then—"

"But—if I were wrong, Fialla—"

"You're not. Not with Bal, *I* know, if you do not. You must trust someone eventually, you know."

"Fialla, you know I do! I trust you—and Gelc, Bor, Fidric. And the Reader, and—"

"Bah." Fialla laughed. "Besides all of us! You have known us for over seven years, that is not trust, merely comfort. Not all hands are against you, you must learn to judge men better than that."

"I—"

"Trust me, if you cannot him. Your very life is safe in his hands, I swear it."

"I—Fialla—"

"Hush. Remember," Fialla added in a low voice, "who you are, who I am. Your own thought is of more danger to you than Bal is, you know that! Or my thought!"

"Not yours, Fialla—"

"No? I wasn't speaking to Gespry, these past several minutes, was I? Remember who you are—Gespry, Archbishop of Rhames, my beloved. Anything else—"

"I know, Fialla my precious." The voice altered, was Gespry's once more. Fialla smiled, caught the hand nearest her, kissed the base of the long thumb. "Now then, it is late, you fight again tomorrow and what of that cut? Here, let me see—and get rid of that shirt, it is absolutely foul."

"Yes, Fialla."

"Yes, Fialla," she mimicked quietly, moistening a cloth at the water jug and working lightly at the dried blood. "I had better take a few stitches in this bandage, it's half off. You were very fortunate, Gespry."

"No. Skilled." Delivered dryly. Fialla glanced up to meet a boyish grin.

"You!" She shook the damp kerchief at the other's nose. "You are as bad as he is!"

"Good." The smile was even wider. "I am supposed to be."

"You are light-headed," Fialla replied sternly.

"Reason enough."

"Scarcely. I thought you nerveless, one learns, doesn't one?"

"Mmmm. Doesn't one, indeed? Ouch." This last as she separated bandage and the lower edge of the sword cut. "You really—you really think he's—"

"My life on it, Gespry."

"It is, you know. Ouch! Need you do that tonight?"

"You can wait until tomorrow, if you want it worse. Consider that the Crown Prince might not be above poison on his blades, and let me finish—and yes, I know it is. My life on his vow. And I still say you can trust him."

"Why?"

Fialla shrugged, her attention fixed on the upper edges of the cut. "Call it Fialla's magic, if you wish."

"Women's sense? Intuition?"

"Don't laugh at it!" she chided quietly.

"No. With my own odd gifts, how should I dare? I—oh well. On your head be it."

"It shall rest there lightly enough, I assure you."

20

NIGHT, WITH FOG easing up the riverbanks, hanging over low-lying bogs. A waxing moon, nearly down behind steep cliffs, glittered on mail, harness and swords—on spear-points, arrows, teeth, nails. Elfrid hunched over her saddle bows, the Archbishop's personal armsmen a watchful triangle about her until she could catch her wind and resume the fight. Cries of wounded men, a howling like that of a dog pack or wolves, tore the air around them.

"That were a near one, Gespry!" Boresin threw back at her; his eyes continuously, rather nervously, searched the damp, heavy grasses.

"Near enough," Elfrid admitted, drawing another deep breath and letting it out slowly, feeling her heartbeat drop back towards normal. Even with the bright moon, it was hard to see; the barbarian had leaped up and forward right under her horse's feet. She had had no time to duck, no time to bring her sword around before the creature was on her.

Thick, strong fingers had grappled for her throat, pulling her dangerously off balance against her mount's neck; fetid, wild breath assailed her nostrils—*hands* at her throat? Her own hands groped, seeking to break the other's clutch, snatched back as they encountered rough, long hair, padded finger ends, long blunted nails—*Elorra aid me, no human man's hands!*—and her inner senses were flayed by a true vision of the Fegez. Neither human nor animal, possessed of inborn and drug-magic that permitted the shift from one to another at will. The horror of it choked her.

Before she could do anything else, the creature was gone, underfoot and behind her. Boresin had pulled up a scant moment later, a Rhamesian short-bow still clutched loosely in his free hand.

"I warned you not to get so far ahead," he'd remarked blandly. "What comes of it—you have armsmen, use 'em." And had been adamant that she rest briefly. Elfrid, her breath still coming in ragged, short gasps, her mind still raw with that final blast of knowledge, was only too glad to agree.

A clashing of weapons, cries near to hand: more Fegez, afoot like all the others, this time coming down from the North. Someone cried out not far away as his horse reared and both fell. Elfrid shook her head to clear it, drew another deep breath, and sat up straight again. "Gelc! Boresin—Fidric—ready? Together, then!" But this time she held back long enough to allow Gelc ahead, settled into place between the brothers. The white horse leaped forward.

Another in the act of rising from the thick grasses—she thrust with her sword, hanging low off her mount's neck. A long-bladed knife caught the moonlight briefly as it spun up, away and out, falling then back into the grass and out of sight. With a choked cry, the Fegez followed. " 'Ware, Gespry—*down*!" Gelc bellowed. Halfway back into the saddle, she flung herself sideways again; a dart tugged at her cape, not far from her ear, passed harmlessly on. She sat up again as the little armsman swung his sword in a ferocious arc, sending a dark, hairy head and hand—blowpipe still clutched in its fingers—flying. *I did not see that*, Elfrid told herself sternly, swallowed hard and turned away, spurring to Fidric's side.

"Nasty things," that worthy remarked calmly, leaning across his mount's neck to search the grass before him. His eyes, his full attention snapped to his left, where three more burly, furclad Fegez were bounding towards them. "They need not shape-change for all of me!"

"No," Elfrid agreed grimly, thrusting aside both dread and inner vision savagely. She dragged her own high-strung mount around to face this new challenge. "They are quite alarming enough by themselves!"

She slashed out: A wildly bearded human face, pale in the moonlight, surrounded by a shock of black hair, was frozen in a cry of pain, gone. Another replaced it—so hairy, she could make out the face only by the glitter of eyes as it came on. The white horse danced nervously to one side, stood motionless as her strong left hand tightened the reins down still further.

Her sword came up, struck, recoiled from the fire-hardened Fegez spear with a shock that vibrated up her arm. Fingers tingling, she struck again. A third time. She moved swiftly then to the side as the Fegez dropped back several paces and threw his weapon, drawing his knife as he did so. A frightened cry from over her other shoulder: She hauled the excited horse down onto four feet by main strength, ran the barbarian through, turned back to search the battlefield behind her.

"Who?" she cried out.

"No harm, Gespry!" an answering, shaken, cry from one of his Beldenians. "Close, though!"

"Watch yourself, then! Before you, lad!" She recognized the voice; Garion, one of the young common soldiers among the Beldenians. *Too young to be out here for his first battle, what was Grolpet thinking of*? The boy sat up, heartened by the Archbishop's words, urged his horse forward at a gallop, sword out and up. Another outcry: his own, followed by that of a Fegez. As Elfrid pressed after, he sagged, fell, slipping from the horse's back. The animal bolted.

"Fidric! See to him!" But it was Gelc, once again to the fore, who leaned perilously across his saddlebows and sat back up shaking his head.

"Too late, Gespry—'ware, to the left!" he cried out, dragging his mount around.

Another wave. Half of these—fifteen or so, though it was difficult to be certain—carried spears, knives, bows: conventional weaponry. The rest—if they *were* Fegez—ran amongst their companions, but there seemed to be shadow on them, or about them—two legs or four? Or did they shift, as they seemed to, between two and four? Man to beast to man—"Hold the line!" Elfrid cried out.

The mercenaries, the Marchers, came around in response to this rally forming a human dam against the new attack.

Time. More than time, lest more half-grown boys die. She rose in the stirrups, brought her hands together high above her head and began the prayer: "By the Two, by Alayya the Blessed, Elorra his Lady, by thee and for the lives of these under my care—*Anayyyadassa!*" The last burst from her lips in an exultant cry. The air was shivered: A gleam of gold swelled between her fingers, bubbling outwards as the space between them increased, changing, growing, swirling like a whirlpool of fire above her head, turning the white hair sullenly red. Eyes closed in fierce concentration, face tilted upwards, arms spread wide, she waited; waited until the light was an eye-searing brilliance.

She cried aloud again, slashed the air with her hands: The Light spiraled upwards, crackling and flaring. Without warning, it lanced towards the enemy.

But the Fegez were no longer there: As soon as the golden Light began to form, they stopped, huddling together in silence. They retreated, then, a step at a time. By the time the Archbishop's Holy Fire was a burning pillar above Elfrid's head, they were in full flight.

With a heartened cry, the Beldenians, the Darioners followed. The northern cliffs loomed suddenly near and blackly to hand. "Hold, men!" Elfrid clung to the saddle-bows; somehow she held her voice strong. Only the Archbishop's armsmen were near enough to see how very drained the effort had left her. "Foolish to follow them—we've traded enough lives with the brutes." She brought the white horse back around: easily now, for the animal was tired, its head drooped. "There are the wounded. Some of you return to camp, bring litters, lanterns. Fidric," she added, "choose some men, go with them. Let Fialla know I am well."

"Aye, Gespry." He gazed across the battlefield somberly. Grolpet rode slowly towards them.

"What shall we do with the barghests?" the Beldenian demanded. Elfrid scowled at him; Grolpet sighed audibly. "Fegez, your Grace," he amended sourly.

She considered this, absently waving Fidric and his four companions on their way with her free hand.

"Drag them to the cliff's edge here. If the creatures want their dead, why should we refuse them? If they do not," she added shortly, "burn them at first light." And with that, she turned away and began the slow ride back to the camp.

Exhausting. More than she'd thought possible. But there was an exultation the weariness could not subdue. *I lit Gespry's Fire. Even he had not been certain*—And under such circumstances.

But—against what? She shuddered, pulled her cloak against the sweat-soaked shirt.

*   *   *

"I am truly amazed, your Grace. How you hold so many men in your hands. Had my Darioners been fighting under Marchham or even my good friend Baldyron—why, they'd have all gone home after the first set-to you had. Certainly after last night." The King scowled into his empty cup; he had not meant to remind himself of that particular fiasco. Though certainly a good fighting man, the King was no tactician, and knew that his lack of ability in that area, the fact that he'd led from within a tight box of guard and not at the fore, had cost him at least a few of his men. He smiled then, with that brilliant warmth he reserved for fair ladies, as Fialla moved to pour him more wine.

"Bah, Sire," Elfrid replied easily. "We learn from these mistakes, I have been fortunate so far, that is all. But I find it like throwing stones at frogs in a pond—one does not miss often enough for it to become tedious."

"Unlike frogs," Sedry reminded her sourly, "*these* throw things back." Elfrid shrugged, refilling her own cup with a mixture nearly as much water as the deep red Embersean vintage. She dreaded these sessions with the openly admiring Sedry, sensing the unease he buried even from himself. If he suspected—if he even *thought* he suspected. Of all those she must play her part with, Sedry was far and away the most wearing.

"So they do. But you underrate yourself, Sire. Or your Marchers. I certainly have no special influence on any of them."

"Do you not?" the King laughed. He was not certain whether he was envious of the Archbishop's undoubted popularity or merely astonished by it. The odd disquiet rose, was thrust aside as he drank deeply. "There is not a man in either camp who would not willing die at your command."

Elfrid shook her head, alarmed. "I should hope not!" she said vigorously. "No man should have the right to such power! Nor are you entirely correct," she added with a slightly malicious grin, "for I am certain your brother—." Sedry groaned but laughed ruefully, shaking his head. "As to why they follow me," she went on, more to herself than to the King, "why do soldiers follow any leader? Hmmm?"

Sedry considered this gravely, smiled finally. "In your case because they love you," he said, adding dryly, "and in mine because I am King and they must. Now Hyrcan—men follow

him, so far as I can tell, because it is somewhat safer to be for
him and under his command than otherwise."

"Only *somewhat*?" Elfrid inquired laughingly. Sedry
shrugged, laughed himself though he did not sound greatly
amused.

"You have seen him," he replied obliquely, turning away to
gaze into the depths of his cup. "Hyrcan," he began hesitantly, stopped. Glanced sidelong at his companion. No, Gespry would not laugh at him, nor would he spread the tale. And
the look of polite interest reassured Sedry. "Hyrcan was
always strange, but grown, he has become a monster. Well,
only for an example: I needed his aid in the North, the people
there for some reason have never taken to my rule—the Two
may understand it, for I do not!—and this past year, he put
down three separate revolts. His own way."

"So I have heard." Elfrid closed her eyes.

"If that is all you can say of it," Sedry exclaimed bitterly.
"I am certain they have heard of the Scourge of Darion in the
lands beyond your eastern deserts!" He subsided again into
gloom. "No one knows for certain how many have died in the
North—noble and peasant alike, Hyrcan sees no difference
between kinds of bodies."

"I do not understand," Elfrid said finally. "Why did you
not forbid him to act in such a fashion?" Sedry laughed
briefly. There was, he realized, a hysterical edge to the sound.
He swallowed wine.

"I? Forbid Hyrcan?" He laughed again. "I forbade him to
challenge you, that alone must show you how much control
any man has over Hyrcan. Hyrcan does what he wants, he
always has." Sedry cast another sidelong glance at his companion, drew a deep breath and plunged on. "And I am afraid
of what he might do; I am afraid of what he has already done.
He—he *is* a monster. He does not kill his prisoners outright,
this is spoken across Darion—in whispers only, I need not tell
you—but I know it for fact. He places them in cells at Kellich,
without food or water, and leaves them to die.

"He left a countess and her young son that way, last year,"
he went on, the words forcing themselves between pale lips,
"whose only fault was that her husband, his father, had opposed Hyrcan's wholesale slaughter of the serfs on his land.
He gave them a bit of raw pork, two ears of corn, a bottle of
water. When the cell was opened, some weeks later," he

whispered, "it was clear that the boy had died first; his cheek had been gnawed upon."

"By the Two," Elfrid breathed. Her hand moved automatically in the Blessing.

Sedry gazed blankly into his cup. "I daresay many have called upon the Two, before madness or death overtook them in Hyrcan's prisons. Did you never hear," his voice dropped to a horrified, unwilling whisper, "that his wife and newborn son died?"

"Aye," Elfrid responded. "Of plague. But—." Something in the King's grim face silenced her.

"So it was given out. *I* know otherwise now." He raised his glance, stared silently for a time through the flap, finally shrugged, turning back to his cup and his companion. "I am not a good King, particularly," he said finally, more to himself than to the one he knew as Archbishop. "I once thought I might be one—at least, I think I did, it becomes harder to remember what I thought, when I deposed my poor old father. It seems to me I thought I could rule better than he."

Coming back to himself, he reddened, buried his face in his cup and drank. When he emerged, he was grinning self-consciously. "No, I am not a good King, particularly. Nor do I care, anymore, so long as I remain King. That is sufficient for me, and I will not be driven from it so long as I live." He pushed his empty cup aside. "But I do take excellent care of Darion in one way that I think no one realizes."

"And that is?" Unnoticed by the King, Elfrid had gone very quiet, her eyes all pupil under the narrowed lids. The King laughed.

"Why—I take very good care of myself, that Darion shall not fall into Hyrcan's hands!" He paused to consider this remark, laughed again, let his hand fall to Fialla's forearm as she again filled his cup. She smiled quietly and in such a manner as to neither encourage nor offend, detached herself gently and vanished back into the shadows. Elfrid's fingers tightened briefly on the table's edge, relaxed again.

"Why not merely remove him from the succession?" Her voice revealed nothing but the most casual interest. "You have another brother, of course—or so I understand. Though rumor in Embersy and Rhames has it he has been ill?" she added casually. Something in this remark greatly amused the King, who threw back his head and laughed loudly.

"Ill! Ill—oh, aye, he has that—confined to his chambers at Gennen for some months now. Very contagious, what Rolend has!"

"Well," Elfrid murmured, "One hopes for his recovery, then." This, of course set the King off again.

"As to your question," Sedry went on, regaining control over his rather grim mirth with obvious effort, "I cannot remove Hyrcan from the succession; only a combined act of the Council and the Witan can do that. And my Witan, my Barons, are one and all more terrified of Hyrcan than I. Save," he mused, "perhaps, Bal—Baldyron. Baron of Korent, you know."

"I know the Baron." Faintly, but the King was too far gone in his cups to notice. "They tell me," Sedry continued, bringing his eyes up to meet hers. "Bal actually tried to fight Hyrcan for you. Was he drunk?"

"Not that I noticed," Elfrid replied gravely. She drank; her throat, her mouth remained dry.

"Besides," Sedry went on, dragging himself back to her original question, gazing the while dolefully at the map under his cup, "Hyrcan might then see no reason not to kill me. Just because I had done that, although I doubt he wants the succession, or that he would care to be King, if he had to. But to take it away from him, that right—no, Hyrcan would kill me for such a thing, out of pique. We are a strange breed," he mused, tracing the line of the road that led from Arolet to Gennen and the southern borders.

"How, strange?" Elfrid prompted after a silence. The King roused himself with an effort.

"We are. Alster's children. More truthfully, Sigurdy's."

"Not so," Elfrid urged, her generous mouth quirking in a smile. "I remember King Alster's visage, I have seen the painting which Queen Morelis has in South Embersy; also, as you must know, he sought sanctuary at Rhames not long before he died. You have his mien, sire." Sedry shook his head.

"Oh, that. Certainly. Save Hyrcan, we all look much like him. And even Hyrcan has a resemblance to Father, enough to be certain of his blood. Though he is more Mother's child than the rest of us." He blinked, drank, licked his lips. "No, I refer to Father himself, not his look. So many of us, and only one was at all like him."

Silence. "Your—your youngest brother, the Prince Ascendant Rolend?'' Elfrid inquired finally. Sedry glanced at her, shook his head.

"No. Though Rolend has Father's consideration for the peasantry; his Trait is more Father's than mine. He has more conscience than the rest of us altogether. Certainly more brains than most of us. No,'' he went on, laughing a little, quietly, as though he savored a memory. "No, I referred to his Bastard. Elfrid.'' He inclined his head towards his companion, weaving slightly. "You have heard of her, of course.'' Elfrid nodded, her face expressionless. "She journeyed to North Embersy with Father,'' Sedry pressed, "You must have seen her.'' *Gods. It needed only this*. Elfrid frowned in an outward show of furious concentration.

"By all that's holy, the Swordswoman! Cyrel!'' she shouted, and fell back into her chair laughing. "She came to the monastery as your father's bodyguard, in the guise of a swordsman.'' She tipped her companion a grave wink. "I hardly need tell you, that is a masquerade not easily held, and she was found out nearly at once!'' Sedry smirked. "Elorra's left ear!'' Elfrid exclaimed. "I was not aware she was kin to the old man—of course,'' she went on apologetically, "she never said so, and he was not in his right mind, you know.''

"No. No, I daresay he was not.'' Sedry sighed. "He had not been for some years. There was nothing else I could do, for Darion's sake.'' Elfrid's hands wrapped around the cup in a murderous grip. Sedry went on, his expression doleful. "It has haunted me since, that I needs must exile him—poor old man. But there were too many in Darion who would have created war to reinstate him—I dared not allow that to happen.

"Another might have had him executed,'' he smiled faintly. "Hyrcan would have. Hyrcan nearly did. But no true man would dare to such a thing. And the girl—Darion was no safe place for her. Bastards among the nobility, royal ones in particular, are not tolerated. She would have been dead within the month.'' He gazed out across the camp through the open flap. "I have often wondered since whether I did the right thing.''

"A difficult decision,'' his companion agreed soothingly, but within a coldness settled around Elfrid's heart: *How calmly you speak of him, Sedry. He loved you, Father did. Could I kill you now, I would. I would kill you twice over*! She pressed such thoughts aside as the King glanced across the table briefly. He was drunk but he had the family skills—they could play her false. *Gespry—I am Gespry*. She turned the litany over in her mind, brought it back to the moment.

"And he died at Rhames—ah, small world that it is."

"There was no pain," Elfrid assured him quietly. "He was old—old and tired, that was all."

"Ah. And the swordswoman—the Bastard," Sedry went on with a casual air that would not have deceived a child. "What became of her?"

"As you can see, Sire," Elfrid smiled faintly, gestured grandly with both hands, "she no longer rides with me." The King laughed. "She went east with us on one campaign," Elfrid continued thoughtfully, one long hand stroking her chin. A faint stubble showed against the wind-tanned skin. "And—let me think, now, she was part of the raiding party against Newldwy. Thereafter, however, she went on south, as a blank-shield. I do not know what became of her. But then, I had no idea she was kin of yours—"

"I am as pleased," Sedry replied grimly. Mere thought of Elfrid infuriated him, sobered him a little. "Though I would not have expected the creature to trade on that kinship. I made certain from the start she knew I would tolerate no closeness with the byplay of Father's sortie into second childhood. So did we all," he added coldly, "save—of course—Rolend."

"Poor lonely child," Elfrid mused. Sedry cast her a reproachful glance.

"It was no concern of mine," he said flatly. "Had I had the choice, she would have been strangled in her cradle."

"Harsh," she replied lightly. "Ah, well. I rather miss her, she *was* an excellent swordswoman, you know."

"I," Sedry said coldly, "know nothing of the sort. Though," he added, almost unwillingly, "Hyrcan certainly has reason to. She nearly killed him in a straight duel when we took Arolet."

Elfrid waited, but Sedry showed no inclination to continue the tale. "Anyway, I tried to get her to join my company, but she would not. She refused me—and *I* am not used to that sort of thing. Gave no reason," she went on, adding another dollop to the King's cup, filling her own, "merely said no, and that was the end of it."

"How very like her." Sedry's eyes were dark with a remembered hate. "Cold. Incapable of any sort of feeling—"

"Well, I could not tell," Elfrid went on blandly. She added

water to her cup, swirling it idly. "She was not a forthcoming sort, I can say that much. However," she roused herself, smiled warmly at the King, who responded in kind, "enough of these ancient matters. My Reader is likely still awake, and has expressed an interest in reading your cards tonight. And you yourself—"

"Ah. Certainly!" Sedry sat up, suddenly very much alert. The one reading he'd had at Arolet had been a short one, an enigmatic one, and he'd had people gazing at him with patent disapproval the entire time. "A shame," he added, pushing his wine aside, "that we have so few seers of any kind in Darion. Our priests tend to discourage them, you know." Elfrid grinned like an urchin; Gespry's charismatic warmth, his familiar gestures came hard for her; but his slightly malicious, boyish sense of humor might have been her own, it fit so increasingly well.

"Who would know better than I? They are greater prudes than the monks in South Embersy, and that, I tell you, is no mean feat!" Sedry leaned heavily against the back of his chair, smiling slackly.

"Yes, it amuses me, your Grace, to see how my mother's priests—even my brother Hyrcan, who kills like a rabid wolf—react to your Reader and your fair lady Fialla. They call your reader 'witch'."

"And Fialla? No," Elfrid chuckled as the King stopped short and colored unbecomingly. "The Crown Prince threw that in my face, it was what set me upon him, as he must have guessed it would. But your Darion priests," she went on, "amaze me. They seem to think service to the Two can be accomplished on such a narrow path: no pleasure, nothing worth having at all, come to think of it. In my opinion, they approach the Two wrongly: such a somber mien in service of those who created the world and the heavens in joy? I cannot think how they intend to enjoy the next life, for in my opinion, a man who neither winbibbs nor wenches in this life will not need an eternal afterlife: This one will last him forever!" She gathered her long legs under her and went in search of the Reader, leaving the King convulsed in silent laughter.

21

THE TAROTS READER slipped quietly into a seat opposite the King's as Elfrid lit another lantern. It cast a yellowish pool of light between the pale woman and the golden haired, red-faced Sedry—a pool of light that swayed as wind gusted around the tent. The King watched, fascinated, as she deftly unhooked the box and brought forth her cards, riffling them expertly several times, then fanning them on the table before him in one smooth motion. "Choose one of the many, Sire." The King blinked, gazed at the gilt-edged iridescent arc before him. After long and diligent consideration he chose one, tapped it, and at a nod from the Reader, drew it free. She reached across to set it face up between them before gathering the rest of the pack to riffle them once more. The King of Dawn, holding aloft his blazing sun, gazed solemnly upwards.

The Reader smiled as she manipulated her pack. "An excellent choice, your Majesty. This is the Tarot of an established Prince, ruler of a nation. One who deals with power and knows well its uses."

"And misuses?" Sedry inquired heavily. His wine seemed to have caught up to him once more. The Reader shrugged, still smiling, set the pack before the King, retrieved it after he had—again with grave consideration—cut it.

"All power is to some extent misused, Sire. Isn't it?" Sedry considered this seriously, nodding absently to himself, then leaned forward eagerly as the Reader began to apportion cards in the most complex of all layouts: A Tree of Life. Two Pentacles, enclosed by a greater pyramid created the body of the

Tree, two rows of three cards each descended from the bottom of the pyramid to make up the trunk. The Reader paused several times as she turned cards face up, frowning now and again as the pattern revealed itself. Sedry watched in fascinated silence.

"These," the Reader began finally, indicating the six lowest cards with a sweep of her hand, "are your base, your foundation, and this," she gestured towards the left-hand pentacle, "is that part of your past which holds influence on your future. This," the other pentacle, "is that future. Surrounding all are the outside persons, deeds, which may control your destiny if you allow them to—or may be shaped by you, to control your own."

"Ah," Sedry breathed, planting both elbows firmly on the table and cupping his chin in his hands. The Reader nodded, bent her gaze back to the pattern.

"Overall, a hopeful reading, Sire," she stated, "though there are many choices you must make to obtain that outcome. Here, in your base, the Princess of Spring. A very young lady, a fair one, and dear to you, perhaps?"

"Juseppa," Sedry murmured as the Reader hesitated. "My Queen."

"By these surrounding her, here and here—Four of Sheaves, Two of Water—she will come to hold you dear as well, though by this—Five of Water, she does not know you yet well, and she is young to have love, other than as a child has it." Her small hand touched the other three base cards: Prime of Blades, surrounded by the Three of Blades and Fog. "A great military victory has shaped you, Majesty. A conquest involving briefly consolidated forces and—," she hesitated briefly, "and treachery." She pressed extraneous thought, Outer Vision aside: The fall of the old King in his own halls was assaulting her from two directions.

"In your past," she went on, gesturing towards the left pentacle, "the Princess of Flames—a woman, perhaps . . ."

"Woman? What sort?" Sedry demanded, grinning. The Reader tapped the card.

"The Princess of Flames, as you see, holds a naked sword. She is not like other women, content with a household, small pets, her needlework. She has her own strengths, although, of course, these need not actually include use of sword." She paused, risked the least of the Inner Vision. Darion's King could not be alert enough, under all that wine, to sense the vision in his mind to be none of his own making,

"The Bastard, by all that's holy!" Sedry exclaimed excitedly, under his breath. Gods, he could *see* her, was that what the Tarots did to you? No wonder some men held fear of them! The Reader gazed at him inquiringly, and he laughed aloud. "Ah, fools, my Darion priests, to scoff! See what you have shown me already!" His laughter subsided, a grim smile twisted his lips. "She was indeed a part of my past, Lady Reader, my father's bastard daughter—but go on, I detain you."

"By your leave, no, Sire," the Reader replied. "I greatly prefer that you ask questions, speak your feelings at my interpretation of the cards. This is of great aid to me, it allows me to see further into your future, and to give you a reading which is of greater practical use to you." She bent back over her pattern. "Also in your past," she went on, tapping the cards as she named them, "and, I would guess by the position still in your present, Six of Water. A dependable man, one who oversees your daily routine, a man to trust with your life—a man willing to sacrifice much for you." *Ah, Nolse*, the King thought, his eyes eagerly following the small white hand across the cards. *She has named thee well, trusted Steward!* "Four of Fire—a treachery, perhaps a defection, by one near to you, trusted by you, that still causes you grief. Here, the Seven of Earth. This can represent a facet of your personality, though I think it unlikely. Or a man known to you—a common man, one comfortable with people of all ranks—"

"Who but my father?" Sedry asked. He brought his gaze up to the Reader, returned it, avidly, to the right-hand pentacle. "And my future?"

"Interesting . . ." The Reader spoke to herself, bringing her attention back to the King with a start.

"Interesting?"

"Indeed—ah, but I disgress. Here, Two of Blades, combined with the Dungeon. Dissent within your ranks, King Sedry, caused by—"

"By whom?" Sedry leaned forward, as though he could wring the meaning from the cards with his gaze. A faint sense of dread tickled his stomach. The Reader squared her pack, dealt additional cards below the pentacle, frowned at them, shook her head.

"Difficult to say. It could be any of a number of men. The reason for it, however . . ." she hesitated.

"Yes?" Sedry prompted impatiently. Dissent? Who yet dared! The Reader glanced at him unhappily, lowered her gaze to the cards again, laid one more, with a soft snap, across the others, sighed, and paused to consider her words.

"A time not long hence, you will find yourself in a position to—do a thing which may cause men to fear you. Improperly handled, this matter can cause Darion to be wrested from your fingers."

"A revolt?" Sedry demanded, astonished. The Reader shook her head.

"No, not as you mean it. A groundswell of opinion, rather."

"Who would dare? No, which of them would not, given what he thought to be the proper motivation? But then," he went on, more to himself than to her, "I need only take care not to do this thing, whatever it may be—can you tell me no more of it?" he asked her. She shook her head with every indication of unwillingness. The Inner Vision, its emotional counterpart, flowed lightly from her, wrapped itself around Darion's King. The flickering dread in his stomach tightened.

"Would that I could, Sire. Perhaps at another time—but even those cards I dealt to clarify the matter for me have only muddied the waters." She hesitated, impulsively added, "Govern your deeds with care, that only can I advise for the moment." Gespry had never forbidden her the right to offer him an alternate course, would not have. Though, like Gespry, she knew it unlikely Sedry would turn from destruction.

Sedry's brow furrowed. Hard to think, the wine was furring his mind. He brought his eyes up from the Tarots to meet hers. "There have been plots—my brother Rolend—"

"The Four of Fire. You had not thought he would turn against you." Sedry's eyes dropped to the pattern; after a moment he shook his head.

"No. Surely," he went on, hesitantly, "surely *he* will not attempt such a thing again?" The Reader bent over her cards for some minutes without answering, dealing out an additional four-cornered layout to one side across the Prince of Sun and Moon. Finally she sighed again, gathered up those cards and returned them to the pack.

"I cannot tell, Sire. He is prisoner, however, is he not? By that much, I hold it unlikely. Though," she added unhappily, risking meanwhile another faint projection, "for some reason which I cannot comprehend, a sense of kindred pervades your entire reading. It is because of kindred, or by the hands of kindred, that you will fall from Darion's throne—if you do so."

"I am warned, then," Sedry remarked grimly, after a rather long silence. In the distance, the Beldenian change of guard around the Archbishop's tent could be heard, and the calls of the nearest boundary-riders, ensuring that the parameters of the camp remained safe. "And these others?"

"The last twelve cards, those affecting your destiny," the Reader replied. "I see the founding of a dynasty, by this," she touched the Nine of Sheaves, "whereby you and your young Queen Juseppa will be long remembered as the force which brought together all Darion, expanding her borders. Sons and daughters to follow you," she went on, her hand grazing across the Seven of Sheaves. Sedry smiled happily, the sense of doom momentarily pressed aside by the lovely vision that formed itself in his mind. No, no trick of *his*, and none, he was certain, of this white-haired lass opposite him. The cards—

"Here, however, the alternative path. The Dungeon, the Lady of the Birds, the Sword. Another choice given to you, whether to act as a servant of the Two, as a ruling King, or as a receptacle of the horrors of Night."

Inwardly, she shuddered. It had taken itself from her hands, as it occasionally did: the price one paid, for any sort of manipulation, no matter how small. Always an exchange, and sometimes—when the Pattern was as far-reaching as this one, the cost of the exchange could be too great to bear. This time—perhaps this beast of a man, who considered even her as a possible object of sex, would yet tread the path of honor. Nothing was predestined. At least, they had warning. Or, she did.

She blinked, shook her head slightly, brought her attention back to the King; he had asked her a question she had not even heard, and as she met his eyes, repeated it. If he had seen—but no, his eyes were full of fear for himself only.

Sedry swallowed past a suddenly dry throat. What had she seen, this Reader of the Futures, to so unnerve her? "And if I do not act as—as a servant of the Two?"

She moved her hand lightly across the King of Night, reversed, on to the next four neatly spaced cards down the right side of the pyramid. "The Priest—reversed. The Keep—reversed. Seven of Fire. Then, Majesty, you will lose all you hold dear." Sedry bowed his head, momentarily subdued.

"I will remember it. And these?" He indicated the bottom of the pyramid.

"Two of Sheaves, the Sun—the Winecup, reversed. Nine of Earth. Those who wish you well vie with those who do not. Beware, King Sedry," she said gravely, "of those who seem yours, and are not."

"Is everyone against me?" the King whispered. The Reader shook her head, but he sensed a hesitation in that motion, as though she saw that same thing and feared to disclose it to him. He stared down at the table then, nodding to himself. If she were right—and she must be right—why, then, any man, anyone he trusted could be an enemy!

He glanced up to meet the Archbishop's quizzical gaze and laughed, embarrassed. Enough! He was warned, but it ill became a man to hold so somber for so long a time!

"Ah, yes. Well! You have given me much to think upon, Lady of the Tarots." The Reader half-rose to give him a courtesy. Sedry smiled, dug into his belt pouch and came up with two gold coins which he pressed into her hand, closing her fingers over them. "No," he said, when she would have refused, "Take them. I know Gespry keeps you well and you lack for nothing, but it is my thanks." He turned away before she could proffer the coins back to him. "Your Grace," he added, holding himself upright with an intense effort, "I bid you good night. I have had a long day, and that is strong wine you offer a man!"

"For yourself," Elfrid replied pleasantly, "I would be sorely remiss to offer any lesser grape. My thanks, Sire, that you accepted my poor hospitality." The King glanced around the Archbishop's sumptuous tent and laughed. "And," Elfrid went on, "that we were of some amusement to you." Sedry stepped forward to grip her shoulders.

"My good friend Gespry—you have been, indeed. I cannot tell you how much I enjoy your company. I shall see you on the morrow." He turned away, took Fialla's hand between both of his, his lips lingering on her fingers. "Nolse!" he called out as he strode towards the flap. The Steward, who had been lounging outside playing at dice with the King's guard and the Archbishop's Beldenian guard, leaped to his feet and aided the King onto his horse. So accomplished was he at this act that none of the mercenaries were aware how very drunk Darion's King actually was, while the King himself remained blissfully unaware of Nolse's careful, rather anxious, attention.

22

ANOTHER MORNING, ANOTHER pale dawn. Elfrid stood, bone-weary, on a steep rocky slope, watching the Fegez that the men of Darion, the Beldenians, had been fighting for hours. They were withdrawing rapidly up the northern slopes of the ravine where they had sprung their trap. From the south, from the only entrance to the narrow cleft, came the sound of a mounted company. Moments later, Boresin and three hundred armsmen thundered into the draw at full gallop, the first rays of the risen sun touching upon spears and drawn swords.

"You came in good time, friend Boresin."

"As swiftly as I could, Gespry." Boresin gazed around them as he slipped from the saddle. "It's fortunate that I was able to get clear of this, and ride for aid. How many did we lose?"

"Fortunate," Elfrid replied dryly, "that for once you obeyed orders and turned when I said to."

She chewed at her lower lip, scowled at the high ledges. "Perhaps a third of our number. But nearly every horse we had. I warned them," she continued flatly, "that it was a fool's maneuver to come this way. Damn Grolpet for two separate idiots, he knew better than this! What was the man thinking of?" Boresin, knowing no answer was expected, held silence, contenting himself with the least of shrugs.

"Do we follow?"

"Do we ever?" Elfrid countered gloomily. "No, of course not; unwise, even on such a bright morning as this."

Fresgkel of Eavon emerged from the trees, leaning on one

of his young armsmen. He was limping: His horse had fallen, almost at the same moment Elfrid's had, but the old man had not been quite swift enough in his dismount. It had taken four of his men to pull him free.

"How is Fialla?" Elfrid waved in the old Marcher's direction and the boy, who had been leading the Baron down the ravine, altered course.

"What would you expect," Boresin grinned at him, "when you have been overnight chasing barghests, and must be rescued at that? Worried, to say the least." Elfrid was scowling openly. Boresin cast his eyes heavenward, in some irritation. "I cannot *believe* that even Gespry of Rhames will not, after all that has passed this month, name the creatures as they are properly called!"

"Which," she replied blandly, "is Fegez. Because one battles them, one need not insult them."

"Huh." Eavon remarked dully, as he approached. "They have cost me this day a son and my best horse. I am not certain," he went on, attempting lightness but failing utterly, "which grieves me more."

"A son?" Elfrid felt the color slip from her face. Eavon nodded, attempted to speak, shook his head and turned away. His armsman, at a gesture, led him to a seat among the rocks.

"Telborn," he finally said, his eyes searching the rocks, the trees across the ravine, not really seeing them. "He was strange, Telborn, but mine for all of that. And my heir. Lands'll come to Dessac now, I suppose." He turned back to the one he knew as Archbishop, smiled, but tears slid silently down his face. "Surprise to the boy, having land of his own. King never cared much for Dessac, and Telborn was a healthy lad."

Elfrid was suddenly overwhelmed by compassion for the old man—and in the early light, under such a load of grief, Eavon appeared old indeed. She closed the distance between them, knelt to hold him close. "The Two guard his soul. My poor friend—how it must pain a man, to lose a child, to lose that part of him he thought would long survive him."

The cold around her own heart loosened its grip. Not Bal, Gods, not Bal. But where was he? It came to her, suddenly, that she had neither seen nor heard the Baron since the ambush began: Bal had leaped from his stricken mount, gathered a handful of men to him, shouted encouragement to his father—and had thereafter vanished. Her eyes searched the valley floor, shied across the fallen.

At that moment, as if in response to some inner call, the Marcher Baron came sliding down from high up on the northern slope, perhaps a dozen arrows and a Darion long-bow clutched in his left hand, the right outflung to counter-balance his rapid descent, occasionally clutching a tree or bush to stay his downward speed. He reached the ravine floor without incident, glanced all around, lips compressed against a clear anger at the loss of so many men, finally started across towards his father.

Fresgkel gazed sternly at his youngest son; his eyes were red-rimmed. "Hast been at it again! Alayya's hangnail, made'st me a vow never to engage in that hair-whitening practice again. Thy father hath enough," he added, running a hand across his long, grizzled locks. "Thou young fool—know'st what he does?" he turned to Elfrid. "He works his way in amongst the barghests, picks them off one at a time as though they were groundbirds and this the season for hunting them!" Baldyron laughed, rather wildly.

"Gently, my friend." Elfrid gripped his arm. "There is too much tension in you. A deep breath, perhaps two." The young Marcher closed his eyes briefly, nodded. His left hand clutched a bundle of arrows so tightly the knuckles stood out white: Black fletched, short—Fegez arrows, the right tight-ened briefly on Elfrid's. She tapped the bundled flights; Bal, jumped convulsively. "Trophies? An odd sort, and certainly not rarities."

Baldyron laughed once again, this time genuinely, grimly, amused. "Trophies? Nay, Gespry, I but use their own weap-ons against them. They are a superstitious breed, the barghests, such a thing smacks of magics to them, and counts as aid to us by that much. But there is more to it, of course. The points—," he gestured with them. Every one was poi-soned. The laughter in his eyes died out as he met Elfrid's shocked gaze. "They deserve no better than they deal."

She shook her head with a hard-eyed determination. "No man deserves such a death," she began vigorously, but the Baron snorted, silencing her.

"No man? Ah, wilt call them men, as a good servant of the

Two must, is that the way of it? Despite the deaths thou hast seen—despite *all* thou hast seen, Archbishop? Thou'd'st still darest to call them *men*?''

"Do you dare to call them less, young Baron of Korent? They die as men do," Elfrid returned evenly. Boresin, alarmed by the look in the grey eyes, laid a restraining hand on her arm. "They run in fear even as other men do, when outnumbered, they suffer pain, as men do, when wounded, and you would call them—would call them what?" Silence. "Or perhaps they are not men, as we know it. Still, do they deserve to be treated as lesser, because they are other?''

"I will not argue philosophies with thee." Baldyron's own voice was level but his dark eyes were terrible. Elfrid fell silent before his gaze and made no attempt to speak again. "Do not ask me to think of them as men." He drew a deep breath, expelled it, and when he resumed speaking, his voice was nearer normal. "They have killed my friends, my comrades and my serfs—my Lady wife, my young daughter—and now my brother, though the Two know he felt no great love for *me*. They made a day and night of my own life a living hell with their foul poisons—they—no, my friend. That thou canst think of them as men, I admire thee for it. But do not attempt to bring me to thy view, for thou wilt not." And he turned on his heel and strode off. Eavon shook off his young armsman and limped after him, expostulating vainly, sparing Elfrid one embarrassed, harassed look.

That he should *do* such things—Gespry himself would have been truly furious and she was no less angry with him. Beyond any ethical considerations—*Fool, if you had died for the playing of such a game!* But that was no thought to follow to its conclusion.

Boresin roused her from a deep study with a light shake. "Come. We brought horses. Some will walk, but you are needed at camp. At once."

"No. Since when does Rhames ride when others must walk?''

"No man will grudge you the mount, you know that. You are needed, and that most urgently. Darion's King has asked for you, there were raids on the camp itself near to midnight, they want your advice and Korent's for increasing the guard. Also," Boresin added in a voice that could not have carried beyond her ear, "there are messages for you. From Carlsport, and from the monastery.

"Ah?" That could mean only one thing—the forces set afloat on that distant time—it seemed years, in this place and moment—in the Archbishop's monastery were beginning to reach their intended shores. The Pattern was bearing fruit. "What word?" she whispered. Boresin paused, his keen eyes wandering, as if in idle curiosity, before he replied. No man within twenty paces of the two, and none interested in them.

"Gennen," he said then, tersely. Elfrid bit back the smile that would have spread across her tired face, the surge of joy that greeted the single word. Gennen! Rolend was free!

23

"FIALLA!"

The Archbishop's Mistress slipped past the closed flap as Elfrid's shout reached her and flew across the packed dirt to the cluster of men and horses. Elfrid let herself down from the saddle with more than customary caution—she was more tired than she dared admit—and clasped Fialla close. "I'm not clean, Lady. Unharmed, however," she added as Fialla leaned back to study her with worried eyes. "Come—a seat first. There is news from Rhames, they tell me."

The guard moved away, two with the horses, a third—at Boresin's order—in search of hot washing water for the Archbishop. Fialla nodded. "Good, all of it. As you wash, I will tell you. Bor said he would bring you swiftly, but I thought another hour, at least—you are certain you are unharmed?"

"Swear it," Elfrid laughed as the main flap fell into place behind them.

"Well, then." Fialla fastened onto the grimed tunic and edged her towards the table; with a final, gentle shove, she pressed her companion into the comfortable armed chair set aside for the Archbishop.

"Unharmed," Elfrid murmured, eyes closed, "but tired, Fialla. Tired to die of it. And damn Grolpet for a fool, I warned him, and he'd have none of it! We lost—Gods, we lost twenty men or more and nearly every horse we had!"

"He had better listen to you next time, then," Fialla remarked quietly. "Here, let me aid you with that." She pushed the swordswoman's hands aside, pulled the tunic free, and began unlacing the lightweight mail shirt.

"He *will* listen to me next time," Elfrid replied flatly.
"Eavon," she went on, "lost his heir last night."

"Ah, poor man!" Fialla had gone from a quiet respect for
the old Marcher to something near the love her father had
never inspired in her. "How is he?"

"It hurts him, though he was not close with Telborn. He—
bless you, Fialla!" This as the Archbishop's mistress loosened
the mail and applied a cool, wet cloth to the back of her companion's neck. There was a comfortable silence as she sponged
Elfrid's face.

"The messages arrived late last night." Fialla spoke next to
her ear, in a hushed whisper. "One of the lay brothers brought
them."

"And the messages?"

"What I told Bor to tell you: Gennen. Rolend is free, he has
the support of Orkry's guardian—you smile?"

"Nothing." Elfrid shook her head, adding, as Fialla waited
for answer, "Merasma always did have an eye to the main
chance, we must indeed be under the protection of the Two,
that she should take his side!" And, as Fialla shook her head,
"My beloved half-sister. Sedry wedded her to the greatest of
the Southern Nobles, as a reward, I think, for keeping an eye
on our brother. That in itself," she mused, still smiling,
"might have been sufficient to press sweet Meras's affections
away from Sedry—that Morelis should sit on the high throne
in South Embersy, while she bears an Earl's brats in the mountains of Southern Darion. What else? You may speak free.
There are none about to heed us. They have their own battle
griefs to attend to."

"Bishop Kreyyes was there when Rolend was freed; through
her the Darion Church has sworn to him. Already word has
gone by Gespry's messengers back to North Embersy."

"Ah. Juseppa."

"The marraige will be annulled, of course—"

"Of course—"

"And they say," Fialla added, "the child is willing.
Whether she becomes Rolend's or is returned is for her father
to say." She shrugged the matter aside.

"Matters progress smoothly, then. So well, I scarcely dare
trust our luck."

"There is more," Fialla went on. "Something between him

and you and the Reader which I do not fully understand. To do with the Pattern, the Reader's manipulation of it.''

"I—all right." Elfrid cast her mind back. Certain contingencies, which only the three of them had dealt with; certain code words taken from the Reader's Tarots. None of them were particularly pleasant, that she recalled. "The rest of the messages, then?''

"King of Night. Princess of Flames. Sword, Prime of Swords, reversed." The pale, tired face so near hers hardened as she spoke.

"Well." Elfrid smiled, rather grimly. "It could be worse. Kill Hyrcan.''

Fialla caught her breath sharply. "Oh, no.''

"It was what *I* wanted, you know that. To trust to the other thing? Foolish. You have seen him since then, Fialla. Would Hyrcan tamely submit to banishment, by Sedry or Rolend? By anyone? No," she went on, brushing aside Fialla's attempt to speak. "There is only one way to deal with one such as Hyrcan. I have tried twice, in my life, to kill him. Third time, they say, wins out.''

"I am afraid," Fialla whispered. "Not for you, just of him.''

"Then it is good you do not fight him," Elfrid replied, her voice still low, flat with scarcely repressed hate. "I do not fear Hyrcan, not like that. You do not dare, if you would fight against him. It is why Sedry never dared.''

"His Trait—''

Elfrid shrugged. "It merely finishes an already overwhelming horror that is Hyrcan himself. I hate no one the way I hate him; I shall kill him with great pleasure.''

"Sedry—''

"Oh, Sedry." Elfrid shrugged somberly. "Sedry was always so obvious, with his little digs, his snubs, his snobbish dislike. His subtlety, which was never subtle at all. Hyrcan, though. Hyrcan simply terrified me when I was a child, and that beyond his Trait. Because even then, I could shield myself from Hyrcan's Trait. His Gifts aren't that strong.

"Sedry would never have dared harm me, for all his talk. He, too, looked always to the main chance, and Father loved me." The grey eyes softened momentarily. "But Hyrcan never thought, he just acted. There was never a main chance with Hyrcan, just what he wanted.''

"He challenged you, even though the King would have lost terribly by your death," Fialla said gravely. Elfrid nodded.

"I hated Sedry for the way he treated me, of course. But that was different, he never gave me cause to fear, not the way Hyrcan did."

"But—"

"You have seen him." The dark eyes gazed blankly over her shoulder, fixed on a distance of time and space. "When I was twelve, I think, one of the grooms told me—Hyrcan had taken one of his dogs down to the cellars and tortured the beast. It had done nothing to merit punishment, it was just—an amusement for him, I suppose." Fialla turned away, shaken. Elfrid laid a hand on her arm. "I am sorry, I should not have told you."

"No. All right," she managed finally.

"For long after that, I feared him, knowing that he would deal with me the same way, given the opportunity. I do not like breathing the same air with anyone who could make me feel as much terror as Hyrcan did." Silence. With an effort, then, she pushed aside the dark thoughts and smiled. "The worst of it is over, Fialla. As you said. Only two small tasks remain."

"Only?" Fialla protested weakly. "Kill a Prince and depose a King—only? And you look forward to your part in this," she added, shaking her head faintly, disbelievingly. Her companion nodded.

"You have known that all along, Fialla, I made no secret of it. Ever. I wanted it so much, I would have come alone, hoping only two deaths before my own was sealed.

"I know there is good in this for all Darion, for the honors of those Hyrcan has slain in his dungeons, for that frightened innkeeper and his family at the Griffin. For the poor souls in Lertondale, alive only in the sense that they still breathe, fearful to do as much as that, lest the King's wrath descend upon them again. To save Darion's young women—I have not missed how Sedry looks at you, the same as he has always looked upon beauty. He was never content to merely look, and only his respect for the Archbishop of Rhames as an ally and a swordsman has kept him from pressing his attentions. I am sorry, Fialla. Everything I say to you today upsets you."

"No."

"A lie, but a well-meant one. Let it pass. I know all those

things, Fialla, and I feel them, but only as one feels another's pain. It means nothing to me, here and now. There is only my shame, my fear. My grief. I am selfish, narrow, I know that, too."

"Never mind," Fialla said. She glanced at the damp, filthy washing cloth in her hands, carried it and the pan of water back to the fire pit. "I have no right to judge you. I have no personal loss, no wrong to avenge. None to whom I owe anything, good or evil. It is easy for me to tell you to look upon the greater picture, that revenge is petty and ignoble."

"Easy, perhaps. Right, also."

"No. Had my beloved been driven mad, died, had a tenth happened to me that has happened to you, there are no lengths to which I would not go for vengeance." She came back down the table, dropped into the chair at Elfrid's side. "Have you a plan, or will you need aid in devising one?"

Elfrid shrugged. "Perhaps—perhaps not. I will puzzle it after I sleep. Unless—Bor said something of a council?"

"Later. There was a little excitement in the early hours, nothing too bad, but the old men are finally stirred up. The meeting will be here, and not until late. I told the King flatly you must rest first."

"Did you really?" Elfrid chuckled delightedly.

"Of course I did! You are his ally, not his subject! And you do need rest, look at you! Bor is bringing bath water for you, come, back into the bedchamber, you know the men drop in unannounced, and I want that bandage from your chest, it is foul enough to be unhealthy." Elfrid sighed wearily as she rose to her feet. With Fialla's aid, she walked the few paces back to the curtained alcove, dropped slackly onto the bed. Two of the Beldenian commons entered shortly after with buckets of hot water, followed by a third with a bathing basin.

There was little further speech. Elfrid undressed and bathed, climbed into clean dry breeches and a loose shirt. The morning sun was already heating the air in the bedchamber. She drew the first decently deep breath she'd taken since Fialla had first stitched the bandage that bound her breasts flat into place, stretched out on the bed furs with a happy little sigh, and was asleep almost immediately.

The after-sunset breeze—surprisingly chill for the warmth of the day—was just beginning to sigh through the camp when the first councilers filed into the Archbishop's pavilion. The King himself did not appear until nearly an hour later, and when he finally did show up, he was preoccupied and out of sorts. Drinking again, many of those present thought, but there was little sign of wine on Sedry. He seemed to find it difficult to concentrate on revised strategies and plans for tightening camp security, however, and finally moved himself to a chair away from the table, near one of the firepits, a winecup at his side. This he drank from rather absently and at infrequent intervals.

If his gloomy, glowering presence affected the other men, they concealed it well, perhaps from ease of long practice. After a time, however, Sedry was forgotten as the meeting got underway. Plans were made, scrapped, remade; maps drawn, marked up, argued over. Tempers snapped, already frayed by the long stay in this valley so distant from Court, from home and hearth, by the ambush on the Archbishop's party and the raid on the camp. Clearly, long contact had not taught them everything about the Fegez, and they were far from second-guessing their enemy. Through the evening, only Elfrid, Baldyron and Fresgkel—the latter's house token reversed in mourning for his heir—remained at all calm.

It was Baldyron, finally, who laid out the ground rules for future attacks on the Fegez, who dropped his own map of the allied camps on the table, marked with new fortifications and changes in the set-up of barriers and guards, and who refused to listen to opposition, finally forcing Sedry's council and the highly displeased Beldenians—to say nothing of the irate Marchers—to agreement. Once assured that his orders would not be cast aside as soon as he left, he took his father and returned to the Darion camp. The council and the captains argued a while longer over minor details.

Elfrid roused herself, pushed to her feet and mouthed polite remarks as the last of them trooped out. Alayya's navel, she thought with irritated irreverence, but it was impossible to work planning sessions around these men! No matter what was decided, or by whom, someone's tender sensitivities were touched upon, and nothing seemed too minor to set one of them off: rank, knowledge of the enemy, the terrain, weapons—how the next morning's weather might turn out, even! She scowled at the last broad back as the flap fell into place.

Her hand came up to scratch at her chest—Gods, Fialla's new bandage was snug!—dropped away again. Leave it!

The King was still an immobile shadow near the fire. As she turned, Sedry's eyes came up, locked darkly on her. "You seem troubled, Sire," she said finally, uncertain what she should say. Need the man stare so?

Silence. Sedry stirred himself with what seemed a great effort, blinked as he set aside a half-full cup. His second only, for the entire evening. That of itself was disquieting.

"I am troubled," Sedry agreed finally, his voice a harsh whisper. "Wrong, all wrong," he added to himself, in an even lower voice. "It is treason to plot the life of an anointed Prince, in Darion."

"In any land," Elfrid agreed. There were long, awkward silences between the King's words, silences into which anything might be read, and her own inner senses caught radiating suspicion, fear, uncertainty. *Alayya, Elorra, if he has suspected, if he suspects—*

"There is a traitor among us," Sedry whispered finally. Elfrid swallowed hard.

"A traitor, Majesty?" To her relief, her voice showed only concern, none of the gut-wrenching fear she actually felt. The King nodded.

"You know it as well as I. Your Reader spoke of it, you were there." Relief left her knee-weak. *Whomever he fears, it is not I!* "I have thought and thought," Sedry went on, "and considered her words, the cards she showed me, the meanings. The alternatives—all of it. I cannot believe that—but there is only one she can—." He shook his head. "I do not know, I only fear."

"Sire—." Traitor, Elfrid wondered, running mentally through the King's reading as he recalled it. No such word had ever arisen, had the Reader dared Vision on him?

"I thought, perhaps, your Reader might speak with me again," Sedry went on. "I must know, you see this, Gespry, I must—know."

"By all means, Sire." Elfrid melted back into the shadows, only then running a sleeve across her damp face. She returned moments later with the Reader. Sedry had already moved to the table, and Elfrid moved a lantern, adjusted the wick so that full light lay between Tarots Reader and King.

Sedry had eyes only for the pale lady as she brought forth

her cards, began to riffle them gently. The supposed Archbishop moved tactfully away.

"You warned me," the King began abruptly, "of a plot
against me. Tell me more of it, Lady, if you can." The Reader
inclined her head gravely, deftly spread the cards and took the
one the King chose: No careful deliberation this time on his
part, he snatched at the nearest, laid it upright before him.

Ah. The Reader squared the remainder of the pack, riffled
them again as she studied the reversed card: Dark clad, her
hair in wild disarray, the Queen of Night gazed back across
her shoulder in terror, one foot poised on the verge of the high
precipice. Fear, fear that pressed towards madness. She closed
her eyes briefly, marshalling the Master Pattern, those few
Options left. She studied the King then, as he bent over the
deck, choosing his cuts with such care his life might depend on
the accuracy of them.

It worked: This Reading would present the final, gentle
push. As for the other: Change could be effected, sometimes
without altering what was desired. Sometimes.

The King watched morosely as she repiled the cards and laid
out the four-sided pattern. As she dealt out the last of it he
slumped, resignedly, down into his chair.

"You fear—a plot—"

"You told me of it, Lady. If not for you, it might have
taken me unawares. As it stands now," he spread his hands,
shrugged. "I know nothing, have no idea who plots against
me. I must know."

"I told you," the Reader reminded him gently, "that the
opposition you faced would be contingent upon a deed."

"But you also said there were those who opposed me,"
Sedry said flatly. "And as to the deed, you could tell me little
of it. If it is a thing already done—"

The Reader shook her head. "No, Sire. I could have told
you, if it were. But—." She bent to the cards. Sedry, with a
weary little sigh, pulled himself upright, leaned forward to
study the images himself, though they conveyed nothing to
him. The central one, though—Gods, a nightmare! What had
such a thing as that to do with him? And—and that one—his
eyes were held, unwillingly, unhappily to the card nearest his
hands: a torture scene, drawn and colored with painful
realism.

"You fear," the Reader began abruptly. Her fingers

brushed the Queen of Night. "And with reason, Sire." Pale eyes met his. "Since you would know the worst of it—." Sedry nodded, swallowed hard. "There is one who hates you deeply. One who feels that only your death will appease that hatred."

"Who?" Sedry's voice cracked. He cleared his throat, drew his cup across the table, drank deeply, thirstily.

The Reader turned over another card, another, studied them thoughtfully. "Who?" The King sounded oddly calm.

"One close to you."

"Close. To hand or by blood?"

He is not truly stupid, this Darion King. The Reader averted her eyes, kept them fixed to the layout. And though he seldom uses his wit, his born Gifts, he is using them now. The Two guide me! She held at bay the tendril of Truthing that sought her mind, turned a third card: Fog. A faint smile pulled at her lips, and she bent lower over the cards to hide it.

"I cannot tell, King Sedry. I am sorry." Literal truth in both statements.

"This?" Sedry's fingers neared the Dungeon, shied off as though the card burned him.

"That—well—"

"I must know, Lady," Sedry urged quietly. "Anything you can tell me, anything at all. I cannot sleep, food tastes of nothing, I fear to drink and there is no enjoyment in wine—I *must* know!"

"One old in death," she said, unwillingness in every word, in her eyes. "There is nothing else I can tell you, I swear that, save to beware. To remember, also, the things I told you during your last reading. It is all contingent . . ." her voice faded away to nothing; Sedry was no longer listening to her.

Silence. The King nodded to himself, several times. The pale grey eyes tore themselves away from the layout finally. "Hast aided me, Lady. I know what I came to learn." He pushed back his chair, pressed to his feet. "It must be, there is no other. But it will be dealt with." Without a backwards glance, without further word to any of those in the pavilion, he turned and strode purposefully from the Archbishop's tent.

Elfrid stared after him, pulling her eyes from the darkened flap with an effort. The Reader was slowly turning cards, continuing the pattern. "Why did you tell him so much?" she breathed. The Reader glanced up, turned back to the table.

"I dared not lie to him, my friend. The Pattern dictated what must be done, I dare attempt no further Changes or the entire thing will come undone. Already—." She stopped. The Princess must not know of *that*! "I told him little enough of what is here, and let him believe what he would of that I told him."

"It is dangerous," Elfrid whispered. "For all of us, for you. For the Pattern."

"No. Not for the Pattern, that I still control." She swept the cards into a ragged pile. "More dangerous to lie in the face of the Tarots." There was a finality to her words.

"There has been danger for all of us, my friend, since we first conceived this strange journey. There is always danger in such a thing, always something taken back when the Pattern is made, something exchanged when it is altered, as I have had to do. Danger in battle, danger in deception. All these things taken together . . ." She shrugged. "You still tread a thin path, but with the least amount of caution, you will be neither discovered nor slain. That I have seen as recently as this morning, and it is truth."

Elfrid turned away from the flap, dropped into her chair. One hand passed over the bandage across her chest, fell to her lap. "I know you mean to reassure me, to comfort me, Reader."

"No. You know me better than that. I speak the truth, from which you may take comfort, if you can."

"But even after all these years," Elfrid went on, unheeding, "I am still of Darion. I have a Darioner's scepticism in full, even with my own Gifts, even when I think I see what you do, I cannot—"

The Reader's eyes were grave; she slipped down the length of the table to lay one long hand against Elfrid's cheek: a rare gesture of affection from one who seldom touched anyone. "You think you doubt," she murmured. "The Princess of Flames does not doubt the clear evidence of her eyes, in the last analysis, that is not one of her faults. Nor does she doubt the evidence of the other senses. The Princess has those also."

"Perhaps." Elfrid patted her fingers lightly and got to her feet, walked slowly to the flap, and pushed it aside. She stood there silently for some time, watching across the Beldenian camp, waving absently as the guard paused just beyond the clearing before the pavilion. "I must move against Hyrcan, soon," she murmured to herself.

The Reader caught the words, faint as they were. "Wait a day or so. Perhaps it will not be necessary." Elfrid turned back to gaze at her curiously but could make nothing of her words. After a while, she shrugged and went back to her silent study of the camp.

24

IN THE DARION camp, the King gained his own pavilion, kicked one leg across his saddle-bows and dropped neatly to the ground, thrusting the reins towards one of his guard. Nolse, ever alert to Sedry's comings and goings, pushed past the half-closed flap and hurried to the King's side. Sedry shook him off brusquely.

"Leave be, Nolse. I am well enough."

Nolse eyed him covertly; oddly enough, the King seemed cold sober. "As you please, Sire." But he spoke to the King's back. Nolse leaped forward, and just as Sedry reached the raised outer flap that served as a sunscreen during the day, the Steward gripped his forearm. Sedry stopped, gazing at him impatiently. "The—Crown Prince is within, Sire. And in a most ugly mood." Silence. "I thought I'd better warn thee."

"To the Caverns of Night with Hyrcan's moods, I am tired of Hyrcan's moods," Sedry snapped. Aura flared around his shoulders, extinguished. Nolse nodded, wordlessly conveying sympathy with the King's words without actually verbally committing himself to a position on the matter. Safest with such a man; Sedry's mood swings were legendary and becoming wider in scope as the years passed. "I think it is time," Sedry continued, "to either sweeten Hyrcan's moods—or do away with them, once and for all!"

The Steward's legendary imperturbability was nearly shattered on the instant. With an effort, he dragged his jaw back into proper place, his eyes darting rapidly about. The King's voice could not have carried to the Crown Prince, and the guard was even further away. He rallied, swallowed, took a step nearer to his King.

"You mean this truly, Sire?" A single nod from the King. *Gods, now what?* But already he was speaking. "It were well," Nolse whispered rapidly, "that it seem accident or illness. At least—yes. Illness." An idea was beginning to shape itself. Risky—well, there were higher risks. And—no, better yet! A smile crept back onto his face.

"Illness, Nolse?" There was mild amusement in Sedry's eyes, though his lips were still thinned, tight. "What are you thinking of, my friend? Already a notion? I have always relied upon thee for aid in deeds I would dare trust to no other man, and you have never let me down." His voice dropped. "Can you help me in this?"

"I—I think so. The Prince is choleric in disposition, such a man might not expect to live to old age, setting aside danger from a chance arrow, a fall from a maddened horse. Now," he went on, drawing the King back from the pavilion, "I have various Fegez darts, given to me by my father. He instructed me in their poisons, and in those antidotes we have for them. "Few," he added, smiling maliciously, "have such antidotes."

"Poison," Sedry murmured, "is scarcely an exact thing. And the barghest poisons do not usually promise a man a speedy end." Nervous fingers shaped a wisp of Moss-Light into a ball, which he tossed rapidly back and forth.

"No," Nolse agreed. "But there are some that are more swift than nightshade. One I recall especially. It paralyzes a man in minutes, to the very words in his mouth."

Sedry eyed him dubiously. "And you have some of this?" The guard, he noted, his native caution reasserting itself, was nowhere to hand. Now that he had returned, the men would move out to make a wide circuit around the tent, but would not mount close watch over the pavilion itself until the second hour after sunrise. Good. As though the thing were meant, as though the Reader had arranged things for him—

He pushed that thought aside hastily. The Reader interpreted events, futures. They lied who said a Tarots Reader could control such things! He glared at his hands; the Moss-Light had faded. Lose control of so simple a thing as the Moss-Light! A crackling, spluttering sound as he reconstructed the pale yellow ball.

"Aye, Sire." Nolse considered a moment, nodded sharply.

"Can you but persuade the Prince to join you for a cup of March wine—it would disguise any taste—"

"Hyrcan seldom drinks," Sedry broke in impatiently. "And even *I* cannot bear the taste of that stuff."

"Nonetheless, Sire," the Steward urged quietly. He had the shape of the thing now; more difficult than providing the King with the women he wished, but not impossible. "That wine is so ill flavored, who would suspect it to also be poisoned?"

"And who," Sedry remarked, smirking, "would waste a better drink on such a mixing ingredient?" He considered this remark, laughed quietly. Nolse chuckled appreciatively. "But Hyrcan does not drink, you know that."

"Then thou—you must find a cause to which he will drink, my King." Sedry shrugged, stroking his narrow beard. "A toast to his kills against the barghests, perhaps." An unfortunate choice. Sedry closed his eyes, shuddered. The ball of Moss-Light faded, vanished for good.

"Alayya, Elorra, what am I thinking of? To kill Hyrcan? I, kill Hyrcan? *I*? On the strength of—." He faltered. Hyrcan meant to kill him, he *knew* so much. Who else in all Darion as old in death as his brother? *It proves I have a conscience, that is what*, he assured himself; he had to set his teeth to keep them from chattering. *Hyrcan will not be so delicate about my death, if I allow him the chance.* "Gods, Nolse," he choked out, "he will kill *me* when he discovers what I have done!"

"By your leave, no. By the time he realizes he has drunk other than a very poor wine, he will be unable to so much as move a finger."

"You swear it?"

"I swear it." The Steward nodded for emphasis. "I myself have seen men fall dead of this poison on the field. Unlike other of the barghest poisons, which only slow a man for them to kill more easily, it is swift and deadly." The King shuddered again. "And who can tell what a man has died of, with no wound upon him? We shall give out he was taken ill and could not breathe, that he suffered a fit and was dead before a physician could be summoned."

"Aye—aye, and we shall. What would I do without thee, Nolse?" The Steward smiled, genuinely pleased, inclined his head. "But I fear Hyrcan."

"You are his match with weapons," Nolse began loyally, but the King shook his head.

"No. I am good, reasonably good, anyway. But Hyrcan is better. And he has an edge over me. For I know he sticks at nothing, and he knows that I know it." He stared at the dimly lit pavilion. "I want him *dead*, Nolse," he added, with whispered violence. Once again the Aura flared with the intensity of his hatred. "Now. Tonight!"

"Then he *is* dead, my friend and liege." The Steward gripped his arm, waited until he was certain he had Sedry's full attention. "You are King. No man will gainsay what you wish."

"No man," Sedry echoed blankly. He shook his head, as though to clear it. "No, of course not. Hyrcan has no loyal men among his following, he does not inspire such a thing. But that does not matter, does it? I am King." Nolse nodded emphatically. "So who will dare doubt my word? Come, Nolse. The wind is chill and I would not keep my brother waiting." Nolse hurried forward to hold the flap and followed Sedry into the darkened pavilion.

The interior of the King's tent was cluttered with low, cushioned couches. One small table, its surface a delicate tracery of inlay, stood centered in the main chamber, and two lanterns hung suspended above it. The room seemed at first deserted; as Sedry gazed around and Nolse turned one of the lanterns up, the shadows against the far wall moved, a darkness stirred on the furthest couch. Hyrcan lay there, hands clasped behind his head. As the light flared he pulled himself up onto one elbow and scowled.

"Where were you, Sedry?" he snapped.

Sedry fixed him with a remote stare. "Is it business of yours?"

"Perhaps it is," Hyrcan grumbled. Sedry's daunting expression seemed to disturb him not at all. "I want to leave for Kellich at first light, but I had to speak with you first." He scowled again. "It is late, I should have been asleep an hour since."

Sedry shrugged, turned aside to fiddle with the small ornaments on his table. "You ignore the councils as you choose, brother, but I cannot. It is one of the penalties of being King. So," he went on casually, eyes fixed on the small bit of crystal and gold he was turning in his fingers. Nolse reappeared with a small tray, wine in a jeweled flask and two filled cups. Moving to where Sedry was between him and Hyrcan, the Steward pressed the King's own elaborate goblet towards him, gave the other a significant look and vanished back into the darkness. "So you do not intend to fight anymore? That is a shame, Hyrcan, you have been of great aid. I shall miss you."

Hyrcan laughed. "Of course you will, Sedry! You always do, do you not?" He laughed again as Sedry cast a wary glance at him. "I leave in the morning. I have killed enough barghests. It is beginning to bore me. And I am sick of your tame barons, your simpering, sneaking Steward, and your precious, dandified Archbishop." Sedry gazed at him across the rim of his cup.

"Do not speak of Rhames to me, I am sick of your harangues against him. And leave Nolse alone, I have warned you before!"

"Or what, Sedry?" Hyrcan inquired easily, grinning as he sat up. "You are not threatening me, are you? That would be foolish of you, brother."

"Why would I threaten you?" Sedry asked mildly, repressing a shudder as cold fear gripped him. Hyrcan grew daily more bold, would any man do other than he was about to, in his place? To his relief, none of his terror showed in his voice. He turned away, drank off his cup at a swallow, refilled it. When he turned back, a pleasant smile touched his face, and his Trait was in full blossom. "I am sorry, brother. This conversation is all at bad points, we had better begin again. I am overwrought tonight, but I did not mean to take it out on you, surely you know that." He smiled engagingly. Hyrcan shrugged sourly, as much an apology as he would ever give. The King's smile widened. "Poor my brother. I have delayed you, thoughtlessly, listening to my fools of advisors, and I ask your pardon for it. And after all the aid you have given me here—indeed since we exiled Father. What would I do without you, brother?"

It was hard for anyone to stay angry with Sedry when he set his mind to being charming, and even the Crown Prince was no exception. After a moment, Hyrcan smiled back, a frightening travesty of his boyhood smile. Sedry raised his own cup in salute and held the other out. "Here—let us drink to your health—let us drink," he added, smiling even more warmly as Hyrcan came forward to take the cup from him, "to your successes in battle: here and in the future."

"I will drink to that," Hyrcan replied and drained the vessel at a single swallow. His face twisted. "The Two bless me, Sedry, but I cannot understand why you guzzle this stuff!"

"An acquired taste, Hyrcan—that is all." *One you will not have opportunity or time to acquire, brother*! "I find it acceptable, though a trifle sour. But there is no point in transporting the good stuff here. However." He dropped into a chair, gesturing Hyrcan towards another, which the Crown Prince accepted. "I know you are tired, but sit a few moments, talk with me. Tell me what you have seen since your arrival. I greatly value your impressions of my baronry, you know, since they are always on their best behavior with me. You see more than I do."

Hyrcan shrugged. "Do you think so? I see mostly fear, Sedry. The Baronry do not receive me to their unmailed bosoms."

He grinned, and Sedry laughed appreciatively, eyeing his brother covertly across his goblet. "Of course they do not. But still—a man of discernment can read more from fear than from friendship, don't you agree? What have you seen? Any of them I might keep a close eye on, more than another?"

"Not really. The March seems strongly behind you at the moment. If you feared a revolt among the bear-merchants, it seems to me most unlikely. They talk of nothing but Rhames," he added sourly.

"Well, you cannot really blame them, Hyrcan," Sedry soothed. "They are rather like their own peasants, my Marchers, and easily impressed by anyone new and unusual." He laughed, lifting one shoulder and turning his hand palm up: Picture of a man overcome by embarrassment. He lowered his voice. "I—tell no one of this, will you, brother? I begin to tire of Gespry myself. He is all show, no real substance."

"I told you so," Hyrcan growled, but he was visibly gratified. *Has Nolse failed me*? Sedry wondered, turning aside and surreptitiously wiping his brow on his sleeve. Had it been a sufficient time? The Two knew it *seemed* hours!

"Well, you cannot blame me," Sedry mumbled, his expression still that of a man made fool. "Besides—you know my weakness for fortune tellers, Hyrcan—"

"It will prove your undoing," Hyrcan responded flatly. Sedry grinned foolishly, averted his eyes. *My undoing? Oh, no, brother, not mine*! "The priests hold it wrong, and against all teachings of the Two," Hyrcan went on primly.

"But Rhames himself—"

"A charlatan!" Hyrcan snapped. "A servant of the forces of Dark!" He blinked, shook his head, stared at his hand blankly. Moved it, cautiously. With an effort he dragged his eyes away from it. "That is a strong wine you drink, brother." His mouth moved oddly. "I—it—" His head came up slowly and with heavy effort. Sedry smiled unpleasantly. "You!" Hyrcan whispered. "What have you done?" He gripped the goblet, gazed into its depths and threw it from him with a motion that brought the sweat out on his face. "*What was in that cup*?" He grasped the edge of the table and attempted to force himself upright. Sedry, alarmed, pushed his own chair back, one hand to his sword. But Hyrcan collapsed, his head lolled against the cushions. Another attempt at movement failed. Sedry, reassured, smiled again.

"Nothing much, Hyrcan. A little wine—steeped in a barghest dart! They say," he went on as he stood, "a man dies in very short order. Shall I say prayers for you, Hyrcan?"

"Why?" The effort to speak was terrible. The Crown Prince's breath came in dreadful, ragged gasps.

"Why?" Sedry mocked him, leaning across the table. "Oh, a mere nothing, Hyrcan! You intended to take the throne from me, to kill me as a mere aside to that intention! You do not lack for nerve, do you? Darion is mine, Hyrcan, you should have left matters as they were and been content with the North, because now you will have nothing, not even breath!"

"A lie! Who says it lies!" The Crown Prince lay suddenly in a flood of dark red, his sometime Aura triggered by pure fury.

"Even dying you would lie to me," Sedry whispered furiously, "but you will not lie to the Two, when they judge you!"

Hyrcan's Aura deepened, flared brightly enough to cast Sedry's shadow against the pavilion's near wall. "I do not lie, Sedry. I have never lied to any man, never." Hyrcan's fingers began to move, slowly and as though they had a life separate from his, crawling across his chest, feeling blindly along his belt to fasten onto his dagger. Sedry, alarmed, leaped back as light flickered on the well-honed blade. "And you believed them. Against me, you believed liars, Sedry? You will say no prayers over my body!" And setting his teeth, he fought once again to rise. Somehow—gasping, his face grey, eyes wild in their pale intensity—he managed it.

Sedry, with a low, whimpering moan deep in his throat, backed away another pace, pulling his sword free with a shaking hand. Hyrcan laughed breathily: A trickle of blood ran where he had bitten through his lip. "Coward! Dost fear a dying man? You always were a coward, Sedry!"

"No, Hyrcan," Sedry replied, trying to hold his voice steady and failing utterly. "I am no coward. But yes, I fear you. I have always feared you, Hyrcan. I have never killed the way you have. You enjoy killing, Hyrcan. You enjoy it!"

Hyrcan laughed again, a horrible, thick sound, deep in his throat. "You never—enjoyed killing, Sedry? What of Lertondale, Sedry? Lertondale?" He choked, would have fallen. Braced himself against the table a brief moment, shook his head, and took a faltering step. Another. Drew himself painfully upright. Air rasped into his laboring lungs, tore its way back out. The dagger gleamed between them. "But I *shall* enjoy killing you, Sedry!" He staggered forward.

Sedry, his sword dragging forgotten across the carpets, backed away, eyes fixed, glazed. Hyrcan stumbled after him, the blood-red nimbus of his Aura lighting his body. The King whimpered. His feet caught on the rugs, he was nearly ill with fear. "Nolse—help me, oh Gods, help me, someone help me." The words pressed against his teeth, made no sound coming out. Something caught at his heels, and with a muted cry, he was down. Hyrcan loomed over him.

"Oh, yes," a faint, viscid whisper, "I shall truly enjoy this, Sedry!" Hyrcan swayed, brought the dagger back and out. Sedry lay transfixed, sword forgotten. A shadow came between him and the lantern, a shadow that staggered, gasped for air. A gleam of metal in the right hand.

Suddenly the Crown Prince froze, dagger still poised. A ghastly squall broke from his lips, blood frothed down his chin, and slowly, so slowly, he toppled forward, falling onto his brother. Sedry, with an airless little cry of his own, fainted.

He could have only been unconscious a few moments, he realized. His face was wet; his hand came away from it red. He choked, coughing bile. Nolse was at his side, an arm around his shoulders, a cup in his hands. Sedry shuddered but closed his eyes and drank. Wine. Good, untreated and unwatered wine.

He turned his head with an effort. Hyrcan lay at his side, eyes wide and glazed, staring blankly at the lantern. Blood still ran from the corner of the Crown Prince's mouth, darkening the carpets, but even as the King watched, it slowed to a thin trickle, stopped. He turned away then, allowed his Steward to aid him to his feet.

"There was sufficient barghest poison in that cup to kill five men within moments," Nolse murmured, wide-eyed. "Here. Sit, Sire. I will bring washing water—can you sit alone?" Sedry nodded, not yet daring to trust his voice. Shivers racked his body. Nolse vanished, returning a moment later with a basin and soft cloths. He sponged at the King's face, plunging sticky hands into the bowl for him. "We will have to burn your tabard, Sire, it is stiff with his blood."

"No. I came to his aid," Sedry murmured mechanically. "Whyfor not?" His eyes moved to the still shape on the carpets, shudderingly returned to his Steward's. "He took ill, and I went to his aid. Of course I went to his aid. Will—will it do?" Nolse glanced over his shoulder, went back to washing the King's face.

"Aye, of course it will do. It smacks of truth. But who would dare doubt your word? Whether they believe or not? And if not, it may teach some of them caution! You are King."

"Aye. I am King." Sedry closed his eyes, shuddered. "I cannot sleep here, Nolse. Find me a safe place, another place, where Hyrcan's ghost cannot come." Nolse gripped the King's arms.

"I shall, Sire. Listen—" Total silence within the tent, but without swift footsteps and excited voices. Something had been overheard. "Ready yourself, my King. Remember you are safe now." Sedry laughed: a hollow sound. His eyes remained fixed on the fallen Hyrcan. Dread filled him. *Aye, I am safe. Until the next of them.*

25

"ANOTHER THREE DAYS like these last, and there'll be no more of the creatures, they'll be dead and done with!" Grolpet slammed a broad, grubby hand to the table; a dirt-and-blood crusted bandage crossed his knuckles, wrapped around his wrist. The Beldenian bow-guard, awkwardly and temporarily fixed over the bandages, skittered to the ground.

"Oh, really?" Nevered's reedy treble voice conveyed a haughty note, even when he least intended it; at the moment, he was terribly remote, a man above dealing with a lower form of life and forced to it all the same. This was not lost on the Beldenian; Grolpet turned the full force of a black-eyed glare on him. "Have you a census of the creatures? For I confess, we who have dealt with them these past twenty years or so do not, and I would be grateful if you would tell me just how many of them you think are left. We can apportion them out evenly amongst us—"

"If you're finished," Grolpet snarled. Nevered eyed him sourly, closed his mouth with an audible snap. Sevric sighed, twisted in his chair to retrieve his brother's wrist-guard, and handed it to him with the same elaborate tiredness. "Does this bore you, Sev? Perhaps you'd be better off counting supplies!"

"We're getting nowhere." Woldeg grumbled in his corner. *Bear-merchant*, Grolpet thought, a corner of his mouth twisting. "Nowhere," the old man repeated sharply. "P'raps one of us can supply a coin, decide the matter that way. For

198

myself, I'm ready for my blankets. Different," he subsided into his beard, "if we were accomplishing anything."

"I think—," Ambersody began loudly.

"Really?" Someone murmured. The Marcher stiffened, glowered around him.

"I cannot," the supposed Archbishop interposed flatly into the momentary silence, "recall what began this particular growling match. Whatever it was, can we either resolve it or table it? There are sufficient things we can argue out without wasting time on things we can't!"

"Mine," Eavon rose to his feet, moved to her side. "And thy pardon, friend Gespry, for the difficulties."

"Yours—oh." Elfrid nodded. "All right." She leaned forward. "We have been here for over a month. I cannot believe we must still test each other's knowledge as though it were a thing unknown!

"Fresgkel knows the barbarians at least as well as any of the Marchers. He knows them at least so well that—well, if he comes to me with a notion that they intend a full battle, one last throw of the wager sticks, then I see it as a matter for serious talk, not as an invitation to spread insult! I," she went on, grimly determined, "intend to discuss it, at any rate. Those of you who do not, may leave and that now!"

"It was my idea."

Elfrid glanced down the table.

"Mine," Baldyron repeated. It was the first he had spoken in three days, though he had arrived each night with the first of the men, left with the last of them. So deep in shadow had he been sitting this evening that most of the others had forgotten his presence. "Sorry, Father. I had not meant thee to take the brunt for me."

"We discussed it together, I feel as strongly for it as thee, else I would never have mentioned it. Particularly," Eavon scowled around the table, "knowing all too well how it would be received." An outcry from several directions, which Elfrid, suddenly irritated, shouted down.

"Thy notion." Grolpet had held to that much of the conversation, even through the ensuing tumult. "Well, then—." He half-turned in his seat, glowered at the half-shadowed young Baron. Baldyron shifted, jumped suddenly to his feet, his jaw set, eyes stony.

"They brought thee here to fight, King Sedry and the Arch-bishop."

"We have done nothing else," Grolpet reminded him, "for over a month. Our losses have been—"

"As great as ours," Baldyron finished for him. "Though none within the camp lately, since thy forces took our advice to heart, how best to avoid ambush."

"Ye—"

"My ideas again. Mostly." The Baron of Korent stood a long arm's reach from the Beldenian captain. "I know the Fegez, better than any in the March. Not even those here who dislike me most would deny that. I played with them as a boy, I studied them. I know them."

"Ye—"

"I *know* them," Bal overrode the mercenary again, with finality. "Thou dost not, for all thy experience at fighting."

"They show no intention of anything," Grolpet finally managed; his face had gone a deep, furious red. "For ten days now, they have thrown themselves at us—at the camp, at any who ride away from it—at any of us, anywhere, in any num-ber," he shouted suddenly. With visible effort, he brought his temper under control. "They die, and more come. And more again. They will continue this until there are no more of them, with no thought at all for the consequences to themselves. That is how *I* see it." And how I intend to continue to see it, his expression said.

"They are not animals," Baldyron said flatly. "However they may appear—in a certain light." Fialla, on her low stool near Gespry's chair, shuddered. It was with an effort she returned to the breeches she was mending: Gelc's, torn from knee to waist by a barghest spear which luckily missed flesh entirely. A long hand lay briefly across her shoulder, with-drew. Baldyron hitched up one lean leg, sat on the edge of the table.

"They are not animals, even if they are not men. They think, even as men do. *Most* men," he amended pointedly.

Sevric grumbled sourly, inaudibly, into his half-grown beard. His brother silenced him with a look.

"They are less civilized than we, in many ways, but no less intelligent," Eavon added. "They are capable of that kind of subtlety. They—all right!" he shouted as half a dozen

Marchers began speaking, loudly and all at once. "It may be they do *not* intend this thing! How wrong to be prepared for it?"

"Why, if we need not? And how prepare?" Woldeg demanded. Fresgkel and his son glowered at the old man.

"Hast protected thy holdings these past years—how?" Eavon inquired dryly.

Baldyron began to enumerate on his fingers, slowly and as though to the halt. "Divide our men into three, perhaps four companies. The same with Gespry's forces. Add to the guard, to the patrols. Send a ten-man patrol, at odd intervals, up the southern ridge wall, it has remained free of enemy and gives a good view over the valley and the north wall, if they intend to attack in force, they must establish a base camp from which to send against us. If—"

"If." Nevered scowled around the table. "I for one tire of thy 'if', Korent."

"Then," Baldyron replied flatly, "need'st not listen, the flap is there, the Darion camp just beyond the River—"

Nevered snapped to his feet. Eavon pushed his way between his son and the older man.

"I," he said bitingly, "tire of thy fool's objections, Nev. Hast learned nothing these past many years, I wonder that thy lands are still of a piece. My son is right, if thou intend'st no sensible contribution to the matter, leave."

"I tire of this pointless arguing," Elfrid cut in sharply. "I suggest we hear this out; comment, whether to the point or not, can wait. Now, we—what?" This across her shoulder as one of her personal guard strode into the pavilion. An armsman, soaked to the skin and so muddied his colors could not be made out at all, stood just behind her.

"Thy pardon, Lords." He cleared his throat, dropped to one knee. Elfrid signaled to Gelc, whispered urgently against his ear; the little swordsman vanished into shadow, came back moments later with a blanket which he draped around the shivering man's shoulders.

"Finzic?" Eavon inquired uncertainly; even close to hand, the man's features could not be properly made out for exhaustion and dirt, but he nodded.

"My Lord. I—the Lady Lillet sent me from Eavon. The way is clear, has been since yesterday morning."

Silence: Those around the table gazed blankly at the armsman, as though unable to take his meaning. Baldyron was the
first to break it.

"Clear—from Eavon to here?" The man nodded. "And—
to the East?"

"Uncertain, my Lord. I—," he shook his head. "They
withdrew from the walls day before yesterday, near sunset. At
first we thought it a trick, but we—you know how well a man
sees from the walls, there were none within half a league, between Eavon and the nearest of the trees. We sent light signals
to Lord Woldeg's holdings, and within the hour had messages
by his birds. The barghests have pulled out; two clans of them
had Gelbenny surrounded. They were last seen moving south
and east. Messages we received from thy holding, Lord, from
Korent—." Baldyron opened his mouth, closed it. "Word
from Korent has it that a large company of barghests were
seen about a league south, crossing that ridge. The Grey
Stalkers still hold Korent at bay; they have aid, but those
within the walls have not been able to make out the clan markings."

"Give up, then, 'at's what 'ee be doing," Sevric avowed
loudly, his Beldenian accent rendering his Ordinate barely intelligible. Baldyron pivoted neatly on one heel, narrowed eyes
fixed on the man. His father pressed him gently back towards
his chair, shook his head at his youngest son, and spoke in his
stead: conciliatory words, certainly a far cry from what the
young Baron had in mind.

"Could be, sir. More likely 'tis only what the'd have us
think." Sevric rolled his eyes, annoyed almost beyond bearing
by this backwoods oaf, only just remembering his promise to
Grolpet not to provoke argument with the bear-merchants.
"Now, I would suggest that all of thee use thy heads,"
Fresgkel went on. One hand slapped the Archbishop's filthy
maps. "South and East of Eavon—here, those of thee who do
not know how Eavon is placed, as against this valley, look.
Here, and here. South and east—so. With not much change of
direction, they could intersect this very spot. Without changing direction, they would wind up—here. Were I a barghest,
and I chose to fight rather than to give up my lands, than to
run, I would choose a single, final battle, knowing the men
who fought against me would consider this unlikely, if they
considered it at all. And, as a base for my men to fight from, I

would choose . . .'' His left hand slid along the map, touched against his right, ''this place.''

''Ye do not know this,'' Sevric growled. Baldyron cleared his throat, spoke out before his father could once again stop him.

''I was not aware that it was necessary for thee who fight for coin to have a certainty first—''

''Ye know little enough—,'' Sevric began hotly, rising half out of his seat. Grolpet, with an irritated growl, pushed him back into it. Elfrid jumped to her feet.

''I have had sufficient of this for one evening—more than sufficient.'' Her face was pale, haggard in the lanternlight. The Beldenian captains exchanged knowing glances: The drawn-out nature of the fighting was taking a toll of their forces, but much longer in this valley would see the Archbishop's death. He had not recovered from Megen Cove when honor forced him to take the Darion King's contract.

She went on, holding the eyes of each man around the table. ''Think upon this, I beg of you—all of you—tonight. Consider the matter, if you can, putting aside personal insult, such things are not worth the loss of time and life they cost us.'' She slammed a fist against the table, toppling her empty cup. ''Think on it, and let us decide what to *do*, we can sit here and quarrel until the sky falls upon us!''

Murmuring. Grolpet and his brother shoved their chairs back, stalked out. Nevered and Woldeg, momentarily united by annoyance with Eavon and his son, tramped out together, followed by their various offspring.

Sedry detached himself from the shadows shortly after and strode silently away, sparing only the least of salutes for Elfrid, the least of bows for Fialla.

Among the group remaining were the six—including Bal—who had been chosen by Sedry to view Hyrcan's body. A poor choice on Sedry's part, had he wished to keep the means of Hyrcan's death secret, for not one of them had never seen a man dead of barghest poisons. Yet Sedry was King, and the King said his beloved brother had died of a sudden illness. And if Sedry altered since his brother's death, if Sedry now saw plots against him under every pebble of the River and started at odd noises and shadows like a man haunted, well, what dared anyone think of that?

Since Hyrcan's death, Sedry had begun to show up half-way

or later into the discussions in the Archbishop's tent, would take a chair in the far corner, refuse wine or indeed attentions of any sort, enter into none of the planning, none of the argument. His dark gaze, nearly unseen in the shadowed corner, would move from speaker to speaker, touching upon first one, then another of his Barons. Without warning, then, he would jump up and leave.

The Marchers were taking this well enough, on the whole, managing to keep the conversation going as the King vanished towards the Darion camp, each gazing sidelong at his neighbors and trying not to be seen at it. Each wondering, uneasily, *Which of us is next*?

Baldyron gazed after the King, turned his attention then to his Father's armsman. Gelc had pressed the man into a chair, put a cup of Gespry's coffee, liberally laced with wine, into his hands. "Finzic. Saw'st any trace of the Fegez, between here and Eavon at all?" Baldyron squatted next to the man. Finzic, eyes closed, shook his head. "Drink, man," the young Baron urged, "thy coffee will be cold and of no use to thee. No trace," he added to himself. "And—between Korent and Eavon?"

"Thy holdings are still surrounded, Lord, or were yesterday," Finzic replied. He swallowed coffee, made a face as he drank. "Beyond that—but the way from here to Eavon is—"

"No!" Fresgkel said forcefully. "Bal, I know what—"

"Father, leave be! I was speaking to thy man, not to thee!"

"No, damn thee, I know what thou hast in mind, and I will not have it!" the old man roared. They stared at each other, aghast. The fire died out of Eavon's eyes. "No, my son, please no. I know what—"

"Father," Baldyron replied intensely. "I must. I had no business to come here in the first place, to leave Korent to its devices—"

"No? Think'st thou to be of no use here? Of more use within Korent's walls? Bal, art not a fool, but this matter of thy holdings is making one of thee."

"That is not so, thou knowest it is not. But—"

"But!" Fresgkel spread his hands "Korent is safe, thy men are safe, thy people are safe! Were it otherwise, this man of mine would have told thee! Finzic?"

"I—my lord Fresgkel, I would." The messenger nodded

his head for emphasis. Neither Baldyron nor Fresgkel, each intent upon the other, noticed.

"Then," the older man began persuasively. The younger
turned away.

"Father. I would not hurt thee for the world. And I—"

"Gespry, tell him he is needed here," Fresgkel cut in. Elfrid
glanced unhappily from one to the other, leaned finally across
the table.

"My friend—Bal, if your father cannot persuade you, at
least let me—"

"Gespry, thou of all of us know that we need information.
A patrol from the south rim, message birds from within the
walls of my father's holdings—useful, but not conclusive. A
man who knows what to look for, where to look for it—"

"Might wind up as dead as one who does not," Fresgkel
finished for him flatly.

"Perhaps. He might die here as well," Bal replied shortly.

"What, did the barghests not manage sufficiently upon thee
last time?"

"Father," the younger man crossed to Fresgkel, laid a hand
across his shoulder. Eavon shook it off. "Father," Bal repeated persuasively. "Last time I was unwell, half dead for
lack of sleep. Trust me, I would not do this unless I thought it
part way safe. Thy man here, he made it safely."

"He—"

"Well then. There is no point to argument, Father. Or from
thee, Gespry," he added, turning to meet Elfrid's troubled
grey eyes. "Take it that I have called for a volunteer and
chosen one. We need to know what passes, need that badly."
Silence. "Father. I need not have thy permission. I would have
thy blessing, if thou'lt give it." Eavon turned away, his head
bowed. Nodded.

"Then," the younger Baron jumped to his feet and strode
towards the flap, "the sooner I am gone, the sooner I return.
Look for me two mornings hence. In the meantime, Father,
Gespry, press further our case with the mercenaries. If they
continue to disbelieve, it will be too late, and—well, Father,
thou knowest how fatal that might be for all of us."
He smiled, faintly and briefly. "I shall give thy love to Mother
and to Elyessa, if the way is yet open to Eavon." He was gone.

Silence. The old Marcher glanced at the supposed Archbishop, turned away with a little sigh. "Always he was headstrong. Even when a boy."

"He is right, though, Fresgkel."

"I know it. Damn the boy. Finzic, can'st find my tents? Good man, go and find a place for thyself for dinner. Give thy clothing to the laundry boys, get some rest." The armsman staggered to his feet, blanket still clutched tightly around his shoulders, and started off.

Fialla glanced up, startled, as flurried movement from the back of the pavilion caught her eye: The Reader, cards clutched, forgotten, in her pale fingers, caught at Elfrid's shoulder. "He's gone, hasn't he?"

"He—." Elfrid frowned uncertainly.

The Reader dropped her cards across the Archbishop's maps: Prince of Flames, King of Dawn, the Madman, Seneschal. "Get him back." She turned to Eavon, gripped his arm. "Your son, Lord. He *dare not* leave this camp, stop him however you can!" So great her fear and intensity, Eavon paled and, without a word of protest, hurried out into the night.

"Why," the Reader whispered, her trembling fingers straying lightly across the center card, "why need he, of all acts he might choose from, take that one? He has set in motion—." She stopped. Her entire body shook. Fialla took the slender shoulders between her hands.

"Reader. What danger? To Bal, or to the plan?" Fialla whispered.

"Danger," the Reader whispered, distractedly. "Danger, Alayya, Elorra, of all the things—"

"We will stop him," Elfrid assured her gently. She had gone pale, her eyes strayed worriedly towards the open flap.

"No." The Reader straightened, and Fialla let her hands drop. "No." She turned aside to gather her cards. "Too late. He—Gods, ah, Gods, I could have prevented—"

"Prevented what?" Fialla asked quietly.

"Dishonor. Pain. Death? Perhaps even that." With a sudden, violent motion, she tore at her hair. Elfrid gripped her wrists tightly, held her close as she suddenly went limp. "I cannot see," she whispered. Tears coursed down her cheeks. "I do not want to see!"

Elfrid gazed at Fialla, frightened, over the pale curls. She turned then, following Fialla's glance: Eavon stood framed in the open flap, shaking his head. His eyes, even at that distance, were clouded with worry.

"Gone. On the fastest horse I have. I sent men after him, but—." He shrugged faintly.

"Gone," the Reader whispered. It had gotten away from her, so complex a matter as this, how had she dared hope otherwise? The Pattern itself yet held. But at such a cost—

26

THERE WAS NO fighting of any kind in the next several days. The Beldenian captains took advantage of the lull to train the Darion troops, as well as they could in the short time allowed them, in the simpler of the field maneuvers that stood their kind in good stead in mounted combat.

Eavon, bereft at one stroke of his youngest and most loved son and the one thing—fighting—that would have kept him from brooding on Bal's safety, spent most of his free time in the Archbishop's pavilion: conversing with Fialla, for whom he'd conceived a strong affection that she readily shared; comparing weaponry, fighting styles and generally talking arms with Gelc (he and the normally taciturn armsman found a good deal in common). And he had volunteered to redo Gespry's maps; they and Baldyron's alike were so worn and tattered as to be illegible.

One day gone. A second. Fresgkel was showing the strain. Elfrid, more drawn and pale than ever, rode full circuit of the camp twice on that second day. A sense of dread descended on Fialla. The Reader was a delicately balanced creature; the Archbishop's mistress had never seen her so upset, so apparently unable to do anything about it. For two days now, she had sat on her blankets, laying out pattern after pattern, scrapping them halfway through, muttering to herself. She was drinking only water and weak tea, eating next to nothing. Sleeping, it seemed, not at all.

It was warm again, the rain gone as though it had never been. Fialla was taking advantage of the warmth, the lull in battle to bring out her fine-work. She and Fresgkel alone were in the blue and yellow pavilion: he laboriously copying a portion of map (lettering required all his attention), she just within the flap, sun falling over her left shoulder as she couched blue and silver thread into a complex pattern of stitchery on a white silken bodice—a pattern that resolved itself to be the Tarot of the Lady of Birds, hands outstretched upwards to a small, eager flock of hovering starlings. One perched on a slender finger.

She glanced up now and again, eyes going often to the old man who hunched over a thick parchment, clenching the long feather quill in a murderous grip. *Poor man. The things we do, to take our minds from ill matters.* She glanced at her bodice impatiently. *And how seldom it works.* (My Gespry, where are you, and how do you fare at this hour?)

She gazed out across the bright, hot camp, turning back with an effort to her needlework. She and the old Baron held a companionable silence for some time. He looked up once, briefly, blinking, forced a swift, tight-lipped smile before turning back to his work. Fialla's responding smile was directed to the top of his grey, shaggy head. *It is as though we wait for some terrible doom that we can neither foresee nor avert. And yet—Bal has skill, and knows the lands. The Two grant him good sense!*

There was a puff of air, as suddenly gone as it arrived. She bent to pick up the packet of threads it blew from her lap. Movement near to hand caught her eye: Gelc, returning from the Darion camp, striding hurriedly through the water. She straightened, frowning. It was not that difficult to leap from boulder to boulder and remain dry. Gelc wasn't bothering, though. Free of the water, he was closer to running than not.

Fialla stood, putting aside her frame, the thread sliding once again, forgotten, to the rugs. Eavon dropped his pen, making a dark blotch across the carefully inked Darion camp as he did so. He scowled at it, swore, kicked his stool over as he stepped back from the table.

"Never was much good at neat work: more a priest's job than an armsman's. What's to do, Lady? Baldyron?"

"Gelc," Fialla replied absently. Her eyes were riveted on the little armsman. Eavon was at her other elbow before Gelc slipped in out of the sun.

"What's to do?" Eavon demanded again.

"Your son's returned," Gelc replied in a low voice. He was out of breath, sweat beaded his forehead. His hand shot out to grip the old man's forearm as Fresgkel tried to slip past him. "Bad news, sir, you'd best be warned before you go to him."

"Bad," Fresgkel echoed blankly. "Baldyron?"

"I met him on his way into camp, sir." Gelc drew a deep breath, gripped the old man's arm even more tightly. "I am sorry. I bring ye sorrow and no time to offer it properly, more's the pity. Your daughter Elyessa is dead." He caught the Baron's other arm, bore him up as he sagged under the news. "A suicide."

"My—my Elyessa?" A faint, choked whisper.

"Lest she bear the King's bastard," Gelc finished grimly.

"No. Oh, *no*." Eavon said dazedly. He searched Gelc's face with glazed eyes. "Where is my son?"

"I could not restrain him, he has gone in search of the King."

Fialla drew a deep breath. "Gelc, where is Gespry." The armsman shrugged, gestured broadly towards the south rim. "Find him, at once. A cool head is needed here, and Gespry's is the best we have. Lord Eavon—Fresgkel, come with me, we will find Bal. Better if he not be allowed near the King just yet. Where is King Sedry, Gelc, do you know?"

"Of course," Gelc replied gloomily. "Not a dozen rods from his pavilion, meeting with his council. Holding audience."

"Then hurry," Fialla gave him a shove and turned to tug on the Baron's arm. Eavon seemed paralyzed "Come, Fresgkel," she urged softly, "We had better find Bal. Don't you think?" The old man started, focused on her with an effort. Nodded.

"I know my boy," he said, almost to himself, as they forded the shallow river—like Gelc, not wasting time on the dry crossing. "He loved the girl nearly as much as her mother and I did. He would have done anything for Elyessa. I fear—"

"Fear what?" Fialla panted as they came onto dry ground again. He shook his head.

"The boy's temper. What he might say in haste, to repent later. But Sedry will give him no time to repent of his words." Fialla made no answer, merely gathered her skirts above her ankles and increased her speed. Eavon forged ahead of her as they neared the dark blue and yellow pavilion. The old Marcher's shoulders sagged. A drooping, sweating horse stood this side of both pavilion and the large crowd gathered before it.

From within the circle, then, they heard the King's voice: "And since it seems to us the barghests be nearly defeated, it is our present intention to return to Arolet within the week."

Fialla let out the breath she had been holding as a sigh of relief, began to work towards the fore of the crowd, drawing Eavon with her. Bal could not yet have confronted the King, they could find him and get him away. She began to plan what she would say to him; they'd have to work quickly, have to convince him in the first few words they spoke, they'd have to—

Baldyron's voice rang out sharply: "King Sedry!" Fialla slipped between two of Sedry's tall householdmen, while Fresgkel, with a low apology for a trodden foot, slid in behind her. Sedry, crowned and robed as though he sat in Reception at Arolet, turned towards the voice, smiling. The Baron of Korent stepped from the crowd.

"You have our leave to speak," Sedry said formally but he smiled with diffidence at the same time, as much to say, 'Ceremony before these, my friend. Though we know it unnecessary as between ourselves.' The smile slipped as Bal made no response in kind: no smile, no warm look, no bow, not so much as an inclined head. He met the young Marcher's eyes, recoiled. The look on his face froze the King's blood.

Is this the next of them? Sedry wondered as he faltered to his feet in alarm. A corner of his mind noted which of his armsmen moved back themselves, which laid hands to hilts. There was a silence as the two men faced each other across a circle of uneasy onlookers. Sedry was aware, suddenly, that his Steward was no longer at his elbow. *Nolse? Ah, no, not he!* "Speak, my friend Baldyron," the King brought out finally, forcing a smile.

Another silence, uncomfortable. "Elyessa is dead." Baldyron's eyes were dark pebbles in an expressionless face.

Sedry lowered his eyes. The smile slid from his lips. *Elyessa. Gods. Why does he look at me like that? Why does he— Alayya's hangnail, he cannot think that I—?* The King swallowed alarm, bile. "Poor maid," he whispered. "The Two guard her soul!" He met the young Baron's eyes, no easy task. "How, Bal—Fegez? But she was within your father's walls— wasn't she?"

Baldyron laughed: a terrible sound. His lips twisted.
"Fegez? Think'st Fegez? Barghests would have been more
kind to my poor sister!" Abruptly he sobered. "Elyessa, poor
sweet." His eyes bored into Sedry's. "Thou knowest better,
Darion's King!" His voice gained strength, rang out across the
stilled, stunned onlookers. Someone edged forward to pluck
at his sleeve; Baldyron shook the man off with a sudden
violence that sent him flying back into the hushed crowd.

"This," Baldyron turned slowly, taking in the entirety of
his uncomfortable audience, "this is that man who speaks
with such loathing of the number of bastards among the
nobility! So moral a man, he, that he would not allow his own
half-sister to remain on the same side of the sea with him!"
Fialla's skin went cold. *Alayya, Elorra, oh, Gods, shut him
up!* Eavon was mumbling to himself hard by her shoulder.
The Earl of Marchham, who had seen him across the open
circle and forced his way around to his friend, had him by the
shoulders.

"Have care," Sedry's words dropped with deceptive quiet
into the silence, "how you speak to me, my friend. I make al-
lowances that you *are* my friend, that you are overwrought—"

"Overwrought? I? Elyessa is dead, as much by thy hand as
her own!" Sedry shook his head; Baldyron took another step
forward, and Fialla could no longer see his face though there
was menace in the set of his shoulders. "She chose that way to
deal with her shame, and thy bastard, Darion's King." The
silence deepened until it seemed those standing within hearing
no longer even breathed.

"Not mine." Sedry shook his head. "No, Bal, not mine, I
swear it to you—"

"No?" The Marcher's whisper carried the circle as clearly
as his outcry had. "And this?" He brought a sheet of tinted
paper, crumpled and much folded, from his tunic pocket.
"Elyessa had no cause to lie to me, my King. Shall I read
what she had written, how you pursued her at Arolet from
the hour of her arrival, how you contrived to be alone with
her, finally coercing her, overwhelming her objections—how
should a child of her years know to deal with a man of yours?
And then, to hold threat of discovery over her head, should
Father learn she was no longer virgin—by the Two, to do such
a thing to her! Juseppa's honor maiden—*my* sister!"

Sedry shook his head again. "Untrue, I swear it," he whis-

pered in reply. Baldyron closed his eyes. A shiver ran through
his body. He backed away from the King, then turned back to
the assembled Marchers.

"All of thee know," he cried out, "how our King prates
against those Lords who debauch among the women of their
holdings, spreading by-blows across Darion. A man should
not lay with the herder's daughter nor the merchant's wife,
lest successions be put in jeopardy, and civil battle result.

"Easy for a man without honor to speak against debauch-
ery with the commons, when he has at hand the daughters of
his Barons! My sister Elyessa is dead! Alive, she would have
born this man's bastard!" He drew a deep breath; his face
contorted briefly. He seemed to pull grief under control by
main, savage effort.

"All of thee knew Elyessa," he went on, his voice echoing
across the camp, "Knew her for a chaste maiden, inexperi-
enced as unwed March women are in the matter of men. She
knew *nothing* to defend against a ruttish man's desires! Which
of your own women will be next, which have already preceded
her?"

"Silence, Korent! I will not tolerate such lies—Nay, do not
dare draw against me!" Baldyron, with an inarticulate cry,
whirled around and clapped a hand to his dagger hilts; the
blade was already halfway from its sheath. The King's armsmen moved, but Nolse slid from the crowd, so near Fialla he
might have touched him, and leaped, catching hold of the
Marcher Baron's elbows and pinning them behind his back.

Baldyron cried out again in fury and strove wildly to pull
away, but Sedry's Steward dug his heels in and held firm:
though a head shorter than his captive, and not nearly as
strong, he had the advantage of a superior balance point. The
young Marcher, with a hiss of pain, went suddenly limp and
the dagger fell from his hand to vanish into the thick grass.

Sedry, still pale and wide-eyed, assured by a nod from two
of the armsmen who surrounded Nolse and his captive,
stalked forward. His open palm cracked across the Baron's
face, backhanding the other cheek. Baldyron, released, fell
heavily to his knees. Blood ran from his temple where the
King's rings had cut him.

Nolse slipped away, reappeared moments later at Sedry's
side. A contemptuous smirk twisted at his lips, his eyes were
directed balefully towards his once brother-in-law. So would

Kressala be avenged, and his father. And he, who had once
had to give this arrogant youngest son the kiss of kinship.

Baldyron made no attempt to move, not even when the King
addressed one of the armsmen closely flanking him.

"His sword, Dorsic. Hand it to me." Sedry's voice was
level, low and cold as death. Fialla's eyes anxiously sought a
familiar face, pale hair that she should be able to see, even
where she stood. *Where is she—where is he, damn him, he
could have averted this, where is he?* She spared a worried
glance for Fresgkel, who looked to be holding to his feet by a
gift of the Two and Marchham's grip only. Cretony was
nearly as pale as his friend.

Sedry's armsman, a contemptuous grin on his young face,
handed the blade, hilts reversed, to the King. Sedry's hand
gripped it so tightly the flesh stood out around his rings. The
point moved, slowly—steadily—Sedry turned it, sliding the
flat of the blade under the Baron's chin, exerting pressure.
Baldyron's chin came up, borne by his own blade.

"Do you see any reason why I should not slay you—now?"
Sedry inquired. The two of them might have been discussing
trivialities over a cup of wine. "To speak to one's sworn lord
as you have is alone worthy of death. But to draw a blade," he
added coldly, "might try the patience of my headsman, how
to best hold you in this world while aiding you from it."
Silence. The young Marcher made no effort to speak; those
surrounding them seemed unable to, shocked and horrified by
the accusations, the all too guilty reaction, the threat of immi-
nent blood.

"It is polite," Sedry continued "to speak, when your sworn
lord addresses you." Another silence. The fallen Baron might
have been made of stone. There was a shuffling of feet among
those encircling the two. Sedry laughed suddenly, brought the
blade neatly from under Baldyron's chin, up and out with a
slicing motion that made the air whine, and whirled away to
slam it into the sod. Bal made a faint, strangled noise, loud in
that unnatural silence. Eavon, white to the lips, was trembling, trying to move forward. Fialla laid a warning hand
across his arm; Cretony tightened his grip.

"No. I will not kill you," Sedry addressed the swaying hilts.
"To aid you from your misery? No. You seek oblivion too
ardently." He turned, sought and found his Steward. "His
bow, Nolse. Get it."

"Sire." Nolse turned and forced his way into the crowd, which moved uncertainly away, allowing him full room to spare when he returned with the Darion ash long-bow and its well-worn, plain, leather quiver. The King took them, turned back to face their owner. Slowly, deliberately, he tilted the quiver, allowing a rain of arrows to cascade to the ground. The bow, then: He gripped it between wide-spread hands, brought it down across his knee. His Aura flared with the intensity of his effort, his fury; Royal Fire crackled from one hand to the other. The bow splintered into shards. Sedry threw the pieces from him with violence. Beads of sweat stood out along his brow.

Baldyron closed his eyes, bowed his head. Impossible to tell, from his face, what thoughts were in his mind.

"You have ten days, ten only." The King loomed over him. "If after that time you are anywhere within Darion's borders, your death will be all I can devise." And in a ferocious whisper, so low even Nolse caught only half of it: "I *trusted* you, I trusted you! My friend Bal, my dear, beloved friend Baldyron! I gave you lands, your title, I cared for you! And this is how you repay my favor?" He fought for control, gained a portion, raised his voice to address the crowd.

"Hear me, all you of Darion and you of Belden here in our aid! I declare this man traitor to our person and to Darion herself, and I exile him from the land! Any man finding him within her borders ten days hence shall bring him to Arolet to await my pleasure. Anyone who dares aid this man shall, I swear, find death a pleasant and welcome thing! *Eavon!*" The old man jumped, but stepped forward firmly, shaking off Cretony's aid, Fialla's fingers. His face was almost as expressionless as his son's. "I know your attachment to him."

Eavon bowed his head, visibly unable to speak. Sedry beckoned, drawing the old man into the center of the circle, so near his disgraced son he might have touched him.

"I wish assurance, Fresgkel of Eavon, that you know where your first loyalties lie. You shall again swear vassalage to me. Here. Now." Fresgkel brought an astonished face up, and Sedry nodded grimly. "Perhaps you have honor, Baron. But I thought your son had it, and look what pass that has brought me to—no." Fire scorched the grass between them. "Say no word to me that is not of your oath!" Fialla closed her eyes as the old Baron slowly, stiffly, knelt, his face crimson, hands held palm to palm before him. Sedry took them between his own, loosely, nodding as Eavon stammered out the words that bound him to his King. There was complete, embarrassed silence among the onlookers, and many had turned away when the proud old Baron knelt.

As he regained his feet Sedry bent a cold gaze upon him. "You know your duty, Eavon. You may give him food, a horse, bedding. Coin for passsage if he has none. *Nothing else!*"

"Nothing else," the Baron whispered. Released, he stumbled blindly away, the uncomfortable crowd parting for him. Fialla pushed her way after. Sedry, surrounded by his guard, Nolse at his side, vanished into the King's pavilion. Fialla came upon the dazed Eavon and Marchham several paces away. "Take Fresgkel to his tent, Cretony. I will bring Bal." She turned back, stopped, her breath catching in her throat.

Baldyron had not moved, seemed unaware of his surroundings. Before him lay scattered arrows and a splintered bow; five paces beyond, his sword still swayed lightly in the afternoon breeze. He started convulsively as Fialla dropped to one knee beside him and gripped his shoulders. "Come, friend Baldyron. Courage! All is not lost. Your father has gone to arrange—," she faltered to a stop. To arrange what? The end of a man's life? As though he had followed her thoughts, he raised his head.

"Lady Fialla, leave me at once. You dare not expose yourself to the King's displeasure!"

"What can he do to me? Gespry is my shield, against the King or anyone else. Come," she urged again, regaining her feet and attempting to drag him to his. "Gespry has been sent for—"

Baldyron laughed terribly. "Gespry? *Gespry?*" He leaped to his feet, gripping her hand so tightly she gasped.

"Baldyron. Your father, you must go to him." And, as he began to shake his head she added, suddenly furious: "Do not and you will kill him! Did he love the maid less than you did? Will you do this to him? Shall he lose both of you at once?" He gazed at her blankly. "You will go to him, Bal, promise me!" Slowly, unwillingly, he nodded. "You have friends," she urged, "remember this, and keep hope, Baldyron."

He released her fingers, turned away from her. "Leave me, Lady. I have chosen my course and thou hast no place in it. I thank thee for thy concern, thy kindness. I am sorry it cannot be of more—no matter. There is nothing can'st do here, save to bring trouble upon thyself. Gespry would be no shield against such as Sedry, did he wish any kind of thing of thee." She hesitated, he turned on her. "My death is a matter of *my* choice, just as it was Elyessa's. Go!"

Tears blinded her; turning, she fled back to the Beldenian camp. When she stopped at the River to look for him, he was already out of sight.

27

"GESPRY—LISTEN TO me. If you—Elorra's earlobe, Fialla, can you *do* something with him?" Gelc turned on one heel, strode to the firepit and knelt with his chilled hands to the flame. Fialla pressed past him, knelt before the chair where Elfrid sat, elbows on her knees, face buried in her hands—as she had since her return an hour earlier. Gelc, unable to find her on the southern rim, had given up at sunset and ridden in only moments since.

"Gespry." Fialla gripped the wiry forearms. "It is not the end of the world, Sedry might have killed him on the spot." Behind the shielding hands, Elfrid nodded faintly. Fialla paused, marshalling her thoughts. Beyond the pavilion walls, pandemonium reigned: Elfrid, Boresin, and Fidric had brought news from the southern rims, though at the moment it afforded Eavon no pleasure in being proven right. Across both camps, Darion and Beldenian armsmen were being drilled in anticipation of the all-out attack that would come the next morning or—at latest, surely—the morning after from the enormous Fegez war camp the one known as Archbishop and her companions had seen in the upper valley.

"I know it." Elfrid whispered. Fialla tightened her grip briefly, let her hands drop away.

"Then—," she began.

Elfrid shook her head. She raised her white, ravaged face. "Fid told me, he had it from that man of Fresgkel's. Bal took nothing with him, nothing but the clothes he wore, no weapons at all, and he left on the same horse he arrived on."

"Gods." Fialla turned away. Anger tightened her mouth. "Fool, thrice fool! His father—"

"Could do nothing with him, more than you could—they told me of that when I came into camp, my dear." Fialla glanced back at her; Elfrid was staring, unseeing, across her dark hair. "They say," she went on after a while, "that he does not plan to leave Darion at all."

"He must," Gelc said roughly. He stood abruptly, a steaming cup in his hand, and closing the distance between them thrust it into her hands. "Sedry will kill him for certain otherwise."

Elfrid closed her eyes, drew a deep breath. "Tell *me* this," she said bitterly. "He rides towards Korent, but *I* know what he means."

"No safety there."

"Of course not. He will never make the walls, never get within a league of them." Grey, anguished eyes met the armsman's. "You know that as well as I."

"Mmmmm. Well—"

"And I just, I sit here," she went on flatly, coffee forgotten between her hands, "while he—"

Silence. "He would take no help," Fialla said finally. "If I could have—"

"By the Two." The swordswoman leaped to her feet in a rising fury. She glanced in some surprise at the cup, set it aside. "By the Two, he will listen to *me*! Gelc—"

The little armsman eyed her warily. "You are *not* going to chase through barghest infested woods after him!"

Elfrid grinned, clapped him on the back, suddenly cheerful. "Nothing other than, my friend." The decision seemed to have taken an enormous weight from her. "Now, don't argue, you waste time, and we have little. If—." She scratched her ear, began wandering absently around the table, "if he is riding a winded beast, he cannot be far—"

"He left nearly two hours past—"

"Ha. So. No, he cannot be far. Now—as I see it, he must take the road towards his father's holdings, at least half way, there are few roads to his own, and none so far south as this."

"If the King should find you gone," Fialla began worriedly.

Elfrid shook her head. "Less difficult than anything else, my dear. Either I have gone to keep watch on the rim tonight —send Bor back, Gelc, as soon as he returns from Grolpet's

council, will you?—or I am sleeping, exhausted, not to be
bothered. Gelc, have any of the Darioners taken the mercenary double-box maneuver to heart?'' The armsman shrugged.

"Hope so. Eavon's man liked the look of it, old Marchham
seemed to approve. Hard to tell. Sevric's working his men at it
hard, though.''

"Good. Now. I'll need a bundle: food, water, you know
what it ought to hold, my friend. Something small, so as not
to cause talk among my guard.''

"You don't think—?'' Fialla began in rising alarm. Elfrid
stopped her now rapid pacing to pat her arm reassuringly.

"No. I trust them, all. But men talk, and odd occurrences
create the most talk. Weapons, Gelc.''

"Right.'' Gelc vanished into the gloom at the rear of the
pavilion. Elfrid gazed after him. A quiet warmth came into
her dark, red-rimmed eyes. "So,'' she whispered, "it comes
full circle.''

"Gespry?'' Fialla moved to her side. The swordswoman
smiled at her, rather absently.

"Full circle,'' she said. "The hunter has become the hunted,
the beneficiary is now the giver.'' She seemed to see Fialla,
then, and smiled warmly. "Odd, don't you think?''

"Odd?''

"Things,'' Elfrid replied vaguely. "Life, if you like.'' Her
head came up sharply as Gelc strode back into the light, an
oblong packet in his hands. It landed with a muted clunking
thud on the table.

"Food, water, a cloak. A small sack of coin from your common supply. A narrow bladed dagger, I recall his was of that
sort. And my second-best sword. Tell that young idiot,'' he
added fiercely, "that I want that sword back when he is done
with it!''

"I shall.'' Elfrid weighed the pack in one long hand,
nodded. "Thank you, my friend. I—Fialla, you anticipate
me.'' She stood at the swordswoman's elbow, a hooded fur-
lined cloak over her arm, draped it across her shoulders.
"Gelc, you had better aid me with horses, I'll need two.''

"I anticipated ye also,'' Gelc muttered. His cape was
already snugged at his chin. "Come. I'll ride out with ye and
slip back later. I'll tell the horse tenders some tale—left the
beast with Grolpet or some-such. All right?''

"Fine, fine.'' Elfrid was suddenly unconcerned with such

details, impatient to be away now that her mind was made up. "Fialla, take care, I'll return late most likely."

"I—." She swallowed fear, smiled. "Take care."

"Always." She was gone, Gelc with her.

The two reined up just short of the guard post at the base of the southern rim. Gelc dismounted, fastened the cloak-wrapped packet behind the Archbishop's saddle. "All right." His voice could not have carried to the nearest tree. "Take it hard the first league, then ease up. Ye know the roads from the maps Fresgkel did—"

"I know them."

"Good. You can reach the North road unseen from here— No, of course you can, pay no heed, I worry overmuch."

"I know it. I don't mind, I know the reason. And I shall use greatest caution." She gazed at the slightly overcast sky; the moon was only a paleness beyond the eastern mountains. "I shall return as quickly as I can, I shall take great care, I promise you."

"I said nothing," Gelc protested quietly. A flash of teeth answered him, a low chuckle.

"You didn't need to."

"I know you," Gelc said. He gave the straps an additional tug. "Even if you had not been the boy's best chance, you would have gone anyway."

"I—"

"I'm not blind," Gelc cut in, "And so you think to make up to me and to Fid and Bor, to Fialla, by extra caution. See," he added in a fierce whisper, "that you do just that! They say the road is completely clear from here to Eavon now, but it needs only one barbarian—!"

"I know," Elfrid soothed. The horse, sensing her tension, pranced nervously, settled as she tightened the reins down. "The sooner I am gone, the sooner I am back safe."

"Good." Gelc swallowed both nerves and the desire, born of them, to lecture further. "That is a good young man, if headstrong, Gespry. He will be a good aid to our cause."

"He—aye, he will." She gripped the armsman's hand.

"The Two guard ye. Go now!" Gelc stepped back, slapped the horse lightly across the withers. Without another backward look, she vanished into the trees, heading west towards a place where she could begin to work her way around the camp.

* * *

It was nearly midnight. Elfrid slowed her horse to a walk, urging it back through damp grasses and low scrubby brush towards the pale slash of road stretching away north under a three-quarters moon. Thin, ragged fringes of cloud obscured it briefly. A wind whined through the upper reaches of the trees, was gone again. Absolute silence. She threw one leg across the saddle-bows and slid to the ground, wrapping both sets of reins over a deadfall. Her mount shook itself vigorously, rubbed its face and neck on the rough bark; the second horse bent his head to crop grass.

The swordswoman crouched beside them. From here, she had a clear view of the road in both directions for nearly a league, and would hear anyone coming through the deep, rocky cleft a furlong back long before they could be seen. *I am ahead of him. I must be.* She toyed nervously with the hilts of her dagger, scowled at her restless hands and forced them to stillness against her knees. *No, I made good time.* She patted her own mount: Its hide was warm, barely damp. *He had a beast already spent, and would take no other. And I was not that far behind him.* She gazed back down the road with sudden, barely restrained hopelessness.

The spare horse pressed against her arm; she rubbed its ears absently. *Have I misjudged?* No. A noise, briefly obliterated by the wind: a horse, walking up the cleft, slowly, and with an unevenness to the stride. The animal was favoring one of its feet.

Elfrid drew a ragged breath, wrapped the cloak more tightly about her shoulders as a chill gust swept down through the pines, and vaulted into the saddle. Shadow edged the cut, and she could still hear the stumbling gait, could see nothing. A dark, smudge moved then. The moon vanished into cloud. She caught up both sets of reins and urged her mount forward, onto the road.

The other did not seem to see her at first; he slouched, head bent forward, taking no interest in his surroundings. *Thank the Gods that the Fegez no longer hold this road,* Elfrid thought grimly. Her horse whickered; the approaching rider started, checked briefly, but seemed to think better—or worse —of it. The exhausted beast shambled towards her.

The exile's head came up once again as he drew even with her hooded figure and pulled his horse to a stop. His face was pale, his mouth set. Elfrid brushed back her hood, exposing her face, the tell-tale hair.

Bal stared at her blankly, uncomprehendingly. The other horse moved forward. "For your aid."

"No." He shook his head slowly. "No," he whispered again. "Do not do this to me!" He swayed in the saddle; Elfrid, alarmed, closed the distance between them to grip his arms.

"Easy; hold. You have friends, you knew that."

"I have no friends, I am exile. To sit where thou sittest is death."

Elfrid laughed grimly. "Who will kill me, Hyrcan's shade?"

"The barghests—"

"The Fegez do not hold this road. Did you also forget that?"

"But—," Baldyron shook his head again. "But—"

"*I* am not bound by any word of Sedry's, who am not his subject."

"No, leave me." The Marcher tried to pull his arm free, subsided as the long fingers bit into muscle. He turned away then, speaking so low she had to lean forward to catch his words. "I am a dead man, for pity's sake leave me to my doom. *Leave me!*" But he was not dealing now with Fialla. Elfrid cast one swift, exasperated glance heavenward and slapped him, sharply. Baldyron stared at her, glassily astonished.

"I know you have not eaten nor slept," she snapped, "and grief has turned your brains—good ones at that—to rabbit's droppings. But the Two damn me if you will speak to me in such a manner! You are my liegeman, you swore fealty to *me*, and I have every right to see to your well-being. Or do you change fealty so often you forget from one day to the next where you are sworn?

"You spoke to me of honor once—do you remember that? —well, where was *your* honor, refusing what was rightfully yours, speaking no word to your father, to me—." The Marcher opened his mouth and moved it helplessly, closing it again as no sound came out. Elfrid's face was stern. "So Sedry did not kill you, oh no! He does not need to, does he? You will save his executioner the wear on his ax, is that your notion? A fool's thought, if thought at all! You will make the

King very happy if you continue this way, Bal—and no one else."

"I—"

"You have suffered a terrible loss, and I grieve with you for it. But that is no way to mourn her, my friend. And if you add your death to hers, *you* will be directly responsible for a third —your father's." With a groan, the Marcher wrenched free and turned away. Relentlessly, the voice continued to assault him. "Darion will so lose two of her best fighting men. King Rolend will lose two good men. I will lose—"

Baldyron spoke up, quietly defiant: "You would not accept my oath of vassalage."

"Oh. Is that how you see it? You swore it, freely. But I did not refuse it." Something in the level voice brought the Marcher back around, dark, doubtful eyes searching the thin face. There was a subtle change in the other. "Will that give you cause for life? I accept it thrice over. There—does that satisfy you?"

But the challenging words no longer held anger. Elfrid gazed at the Marcher for a long, tense moment, as though she could convey what she could not speak. She turned away finally, to glance back down the road, slipped from the saddle, pulled the pack free, handed it to him.

Baldyron dismounted slowly and stiffly. He placed it between them on the road, and knelt to inspect it. His hand strayed across the packets of dried meat, fruit, the small loaves, waterskin. They stopped short of the plain, serviceable sword. "Gelc's," Elfrid responded to the inquiring look. The wide mouth moved in a faint, nervous smile. "His second best, and he sends you word he would have it back unharmed."

"Ah. I had—better take care, then." Baldyron essayed a shaky smile.

Elfrid's laugh was no less shaky. "Keep yourself and the weapon in one piece. Gelc is a hot-tempered man, and fond of his second-best sword." There was another tense silence. The two gazed at the contents of Gelc's neat pack. Baldyron reached then, gripped the other's hands.

"Hast convinced me. I am thy man, my Lady." She started, gazed at him half anxiously, half-warily, gripped his hands in turn. "Tell me what thou hast in mind, where I must go."

Elfrid bowed her head, thought hard. "To Rolend."

"Rolend is at Orkry, but in prison. Thy—half-sister, her husband, hold him."

"They did. He has been free a number of days now, though he remains at Orkry so as not to alert either Sedry or Nolse's spies. He will remain there until he has finished gathering his force together. To maintain secrecy, he is adding to his troops by small numbers."

"I see. How long before he moves against the King?"

"Another—five or six days. No more. At the end of that time, Arolet and Lertondale will be in his hands. The Church is already his."

"Not good." Baldyron shook his head. "Sedry thinks to return to Arolet within the next day or so."

"He will not be able to. Did you not forewarn of the attack? The barghests are readying a last, massive battle and wagering all upon that."

"So I said, but—"

"You were right, you and your father. There will be such an attack. Sedry will not wish to appear afraid, and will lead the Darion armed."

"Oh? And you know this—how?" The Marcher eyed her warily.

Elfrid smiled. Her hands lay, seemingly forgotten, in his. "The Reader, of course. It is I, my friend," she reminded him gently, "that is the fraud." She smiled again, diffidently. "More to the point, however, we saw the camp late this afternoon, Fid and Bor and I." She shrugged. "Sedry will not leave for Arolet until it is too late."

His hands clenched. "How mean'st thou—too late?"

"You are hurting my fingers—thank you," she added quietly as he released them with a faint oath. "Only that Rolend will be King and Sedry deposed, with choice of exile or prison. What did you think?"

"I did not think," he replied grimly. "Merely feared, and not for him." Silence. "Well? Wouldst have his life, wouldst not?"

"I told you—for what he has done to me, for what he did to Father. And to you, your poor father. But *Rolend* does not want him dead, so what I would have does not matter. Does it? Save in one thing," she added rather flatly, gazing at the trees, and then up the road. "I would have you live, who aided me on a time in that same endeavor."

The smile slipped from his face. Swiftly, she turned back, caught his hands between her own. "No, Bal!" Her voice dropped to a whisper. "Are you the only one who has lost a loved one because of Sedry? The only man in Darion whose beloved sister was prey to his appetites? She was dear to you, I know that, I remember how you spoke of her. Her death could drive you mad with the pain of it, with the helplessness, I know that, too. *I know*."

"Elyessa," Baldyron whispered; tears blinded him.

"Elyessa," Elfrid replied gravely. "Mourn her, my poor friend. As I mourned my father. Mourn her, but avenge her as well. Poor maid, she never deserved such a death. Avenge her." Another silence. He swallowed, nodded.

"Tell me what I must do to aid thee. The rest can come as it may."

"To Orkry. Ask for the Chatelaine. That will get you within the gates; you may need repeat the request many times, and to many folk, but eventually you will fetch up against one of Gespry's monks, who will tell you that she has left Orkry. Then you must ask, "Has she gone to Rhames?""

"Orkry. Ask for the Chatelaine. Someone will say she is gone, and I ask if she has gone to Rhames?"

"Good man." She pushed to her feet. "Give Rolend my love. Of all my half-siblings, only Rolend treated me as human, and I have not forgotten it."

"I shall. Give my love to my father, and do not allow him to worry. Tell him what I have done, and why." He refolded the pack and strapped it into place, buckled the sword to his hip. Elfrid, already remounted, watched expressionlessly as he dragged the saddle and bridle from his lamed horse, climbed slowly, stiffly onto the animal she had brought.

There was a long silence. Marcher Baron and false Archbishop gazed at each other, unwilling, suddenly, to separate; uncertain, both, what to say next. "Take care, my—my liegeman," Elfrid said finally. Her color was high.

"My Lady. I swear it." On sudden impulse, he urged his mount to her side, took her face lightly between his hands and touched his lips to hers. "The Two guard thee, my Lady!" He was gone, then, back the way he had come, lost to sight almost immediately in the narrow, shadowed cleft. Elfrid gazed after him in still wonder long after the hoofbeats died away.

28

ELFRID RETURNED TO camp in the dark hours after moonset. Gelc was waiting, huddled into his cloak against the chilling damp under the trees.

"Ye found him?"

"Yes." Elfrid seemed unwilling to comment further. They entered the Archbishop's tent, dimly lit, warm after the chill night breeze and damp ground. It seemed deserted.

"Fialla," Gelc said as the flap dropped into place behind them. "is with Fresgkel. She said she would tell him nothing, lest you should somehow fail. Also," he added as he poured wine and brought it to her, "we thought that your place."

"Of course," Elfrid whispered. She stared blankly at her hands, rousing as Gelc pressed the cup into them. "Bor and Fidric—where?"

"Yonder," Gelc waved an arm in the general direction of the south rim. "We thought it better to have men we could trust for an honest count on that ridge tonight, there was too much hysteria on both sides of the River. They will return in another hour. I am to ride out then until first light."

"Good. I think I will rest, so that I can ride with you. Sleep is not in me, not tonight. Rouse me when you are ready."

"I—all right." Pointless to argue. In many ways the tall, white-haired figure might as well have been Gespry. Gelc watched as the swordswoman stood, yawning and stretching, then turned to stumbled away towards the alcove. A brief smile lightened his normally bleak face, he nodded, and strode purposefully to his own blankets.

* * *

The sun was an hour over the north rim of the valley when Elfrid and Gelc returned to camp with a warning that had preceded them: The Fegez had broken their enormous camp. They had counted over two hundred fires on the wind-shielded, leading edge of the bare ridge; more visible but undistinguishable, hid behind the trees. Gelc and Elfrid had pulled back only when it became clear that the entire camp was preparing to move towards the valley.

There was frantic activity on both sides of the River: Elfrid sent Fidric personally with messages for the Darion King.

The armsman slipped back into the bedchamber as Elfrid struggled from the shirt she had now worn for two days straight, the stiff, dirt-caked breeches. Fialla stood expressionlessly before her, clean shirt ready; she swiftly, deftly checked the bandages across Elfrid's chest, helped her into the soft brown fighting shirt. Breeches then; they were slightly damp, and Elfrid made a face at which she shrugged.

"You have only two pairs left, which I must have washed in turn. You should not be riding with the first party at all, you need sleep!"

"So do we all, Fialla. I am needed in the fore. I am Belden's battle flag, did you forget?"

Fialla sighed heavily. "You will be no one's battle flag soon, do you continue to fight when you are half-dead from lack of sleep!"

"What difference," Elfrid inquired patiently as she laced the breeches smoothly to her calves before donning her boots, "will another hour's sleep make to an already tired man? And how well should I sleep for the worry?" She turned to Fidric, who stood patiently at her side, mail shirt in his hands.

"The King says," Fidric said in response to the questioning look, and with the air of one quoting verbatim, "that he will come here as soon as he is clad, that you and he may ride into battle together, so as to hearten our men and bring fear to the enemy." Elfrid only just managed not to cast an 'I told you' look at Fialla, who sighed again.

"Well," she said heavily as she led the way into the main chamber, "there are none here but ourselves for the moment, we can dispose with the shaving I suppose, but you need coffee. Here, sit at least, will you?"

Elfrid yawned, shaking her head. "I dare not sit, I am not nearly awake enough. And for the coffee my thanks, but even moreso for the other thing.'' She ran a hand over her chin, and Fialla, in spite of her dread, giggled like a girl.

"For shame! I have shaved Gespry for years now—!"

"Aye.'' The other laughed in reply. "You have reason to be careful of *his* throat, Fialla; mine might be another matter! But think! What if our positions were reversed, and I had that sharpened blade in my hands. How safe would your neck feel?"

"No." Fialla came back with a steaming mug which she pressed into the swordswoman's hands. "Oh, no! I should invent a quite plausible reason why no beard grew upon my face—"

"Oh? There are only three I know of,'' Elfrid returned, grinning cheerfully. She enumerated on her fingers. "One: too young. Two: a—shall we say delicately, an accident? Also, that means whereby boys are made able to sing with a woman's range into their older years . . .'' The grin widened as Fialla blushed and whirled away. "Third, of course: that one is not a man at all. Your choice, my dear."

"I should think of something,'' Fialla replied stubbornly. Her cheeks were still abnormally red. "Magic. A—a miracle, perhaps."

"Coward,'' Elfrid murmured sweetly before bending to inhale the fragrant steam rising from between her fingers. There was a noise of many horses outside and Boresin leaned in through the flap.

"By your leave, Gespry—King Sedry is here." Sedry clapped him on the shoulder in passing as he strode inside. Impending battle had pushed aside his terrors and he looked every inch a King.

"You will ride with me, won't you?" he asked, his most winning smile gracing his face. Lantern light, or possibly the faintest of Auras limned his tall frame; Trait practically flowed from his fingers, unforced for once. Elfrid felt the sudden, strong pull men had felt for their father, for Sedry himself despite all he had done to Darion's harm; it hackled the hairs along her forearms. *You could have been a great King, Sedry. The Reader was right in this also.* "Together we will sweep them from Darion,'' Sedry began bravely, but stopped, abashed. "Well—from this valley, at any rate!"

Elfrid stepped forward to grip the King's arms, and her smile was at least as warm as Sedry's. "So we shall, King

Sedry. So we shall. At least," she added firmly, "after I finish my coffee, for I warrant there has been time for nothing else since Gelc and I came down from the ledges this morning, save a change of shirt."

Sedry inclined his head, moved to Fialla's side to kiss her fingers, holding them, as he always did, perhaps a little longer than good conscience or manners would dictate. With a wave of his hand, then, he went back out to his household armsmen. Elfrid drained her now lukewarm coffee at a swallow, allowed Fidric to install her in the mail shirt while Fialla buckled on the long, narrow-bladed sword. She was still strapping the dagger into place as she walked out into the cool morning.

Fialla slipped out behind her, standing to one side to grip first Gelc's arm, then Fidric's, finally Boresin's, as the armsmen moved off to garner their mounts and Gespry's. The King was speaking to his personal guard. With her mind blurred by lack of sleep, worry, Eavon's grief which she had striven to assuage for so many hours the past night, Fialla was unable at first to follow what Sedry was saying: ". . . of Rhames at our side, we shall be victorious, and drive the Fegez so far back into their mountains that our children's children will think them mere myth!" Aura blazed briefly, brightly. Elfrid inclined her head to the cheer that greeted this, a cheer echoed by the Beldenians who had gathered to one side.

"So we shall," she said then, turning to face the King. "Darion and Rhames!" she cried. The two drew as one, holding their blades aloft and touching the points for luck. The Archbishop's Holy Flame crackled from sword to sword and pillared briefly skyward. A great cry followed, a loud clash as many of the armsmen struck swords with their neighbors.

The mercenary troops drew back as Elfrid, now mounted on the Archbishop's favorite white horse, Gespry's three armsmen about her, moved to the fore. The Darion King was no more than a man's length away, his own guard strewn out behind him. Gelc stood in his stirrups, crying out, "Gespry and the King!" His harsh voice echoed across the valley.

"Gespry and the King!" came back at him, a roar from a thousand throats, and the allied force began to move out— slowly at first, gathering speed as it passed the last of the tents and crossed the River. Fialla turned away, eyes dazzled by sun on so much metal.

29

ELFRID SETTLED INTO place between Gelc and Boresin, Fidric
taking the lead as they splashed across the River and onto open
meadow, its high grasses long since trampled flat. Fidric held a
good pace at first, so that the Archbishop's company led, the
Darion King several lengths behind and to their left. Directly
behind Elfrid herself rode Zormerian, proudly bearing the
blue and gold banner that was Rhames' token. To his left,
Sedry's arms were borne by one of his own young equerries:
Vert, a gyrfalcon or, enclosed within a border, double-tres-
sured, argent. To Zormerian's right rode another Beldenian,
carrying the arms of the mercenary force: gules, a sword
argent.

Another great cheer echoed across the mounted force as
they gathered speed, spreading out as they moved towards the
eastern end of the valley, towards the narrow gap, no more
than wide enough for three men abreast, through which the
enemy must come to engage them. There, they hoped to contain a large percentage of the Fegez.

They passed swiftly into the shadow of the overhanging
cliff. Elfrid lowered the hand she had been shading her eyes
with as Boresin cried out, "There they be!"

"Aye." She drew her sword, reining back to allow the mercenaries around them. From where she sat, the cleft in the cliff
face was clearly visible: Fegez poured from it like bees from a
destroyed hive.

To the far left, half a hundred Darioners wheeled sharply
away, galloping wildly towards the cliff. These were to watch

carefully, turning back at the proper moment to seal the gap and prevent the barghests already in the valley from returning to their camp. Preventing, also, more of the berserkers from joining those already engaged in battle.

"Timing," Elfrid fretted under her breath. So much depended on it: too soon and they'd be trapped themselves, these young Darioners. Too late, and the maneuver would be a gesture only: Pretty in its execution but pointless—and likely to cost them every one of those young lives. Bal was to have been in charge of the sortie. As it stood now—

She squinted, tried to tell who led it instead. Useless: Too far to see in any case, and a fine haze of dust already hung over the open ground between them. Even as she stared, they were one and all totally lost in shadow.

King Sedry and his personal household guard were once again close to the Archbishop's banner. Marchham was visible among these; Eavon himself was nowhere in sight, though his house colors were prominent among those who had ridden off at a tangent. "Timing," Elfrid muttered again, half-chanting as though it were prayer or incantation.

"They'll do," Boresin shouted. " 'Ware, Gespry, barghests on your right!"

She scowled, shrugged then. What did it matter? No sense in humanizing those you intended to slay with the little compassion you might give mice in a pantry. She stood in her stirrups as the first cries told her battle was joined, raised her own voice above the noise. Zormerian dipped the banner twice to signal those who could not hear.

The Beldenians responded. Three hundred horsemen fanned smoothly out to the right of the Archbishop's banner, forming a line several men thick along which the Fegez must fight. At a cry from the Earl of Marchham, the Darion force —less experienced at such troop movements and so more clumsy—began the same maneuver, holding to a shorter, deeper line.

"Who rides there?" Elfrid shouted at Fidric, gesturing towards the sortie, now entirely out of sight under the overhanging cliff and totally in shadow.

"Three of Woldeg's sons, best we could do. Good lads but impetuous and none too bright." He spared a glance in the direction of the waiting sortie. "Hope they've sense enough to wait, we warned 'em enough!"

"Aye," Elfrid replied. "Forward!" she shouted then, gesturing over her head with her sword. Flame touched it, briefly. Fidric spurred his horse towards the gap that had opened between the Darion and Beldenian lines under the fury of barghest spearmen. The swordswoman was right behind him and, a scant moment later with a curse that blistered the air, so was Gelc.

Elfrid sheathed her sword as she came into the front ranks, nimbly untied the Darion bow that hung by her left knee, fitted an arrow from the leather cache, and let the whole dangle loosely in one hand as her eyes searched the battle before her for an opening. Her left hand slid the silver thumb ring on her right hand, moved to adjust the patterned leather wrist-guard.

"A Darion grip?"

Elfrid started, turned to smile briefly at the King, who had stayed with her through the latest charge. *Seven Hells, he would take note of that!* "More accurate from a horse, Sire. I have used the thumb pull for most of my life. It is also faster: My mercenaries with their blasted cross-bows—"

Whatever the King replied was lost as, with a howl that set her teeth on edge, at least twenty Fegez slipped past the Beldenians and into the midst of the allied force. Elfrid pulled up in her stirrups and loosed four arrows before the fighting became so intense she dared risk no more. Even so, four of the barbarians lay on the ground, still, as she hooked the weapon over her saddle-bows and drew her sword. Gespry's battle cry, "Rhames!" echoed across the field, was answered by a cry from Beldenians and Darioners alike; the Fegez warrior who had snatched at her bridle fell to the ground, throat cut. A second—stunned by a burst of the Fire—went under the horse and was lost to sight.

The last of the small infiltrating force was cut down in short order. Elfrid urged her horse back into the front line, Gelc behind her protesting furiously. But it was where she belonged, where she was needed. Where Gespry would have been, at the same moment.

The Fegez were as numerous as count the night before had guessed them. And most were mounted, making the fight a new thing, a different kind of battle than they had become used to, though enough of the barbarians still moved on foot with blowdarts and knives to constitute a serious hazard.

There was this much to be thankful for, Elfrid realized, that the Fegez had taken the challenge of the Darion/mercenary force and joined battle during daylight hours: There would be no shape-changing.

Odd, how easily she could sense the *real* of them—this near-human shape they wore under the sun was no more theirs than the wolflike beast shape they assumed in the night. *They cannot bear full light in their native form. The Gods be thanked they are more proud than most, and seek to defeat us on our own terms.*

Away to the right, deep in the Beldenian ranks, she could hear Boresin shouting: "Pull in, pull *in*, I said! Ye know the maneuver, count of three, divide at the mid and back in! You are spread too wide, they will break through the lines!" To her left, Marchham's high, gravelly voice: "Aye lads, lay to 'em! We'll see the last of the creatures yet—hold that line, damn thee! Thee in front, know'st the signal, *use* it before pulling back to let those behind take the fore! I'll see no holes there!"

Nearer to hand, a scant moment later, Nevered's treble voice cried out: "What? What are they doing there?" And, urgently: "Signal 'em! They've started too soon, they'll be killed, all of 'em!"

One of his sons protested, "Father, they'll never see the flag—"

"Wave it anyway!" Nevered roared back.

The boy was right. The sortie could not possibly see any signal at such distance. Elfrid could barely make out the double line of horsemen streaking towards the gap. Part of the Darion force, alerted to the peril their comrades faced, surged forward but dropped precipitously back as old Marchham galloped recklessly into the open and across in front of them. "Stay put!" he bellowed. "They knew the chance when they took it!" Marchham regained his own line in safety: Elfrid could not see him, but there was an intense cheer at the far end of the Darion line moments later.

Elfrid once again sheathed sword as a space opened at the fore, pulled the bow up at the same time. Hauling the string back, Darion-fashion, with her protected thumb, she loosed several more shots before allowing Gelc to replace her. The little armsman was beyond speech, cast her a reproachful look before adjusting his own plain three-fingered guard and setting an arrow to the string.

More poured through the gap, and more still, but the Beldenians were holding well despite furious attack by the barbarian
forces. Of the sortie, there was nothing to be seen. Heavy dust
obscured most of the northern cliff.

"Back!" Grolpet howled, hauling up in his stirrups and gesturing ferociously. "Are you posts, are you trees? Give way,
double-box them!" Reluctantly, it appeared, the mercenaries
began to draw back, splitting near the midpoint of their line
like a double gate, half of the original protecting the flanks of
the Archbishop's party and that of the Darion King; the other
half forming a three-man deep rectangle a short distance
away. Into this opening Fegez poured, milling to a sudden,
confused halt as mercenaries galloped around to close the box.

Not for long, of course, for the line was necessarily thin,
and the barghests soon broke out on both sides. But there were
considerably fewer of them to reach their comrades or open
ground again.

Elfrid rubbed sweat from her eyes with a hand and sleeve
thick with dirt, forced her arms to drag back once more on the
bow. The dart missed its mark by several hands. She blinked,
was suddenly aware that Boresin was shaking her arm. "You
are worn," that worthy shouted. "Return to camp, now!
No," he added as she opened her mouth to protest. "Particularly if you head the relief force this afternoon. Did you
forget: A man must rest, if he's to do such a fool thing!"

He leaned forward to grasp the reins Elfrid had slung
around the saddle-bows so as to leave both hands free. She
gave him a hard look but met eyes as determined as her own
and nodded. At Boresin's gesture, several of the mercenaries
and two Darion bowmen joined them, forming a rearguard.
Elfrid, with what dignity she could muster, regained control of
her own horse.

The rearguard was needed for no more than a few minutes:
The fighting, though the allied force had lost some ground,
was still contained in a narrow belt. Elfrid and Boresin
reached the easternmost of the earthworks in short order and
a cheer went up from those watching. The swordswoman
dropped stiffly from the saddle, led her tired horse into camp.

"Best I stay here. Since I return to the field in a short while.
I will sleep, if I can; rest otherwise."

Boresin shrugged. "Of course. You always do. I will tell
Fialla that you are unhurt," he added, "and bring fresh horses

for this afternoon.'' He clattered off towards the blue and white pavilion. Elfrid did what she could to fill in the waiting men, drained a proffered dipper of water at a swallow. A quick swipe at face and neck, then, with a damp cloth, more for coolness than for cleaning.

Unnerving to sleep with the men, however necessary. *If Gespry's Semblance did not hold, if my own poor additions to it slipped while I was asleep*—she shook that off with an effort. It hadn't, yet. And under severe circumstances, once or twice: the resemblance, strong enough by itself without Gespry's aid, held. The semblance of beard—Gespry's work, originally, her own strength, now—appeared when it should, as much as it should. Fialla had not shaved her this morning, by mid-afternoon there'd be shadow across her upper lip and cheeks.

Odd, that *that* should not be unnerving of itself. Perhaps if she had been able to *feel* it also—

Ah, well. She sighed deeply. She *was* tired, perhaps tired enough to set aside worry for her part, the slight, nagging worry for Fialla that was pressing her of late—Bal, who, the Two knew, could take care of himself, and very much without her aid. A hand touched briefly, with remembered warmth, and something of surprise still, at her lips.

She sighed again, lay down in what shade she could find and closed her eyes.

They lost ground again in the afternoon, considerable of it. Elfrid, when she dared look, could clearly make out individual Darion tents. But the allied force managed to regroup, dragging its tattered lines together long enough to drive the Fegez East once more. With sunset, the barghests melted away, retreating swiftly up the narrow gap, and it was with some effort that Elfrid, Sevric, and Eavon held the immediately heartened troops.

As full night set in, with the last of the Darioners and Beldenians behind the earth ramparts at the eastern end of the camp, Elfrid and Eavon scaled its heights and gazed out across the meadows. Fires burned out there, a long, ragged line of them. Distant, but not distant enough to please either one.

''We'd better post heavy guard tonight,'' Eavon murmured. Footsteps crunched behind them, sliding on loose rock and dirt: Gelc. Elfrid gripped his shoulder before turning back to gaze out at the fires. "Full rotation and by fours, full parameter," Eavon went on. "They might attack, thinking us unprepared."

"Aye." Gelc chewed gloomily at his moustaches. "Half the sortie made it back, mostly your lads, sir," he said. Eavon shook his head unhappily.

"Woldeg's boys?" he asked.

"Youngest made it clear. Hurt bad, but he'll live." Silence. Gelc shook himself then, clapped the old man across the shoulders. "Things'll turn out, sir," he added cryptically. He turned away, slid down the inner face of the embankment and strode off. Eavon stared after him.

Another, friendly, silence. Supposed Archbishop and Marcher Baron stared across the darkened valley. "If you like, I'll take first watch with you, Fresgkel."

The old man nodded, a genuine, if faint smile touching at his lips. Gods, it all went wrong, and at once when it did! "I would welcome thee, Gespry. Cretony is aiding me in setting the others. We can take the first, thee and I, after supper." Elfrid nodded. The Marcher Baron, with sudden energy, scrambled down to level ground and vanished in the direction of his tent. Elfrid, aware of the smell of cooking food from various quarters, started briskly towards the Archbishop's quarters.

Fialla met her outside the pavilion anxiously. "You are well?" She relaxed as Elfrid nodded, drawing the swordswoman's arm around her shoulders as they went inside. "You've visitors to share attention with your food," she went on tartly, "as usual."

"Fine." Fialla's eyes had held equal parts indignation and warning; Elfrid gripped her fingers briefly, nodded her thanks.

Grolpet and his half-brother Sevric sat within, still in grubby fighting garb—though Grolpet appeared to have smeared water across his face, possibly to have plunged his head into the River. Water dripped from his greying hair onto his leather-and-mesh shirt; his face was clean and red in patches. Beyond them, a young Darion armsman in the red and white of Marchham's men sat in silent awe, clutching a list in his fingers.

"Gespry, I know you're a tired man and a busy," Grolpet began apologetically. He pushed to his feet, sinking back into the chair with a sigh of relief as Elfrid waved him down. "The plans for tomorrow, however—"

"We can discuss them while I eat. Have you taken meat yourselves?"

"Will," Sevric grunted, "with our men; we are expected."

"Then I will not detain you more than necessary." Elfrid dropped into her own chair. Fialla gave her an exasperated look. Two of the young mercenaries came from the fire, one with a bowl of water for the battle-grubby hands, the other with a plate of stew. The swordswoman ate swiftly, scarcely tasting her food, paying close heed as her captains traced out strategies across the map, incorporating what scant new knowledge they had into the plans, adding an occasional comment of her own. Both declined wine, rose, and left as Elfrid pushed her empty dish aside, and beckoned Marchham's man—a page scarcely come to his teens—to her side.

"You've the lists from Cretony for tonight's guard?" The boy could only nod. Soft brown eyes were impossibly wide. "Have you eaten?" Elfrid asked as she unfolded the paper. The boy nodded emphatically. "Now," she chided gently, "You have done no such thing, have you? And you ride tonight with the watches, don't you? Of course you do. Go on, lad, back to your company. And give Cretony my thanks, that was quick work." As the young armsman dropped to one knee, her hands came out, touched lightly the curly head. The warmth of the Blessing glowed briefly around the boy, and he smiled tentatively, a smile that warmed as Elfrid returned it. He was gone then, breaking into a run just beyond the flap.

"Gespry, you must rest," Fialla began quietly, urgently. She dropped into the nearest chair, took the long hands in her own.

Elfrid sighed, closed her eyes briefly. "I know. But there will have to be time later. Eavon will be here in moments, he and I are taking watch together. I have much to say to him."

"Ahhh." Fialla shook her head. "He was so hurt," she whispered. "Not by Bal, though; by Sedry. Odd, since he never trusted the King."

"Not odd at all, really; a man like Fresgkel could never understand the depths of one like Sedry. Fialla—"

"Gespry?"

"Take care of yourself, Fialla." She pressed the small hands gently, held them against her cheek.

"And so I do," Fialla replied, startled. There was more than casual concern behind her companion's words.

"I mean nothing in particular," Elfrid went on, as though she had followed Fialla's thought. Her eyes were fixed, absently, on the smouldering firepit. "It is not the Fegez I fear, I do not know *what* I fear." An embarrassed smile creased the thin face. "And yet, there is something, and it centers about you—it worries me. I—better, I thought, to warn you, even though I have nothing to warn you *of*."

"You should obtain Tarots, you are wasted as swordswoman," Fialla said gravely. Elfrid laughed.

"I daresay! Or I will become another Sedry, starting at shadows, and fearing anyone who will not meet my eyes, anyone who says seven when I think he should say six—"

"You beware the King!" Fialla broke in with sudden energy. "He has been morbid since Hyrcan's death, but now, with Bal, he fears anyone who might wield sword against him. And that is to say anyone with one hand!"

"I know it. I have an eye to Sedry, Fialla." Elfrid turned as a horse snorted just beyond the canvas wall. "That will be Fresgkel, I am off."

"Promise me," Fialla said as she followed the swordswoman, sparing a brief, warm smile for the Baron of Eavon, "*promise* me that you will not stay at this the entire night, my Gespry. Do not let him, Fresgkel, he needs sleep!"

"Well—what I can do," Eavon began. Elfrid laughed. The horse—a cobby dapple—pranced sideways, settled down as the reins tightened.

"I promise, Fialla. But I will sleep against the eastern earthworks, lest I am needed tonight."

Fialla shook her head, casting her eyes heavenwards. "I knew it, I just knew it," she murmured hopelessly, adding, "take care!" as Elfrid and the old Baron turned and rode off.

There was a long, companionable silence. The Marcher led, letting his horse pick a slow route beyond the outer parameter guard, working slowly around the camp. From this angle, the barbarian fires were only a glow at the edge of sight. Elfrid let the reins drop as her horse settled down to follow the other now and again, she waved as some armsman recognized the blue cloak and spoke Gespry's name.

For the most part, the camp was quiet; few men moved

about save for those on guard. But few of those blanketed
forms they could see, Elfrid would have wagered, actually
slept. The disquiet was almost a thing to be touched.

They moved further out, after a while, into open meadow,
following a trampled path that led from the mercenary horse
lines to the River.

"Fresgkel." Neither had spoken for nearly an hour; the
word was not much above a whisper but the old man started
sharply. "Your ear, Fresgkel."

"Thine, my friend." In the faint light of distant fire,
Eavon's face was that of an old man, indeed; Elfrid could suddenly have wept for him. She reached, caught at his fingers.

"Ride close, if you would. My words are not—for general
sharing." Eavon eyed her sharply but did as she asked.
Elfrid's voice dropped. "He's well. Bal is."

"He—." The old man shook his head, unable to continue.
Elfrid gripped his fingers.

"Well, I swear it. I—." She marshalled her thoughts firmly,
began again. "I heard from Fialla, from Gelc, after I returned
to camp. I went after him, took him a horse, weapons. Food
and water."

"He would not seek exile. Sedry will—"

"No, Fresgkel. Hear me. He took what I offered, took also
the task I set him. I cannot say more of that—but he is safe.
There was life in his face when I left him. He sent his love to
you."

Eavon's fingers tightened on hers, hard. He drew a harsh,
shuddering breath. "Curious," he whispered finally.

"How so, my friend?"

"That thou should'st give him such aid, as he did thee, after
so long a time." He wrapped her hand in both his; the fingers
were tense. "Thy secret's safe with me, I was thy father's man,
remember that. And for thine own self, the person I've grown
to know these past days, for that alone, I'd keep the secret."
Silence again, again a companionable one as Elfrid let out a
held breath. "Bal told me, all of it. His—his aid to thee, when
my poor friend Alster was exiled and thee with him; how he
knew thee here, and nearly died of his foolishness—all of it."

"I—when?"

"A time since. After Telborn died, we spent the night talking. A thing we hadn't done in much too long. It came out
then."

"So long as that—old dissembler," Elfrid said faintly. Eavon laughed.

"I have been at such things since thou wert a girl—longer, since thy father was a lad. For one reason or another." He eyed her frankly. "Hast something of thy father about the eyes, but little else in this guise. 'Tis not a difficult thing to remember, that thou'rt Gespry."

"You have a right to know the rest, then. Rolend's free, Bal's gone to his aid. They should take Lertondale and Arolet before long. Sedry will return to a great surprise, if all goes as we plan."

The Marcher stared at her, stunned into silence. He turned to guide his horse across the stream, covertly eyed his companion. *No accounting for children; I would have pledged my Bal to Alster's daughter eight years ago, and he'd none of it. Insult, he said. Was it then, when she fought Hyrcan, or since she returned to Darion? He would not live for me after Sedry broke him, only for her*. Eventually, he knew, he'd be proud of his son; at the moment, he was more exasperated than otherwise.

But—a years-old weight rolled from his shoulders as the rest of her words struck him. Surprise? Surprise, indeed! "How do I aid thee? Remember that if thou hast need of aid, or of men, I am thine, and my following." He considered. "And Cretony. He is of my mind, if thou'd'st give me right to speak to him, I'll do it, and put him to ready. In case there is need."

"I—good. Do it." *In case there is need. Another Gelc, but better to prepare against the worst*.

Fresgkel nodded. "I shall, as soon as may be. Now. There are none close to us at this point—"

"None I can see. We've moved away from the guardline."

"Then hold. I will swear, now, to Rolend's aid—"

"Fresgkel, there is no need—"

"There is," the old man interrupted fiercely. "To remove the taste of the last swearing from my mouth, would'st deny me that?" To that, Elfrid could make no reply. She drew her mount to a halt and slid from the saddle, caught the Marcher Baron's hands between hers as he knelt and spoke again the words that would bind him as another's liege man. This time there was life in his voice, and hope.

30

THE SKY WAS still a clear, slate blue, only the orange edge of the overhead clouds hinting at the sun and heat to come. Elfrid yawned, staggered to her feet to stretch and yawn again. A voice from behind made her jump: Gelc's.

"Ah, hah! And how much sleep had you last night?" The armsman stood before her, two steaming mugs of coffee in his hands. But as the swordswoman reached, hungrily, he drew them back, his expression daunting. Elfrid sighed, a rueful smile pulling at her lips.

"I slept. Well—some, anyhow."

It was Gelc's turn to sigh, but he handed over one of the coffees. Elfrid buried her nose in the steam, closed her eyes happily. "You will be the death of yourself," Gelc went on sternly. "This is no garden party—"

"Such as Megen Cove?" Elfrid asked pointedly. "I was there, remember?" Gelc shrugged as he downed half his coffee.

"Not under the burden you carry now." Ever cautious, he glanced all about them before continuing, lowering his voice as he went on, even though the few men near to hand were still asleep. "How is Fresgkel? I have not yet seen him this morning."

"Better." Elfrid lowered her own voice which—when she chose—had no carrying power at all. "But he already knew—"

"Of Bal?" Gelc asked, startled. Elfrid shook her head. Gelc gazed at her blankly, then: "Oh. *That.*"

242

"Yes. *That*. He—his son told him, of course."

"Well—." Gelc considered this, seemed to find no cause for fresh worry in it. "And Fresgkel?"

"Wanted," Elfrid replied with a genuine, if tired, grin, "to swear to Rolend's service, through me, on the moment. I told him the intent was sufficient. He then asked permission of me to bring Cretony into his confidence. Says he can trust the Earl with his life—"

"Let him, then," Gelc said grimly. "We may need all the aid we can get before this mask is finished."

Elfrid laughed. "Poor my friend; battle does indeed affect you adversely!"

Gelc snorted, drained his coffee. "We may," he reiterated, even more firmly. "I merely seek to close all stray passages. You," he went on, mildly accusing, "are as bad as *he* is: Folk like you need men like me. To keep your feet attached to the ground while your brains are soaring." Elfrid gazed at him in astonishment.

One of Marchham's grandsons came around to bring them bread and meat, a barely ripe apple each, a cup of purple fruity wine. Elfrid's thanks brought a shy smile to the child's face before he hurried back to the food trestles.

"You are right, of course," Elfrid mumbled around a bite of the rather tough bread. "We need all the friends and allies we can get in a game such as this. I took the midnight watches with Grolpet," she added. "After yesterday, the poor man is nervous as a mother cat and wanted to worry plans with me once again."

"And?"

"What d'you think? We got nowhere, save to agree to allow no more sorties to young fools."

"Which we'd decided before already. Man worries too much, ye'd have done better to sleep."

"Aye." Elfrid yawned, covered her mouth with the crook of her elbow. "But I could not properly have refused him, he is an ally, remember. And he might've had something intelligent to offer."

"Doubtful. He's Beldenian, after all."

Elfrid laughed, nearly choking on a mouthful of apple. "For shame! You are too hard on them. I grant you come from an educated household—"

"Illiteracy is not the question," Gelc mumbled, "stupidity

is." The swordswoman's dark grey eyes were alight with mischief.

"If you are *very* nice to me, I will repeat none of this to Fialla—"

"Hah!" Gelc grinned crookedly. "I will be nicer than ye deserve, I will say nothing of how little sleep you had last night, and after you promised her, too! You left Grolpet when?"

"Just past middle night. I think."

"Not so bad. You had five hours—"

"Well—not exactly," Elfrid bent over her food. "Old Zorec came by only moments after I returned, looking for someone to share his watch."

"And you," Gelc said sarcastically, "of course, went with him."

Elfrid shrugged, tore off a chunk of bread, wrapped it around a bit of meat and stuffed the whole into her cheek. "It seemed a good idea. The kind of thing I would do, in any event. But the man saved my life, if you recall—"

"How could I forget?" He glanced around. Low conversations, mostly a distance away, as men washed, began to arm themselves or saddle their horses for the first assault. The eastern sky was growing lighter, there was now a patch of yellowish blue where the sun would make its appearance. "Ye have indeed done well, that men such as Zorec see you as Gespry."

Elfrid scowled. "I am not certain. He was concerned, terribly so. He sees a difference in me, Gelc—no, not what you think," she added as the armsman sat up sharply. "No. He thinks I was wounded in some way I am trying to conceal."

"Ye persuaded him otherwise, I hope?"

"Hard to tell. I think so. We spoke mostly of his nephew thereafter. Young Zormerian."

Gelc nodded his approval. "A good lad. A bit green, and more brave than skillful. Good, though. When did he come by the banner?"

"Took it up about five days ago, and has simply held it since. Perhaps I should give him the right."

"Perhaps. Dangerous for him. They are wasted on Grolpet's company, both of them. He and Sevric are barely aware of them. Zorec should long since have been captain, and look at him! Penalty you pay," Gelc added, "for serving in an army the size of this."

"Not like your own service," Elfrid grinned. Gelc shrugged.

"I reap my mistakes in full, but what I do proper is noted." He eyed his companion sternly. "Did ye get *any* sleep at all?"

"Of course," Elfrid began indignantly, spoiling it with another yawn. Gelc laughed sourly. "Enough to fight on."

"Only you can know this for certain," Gelc warned her. He jumped to his feet. "I will fetch our horses. Do you need aid before I go?" Elfrid shook her head. "Fialla said to tell you, she will be here with food and drink for you after the first assault," he added, turned and strode swiftly away.

Alster's daughter yawned again, stretching until her joints cracked. It was, suddenly, a terrible effort to stay upright. *I am so tired, tired to my very bones, and not just from lack of sleep this past night. My breasts hurt, even though Fialla stitched the newest bandages with care. And I weary of playing a part to which I am so poorly suited.*

No, she ordered herself sternly. *This was your choice, to take this part, when you could yet have come alone as you first wished.* She stretched again, pressed Elfrid deeply down inside the persona of Archbishop, and smiled at the armsmen who passed her.

What did it matter? A week, perhaps less. Certainly no more. It would be over. Done. *And then?* Unprofitable thought, that last; like the others, it was pushed aside impatiently.

Gelc appeared in the distance, leading two horses. With him, Fidric and Boresin, Zorec, who had attached himself to the Archbishop's personal guard and who was carrying on an animated conversation with Bor. Behind them all, mounted already, Zormerian, the Archbishop's colors attached to his saddle-bow. His expression was casually defiant, as though he half hoped no one would notice his taking of the banner, half hoped, also, that someone would, so giving him cause to defend his holding of it. *I had better give him actual right. It is dangerous, but he will not abjure it for that.*

Sunlight lay cool and pale upon the trees on the south ridge. From the center of the Darion camp now came Sedry and his personal guard of ten. Elfrid repressed a sudden desire to laugh: *Ah, Sedry, guard your person how you will, it will not prevent your undoing!*

Sedry dismounted, clasped her arm, and the men in the sortie cheered loudly.

"Gespry! Gespry!" Fialla came running up behind them. Sedry, half onto his horse, dropped back to the ground. His pale eyes were sharp, alight as the Archbishop's mistress, hair undone, bosom rising and falling rapidly as she sought to gain her breath, her face flushed, dropped him a brief courtesy. "Gespry, thank goodness I caught you; urgent—ah, a moment—urgent messages from Rhames." Elfrid took her hands, kissed the fingers, glanced at the King.

"We dare not hold up the force, Sire. I will catch you up in moments." Sedry sketched a brief salute, brought his horse about as he cried out: "Darion!" and set out at such a pace his armsmen were some moments catching up with him.

Fialla's whole attention was for Elfrid. "Gennen. The Prince of Flames—upright. The King of Dawn, reversed. The Lantern. The Keep."

"Rolend rides against Arolet, within the day," Elfrid whispered. "Anything—else?"

Fialla shook her head. There had been more, but—the Priest. Gespry, *her* Gespry, well and in Darion? No, that she would hold to herself for now.

"The Prince of Flames. *He* rides with Rolend." Elfrid turned, dark eyes gazing across the valley to west and south. Her pale face was suddenly flushed.

Fialla nodded. "Of course he does. You told him to."

Elfrid tore her eyes away, favored Fialla with a brief, unfathomable look.

"Rolend is free, and Arolet must fall in a matter of days. Sedry remains here yet—our plan holds so well, I dare not believe in our luck." She gripped the small hands, hard. "Take care, Fialla."

"I? You are the one who must take care, my Gespry—see that you do." She stood back as Elfrid mounted, watched as Gelc fell in to one side, Boresin the other, and Fidric spurred ahead to set the lead.

31

THE DAY WAS humid, sultry, and there was no dust, as though the damp-laden air could not hold it. Marchham was again well to the fore: Elfrid could see the old Earl's colors and frequently hear the man's astonishing bellow above the din of battle. The line was holding, despite the sapping heat. It affected the Fegez as well, however: They were not moving as quickly as they had throughout the morning. Many of them had shed furs to fight in little more than loincloths and body paint.

Elfrid moved into the midst of the Beldenians, who gave a brief but heartfelt cheer at sight of the Archbishop's banner.

A shout from Grolpet; the mercenary force broke in the center of its line as it had twice the day before, once early in the morning. The Fegez had still not learned the mistake of falling for this simple trick, and again they poured into the breach, stopping dumbfounded as the mercenaries closed about them. Ignoring Gelc's furious protests, Elfrid was always in the front line making good use of her bow before the fighting became too intense to risk further arrows.

Grolpet shouted again: a high, wordless cry. Elfrid snapped around. The Beldenians' leader stared in shock at the long, heavy-bladed knife that protruded from his belly, lodged neatly between the patches of reinforcing ring mail on his leather jerkin. With a terrible cry, he launched one last long swing of his broad sword at the Fegez below him before he toppled dead from his horse. The Fegez fell headless across him.

The Beldenians, bereft of their captain, panicked; the Fegez formed themselves into a tight group and drove through the way they had come. More replaced them. The mercenary line disintegrated completely.

Elfrid's bow fell unnoticed to the ground as she gathered the reins back into her hands, pulled her horse about, and pressed back past Fidric before the man knew what she was about. She stood in her stirrups, cried out: "Belden, to me!" in a voice that pierced the battle around them. Zormerian was right behind her, one strong young arm moving the standard in signal, the other capably wielding a Beldenian short, broad-bladed sword. Elfrid could hear Gelc cursing imaginatively just behind her, but so many responded to her rallying cry, her own guard could not get through. She wound reins back about her saddle-bow, slapped at her cheek as something bit, waved another cloud of biting flies away with her free hand as she drove her sword downward, into the press.

"Gespry, damn ye, get *back*!" Boresin bellowed.

"When I can!" Elfrid shouted back. One of the persistent flies bit her neck, she brushed it angrily away. Damnit, they *hurt*! Another Fegez, and yet another to take his place as he fell. She bent forward to free her blade, swung it in a short, backhanded arc. Out of the corner of her eye, she could see one of the Beldenians edging forward to cover her retreat. "Not yet, lad. Wait for an opening behind me and call it for me. I don't dare look for it."

"Aye, sir!"

The Beldenians were rapidly reforming, cutting off, boxing in the enemy. Elfrid scanned the front line: Gelc there? That was Gespry's armsman all right, dangerously in the open, furiously reorganizing the mercenaries. She shook her hand as something bit deeply: *Elorra's left ear, I will itch tonight!*

The barbarians milled in confusion as Gelc led a picked wedge forward. Several fell, the rest fled, wildly attempting to cut their way free of the encircling Beldenians. Gelc had to shout orders several times before the mercenary line parted. Those around Elfrid surged forward, sweeping her, the Arch-bishop's banner with them.

A cheer rang across the mercenaries, rippling down through the Darion ranks and back again. Elfrid drew her horse to a halt. The boy had stayed with her through the last few min-utes' mad confusion, had managed to work an opening for his

Archbishop to fall back. She drew to side, pulled back as the
Beldenian slid into her place. Only then did she dare glance
around. It was the first moment's rest she'd had for over an
hour.

Gods, it was hot! She pushed the hair away from her brow.
The line before her was engaged, not heavily. Most of the
fighting seemed to be at the ends of both lines. They'd held,
though. So far as she could tell—hard to think, to remember
—they'd lost no ground.

Clouds boiled over the eastern ridges: not at all surprising,
considering the feel of the air. Not far away, Sedry was
resting, leaning across his saddle-bows, breathing hard. His
household surrounded him in a tight circle. Fresgkel—there. A
long cut ran across his cheek. She automatically slapped at her
arm as something bit deep. Fire ran across her palm, her
fingers clenched convulsively.

She brought the hand up, stared at it blankly. A long,
ragged cut ran from the base of the thumb across to the opposite side of the wrist: The entire hand had gone numb. "Oh,
Gods, no." It was with difficulty she forced her suddenly terrified gaze to her forearm.

So small a thing. Like the one Baldyron had shown her in
the quiet of Gespry's tent. Three of its four corners projected
from her flesh: They, and by the cold racing up her arm, the
one embedded in muscle, were a mottled brown. Her hand
burned the length of the cut. With a faint moan, she hunched
over her saddle-bows.

A hand gripped her shoulder: Fidric, a concerned Boresin
right behind him. "Gespry, what?"

"Nothing—all right," she managed to whisper, even
managed a faint, deprecating smile.

"All right? Alayya's thumbnail!" Fidric's grip tightened.
His keen eyes found the dart, and he reached with one of his
bare hands, checked. "Poisoned?" Elfrid nodded, closed her
eyes. Her face twisted with the effort not to cry out.

"It's gone cold, Bor. My hand—"

"Gespry?" Eavon, face dark with worry, appeared at her
other side. The old Marcher turned to shout for a guard. He
leaned forward to grasp her hand, squeezed it hard. Elfrid bit
off a cry; blood ran down her fingers. "May drain some of the
poison, has it been long? No? If that was the only—no, wait. I
see it."

His eyes followed hers; Gloved fingers gripped the tiny caltrap. He tore the glove from his hand, dropped the dart inside, and tucked it into his arrow sheath as he drew his dagger. "Turn thy head, man," he ordered fiercely; Elfrid drew a deep breath, closed her eyes, hissing as the blade bit twice, deeply, into her forearm.

She opened her eyes, wished she had not. The battle before her blurred.

"What—," she swallowed, tried again. "What poison?"

"Nightshade, by its color," Eavon replied. "But it was small, not deeply set. Thou'lt not die."

"Nightshade." Gods, think! Terror, as much as pain, was freezing her thoughts. "They say a man talks with nightshade. If I talk—." Her sword hand gripped Eavon's fingers tightly. Eavon shook his head, looking more assured than he could be feeling.

"We'll protect thee."

"Sedry—"

"Do not think on the King. Come, we must get thee back to camp. The nightshade will not kill thee, but dost not belong here." Gelc, alerted by the suddenly intense group gathered around the Archbishop's banner, fought his way to their side. Eavon motioned three of his men to them, grabbed hold of Elfrid's reins, and began to draw her in the direction of camp.

It was no easy task: The Fegez had been dealt a severe blow by the mercenaries, but there were many behind the lines. Elfrid clung desperately to the saddle-bows, trying not to look too closely at things, since anything she did look at closely seemed to change subtly, to become something slyly evil, terrifying.

Gelc's sword tore through a Fegez throat, an arc of blood splurting out behind it. She cried out in horror and closed her eyes tightly.

What is wrong with me, what is—More and more difficult to think, to remember who, what she was. Eavon's voice ran reassuringly against her ear, fading now and again—again, the drug? "Relax if thou can'st, my friend. I know nightshade. Relax, allow it to run its course, do not try to fight it. That way lies madness."

Madness. A word, among all of them, to grasp. "Was that what drove Father mad?"

"Shhh. No, no do not think on it. Do not fear. We'll see thee safely to thy tent. Fialla is there."

"Fialla."

"That is right, think of Fialla," Eavon urged quietly, adding aloud, "Hist! The King!"

"Blast!" Gelc snarled between his teeth. His hair was plastered to neck and brow. "If *he* comes with us—"

"Can you stop him?" Boresin inquired sourly. Gelc scowled at his fellow armsman, pressed nearer to the false Archbishop.

"No, we'd better slow," Fresgkel advised quietly. "Allow him to catch us up. Sedry suspects bad motive of everyone around him, we dare not allow him to suspect Gespry."

"Gods no," Gelc muttered to himself. Elfrid straightened herself with an effort, forced her eyes open. *Why do they look at me so oddly? What have I done to them, that they look at me in fear?* "Do not fear me, you know me," she whispered faintly. Gelc gripped her sword hand briefly, forced himself to smile reassuringly.

"Gespry, dear friend, we fear *for* you. You are ill. Can you make camp?"

"Camp." She swallowed, and with visible effort pulled herself upright. "Gespry," she whispered to herself, "*I* am Gespry, Archbishop of Rhames." And, in an only slightly stronger voice, "Of course I can." A feeble smile twisted her lips. "I had but a scratch, until my leech here made it a real wound!" Eavon smiled in appreciation of the joke, though his eyes were worried indeed.

"Of course canst reach camp, Gespry. A scratch, as thou sayest. We are here to aid thee and to protect thee from the barghests." Elfrid closed her eyes again. Easier not to look upon any of them: Their faces were shifting under her gaze, as though underwater, becoming evil, untrustworthy. But— something—of course.

"Fresgkel, for shame. Fegez," she whispered; she managed a faint smile. Eavon chuckled. Opened his mouth to remonstrate lightly with his companion and so lighten the moment for all of them. Horses behind them, then. He turned, turned back again to grip Elfrid's leg.

" 'Ware, Gespry, Archbishop of Rhames," he enunciated in a low, careful voice. "The King comes here."

"The King—." Elfrid frowned. Her mind had gone suddenly blank. Who were these? And who—? "King? Father? No, he cannot be here, he's gone mad—." She drew a sharp breath as Gelc exerted pressure on her torn hand.

"Have care what you say!" He hissed. There was no time for anything else as Sedry reached them. Elfrid swallowed hard, nodded. Closed her eyes. She felt the horse begin to move again, risked a glance. The camp, which moments ago seemed less than a furlong away, receded beyond reach.

"I shall never make it," she whispered to herself. No one else seemed to hear. A familiar voice broke through her despairing thoughts. *I know that voice; oh Gods, no, not Sedry!* There was nothing of Gespry left; a frightened Elfrid hunched lower on her horse.

A hand lay lightly on her right shoulder, by now throbbing harshly as the nightshade spread up her arm. "My friend Gespry, tell me you are not badly hurt!" *Gespry? I am Gespry. I am Archbishop of Rhames, Gespry.* The litany washed through her, reassuring, momentarily holding the nightshade back. She opened one eye, recoiling with a faint cry of terror from the King's face, not a hand's distance from her own.

Sedry drew back, startled and confused. Gelc reached out in reassurance, whispering against her ear; reassuring words, soothingly uttered, though he'd never felt less in the mood for it and could never recall any of what he'd said. Eavon, used to dealing with Fegez poisons, stripped off his remaining glove, took her earlobe between thumb and finger and gave it a savage pinch.

"It is not a bad wound, Sire," Gelc was telling the King. Someone, he reasoned unhappily, had to; the Marcher was busy and Gespry—*Gespry, damnit!*—was beyond rational speech. Gods, what had they done to themselves, coming here? None of his fears showed in his voice, at least. "But the dart was poisoned and he cut his hand on it as well."

"Will he live?" Sedry demanded anxiously. Gelc shrugged, then nodded gloomily. On Elfrid's other side, Eavon now spoke against her ear.

"Gespry, pay heed, this is Darion's King, King Sedry." Another, milder, pinch to the earlobe. Dark grey eyes slid sideways to meet the Marcher Baron's. Eavon nodded emphatically, barely restraining a sigh of relief as he saw understanding in them. Elfrid managed a shaky smile for the King.

"Sire—my apologies—"

"Not needed, your Grace." Sedry waved apology aside. Grave concern had replaced his wary expression. "If you need my physicians, my doctors, anything—"

"No, I thank you, only—Fialla—." She closed her mouth firmly, caught her lower lip in her teeth, lest she say something, anything, to arouse the King's easy suspicions. Closed her eyes again as the landscape took on an intensity of color and shape that made her ill.

"I have some antidotes, Sire," Eavon said. Sedry frowned briefly, remembering he was not on good terms with the Marcher. Eavon appeared to remember this also and there was an uncomfortable silence before Sedry shrugged it aside in his fears for the wounded man between them. *If Rhames were to die in Darion*! Cold terror shot through him. But no; Eavon knew how to deal with barghest poisons if any of them did. In that much he could surely trust the old man. Gods, he had to!

A lump formed in his throat as he watched the tall, overly thin Archbishop struggling to hold himself upright. He liked this man, better than many he knew. But if he were to die in Darion—Sedry flinched away from the thought. His keen ears picked up faint words: "A little further and we can rest; do not fear, I will take care of you." The Archbishop, mumbling to himself—to another? But what was he saying? Sedry edged nearer.

Gelc turned a worried face toward the King, swallowing past the lump in his own throat. "He'll be well, King Sedry. He needs rest—"

Sedry drew his attention with effort from Elfrid's muttered speech. Fought against that prickling along his inner senses that was returning more strongly than ever. What was it about Rhames's Archbishop that triggered a sense of *familiar*? He looked at the visibly upset armsman, then, and was ashamed of his stray thoughts. "How did he cut his hand?"

"Don't know. Fresgkel bled it, I had not the sense." To his other side, he could hear Elfrid's whispered: "Birds, I knew they would come, I knew it, he does not intend we reach the sea." Eavon gripped her shoulders, as though to keep her from toppling over, drew woman and horse a few paces away. Gelc could almost hear himself sweating. *Alayya, Elorra, shut her up*! Somehow he kept a running conversation with the King, scarcely aware of what he was saying; Sedry would have needed four ears at the very least to follow Gelc and Elfrid both. Fidric, alerted by that sixth sense that made them such good comrades in arms, dropped back to help Gelc distract the King.

Their progress was slow, slowed more as the poison took effect. Elfrid swayed in the saddle, now leaning heavily against Eavon as pain, chills, wracked her body. She could no longer recall who she was, where she was. Why. Her arm throbbed, the left hand burned, stung whenever it brushed against anything.

Fresgkel held her as gently as he would a child, keeping up a constant, low, reassuring murmur. Sounds became words again, strung together to make a little sense. "We are nearly there, Gespry. It will be all right, Gespry, believe me. A little barghest poison, not enough to harm thee, Gespry." *Gespry. That is me; I am Gespry, Archbishop of Rhames. Remember that—remember, even though the world is falling from beneath me—*

A terrified shudder tore at the thin body as Sedry barked out commands, directing armsmen to race to camp, alerting Nolse to his return, warning Fialla of the Archbishop's. "The King is concerned for thee, Gespry," the Marcher soothed, "the anger thou hear'st in his voice is fear for thee."

"It is my fear," came the whispered, trembling response. "I lied to Fialla, I said I never feared Sedry, but I did. I feared him when I was small, I still fear him. He hated me, he always hated me."

"Shhh," Eavon soothed, casting a worried glance about him, meeting Gelc's eyes. The little armsman was terrified, but was managing to hold it in. Only one who knew him well would see it. Good. Gelc turned back to once again distract the King's attention. Eavon returned his attention to Elfrid. "No. Didst not any such thing, nor dost thee now. Thou'rt Gespry, Archbishop of Rhames, whom shouldst thou fear?"

"I am Gespry." An even fainter whisper. The lean body went limp, and Fresgkel, who had nursed any number of men through nightshade, recognized the second phase, a period of lucidity, when it seemed, if only briefly, that the stuff had run its course. *Pray the Two it lasts until we are safe in Gespry's pavilion*!

Sedry's gaze fastened on the one he knew as Archbishop; he turned his eyes away then, in what he hoped was a casual movement. It was not *wrong*, surely, to just try—a little. He set his mouth in concentration and reached within.

Strange thoughts pattered frantically across Elfrid's mind: little creatures, too tiny to see, tinier than the battlefield flies, under her skin—she swallowed, fought the urge to tear at her arms, knowing it for the nightshade. The air was too thick to breathe: For one terrifying moment, her lungs froze. It took concentration, hard concentration, to make them draw in, expell. She forgot about them, suddenly, as another thought touched at the edge of her mind: not *hers*, no, and not the drugs! That he'd dare—! Sheer fury gave her strength she might not otherwise have found; her mental shields slammed into place.

Across the Archbishop's armsman and his own Baron, Sedry cast a sudden, sharp glance at the wounded Elfrid. Gelc had his attention before he could try the Truthing a second time.

They made it across the earthworks, Eavon and Gelc holding the now helpless Elfrid upright between them while Fidric led her horse. Horrified armsmen watched silently as they rode slowly by. Now the River. Thunder rumbled ominously in the distance as they reached dry ground once again.

Fialla cried out as Elfrid half fell from his saddle into the old Marcher Baron's arms. The swordswoman swayed back into her mount. "Why are we here? Is this where Father—no, he's mad, he cannot be here!" Gelc leaped from his horse, darted a quick glance at Sedry, who was wide-eyed with consternation, a frown creasing his brow as he sought to catch, to make sense of the Archbishop's words.

Silence. Elfrich clenched her torn hand, slowly and deliberately. Pain cleared her mind and she gazed, stricken, at those around her. *See how frightened they are. Because of me! And look at Sedry. Gods, did he attempt Truthing on me, does he suspect me—or was that my own fear playing me false? Alayya, Elorra, what have I said, and what only thought?* The nightshade swirled heavily through her veins; this could not yet be the worst of it. Not just her own death, but that of all of them—

She met Fialla's frightened gaze, closed her eyes and clutched at the saddle. "Help me," she whispered, so low only

Eavon heard her. The old man nodded, very faintly; his fist came up and caught her just below the ear. Fialla screamed as she fell, threw herself protectively over the unconscious Elfrid.

"What have ye done?" Zorec, who had ridden back, nearly unnoticed, with them, pushed past the stunned armsmen.

"I? Nothing," Eavon replied levelly. "Save to spare him a quantity of the misery he yet faces." His glance crossed the mercenary's, locked hard on the King's. Sedry was pale with fury, but the old man was equal to him at the moment. "Hast seen a man run the full horrors of nightshade, Sire: Any of thee? I have. I have seen men die of it, or go completely mad!" Fialla cried out again, her face against the white hair. The old Marcher dropped stiffly down beside her. "He will not die, Lady, I promise thee. But the poison will hold him in its grip until sunrise tomorrow, at the very least." He glanced from one to another of his silent audience. "Dost think, any of thee, that he did not welcome what I gave?"

"No." Fialla forced the word between sobs; tears coursed down her face. "You did what was best."

"No, dear Fialla," Eavon replied gently. "Only what I could. Come, Boresin, my good friend. Go with these lads of mine. Korvegken, fetch out my sack of antidotes, all of them. Give them to Bor, send him back with them. Go on, man. We'll get him inside." Boresin pulled himself together with visible effort, remounted, and clattered off with Eavon's men.

Sedry moved forward to slip into the gap the four had left, knelt beside Fialla. For once, he was not drunk on her presence and concern for Gespry had driven out every thought not centered on the fallen Archbishop. This was his friend, a man he knew and liked. He was more ashamed than ever for his doubts: Of course a priest would sense the Truthing and shut it out—and rightly so! And if Gespry, his good friend Gespry, were to die—

"If you need anything I might have, sweet Lady, you have only to send. If I do not have it, I shall obtain it. I swear to you. Will you remember?" Fialla nodded, dabbed her handkerchief blindly at her face, swallowed, finally managed to whisper thanks.

"No thanks needed," Sedry replied. "If I could do more, I would, believe that." He patted her fingers; reached then to lay his hand in unaccustomed, and so awkward, affection upon the Archbishop's thin cheek. Gelc and Fidric picked up the unconscious woman; Fialla stumbled after them like a sleepwalker.

Sedry turned away, motioning his men to follow, to bring his horse. He rubbed his chin thoughtfully. Gods, what had Gespry been babbling about? Madness, wild beasts, attacking birds—nightshade must make a hell of your mind indeed! Sedry shuddered. And then stopped in his tracks, so suddenly his armsmen gazed at him in concern. A chill walked across his shoulders.

He waved them on. "Go back to our camp, I will follow. Go on!" He spun about on his heel as they splashed across the River, picked Zorec out from those still waiting outside the blue and gold pavilion and, catching his eye, motioned the old man to join him.

His hand moved, unwillingly, back to his chin. It itched, damn the flies. Worse, it was prickly: he needed a shave and that badly. So did all of his men, those who didn't wear beards. And the old man bowing before him right now: His chin and cheeks were covered with a grey stubble that matched his heavy, short moustache.

Gespry's cheek, just now, though Sedry had seen beard as heavy as his own, had been as one just shaven moments before.

"Your Grace?" The man's accent was heavy, but his Ordinate was understandable. Sedry, normally a stickler for form, ignored the misuse of the honorific. There were other matters, suddenly, much more important.

"You have served with Gespry before."

"Aye, your Grace: Twice, I did. When the Coastal Lords were having pirate troubles, first time he came to Belden. And then, Megen Cove, I was aboard the *Wave Cleaver* with him—"

"Of course, of course," Sedry cut him off brusquely. "Tell me then: Has he—," Sedry hesitated. "Has he always been beardless?"

"What, Gespry? Always been clean-shaven, Gespry has."

"Not my meaning," Sedry snapped. He drew the old man further from the Archbishop's pavilion. "He has *no* beard, none at all. Look at my face—feel your own, man! Gespry has none!"

"But he has!" the old Beldenian began indignantly. Sedry shook his head in a fury, effectively silencing him.

"Appearance, nothing but appearance! His beard is nothing but sham, his cheek as smooth as a girl's!"

"Oh, Gods." To the King's surprise, Zorec's eyes filled with tears. The old man turned from him to blink them away.

"What?" Sedry glanced up as a horseman tore by: Boresin, returning from the Darion camp, a small, brightly red bag clutched in his hand. "What is it, what's wrong?"

"I feared it," Zorec replied flatly. "He looked so odd to me from the very first. As though—as though he were not Gespry at all!"

"Not—?" Sedry began in rising alarm. Zorec went on, lost in his own misery.

"He's thinner, his hair's gone all white." He swallowed again. "Seemed he had always to push himself, to prove himself. Unlike Gespry, and tense. He just didn't feel *right* to me, this time. Last night, I asked him what was wrong, I *knew* there was something. He wouldn't say, just reminded me he'd been bad hurt."

He turned back to the tensely silent Sedry. "I knew that. He'd ought to've died that first night: Bones broken, his back all twisted, innards broken up. He was burned, too, burned terribly. But I never thought then—"

"Thought *what*?" Sedry kept himself from screaming with an effort that was near to pain.

"Why—how else would a man's beard cease to grow? He always had a stubble after a day's fighting thick as your own!" Zorec's eyes blurred. "Poor Lady Fialla, these past three years she's been mistress in name only." He drew a deep breath. "The mast, your Grace. It unmanned him."

32

"GELC?" THE FAINTEST of whispers but the armsman was alert. Elfrid, face nearly as white as her hair, made one feeble attempt to press up onto her elbow, but fell back again. Gelc was at her side.

"Myself," Gelc replied. "How d'ye feel?"

She closed her eyes, nodded. "I've felt better." One eye fixed briefly on the armsman; she nodded again, a weak smile creasing her lips. "You look yourself again, and no monster."

"Good. D'ye want water?" Elfrid let the eye close, nodded. "Fialla is out and about the camp with the Reader, assuring the mercenaries ye intend to live." Water splashed into a cup. The armswoman gratefully accepted Gelc's supporting arm about her shoulders as she drank, even more gratefully lay flat again. "The Fegez broke just before the storm did." Gelc needed no words to know his companion's next concern. "Not that there were many left by then. They tell me the men went wild after we took you away. Barghests didn't stand a chance. Some of their chiefs are meeting with the King this morning to talk a truce."

"How long have I been here?" Elfrid felt her arm gingerly. Her left hand was thick with bandage and stiff, but not painful except when she tried to clench it. The arm hurt only where it had been cut.

"Nearly two days. No," he added sharply, pushing her back flat as she struggled to sit again. "You're to stay here. Fresgkel says nightshade weakens a man, beyond what it does to his—"

"As you love me," Elfrid whispered, "do not speak of nightshade!" She gazed, stricken, at her bandaged hand. "Two days!"

"It took that long for the stuff to run its course. Fortunate for us all Fresgkel was near to hand, ye'd have died otherwise. No. You're to stay here. You're weak, and could easily take ill. And it would not do for the barghests to see you. Cretony tells me they think you an ancestor spirit."

"An ancestor spirit. What," she demanded, curiosity momentarily pressing everything else aside, "is that?"

"The King's great grandsire or some such thing. Few of their men, he says, reach an age for hair white as yours. Men that old among barghests do not ride to battle. By their thinking, you are not a living man."

Elfrid laughed shortly. "I do not believe it. They tried to kill me—"

"So? A man tries, doesn't he? But if they saw you now, it might ruin Sedry's bargaining position." He felt her face, pushed damp hair off her brow. "Fialla left a broth over the fire, ye'd better have some."

"I had, I suppose. Wait a moment, though." Elfrid rolled to one side, propped herself carefully onto one elbow. "I—tell me what chanced, I recall little, save—that Sedry was with us, I remember that. And Fresgkel tried to keep me away from him. I was afraid, I remember that, too, because when I opened my mouth words came out, whether I intended it or not." She closed her eyes. "What—did I say?"

"Gods," Gelc demanded despairingly, "what did you *not* say? Though," he went on hastily at the look on the already pale face, "we kept the King occupied enough, I think, that he heard little or none of it. And ye kept your voice low, I'll give ye that. Eavon did what he could, precious little, but I'd give oath Sedry heard nothing he should not have."

"Ahhh." With a sigh, she rolled back, closed her eyes again. "I think I could eat something, Gelc." But when the armsman returned, balancing a bowl carefully between his hands, she had fallen asleep again.

Across the camp, on the wide, trampled meadow before the King's pavilion, a parley was in progress: The King sat in his high-backed chair, pale blue canopy shielding him from the sun. Nolse stood behind him, two of his personal armsmen near to hand. A tray, near his right knee, held wine and a dish of confection.

Not far away, on chairs and stools brought from the King's table, sat those brought to witness the truce for Darion: Marchham on his right hand, and beyond him Eavon. Though Sedry was not pleased with Eavon, he dared not leave him out of the parley: he had saved the Archbishop's life. As importantly, the Fegez knew him and insisted upon his presence. They were already affronted by Korent's absence, Sedry dared risk no further insult to them.

Two of the other Marcher Barons held places beyond Eavon: Ambersody, and next to him Woldeg, his face a sleepwalker's, hair hacked short in mourning for his sons. *By the Two, they are as barbaric, my Marchers, as the barghests!*

The Beldenians were no better. Sevric, now leader of the Beldenian force, wore a broad band of red about his sleeve from which depended Grolpet's braided war-lock. Beyond him, two of his lieutenants had bound their own war-locks and sword hilts with red threads.

The Fegez were grouped loosely to Sedry's left. Seen close to hand, by daylight and unarmed, they could almost have passed for normal men: Eavon himself was tanned more darkly than many of them. The younger retained a berserker appearance: untamed manes of hair, fur cloaks over coarsely woven, embroidered and beaded breeches, most of them heavily bearded. Of one or two, only the eyes could be seen, glittering, dark points in a tangle of wild hair. The eyes were not, quite, human. Looking at these, it was not difficult at all to believe in the shape-changing.

Their elders, by contrast, were clad plainly, in breeches that could have been woven in Darion or Genneldry. Plainly—if colorfully—shirted. Only one, eldest by his white hair, had enough of the stuff to pull back in a thong, much the way the Marcher Barons did. The other two had cropped iron-grey hair to just below their ears. All three were clean shaven.

Clean shaven—Sedry rubbed his chin, shaven within the hour and so smooth as young Juseppa's. He was concentrating on his part in the parleys with great difficulty, relying heavily on Nolse to keep abreast of the many conflicting threads of conversation, to alert him to what he must say when speech lagged and men turned to him.

He could not think! Had that old mercenary been right, had

Gespry lost his manhood at Megen Cove? Poor Lady Fialla, indeed, then! But—no. She did not have that look, and Sedry of all men knew it well, the look of a woman whose man no longer attended to her needs. No. Nor did she have the mien of a woman who turned to other men—Sedry knew *that* kind of woman also, and he was powerfully attracted to Fialla—he tore his thoughts away. Enough, he would have known!

Why had the Archbishop, even heavily drugged, had such a tight grip on his thoughts? As though *he* were afraid. *Afraid of me? But why? What does he know that I should not?* Priestly matters, of course—but in Gespry's placing, at that moment, how much would things priestly have mattered? No, he'd been afraid, hiding something. Why else would a man react so swiftly against Truthing?

The old man's words circled in his brain, as they had over and over these past two nights, breaking his sleep, leaving him to stare, blankly, at the roof of his tent, rippling in the light breezes: ". . . as though he were not Gespry at all . . ."

Not Gespry? Not possible! And yet—he shifted in his chair, rousing at a touch and a whispered word from Nolse, interjected a comment into an already warm discussion, adding another remark as things settled down and Eavon brought up yet another matter to be considered. No! How could any man impersonate Gespry of Rhames? A man as well known as he? And why?

Why? Well, that was easy enough. The man'd been hurt badly, everyone knew that. Perhaps the rumors were right; perhaps he'd died and his following had decided to keep him alive. But to find another man who looked like Gespry, at least sufficiently for priestly magic to bind the appearance—

Sedry roused again to speak briefly to the eldest chief, repeating the barghest words Nolse whispered to him. Satisfactorily; the old one nodded, turned away to speak to his comrades. But—the inner conversation raged on. Sedry had never seen the Archbishop himself, not until this campaign against the barbarians. No one in Darion knew Gespry from before Megen Cove, few knew him at all, save as Sedry did, by reputation. Gespry's Beldenian allies had not seen him for three years, and a man could change greatly in three years. According to the old Sergeant, he had, in fact. But—if he were not Gespry, who would suspect? Only his height, his build, his style of fighting and skill with weapons must not change—who then would gainsay that this was indeed Gespry, Archbishop of Rhames? One would see only Gespry with his familiar armsmen, his mistress, his Tarots Reader.

And if not Gespry? Mentally the King shrugged. Anyone. Anyone of that build, perhaps; who was he to say how limited the Priestly Gifts were? And so—any number of men in his own household were tall and thin like that; Bal had been, if not quite so thin. Ambersody's second boy was—even Rolend. Why, even the Bastard had been of a similar size, the last time he saw her!

Nolse gripped his shoulder and Sedry blinked, brought himself back to the moment as the three Fegez elders came forward. They did not bow, but he had not expected it. This was a truce, not surrender. Though it came to the same thing: He lost no lands from it, while they lost nothing which had not been taken from them six years previously. Eavon translated haltingly as the old men spoke the parting, slowly from Ordinate to barghest then, as the King replied in kind. They would return at first light. Sedry would welcome their presence. The Fegez turned away, strode to their horses and rode out eastwards towards their camp without another backwards glance. Sedry gazed after them, unseeing, rousing only to follow Nolse back to his pavilion. He sighed, settled into a well-cushioned couch as his Steward dropped the flap into place.

"Wine, Sire? You look as though you'd slept poorly." Nolse deftly propped a cushion behind him, moved away, returning moments later with an unopened jug and two cups. He poured, drank a little himself before pouring any for the King. "I spoke with Gespry's armsmen before the parley," he went on, holding a cup out to Sedry. "They say Rhames will be well enough to walk about tomorrow."

"Good. To have him die here—." Sedry pushed his wine aside, untasted. "Nolse—"

"Sire?"

Sedry fussed with his rings, called up a wisp of Moss-Light, let it fade. He was embarrassed, uncertain he wanted to speak, afraid not to. "I—he spoke oddly, when we brought him back here to camp, did I tell you?"

"You did, Sire." Nolse dropped onto the only other remaining chair in the pavilion, a plain, three-footed stool. "That was the nightshade, Sire. I have never been so un-

fortunate as to encounter it myself, but my brother did. He
saw monsters three days and nights and was never the same
again.''

Sedry waved Nolse's brother aside impatiently. "It was not
monsters the Archbishop saw, save in myself. He cried out in
terror every time he set eyes on me." Sedry stared blankly at
his hands. "On me—only."

Nolse frowned briefly, shook his head. "That might still be
the belladonna, Sire. Jansek told me later that when he looked
at any of us, we seemed strange to him, evil. As though we
meant to conspire behind our smiles, and set upon him and
murder him in horrible fashion—something like that," he
finished lamely. "He could never clearly explain how he felt."

"No. He—." Sedry reclaimed his cup, drained it at a
swallow, and pushed it back towards Nolse for him to refill.
He could not, somehow, bring himself to admit aloud he'd
tried to read an Archbishop of the Two, not even to Nolse.
There was, he was certain, a point at which even Nolse might
balk. "I—perhaps *I* am seeing conspiracies where none exist.
But he was odd, Nolse. So very odd. I do not yet understand,
and I cannot put into words what is wrong. His own men, even
Eavon, he leaned on for support, even though it seemed as you
say, he dared not look at them, because they changed in his
eyes. Me, though. He cried out when his eyes lit on me, he
would not look on me at all."

"Perhaps it *is* nothing, Sire," Nolse ventured tentatively.
"Even if he saw some special fear in you, what could it
mean?"

"I don't know. And yet—"

"He cannot—what?"

"I don't *know*," Sedry cried out. "Since his Reader warned
me—by the Two, I had rather never known! Which of them,
Nolse? Who plots against me, who would have my throne?
Besides Hyrcan?"

"My Lord, none of them. You know that."

"No," Sedry whispered. "She has given me that same
reading again, last night, they plot against me. I did a wrong
thing against Bal, even though I had no choice. My fate is
sealed."

"By your leave, Sire, not so—"

"Oh," Sedry shrugged. He drained his cup suddenly, held it
out for more. "Not in that sense, no. That my acts are foreor-

dained, that there is no change possible to them? No. But I am
boxed in, my choices dwindle, they plot against me, all of
them, and I cannot see—''

Who dares cross you, even with a look?'' Nolse demanded.
''Why, none of them! No one would plot against you, my
King, they are none of them such fools as that! Your
Marchers, all of your nobles, your commons—they know,
every one of them, that you will tolerate none of it, they dare
nothing. Nothing!''

''Aye. But Rhames is not one of mine.''

''No.'' Nolse paused to find words. He could not understand Sedry—why would he not simply accept that Fegez
drugs altered a man, however temporarily? This new line of
thought had better be squelched at once! ''Gespry is not one
of your vassals. But he has aided you at great personal cost,
and at great cost to those who follow him. You cannot suspect
him of ill intention, Gespry of all men? Why, then, would he
allow his Reader to tell you what she has?''

''A Reader cannot lie,'' Sedry whispered into his cup. ''The
Gift goes from one who lies in the face of the Tarots. Even I
know so much as that.''

''Well, then Sire, perhaps Gespry really *is* your enemy.
Perhaps''—Nolse dredged up the most fantastic thing he
could think of on the instant—,''perhaps he was bought by the
Merchants of Lertondale, who paid more coin than you did,
giving him a contract to murder you?'' As he had hoped,
Sedry tipped back his head and laughed heartily.

''No, of course not. Suspect Rhames of—of what indeed?''
And he drained his cup, holding it out for yet another
draught. ''All the same,'' he mumbled defiantly into its depths
moments later, as Nolse went in search of his midday meal,
''there is something not right in the Archbishop's camp, and I
will find it out!''

33

THE NEGOTIATIONS FOR the treaties dragged on; two days, a third. Sedry, never a patient man, chaffed. He had been too long from Arolet, too long from the center of things with only his messengers, his birds to keep him apprised of happenings. He should have never come, he should have left after the first day or so, but now the Fegez were willing to treat with Darion for the first time in recorded history, he was forced to remain.

Messengers deepened the ruts in the long road between the King's pavilion and Arolet, bringing sheaves of documents to him and his advisors, matters which the Witan deemed most pressing, those requiring the King's signature and seal. Tributes and signed documents from Lertondale—the first sign of defeat from the proud Guildmasters. A small rolled paper, bearing the seal of the gaoler of Orkry: By this, Sedry was assured, the Prince Rolend was still under lock and key, and the South extremely quiet.

All quiet, all things under control. Still—

Since Hyrcan's interment at Killech, the North had also become quiet. Another message, this from Sigurdy, announcing that she was retiring, voluntarily this time, to Elenes, where her daughter Sigron had taken priest's vows. *Of all of us*, Sedry reflected as he crumpled the note impassively and tossed it onto the fire, *she loved Hyrcan best. Or does she suspect that I had something to do with it, and thinks to see to her own safety?*

The Reader's interpretations of his cards ate into his mind.

Who is Rhames? It haunted Sedry during the day, brought him awake and sweating at night.

The old Beldenian's words, which had struck him so strongly at the time, no longer made sense: If Gespry were indeed beardless yet with a deliberate appearance of one, there was a reason that had nothing to do with fallen masts! No. That a woman as young, as beautiful, as Fialla would hold to such a masquerade for three years, merely to protect his manhood from untoward rumor? Hah. He, Sedry, knew women better than that!

He visited the Archbishop's camp seldom, but Elfrid, recovering from the effects of the nightshade, was allowed few visitors and only for short periods by the watchful Fialla. One morning, Sedry dropped by to consult with the Reader, stayed to speak a few moments with the one he still more than half-believed to be Gespry. Elfrid was weak and had lost weight since coming to Darion: Her forearms, exposed by the under-jerkin, were all skin and tendon. Fialla was shaving her in the sunlight before the tent. Gespry's armsmen were all close by, alert; two of the Beldenian lieutenants were discussing battle strategy with her in an offhand, extempore fashion.

The King remained only a few minutes. The Fegez would arrive very shortly, and in any event he had nothing to contribute to the conversation—Sedry was no tactician and knew it.

Unfortunate that Gespry could not attend the parleys with the Fegez, they'd get less from Darion, Sedry was certain of that! But one of the first bargains struck by the barghests was that the white-haired ancestor spirit be returned to the dead. So the Marchers carried on as best they could, Sedry sat, morosely silent for the most part, on his Royal seat, and Elfrid stayed carefully out of sight.

He walked alone back to the Darion camp, blind to his surroundings, his mind occupied with the scene he had just left: Gespry, his face covered with soap, Fialla drawing a razor across a face that had no need of it.

All this to protect a man—against what? *Would I, if I were unmanned, would I not become terribly protective, lest other men find it out and hold it against me? But what does Rhames need, beyond the beautiful Fialla?* And *why* does the Truthing warn me around him, why is that, and why can I not read him at all? Granted my Gifts are seldom used, the Truthing serves me often enough, why does it warn me and then fail to serve? And the Reader—Gods! Sedry reached his own pavilion, poured himself wine, and drank it down at a swallow before sounds of men and harness without advised him the Fegez had arrived.

The rest of the morning passed very slowly. He managed to maintain an appearance of interest in the negotiations, in Eavon's painful translation, though he could not have said what any of them spoke about. Thoughts chased themselves wildly through his brain.

Hyrcan never lied to me. Never. Why would he, who feared no man, least of all me? Rhames lied for Hyrcan, but Hyrcan gave me the truth even then, knowing I could have had him killed for it. With an effort, the King brought his wandering attention back to the present as one of the younger Fegez laid a bear's skin, still clawed, before him. Nolse, who had been carefully briefed by Eavon and Marchham, had the neckpiece of silver and polished shell for the exchange, had the correct words to whisper to the King, who spoke them aloud, proffering the gift. The Fegez returned to the elders with the jewel, a soft buzz of conversation floated over their huddled bodies, over the Marchers. Sedry slipped back into his gloomy thoughs.

Hyrcan did lie to me, though! But, did he? He was already dead, poison tightening around his heart, he knew he was going to die, look how he spoke then! The King repressed a shudder. *For Hyrcan to go to the Two, unshriven and with a lie upon his lips? Never! But if that is so, then the Reader lied! The Reader?*

But a Reader couldn't lie! No, wait, what she'd said—she'd said—carefully, Sedry, he admonished himself grimly, caution in interpreting the words she gave you, you didn't do that, did you? Thought you did, perhaps, but—one of kindred, one old in death. That was what she'd said. No names. Old in death, well—one who killed frequently. Hyrcan. But a soldier, an old soldier, would be old in death, too, by that reckoning, wouldn't he? Not Rolend, he has never killed anyone, that I know of. Damn, there *are* no old armsmen in our family, Father's or Mother's, either one! Cousins, uncles. None alive —Father might have been, but—

But, by the Two, there were none left, save the Bastard! No, oh, no! Never that! She was dead, she must be dead. There had been no word of her, not since she'd managed to escape Darion with the old man, save the bits he'd gotten from those he'd put against her in South Embersy, and of course the little Gespry had known of her.

Gespry? Sedry glanced around, a little wildly, certain he had cried the name aloud. All eyes were on Eavon, laboriously translating for the Marchers as two of the Fegez elders argued. "No," he whispered to himself. "No woman could ever impersonate a man. Never like that!"

A voice from long ago echoed through his mind: Morelis, speaking in the Princess Tower the night he had brought her and Merasma into his plans: "The creature is positively mannish . . ."

Ah, that was one thing! But to battle as a man, to live with men as one of them, and then, to hold to that illusion, day after day?

Sedry shook himself. The Fegez were leaving again, and Nolse had dropped a hand to his shoulder. The King roused himself sufficiently to speak with his Barons before returning to his pavilion. It was hot and windless without, stifling within. Nolse poured him wine, silently set his midday meal before him, vanished briefly. Sedry drank deeply, picked at his food, pushed it aside.

"You are not hungry, my King?"

"No." Sedry gazed at his Steward, rather wistfully. "I am concerned, my friend, and afraid, I admit it. Help me?"

Nolse sat. His black, rather opaque eyes fixed on his King. "You have been preoccupied for some days now."

"It—shows?"

"Only to one who knows you very well," Nolse reassured him. Sedry sighed, leaned back in his chair. "Let me aid you, Sire, if I can."

"What would I do without thee, friend Nolse?" Sedry murmured. His Steward colored, busied himself with refilling the King's cup.

"Ah—aye, well. I am thy man, my King; thou knowest this. Thou hast given me everything I have, what little I can give to aid thee is all I have in return, and it is thine. What trouble hast thou?"

"Gespry," Sedry replied simply. Nolse pondered this
briefly.

"Hast not solved the matter to thy satisfaction. And yet
—what the old man told thee—?"

"Wrong, all wrong." Sedry drained his cup at a swallow
once more, held it out. "Oh, he believes it, the old mercenary.
It took little enough of the Truthing to tell that. But does that
make it truth?"

"Well—no."

"And why? Why such a charade? If the thing were true, if
Gespry were—were a eunuch, since Megan Cove, would *you*
hold it against him?"

"Not I," Nolse replied readily. "But, if I lost that of my
manhood, I might myself go to great length that other men not
know." He shrugged. "It is not the kind of thing a man would
want known of him. Any man. In that case, he might affect
shaving, where no need existed. And, if he could, he might
show beard, where none really was."

"I cannot see it," Sedry said, shaking his head. "This is
Gespry, Archbishop of Rhames—"

"All the more reason, knowing how many men follow him,
how men feel about him," Nolse began. He fell silent as the
King shook his head again.

"Perhaps. But I have another reason." The King pushed his
cup across the table; Nolse drained the bottle into it and went
in search of another. Sedry gazed unhappily, blearily, into its
depths. Better, perhaps, not to drink so fast, his head was
spinning. But the fear in his stomach was loosening its grip.
Nolse slid back into the chair opposite him, chipped the King's
seal from the bottle, poured. "A reason which fits all pieces of
the puzzle, leaving none aside." He drank. Nolse waited patiently. "If Gespry—were *not* Gespry—"

"Why?"

"If Gespry died after Megen Cove."

Nolse considered this. "Possible. Likely, even. A man hurt
so badly could die, and who would hear of it, if the priests did
not allow word out? Not like a town or a holding, where
people talk and move about freely." He considered it further.
"Gespry has been good for Rhames, for the King and for the
Church there. If he died, there would be loss of revenues, loss
of a certain prestige, and Rhames would lose, also, a certain
bargaining piece in trade, not having Gespry anymore to keep

its borders tame, or to lend to those who need aid in taming their own.''

"As I saw it.'' Sedry filled his cup again, pressed the bottle on his Steward.

"But—no.'' Nolse, cup halfway to his mouth, paused, shook his head. "Who replaced him, if he is dead?''

"Had you seen him before?'' Sedry demanded.

"No—but the Beldenians had, most all of them. Or—Grolpet and his brother might be in on the thing—''

"Unless the man bore some resemblance to the real Gespry. He has changed a deal, they all tell you that, you know.''

"Well.'' Nolse drank. He was silent for some time, then, eyes fixed on his hands, mind turning possibilities. Sedry emptied his cup, was half through another draught before his Steward spoke again. "He is a type, I suppose. Hair can be colored, women do. My sister, the red-haired one, Alixes, was not red-haired a year ago.''

"Dark hair could be made white, then?''

Nolse shrugged. "I imagine. The women who serve your Lady Queen would know that better than I. But beyond the hair, what has Gespry? A certain height, a certain breadth, and they say he was not so thin before.''

"They say.''

"Dark eyes, a man might find certain spells to alter that, but it might be unnecessary. A certain kind of face, bones, mouth. Hands. Things that do not readily change for illness or injury. His style of fighting—''

"Which could be taught,'' Sedry interrupted.

"Of course. What we have, then,'' Nolse smiled faintly, "is a man who could, and not with great difficulty, be matched by another. He is not overly tall, has not one blue and one green eye, is not missing a limb or an ear—and so, perhaps, he could be not Gespry. But—if not Gespry, then who?''

Sedry licked dry lips. He felt, suddenly, defensively, foolish. "If—say, perhaps, a woman—''

Nolse eyed him warily. "Impossible, flatly impossible! Out of the question, Sire! You have seen Gespry fight—Elorra's thumbnail, hast fought with him! I have seen him myself! No woman could hold to such a disguise! By the Two, no woman could wield a sword like that!''

"And you come from the Marches,'' Sedry laughed. "Even I have heard how the Chatelaine of Aldion drove the Fegez from the castle while her Lord was absent: Not from the rear, no; clad in mail and wielding a sword.''

"I know all that, Nalleyta was an exception, Sire. Women do not wield sword and bow like that!''

Sedry laughed wildly. ''She was an exception, was she? And the Bastard, my friend?'' He laughed again. The winecup flew from his hand, rolled across the table, its contents spilling across the rugs. Neither man noticed. ''At fifteen, she could wield a bow better than I can yet. At seventeen unarmored and barefoot, she nearly killed Hyrcan!''

"Sire, use sense,'' Nolse urged quietly. He ran a hand through his hair. ''She had luck on her side, that was all. Hyrcan was such a wild man that night, your old nurse Panderic could have killed him!''

"No.'' Sedry clawed his cup upright. ''Bal told me of it later. He was good even then. Better than I was, better than you.'' Nolse shrugged. He had never cared much for sword and took no affront at being reminded of his lack of skill. ''Baldyron said,'' Sedry went on pointedly, ''she was skilled. Very much so. She had, at that time, not two years' lessoning. Hyrcan had eleven. I agree,'' he went on, holding up a hand for silence as Nolse strove to speak, ''I agree that Hyrcan's state of mind worked to her favor, but she still held him off. Could you have done as well?''

Nolse shrugged. ''Know'st I could not.''

"Who,'' Sedry continued, ''recently, not only held off Hyrcan in another of his murderous furies but gave better than he got?'' Silence. ''Gespry.''

Nolse watched as the King poured himself another full cup. ''That does not make it,'' he said stubbornly, ''that Rhames and the Bastard are the same person. Sire, he has been here for—what, three months? To continue a mask of that nature for so long? No woman could do it!'' Sedry eyed him flatly, as stubbornly, across the table. Nolse sighed. ''All right then. Why not ask him, if it is such a bothersome matter?''

Sedry laughed. He swayed, put both hands down flat on the table to steady himself. '' 'Pardon me,' '' he lisped, '' 'have we not met before? You are King Alster's Bastard!' ''

Nolse shook his head impatiently. ''Dost not understand—''

"No. I understand you. I think. But how does a man go about asking such a question? Particularly,'' he went on moodily, "after today. I walked to his tent and there he was, sitting in the sun, soap lather covering the lower half of his face and the fair Fialla drawing a totally needless razor across his cheeks! I—what could I say?"

Nolse considered this. There was a long silence, broken only by an occasional call, the occasional clink of harness beyond the pavilion. His eyes narrowed then, his head tipped to one side. Sedry became aware he was holding his breath, let it out with a quiet sigh. He knew that look; Nolse had worked out a plan. Nolse would help him. "No, my Lord. There is but the one way to do it. You must," the secretive smile widened, "ask Gespry."

Sedry scowled at him, but the Steward, caught up in his thought, was unaware of this. His eyes narrowed even more. "If," he went on dreamily, "thou had'st a thing in thy keeping, a thing Gespry wanted, a thing for which he would answer any question, do any manner of thing. A thing—a person, perhaps—dear to him."

"Alayya, Elorra, the Lady Fialla," Excitement welled up, catching the breath in Sedry's throat. A smile twisted his lips, spreading to his pale eyes. "If—if I had *her* in my keeping, then Gespry would *have* to tell me who he truly is, or what he is—to regain her. Would he not?"

"And if he is, truly, Gespry, then she is dear to him."

"Or if he is not Gespry, she is still dear to the real Gespry, if he lives."

"She is beloved by the armsmen who follow Gespry in any case."

Sedry laughed, his voice cracking like a boy's. "He must tell us, he must!"

"Of course. It is a delicate puzzle, Sire. But not beyond our means to solve. With caution—if, mind, it is Gespry—there will be no false step to anger him, and if not, none to anger his allies. Then again," the Steward continued slowly, "if thou dost truly think Gespry is the Bastard Elfrid—"

"No." Sedry gripped his cup with both white-knuckled hands as the color drained from his face.

Nolse tried to smile reassuringly but managed only to look uncertain. Why was Sedry so plainly terrified? If *that* was what the Reader's fortune-telling did to a man, he wanted no part of it! "Sire, if thou think'st—"

"I—it cannot be, no, it cannot! I cannot think it straight,

Nolse, but it is not that! She is dead! Father is dead, she *must* be! By the Two,'' Sedry went on, his voice a thick, scarcely intelligible whisper, ''I hated her always, I hated her enough she should be dead!'' To this, Nolse found no answer. Sedry glanced up, blurred eyes briefly crossing his Steward's, before he collapsed across the table. The cup slipped from his hands a last time: The remaining drops of liquid pooled around his fingers.

34

ANOTHER DAY, A second. Elfrid was up and about again, apparently little the worse for her injuries, her brush with drugged death. With the Fegez returned to their camps and herds, she rode freely about the camps, the Archbishop's distinctive blue and yellow cape, the white hair pulling the men to her.

But there had been a change: Elfrid now sat as much in command of the physical being as did the personality she and the real Gespry of Rhames had fashioned for her. *The Two grant my part in this soon over*. It had become a litany, of recent. And surely, Rolend would soon gain control of Arolet, Sedry would return there unsuspecting—*nothing further can go wrong!*

So much nearly had gone wrong, had been saved by merest chance. *I could have died*. Fresgkel had saved her: from Sedry, from herself, from the barghest poison. *I hadn't realized how much I cared for living, until nightshade nearly took it from me*.

More and more often she pulled her gaze impatiently away from the West. *He* rode there. Unless—no, she dared think no such things. Rolend surely would take his service. And he was no fledgling boy of an armsman, to take foolish chances and die of them. But to not know what passed—*that* ate at her.

Sedry was impatient to return to Arolet: The most recent messages were reassuring, but so much could go wrong, and he had been gone far too long. But this matter of Rhames—

no, he could not leave with the riddle unsolved. More, he feared, might depend on it than the satisfaction of his curiosity.

Because Hyrcan had *not* lied to him. How he could have thought it of Hyrcan—but a man had strange thoughts sometimes, particularly when he was frightened. And he'd been frightened, and with cause. The Reader had told him things that would have frightened anyone!

But the Tarots Reader had not lied to him, either. She would not risk losing her Gift that way. She might, of course, have selected certain true things to tell him, withholding others —still wasn't that also a lie?

Wrong, all of it, and nothing made any sense anymore! Out of his uncertainty, he clung to one thing, whether it made sense or not: The kinsman he had to fear was a woman. That Elfrid was involved deeply in a plot to deprive him of Darion —oh, yes, he could believe that, did believe it. She'd sworn vengeance, she'd would live to see it accomplished, she'd that kind of spite in her.

That she was Gespry himself, though—impossible! He had ridden, fought, drank with the man! Whatever he sensed about Gespry—no, by all that was Holy, it could *not* be that! And—even if it were true, he assured himself, he would know *her*, man's guise or no!

The camps were shrinking, slowly, as the Marchers returned to their holdings and the mercenaries, in small companies, set out towards Carlsport and the ships that would take them back to Belden. Elfrid remained, having Gespry's business to conclude with Sevric. She rode frequently with the Baron of Eavon, who had kept his personal armed guard in the camp as protection for the King and the Archbishop's party.

Day followed slow, hot day. He must do something! Sedry lay awake nights, thoughts spinning wildly through his aching head. Something, but what? Any day, now, Gespry would leave, and that would be the last of it: Sedry had extended an invitation to the Archbishop to return to Arolet with him, an invitation which had been smilingly refused. *Then he will be gone. I must be wrong to see plots in the man*, he told himself. But unbidden, another thought answered: *Aye, or what he plots, what is plotted, will be done in a short time*! He must discover Gespry's secret, and that soon. But he and Nolse could, as yet, devise no plan which would allow them to take the Archbishop's mistress without danger to themselves, nor could they think of another course.

In the end, all their planning proved unnecessary: Fialla fell as neatly into the King's hands as though she herself had devised it.

It was late on an airless afternoon, nearly time for evening meal. Sedry, tired of the fruitless circle his thoughts pursued, sent Nolse for a bottle, moodily watched him unstopper it and swallow the first mouthful. He filled his own cup only then, drained it swiftly, refilled it, and settled into a morose study of the table.

A gentle, apologetic cough roused him. Fialla stood framed in the open flap, the rays of the late afternoon glancing blue on smooth black hair. Sedry's smile was automatic, genuinely, warmly pleased, and he leaped to his feet, grateful that he was still sober enough to stand without swaying. "Dear Lady, you do me honor! Enter, please." She inclined her head, moved out of the patch of sunlight, through shadow and into the light cast by the lanterns over the King's table. Her hair had been drawn loosely back from her face with a ribbon; a dark blue saque, cut low and nearly to the outer curve of her shoulders, was laced loosely from bosom to waist and fell in pleats down her back, spilling over the light blue underdress and a wide circle of petticoating. Sedry's heart beat faster, he smiled at her fatuously. *Alayya, Elorra, for a woman such as this one, what would a man not do?* Fialla bent her head, her skirts rustled softly as she curtsied. Sedry took her fingers, held them to his lips, momentarily lost in her scent: a compounding of roses, spice, violets.

"King Sedry, I am very sorry to intrude upon you—"

"Not so, dear Lady. You have saved an otherwise boring afternoon. And how could you bother a man?"

Fialla smiled politely, a little diffidently. She would, she thought, be most glad to leave behind the King's rather heavy-handed manner. "I have come begging, I fear. A time since, you offered me chocolate, and I refused it, like a fool." She shook her head and laughed; the hairs on the King's neck tingled, blood warmed his cheeks. Gods, did not the woman realize what she did to a man? "And now," she went on, light dismay in her voice, "there is nothing in Rhames's tent save wine, Gespry's coffee, or cold spring water from the south rim!"

"Poor my Lady," Sedry replied gravely, "you should have come to me sooner, for I would consign no one to drinking any of those things." He winked; Fialla, uncomfortable with her errand—*I should have gone to Fresgkel, surely there is one of his men who has teas, even though he himself drinks nothing but wine!*—horrified herself by giggling like a girl.

"The Two alone know how Gespry acquired such a taste," she said, finally, "for I do not." A smile, brief, embarrassed. "And so I have come to ask you for chocolate. I did not like to ask, for I did not know whether you had sufficient of it yet to share, but," another smile, "as you see, I have no choice."

"But for so fair a Lady," the King murmured against her fingers, "it would be an honor." Fialla was becoming more disconcerted by the moment.

"Sire, you'll have me face-proud do I listen to you." *Damn fool, keep silence if you can only babble!*

"Remember also," Sedry added gravely, "that I leave for Arolet shortly, and they brought more than enough for my wants. Nolse! Nolse?" The Steward appeared, suddenly and silently, from the shadowed back of the pavilion. "Nolse, I have a guest. Lady Fialla!"

Nolse smiled, a turning of the corners of his full mouth Fialla found disagreeable. *Poor man, can it be his fault he has a sly face?* she chided herself, and to compensate for the unkind thought, the smile she offered him was warmer than it otherwise might have been.

"Ah. Yes." Nolse's smile broadened briefly, vanished completely. "The Archbishop's Lady." Sedry, for some reason, found this amusing. A faint line appeared between Fialla's brows— Sedry, by the smell of his breath, had been drinking, but were they both drunk?

"The Lady has come in search of chocolate, Nolse. It seems to me I have an untouched box of it. Not here, no. In the cook tent. You had better go for it yourself; they will be hard at work on my dinner at the moment." Nolse turned on his heel and slipped from the tent. Fialla gazed after him, still vaguely troubled. The man was entirely too quiet on his feet, and his attitude—she shrugged it aside. Attributable, all, to her own intense dislike of begging, and particularly from this man whose attention barely stopped short of insult.

She brought her gaze back to the King, who was smiling at her, as he held a chair. "He will not be long, dear Lady."

She inclined her head, still out of countenance and voluble because of it. "It is of no great moment, Sire. I just thought, for tonight, since it was so cold last night. Wine, particularly that we have left, is not sufficient to warm me."

"The chocolate is an excellent drink for a cold night. How does the Archbishop, I have not seen him today?"

Fialla waved a hand vaguely in the direction of the River. "He and the men are off with Sevric, there is a new contract already. Against the pirates, south of Belden."

Sedry shook his head gravely, "The Archbishop will find that taxing, will he not?" He poured her wine, pressing the cup towards her so that she felt to refuse would be an insult. "He does not look strong, these past days—your pardon, it is not my place to say, of course." He refilled his own cup, raised it in a salute, smiled as she raised hers in reply and drank.

Nolse, he knew, was outside, setting the King's personal guard and his own men in a tight watch about the pavilion, giving them the tale that would keep them in place, any who wished to pass beyond their circle. *And she suspects nothing —nothing!* Somehow, he kept that from his face as she took a very small sip of her wine, pushed it aside.

"Gespry will not fight with them this time. He was gone from his monastery overlong for a man still recovering from his last battle."

"Megen Cove," Sedry agreed gravely enough; a manic corner of his mind gleefully followed Nolse as he placed carefully picked men about the pavilion. He could almost feel the pulsing of his blood in the tremor of his hands, carefully moved them beneath the edge of the table.

By the Two, this was a hunt indeed! As stimulating as any of his various women had been. *I know how this will end, I alone, not even Nolse suspects what I intend. Look at her, she is tense, she sits on the edge of her chair and any moment now will make excuse to me. And yet, she does not actually suspect!*

"He must," Sedry went on, "have been badly hurt indeed. That was over three years ago." Without appearing to do so, he watched her intently over the rim of his cup, through partly closed eyes.

"He was, though he is nearly well, in truth. But he has been overlong from his monastery, and though he handles much by

messengers, he cannot continue to do so. He has a duty in
Rhames, and Gespry is not one to shirk his duties." *What is
wrong with me? I am as high-strung as a hunting-bird! What
do I fear, for it is fear indeed that makes me talk so much?*

Sedry looked up as Nolse let the flap close behind him, set a
small, plain box in front of the Archbishop's mistress, bowed
gravely when she met his eyes. Fialla turned away; Nolse
nodded once. Sedry smiled as Fialla took the box in both
hands, waited for the King's Steward to see to her chair.
"Well—I must not take more of your time, King Sedry." Suddenly uncomfortably aware of the closeness between herself
and the King's man, she stepped aside. She could smell stale
wine on his rather uneven breath. Sedry leaped to his feet, his
face dismayed, though something else vied with dismay, something she did not care to try and identify.

"Surely you—you need not leave at once, Lady? Come, ah
—come, sit again, have wine with me, you scarcely touched
what I gave you—"

"By your leave, Sire." She inclined her head; another frown
touched her brow. "There is much packing to be seen to
before we leave. We do not carry Gespry's pavilion ourselves,
of course, but I must have it readied for Sevric's men to return
to Belden, and Gespry has a shirt—." She stammered to a
silence, the words fading from a determined brightness, to a
whisper, to nothing. She recognized the look on Sedry's face
now. It was that of a small boy who has done something forbidden and gotten away with it. She clutched the box to her
breast and with a curtsy started towards the clean outside
world.

Nolse was no longer at her side, but as she neared the entrance she slowed. The King's Steward stood before the flap,
his face unreadable in the shadows. He made no effort to
move aside, to hold the flap for her. She swallowed.

"Sir. You block my way." Softly spoken, levelly—to all appearances unafraid, but her heart lurched painfully, pattered
rapidly against her ribs.

"I do." A presence at her back: Sedry stood there, and she
was caught between them.

"Surely," Sedry murmured, repeating himself with deceptive, mocking, mildness, "surely you need not leave at once?
Lady?" His hand clasped her shoulder: The palm was damp,
the fingers trembled. Fialla closed her eyes, fought the breath

from her paralyzed lungs. In again. The hand tightened.

"No," she whispered. "No. I—suppose I need not." A corner of her mind railed at her: *Fool, what have you done*! as she moved, with feigned calm, to sit at the King's table again. Silence: King and Steward remained close but clearly waited for her to speak first. Only when she was certain of her control over her voice did she attempt it. "This will not do, King Sedry. I wish to cause no incident, but you dare not keep me here against my will."

Her chin came up, her voice steadied. "I do not know what you intend, or if you are merely drunken and so not responsible for your actions. But if you and your man do not allow me past that flap by a count of ten, I will raise a cry that will be heard halfway to Lertondale!"

Sedry laughed, delightedly. "Do you hear that, my Lord Steward? She will raise a cry! I like a woman with nerve, dear Lady. But who will hear you in a half-deserted camp? And how," he went on urbanely, "will any who hear—and come to your aid—get past my guard?"

"Your—guard."

"Surrounding this pavilion, with word," Sedry glanced at Nolse for confirmation, "that the Archbishop's Lady has come for a dalliance, and we would remain undisturbed. Under any circumstances." He laughed, a high, thin giggling noise.

"Gods!" Fialla whispered. At that moment, had the King touched her, she would have fainted. A terrifying lassitude gripped her muscles. Sedry eyed her, shook his head.

"You may put away your expression of distaste, fair Lady. I have no intention of touching you."

"What do you want?" As if she could believe that! Her skin was cold, only a stubborn pride kept her from shivering. *Let him see nothing*!

"Why—information. There, you see? A mere nothing!"

"Information," she echoed. "I have no information that I could give without Gespry's permission. And Gespry will—"

"Ah. Yes. Gespry." The King found this amusing. He and Nolse caught each other's eyes and laughed. The Steward moved quietly back into the shadows near the flap. "What will he do, Lady Fialla? Your Gespry?"

Fialla swallowed, forced sufficient air into her voice to keep it from quavering. "I do not know, but I do not think you will like it. This goes beyond misusing a woman of Darion. Remember that Gespry is not your subject. *Nor* am I!"

"No," Sedry replied agreeably. "But Gespry—you are right, of course. Gespry is the one to answer my questions, not you. Of course, you might tell me yourself, if you wished. Who is Gespry, or what? No comment? I feared not. In that case, you, dear Lady Fialla, will remain here, until Gespry himself comes to give me the answer I want."

Worse than she had feared! *What does he suspect? And how do I win free, she—Elfrid must not come here*!

"He is, as you have seen him," she replied coldly. "He is Gespry of Rhames. Your ally, I thought your friend! But if not," she added pointedly, "a man who has many years' practice with sword. A man with skills to equal those of your brother Hyrcan."

"Is it a threat?" Sedry crowed gleefully. "The Lady has nothing to fear, could a man doubt it? Clean conscience and no terrible secrets, eh? Well, we shall wait for Gespry, then. Go, Nolse. Send your note to the Archbishop's tent—send one of the guard, return yourself immediately." Nolse vanished; the King turned back to Fialla. "There will be time, Lady. Plenty, if you spoke truth earlier—?"

"Gespry is, as I said, away," Fialla said flatly. "I do not lie."

"In that, no." Sedry turned away, "I read that much in you. For the rest, you guard your thoughts rather closely for a woman who is merely mistress, and not part of—well, Lady Fialla, of what?" Silence. "Since you are my guest—perforce, but that will not bother you, I hope—will you finish your wine?"

"I will take no more wine of yours, men die of it and I would live a while longer, so please you!" She drew her breath with a little cry as Sedry turned on her furiously, dragging her to her feet. "You are hurting my arms," she gasped. The fingers tightened.

"What—afraid after all?" Sedry laughed low in his throat. His mouth hovered near hers. Fialla drew back, twisted her face aside. His right hand moved around her shoulder; the left moved lightly, barely touching the skin of her jaw, her shoulder, the prominent, delicate, collar bones. The breath stuck in her throat. Sedry laughed again, a low, unctuous sound. *He cannot know what he is doing to me*. Another moment and she might be ill in truth: There was a sour taste in her mouth. The King's lips grazed the hollow between collarbone and throat. "They say a man may as well be hanged for a whole loaf as a slice."

Sudden fury released her; she twisted in his grasp wrenching half-free. "Beast!" She tore her arm free, slashed wildly. Sedry ducked but not quickly enough. Blood ran down his cheek.

Nolse darted into the light; Sedry motioned him savagely back. "I will handle this, my friend!" Fialla cried out as the King's hand cracked across her cheek; his fingers gripped her chin. "Look at me. *Look at me*, I said!" Unwillingly, terrified, she met his eyes, less than a hand's distance from her own. His left eyelid was badly cut. *I hurt him, at least I did that!* It briefly gave her back lost courage. "I have no idea what you intended to accomplish, sweet Lady—"

"I? Nothing!" She laughed, knowing that would upset him the most, unable to care at this moment. There was agitated movement just behind her.

"Sire—"

"Shut up, Nolse." Sedry did not even look at him. Fialla's momentary triumph slipped away; she shook. Somehow her eyes held steady. Sedry loomed over her. "Why," he went on to himself, "should I wait for Gespry? Tell me that, my dear."

"But we—." Nolse was suddenly apprehensive.

"Aye." Sedry's voice was faint, dreamy, his eyes vague, pale grey lights. "That was to be our plan. That Gespry must give his true name and purpose to redeem this fair woman." His smile settled like ice in her stomach. "*You* will tell us," he ordered flatly. Fialla shook her head. The King struck her across the face with his open palm, again with the back of his hand. "I will know it," he went on dispassionately. There was nothing but a mild curiosity in his gaze as he brought his hand up again. With a faint cry, she flinched away from him.

Sedry stared down at her with rising awe. By the Two, he had never known such excitement! Was this how Hyrcan had felt? This—this kind of strength? There was power in seducing a woman, certainly, and particularly one unwilling—power in holding it over her, later: silence for more favors. The Gods knew he'd gotten enough excitement from it, all his grown years.

But this! Nothing, ever, had made him feel so very, trem-blingly, alive. *I hold her death in my hands, and she knows it*! Something of what was passing through his mind must have shown on his face, for Fialla paled even more and fought desperately to free herself, but there was no real strength left in her. Sedry tightened his grip; she crumpled weakly, loosely against him.

"I will hear what it is you know of Gespry." Sedry's words dropped like darts in the charged air. "Or," he corrected himself gently, "say rather, of the one who claims to be Gespry. And have care what you say to me, for we both know, you and I, that is *not* Gespry of Rhames. A name." Silence again, save for the rasp of Fialla's breath against her tight throat. Sedry's left hand released her shoulder, fastening in her hair and dragging her head back. He brought his face down to hers. "A name, Lady Fialla."

She swallowed, forcing a whisper past dry lips. "He is Gespry, Archbishop of Rhames. Ah!" Sedry struck her again, with the flat of his palm. "I have told you, whatever it is you want, I do not know and cannot give!" She brought forth a weak, ragged whisper of a laugh. "Poor frightened creature, you start at shadows and think them real! Perhaps it is your dead brother Hyrcan, the one *you* killed! Perhaps he has come to drag you to the Caverns of Night!"

"A name," Sedry said flatly. "Do not think to distract me, Lady, I am in no mood for it. A name, and that quickly! Shall I set my Fire to you? A name!"

"Sire, listen to me—." The shadow near the flap moved uncertainly.

"Stay where you are, Nolse, lest anyone somehow pass the guard, and keep silence, damn you!" Sedry retreated further into the tent, dragging her with him. At the very edge of the pool of light cast by the lanterns near to the firepit, he stopped again. "Do you think I cannot wrest what I want from you?" he hissed. "You are lying to me, I *know* it!"

"Gespry will kill you for this!" Fialla whispered.

Sedry laughed wildly. "A man dies only once, woman. I think *your* Gespry will kill no one, by that measure! A name, Lady Fialla!" He let go of her suddenly, and she tried to move, to dart aside, but he leaped forward, pinned her arms behind her back. "A name, that only. Come now," he urged with deceptive mildness.

"He is Gespry!" she choked out. Sedry exerted a light pressure against her wrists that tore at her back and shoulders. "Would you rather a lie?"

"You lie now!" Sedry snapped. "Once more, that only. Your last chance, because I have little time and no more patience." He pushed savagely upwards. She shrieked, fell to her knees. Tears flew as she shook her head. "No?" He was beside her suddenly, body pressed hard against hers, one hand gripping both wrists as the other reached for the ribbon-bound hair at the nape of her neck. "Remember that you have brought this upon yourself, then!"

Her eyes flew open at the sudden, unbearable warmth against face and shoulder. "Ah, no!" The airless little cry escaped her lips, made no sound at all. The glowing embers of the smoldering firepit entirely filled her vision. Sedry's hand, wrapped in her hair, pressed inexorably downwards. Warmth became heat, heat mingled suddenly with the scorching smell of burnt hair. Her arm jumped, her whole body arched, jolted insupportably as skin touched the hot stones. The King's hand held her face, implacably, inches above the glowing, shimmering fire. "A name. Or who will look upon you with pleasure when I have done?" he whispered.

"Hold." A voice trebled waveringly above her, was followed by the scree of a drawn sword. The pressure on hands, on neck, was gone, but for the moment she was unable to move, could only kneel where Sedry had left her, the breath jerking into her body. Somewhere far above, the voice went on.

Sedry rose to confront his Steward, his own sword, his dagger, already in his hands.

"How dare you?"

"I, my King? I dare? I? This was not the plan!"

"I changed it! She will tell us—"

"Nothing. *I* understand that much of an honorable woman. But I will not allow you to continue this way, Sire, whether or not you can buy what you desire with this coin!"

"You will not allow—by the Two, you have no say!"

"No? Then I take one." Nolse was edging, a nervous step at a time, working himself to a position between King and Archbishop's mistress. "This is no woman such as Elyessa or Calla'andra, you cannot lay hands upon her as you did them. If you harm this lady, my King, no man within Darion's borders will remain yours." He smiled then, a bitter, ironic twisting of his lips. "As for myself—for the first time in my life, I find I have a conscience."

Sedry began to laugh. "You—*you*?"

"It *is* funny, is it not? I have aided thee in every deed, every plot ever thou didst conceive, my King. When thou struck against Arolet and thy father, I aided thee in obtaining funds, in garnering men, in determining which of the Baronry to approach, which to leave unknowing. When thou planned the assassination in Arolet, was it not I who suggested the men from Carlsport? Willing to murder any man—*or* woman—for enough coin, impossible to trace to thee. Whenever thou saw a burgher's wife, a Baron's lady, and wanted her, I arranged it.

"More men can lay their deaths to me, to information brought thee by my spies, than I can count." He drew a breath, let it out slowly. The sword in his right hand ceased trembling, his voice steadied. "I have served as thy hands, thy mind, in each thing thou hast done. I even bled a caltraps into a cup of March wine, all for thy service."

"No man held thee to my service, so," Sedry broke in sharply. His own March accent, a seldom thing, was momentarily strong.

"No. And do not mistake me, I felt no remorse for anything I did for thee, I do not now. But this—this stinks to the heavens, and *I* say thou shalt not do it!"

Sedry laughed wildly. "And who is to stop me? You?"

"With my life," Nolse replied flatly. He gasped, threw up his scarcely tried blade to block the King's slashing backhand to his body.

Get up—get up, weak fool! Fialla railed, cursed at herself, but fright and pain left her weak, dizzy. With a terrible effort, she pressed up on half-numbed arms, away from the firepit, and fell back onto the carpets. The sound of fighting, the pavilion itself, faded.

Sedry held his temper under control; he must, he knew, or even a fool such as this one could have him. Only such as Hyrcan fought on anger. He laughed as Nolse, clearly terrified, backed away warily, sword gripped awkwardly in his right hand. The table was between them. "You should have kept still, Nolse." Sedry feinted, lunged across the table. A chair tottered, fell. Nolse cried out as the King's point bit deeply into his shoulder. "You should have remained where you

were." Sedry feinted again, lunged. Nolse drew back; blood
rose in a thin line across his cheek, dripped to his shirt.
"Fool," Sedry hissed. "Fool and traitor!"

Nolse upended the table between them, fell back hastily as
the King leaped across it. There was a harsh clash of blades,
sudden silence. A dreadful, hoarse cry. Fialla dragged herself
onto shaking arms, eyes staring wildly into the darkness between her and the flap. Nolse staggered a step, another;
swayed between the lanterns. His sword fell from nerveless
fingers. He pawed for it, clutched at the last standing chair.
Both went over.

Sedry stalked around the table, sheathed his blades. Blood
dribbled onto his fawn-colored breeches. He ignored his fallen
Steward. A step, another. His boot toes rested against the spill
of her robes. His breath came harshly. "We have unfinished
business, Lady." Movement at the flap drew her attention
away from him.

"Darion's King! What would you discuss with me?"

Fialla cried out weakly, Sedry whirled. Her hair reddened
by sunset glowing sullenly through the now open flap, Elfrid
leaned upon her drawn sword.

35

"WHAT—WERE YOU unable to decide, Sedry?" Elfrid gave the King a flash of teeth, a tight grin that did nothing to erase the cold fury from her eyes. "There was a note in my pavilion, offering an exchange of Fialla for a single name from me—but your armsmen were so very reluctant to allow me entry just now." Silence. Sharply: "Fialla! Fialla??"

"I am here." She forced words past a dry throat, chattering teeth. Elfrid darted a glance in the direction from which the voice came.

"I cannot see you, are you—are you injured?"

"No." She could manage nothing else.

Elfrid's eyes went back to the King. "I hope not, sweet Lady, I do hope not."

"How did you get past the guard?" Sedry demanded. The other laughed grimly.

"Oh, that. They found another matter to engross them, how best to avoid argument with Fresgkel's men. What, surprised? You didn't, surely, think I would come *here* alone?" A taut silence, which Elfrid again broke. "I feel compelled to point out to you, that is my woman you have been handling, and none too nicely, I would say."

Sedry began to laugh, a faint, helpless, airy giggle that edged his speech: "Your woman? *Your* woman?" And then the hysteria was gone, in its place a fury that made the dagger in his right hand shimmer under the lanterns. "You lie!"

Elfrid smiled coldly. "Truthing? Against me? When has it yet served you?"

"You are not Gespry!" Sedry shouted. And you will tell me who you—no, do not dare to move, I am still between you and her!" His heel grazed Fialla's foot; she drew it back sharply, huddled away from him. "You will tell me why she daily shaves a chin as needy of it as her own!"

"Why, King Sedry," Elfrid replied gently. "You are trembling. What do you fear? Me? I am your ally, do you not recall? You are unwell, perhaps—"

"Do not play with me!" Aura flared around Sedry's shoulders. "Give me the truth, or I will set my Fire to her!"

The swordswoman moved forward, stopped abruptly as Sedry lunged towards the huddled woman at his feet. "Your fire isn't worth much, King Sedry and we both know it. But if you insist upon the truth—you will not like it, I fear.

"Yours was not the only message to reach Rhames from Darion, asking my aid—did you know that? No, of course not."

"Message—." Sedry's brow puckered. "Rolend," he breathed. Elfrid grinned, without humor.

"Prince Rolend," she amended gently. "I took counsel with my armsmen, with the Reader. After some time, we decided I must come to the Prince's aid, and so to Darion's. But I could not just ride into the land in open challenge. Another way was therefore found."

"No."

"Rolend is free of Orkry," she continued. Sedry shook his head, disbelieving, unwilling to believe. "You will tell me you know better." Another flash of teeth. "Shall I tell you, word by word, the last message you received from your brother's warder, the note written by your sister?"

"No."

"All truth, you know it for truth." Elfrid gazed, with apparent concentration, on her fingers. "By now, Prince Rolend has taken Arolet, and has persuaded the Witan and the Councils to his side. The Church is already his. You are no longer King."

"Lies! All lies!" Sedry shouted.

"No. Whyfor would I lie? Your men, those who followed you here, those guarding your pavilion, have been restrained by Eavon and Marchham. You have one choice at this moment: Lay aside your weapons, freely abjure the crown."

"I—abjure?" Sedry began to laugh. "To *you*? Or to old

Eavon, he would like that, would he not?'' The laughter was, abruptly, gone. ''You lie. Gespry of Rhames has never interfered with civil matters. Never.''

Elfrid shrugged. ''Until now. Everything has a first time.''

''No.'' The King glanced down at Fialla who lay still at his heels. ''But—say that I believed you, say that Rolend has somehow escaped Orkry, has somehow wrested Arolet from me. Even,'' he drew a deep breath, expelled it harshly, ''even that he holds Darion as a gift from *my* Witan, *my* Baron's Council. That can be remedied. And will be, now that I am forewarned.''

''Think so, if you wish.''

''I would be a fool to give myself tamely into the Marchers' hands. I care for life more than that!''

''You know your brother. Prince Rolend does not want harm to come to you.''

Sedry laughed, dryly. ''And you? There is another thought in *your* voice—I did not harm her, not in the way you think!''

''I think nothing—''

''But she is not—the reason—,'' Sedry went on, haltingly. Painful to push the Truthing as hard as he must; draining also. But, Gods, he needed it! ''No, she is not why you want my death—and you want it, I see it in your eyes—''

''Perhaps.''

''Perhaps,'' Sedry mocked harshly. ''No, there is a thing wrong here, wrong from the first. But I chose to see what you wished men to see, and put aside what I *knew*!''

''More fool you, then,'' the false Gespry gave him another humorless flash of teeth.

''Fool to trust, indeed. *You* are the one who seeks my death.''

''No. Prince—King Rolend has decreed otherwise, I am bound by that.''

''*Who are you?*'' Sedry had gone very pale in the last few moments; the one he had known for so many long weeks as Archbishop no longer held his mental pressure at bay. Almost as though *daring* him to see—!

Elfrid laughed, took another step into the light. When she spoke, her voice was different: inflectionless, the Ordinate unaccented. ''Why—you are afraid! Odd, to see fear in *your* eyes.''

''Who—?'' The King retreated a step, nearly fell as his heel caught on the silken skirt sprawled across the carpets.

"I was never afraid of you, Sedry. Never. Not when you plotted my death with your lovely sisters—*our* lovely sisters, aren't they—I knew of that, are you surprised? I was not afraid when I stood between you and Father, and saw his death in your eyes."

"No." Sedry retreated another step, shaking his head frantically.

"Vengeful—yes, I was that. I swore your dealt, Sedry. Then, and every step of the way to Carlsport."

"No! It cannot—you are not—!"

"No?" Aura limned the slender figure, the drawn sword. "Well, then, perhaps I am not—not what, Sedry?"

Sedry's face was dead, slackly white. "Bastard." His lips formed the word, no sound came. The other bowed deeply, mockingly; her sword was at the ready when she straightened.

"Eflrid," she corrected gently, "Brother."

"You thought to fool *me*?"

"I did so. You and all others here." Sedry grew a deep breath and his eyes went hard with purpose. Elfrid laughed. "What, would you call for help? Go ahead, Brother, call all you want. Well? Of course, I doubt you will get what you hope for, if you do. I told you—your men no longer hold the parameters of this pavilion, Eavon and Cretony's men do, and they are sworn to me."

"To—"

"More precisely, to Elfrid, Alster's daughter, and through me to King Rolend. They know, you see." Sedry's shoulders sagged. "Though none else will—no," she added warningly, "I would not bother, really. You think somehow to extract yourself from this moment by crying out for all men to hear that Gespry, Archbishop of Rhames, is really old Aster's bastard daughter, returned from exile to wreak vengeance upon Darion's rightful King?" Silence. "You had better leave tactics to others, Sedry, you have no head for them."

"My men will not stand for—"

"Your men willl not believe you," Elfrid interrupted him coldly. "What? That a *woman* wears Gespry's mail and fights at the head of the mercenary force? That a woman hid her sex under Rhames's colors? No, Sedry. My armsmen, my Lady, my Reader all deny this crazed thought of yours. No one could possibly believe you, they would think the pressures of this past year, your misdeeds, have driven you mad. Mad—like your father.''

"They will believe me," Sedry shouted, color flooding his face, "when I display your dead, naked body!" A white-knuckled hand clenched his sword, he sprang to the attack.

Elfrid laughed, held her ground. One hand swept the fallen table aside. "I hoped for this, oh, Gods I did! Try, Brother, try your blade against me! I will tear your heart out and laugh as you die!"

"Elfrid, no!" Neither heard the faint whisper. Fialla fell back to the carpets as Sedry threw himself onto his opponent.

She could not have been unconscious long, the two were still fighting beneath the silver lanterns. Moments later, they vanished into the dusk. Beyond the gaily colored canvas, she could hear men calling out, shouting in Ordinate and in the heavily archaic Marcher accents; running feet.

She dragged herself a few more feet from the firepit, stopping only when she could no longer feel its warmth. A moan escaped her lips as she put weight on her arm: It throbbed wildly, the hand ached, twitched. She set her teeth, turned her head: a hole the size of a silver pence in the velvet saque, the skin under it blistered and weeping. Not as bad as she would have thought, the way it hurt. She balanced cautiously on the other arm, pushed herself to a sitting position, swayed slightly as she touched her hair. Harsh ends pricked her fingers where it had burned, but she had not lost much. *Vanity. A woman who fears more for her curls than her hide cannot be badly hurt!*

That brought a thin smile to her face, but she still trembled too much to gain her feet. And she dared not wait here, Sedry must not die! And Elfrid—Gespry—she rolled to her hands and knees, dragged the voluminous skirts from under her legs, and began to crawl towards the flap.

She slowed as she passed Nolse; he was dead, huddled on his side, eyes staring beyond, through her. Blood soaked the rare, cream-colored carpet beneath his body, erasing the delicate pink tracery of flower and vine. She shuddered, moved away from him as quickly as she could.

She made it no further than the end of the table. The flap loomed four paces away; it might have been four leagues. *Rest. Just for a moment.* She could hear the men outside, the clash of swords. *I can stop it, I will stop it, if I get so far. But* —she tried to force her breathing to normal.

It caught, raggedly, in her throat: A tall man, heavily cloaked and hooded, was inside, outlined by torchlight. He hesitated, the flap dragged across his shoulder. A faint cry forced itself free, one hand came shaking upwards, her last and only defense as he took a step and the flap dropped behind him.

"Fialla?"

"Gespry?" she whispered. "My Gespry?" With one swift motion, he swept aside his hood, knelt at her side: Lantern and firelight fell upon thick white hair as the true Archbishop of Rhames gathered his mistress to him.

36

"THERE, MY SWEET. Myself, in truth, dearest Fialla."

"Gespry." She could only cling to him at first. "How did you come here?"

He smiled, rather smugly. "I told you all I improved daily, you would not believe it, would you? I felt well enough to come personally to Prince Rolend's aid, that is all. And so, I did. Why?" he asked, kissing her fingertips lightly, "are you not pleased to see me?" Fialla, for answer, gripped his arm and leaned against him.

It required a tremendous effort to sit up again—how much easier to stay there, safe and protected! "Gespry, Sedry knows."

"I see—"

"She—would not have fought him, she had no choice—"

"No, you need not reassure me, Fialla. I had her word. But Sedry— that is bad. When did he learn, how?"

"When, I cannot say. A while since." She shrugged, wincing as pain coursed through her shoulder and settled in her stomach. "He has been a madman this past month, fearing everyone. The Reader did her work too well. But that he believed Gespry was not Gespry—we had no idea, or I would never have come here." She swallowed. "He tried to learn, from me." Gespry's pleasant face was, briefly, murderous. His lips brushed her forehead.

"He hurt you. How badly, my sweet? No—no, I see that, it is painful, isn't it? I know it is."

"Sedry—"

"Roland is here, I came with him. Sedry is finished." He pulled the concealing hood over his face; Fialla wrapped her arms around his neck as he picked her up lightly, started outside. He set his shoulder against the flap, bent to kiss her, to murmur against her ear: "We dare leave nothing to chance. Remember who is Gespry here." Worried eyes met hers. "Can you, my own?"

"Of course. And must, I know that." She fell back against his shoulder as Gespry, now merely another of perhaps twenty anonymous monks, strode towards the armsmen who clustered several deep in a rough half-circle. Men parted before them, stared after them, shocked into silence. So that was it— Sedry, in despite of reason or sense, had given in to his desire for his ally's lady, and when rebuffed, had resorted to force. Why else would the Archbishop fight him so furiously?

Fialla, eyes tightly closed, lips set against the pain that jarred through her arm with each step, did not see the change which came over Sedry's few remaining followers as the monk carried her through the crowd, stood her gently on her feet, held her upright as she swayed.

Fingers gripped hers, a clear warning. She blinked. Sedry there, bleeding from a long cut on his face, another on his forearm. Facing him: "Gespry," she whispered. The fingers tightened reassuringly, were withdrawn. The one she must see as Gespry stood a length from her, blades still at the ready. The shirt was torn at the shoulder, blood trailed down the sleeve onto the long fingers.

Beyond the two, still mounted, sat a young man, his hair the pale gold Gespry's had once been, a darker gold moustache hiding his upper lip. A thin silver band confined his hair; a fur-lined cloak of green and gold—the same colors as the standard at his shoulder—flared in the evening breeze. "Roland," she whispered. "King Roland."

Roland was speaking, she realized then; had been speaking for some time, urging some course of action to Sedry who, to all appearances, might have been deaf, for his eyes, his whole attention, were fixed on his sword opponent.

"I am King of Darion," Roland said quietly. "The Witan has confirmed it, the Baron's Council has ratified it. The Church is mine." Silence. Men eyed each other uneasily. What was wrong with Sedry? "You did the land great harm, brother. Between you, you and Hyrcan tried to make her a charnel."

"You are King." Sedry had, after all, listened. His eyes still flatly held his opponent's. "And I? What of Sedry, once Darion's ruler? Answer me that, Brother!"

Rolend shifted uneasily. "The choice is yours, Brother. I do not wish to be unjust, but I cannot allow you freedom of the land. You may take the road to Carlsport and so to Embersy, with full escort. Morelis is willing to give you shelter. Or you may have residence at Kellich—perhaps Orkry. With what freedoms of movement I dare allow you—." He stopped; Sedry was laughing.

"You would not be unjust," he mocked. The laughter vanished; he threw aside his sword, took three swift steps forward. Elfrid held her ground, sword dangling loosely, almost forgotten, from blood-stained fingers. "You played with me," he whispered. "You brought me to this! All of it—*your* planning!" He brought up one hand, threateningly. A bluish spark faintly colored his fingers, but the Fire was long gone from him.

"No. *I* would have planned differently." The two might have been alone.

"Would you?" Sedry laughed again. "And now you think—you think I will go with this—this boy? A prisoner, a pet?"

"That was his choice, never mine." Elfrid's voice was pitched so low, the nearest of the armsmen could not hear them. "I would have cut you apart one screaming finger's worth at a time, and that would still have been better than you deserved. You brought all of it upon yourself, Sedry. All of it. And what you now are—that is a matter for Rolend, and for the Witan to decide."

"No." Sedry's eyes darted across the silent crowd, assessing the still faces. "No. There is another choice." He spun on one heel, pale eyes catching Rolend's as the young King slid to the ground. "I will not live, Brother, as a butt for all *thy* Witan would blame upon me. Nor by *her* mercy." Rolend moved towards him warily; Sedry backed away. "No. I am yet my own man," he whispered, "and the choice is *mine*!" He spun away, clutched the dagger two-handed. Before anyone could stop him, he buried it to the hilts in his throat. Rolend's arms were about him as he fell.

"Gespry!" With a wild cry, Fialla threw herself forward, past Rolend, who lowered his brother to the ground, knelt over him. Elfrid started, tore her stunned gaze from the two men; sword and dagger fell from nerveless fingers as she caught her, gathered her close. "Tell me you are not hurt, my Gespry, tell me he did not hurt you!" She was weeping, shaking, unable to stop. Elfrid stroked the glossy hair, her shoulder, kissed her brow.

"Not hurt at all, Fialla. But you! Ah, no—what did he do to you?" Fingers trembled across the scorched sleeve, snatched away as she cried out. Fialla shook her head, but it was several moments before she could speak again.

"I—when I refused him," she choked out finally, "I refused him, and he—he hit me, hit me. He—swore to set—my face against the fire—." Unlike Elfrid's, her voice carried across the clearing. There was a murmur of angry, shocked speech among those surrounding them.

"He cannot hurt you now, nor ever again. He is dead, Fialla, and by his own hand." Oblivious to the crowd, she bent to hold Fialla close again. The Archbishop's mistress closed her eyes, leaned into her with a grateful, shuddering sigh.

Elfrid gazed blankly over the small, dark head. The odor of burnt hair assaulted her nostrils. *I should have killed him.*

And yet, she had not, though she could have, more than once while they were fighting. *I would have been another Sedry, another Hyrcan, was that why? Or that Father, even after everything, would never have wanted it? Or was it the knowledge that death would hurt Sedry less than exile? Or was I simply, at the last, unwilling to kill again? Did Gespry know what I meant to do? And that, when the moment came, I could not?* She closed her eyes, sighed wearily.

Gespry. I am Gespry, Archbishop of Rhames, and this is my Lady, the Lady Fialla. How often these past months had she told herself that? How much longer must she continue to do so? And—what was left, after that? Sedry dead. Hyrcan dead. Alster dead, long since. Seven years dead, and only now avenged. *The past eight years, each moment of them, has pressed itself to this hour. Now that Sedry is dead, why is it I can only feel a relief that my hand did not hold the blade?*

She was tired, suddenly. So terribly tired.

Rolend pushed slowly to his feet, closed the distance between them. The pale grey eyes that beyond doubt marked him for Alster's were blurred with tears; he swallowed, hard, as they coursed silently down his face. "You are Gespry, Rhames's Archbishop, are you not? I am Rolend."

Elfrid inclined her head. Her arms were still wrapped protectively around Fialla. "I am Gespry. You come unexpectedly, Sire, but not unwelcome. My Lady," she continued. "The Lady Fialla."

Fialla opened her eyes with effort, attempted to face Darion's new King, to give him proper courtesy. She could only cling, weakly, to her companion. "Sire," she whispered, letting her lids close again, "your pardon, I am unwell." Rolend moved a step closer, a concerned hand going to her arm, one to Elfrid's shoulder.

"She is indeed pale, your Grace, and injured also, I see that. Nor do you look well, sir. Can you reach your pavilion? I will send men with you—no? You had better get the Lady to bed, then. I know," he went on rapidly, "that you were an ally of my brother's. By all rights, any man who served Sedry should be suspect by me and mine, but I see no reason or need for distrust between us. When matters here free me, I will come to assure myself that you and the Lady are well."

A pale shadow of Gespry's warm smile lit the thin face. "Sire, my thanks. You are welcome whenever you come." Rolend dropped to one knee, bowed his head. Gespry's blessing shimmered across the smooth, golden hair. As the King stood, Elfrid inclined her head deferentially. In that moment, she whispered against Rolend's ear: "Fresgkel of Eavon, the Earl of Marchham, and any they swear to are truly yours, kinsman. My word on it." Rolend met her eyes with understanding.

Elfrid turned away. A priest, clad in the rough brown of Rhames's monastery, knelt before her. "My Father, shall we begin the prayers for this man's soul?" She nodded, realized the long hood precluded her being seen and spoke the permission as she turned away. The monks began to chant the last prayers over Sedry's body. Fialla, glancing over her shoulder as she was led into the silent crowd, saw Fresgkel kneel before his new King.

37

HER LEGS WERE beginning to shake: the Archbishop's pavilion, glowing like a beacon, receded in a teary haze. Her companion held her upright with a strong right arm but did not speak, seemed, in fact, scarcely to breathe, and walked as though stunned by events. It seemed hours, could only have been moments, before three of Eavon's men caught up to them. One of these carried her, the other two supported, half-carried Elfrid.

The noise level, the warmth, brought her eyes open as the armsman carried her past the open flap: Both fires, all the lanterns, were burning high, and what seemed dozens of people milled in the large main chamber; voices verging on hysteria topped one another. Speech died away as Fialla was deposited gently in a chair. Elfrid shook off her helpers, not unkindly, to lean against the table. Gelc and Boresin pushed through the crowd.

"I am fine. Don't worry me. But Fialla—." Her voice, a tired, flat whisper faded. "He hurt her. Gelc, go and find Zorec, he dealt with my burns three years ago, we need him." The armsman cast one frightened glance at the charred velvet saque and left the tent at a dead run.

"Gods," Fidric whispered as he knelt at her side. "Fialla, you had better lie down—"

"No." She shook her head. "*He* needs me here. The— Sedry cut him, Fid, see it's not bad."

"I'm fine," Elfrid insisted. She knelt at Fialla's other side. Sevric, two of his aides, stood in gape-mouthed silence on the other side of the table; behind them, Eavon's men, several of the Beldenian guard. *Use care, what you say*, she reminded herself. *Ears everywhere*. And, despairingly, *I cannot, I cannot, no more of it, I cannot—*. She shook herself angrily, pulled herself together. Tears trembled at the corners of the dark grey eyes. "Fialla, my dear—"

"Gespry?" Tears spilled down her face. "It hurts, beloved!" Elfrid took the tiny hands lightly between her own.

"I know. I know it does." Private speech was impossible. Zorec and Gelc pushed through the crowd moments later; close behind them were three men wearing Rolend's colors.

The old Beldenian shooed the onlookers well back. "A man needs room to work, ye distract me!" And, to Elfrid, "Ye had better move aside, my friend. She will be braver without ye. Bor, Fid—get the man into a chair, he's about to collapse!" It was true: The armsmen pulled Elfrid to her feet—she seemed incapable of so much movement, herself—and dropped her gently in her favorite chair. She sat as they left her, staring blankly at the milling, silent onlookers; with a groan, she suddenly buried her face in her hands. Gelc hesitated, moved back to her side, whispered urgently against her ear. The other two moved, at Zorec's imperious gesture, to aid the old Beldenian.

"It cannot be too bad," Fialla whispered, attempting to lighten the burden on those around her. Zorec hesitated, fabric in one hand, a slender-bladed knife in the other. "I fear more for my sleeve than my skin at the moment." The old man smiled at her, unexpectedly gentle.

"I'll cut as little as I dare of it. No," he added, peering closely at her arm, " 'tis not so bad. Damned sore, I'll warrant—your pardon, Lady Fialla—and will be for a few days." He bent over his bag, brought out the small, flat box of ointment. "Bor—." Boresin took her fingers lightly in his.

He was deft, careful. Fialla cried out only once as his fingers touched her elbow, a distance from the burn itself, and set off a reaction like lightening up and down her arm, curling her fingers in a sharp spasm. She closed her eyes and bit her lip against further outcry. He bound it loosely, set her arm in a sling so that she would not use it. She opened her eyes then, though it took effort—all she wanted, now, was to sleep—and thanked him. He waved thanks aside, moved to the table. Elfrid was a less willing patient than Fialla but finally allowed the Beldenian to wash her cuts.

Boresin materialized between them with wine. "Drink, both of you," he ordered flatly. He glanced around as they did so: Gelc, Zorec, and Zormerian were clearing most of the excess people from the pavilion. The Reader had materialized from the quiet back chamber to kneel beside Fialla's chair.

"Gespry." Fialla held out a hand. Elfrid's head came up slowly, but it was several moments before she focused on Fialla. She stood, swayed, and caught herself against the table; Fidric pulled her chair nearer Fialla's, rather roughly bestowed her in it. Elfrid spared him a tired smile that fell far short of the dark grey eyes, turned back to take Fialla's near hand in one of hers. The other touched, gently and briefly, against the Reader's white hair.

"That he hurt you—I would have killed him, Fialla."

"No. It would have been wrong."

"Perhaps. In any event," she said, wonderingly, "I didn't. I'm glad of that—I think I am. It's hard to be certain of anything just now. I think I'm glad." Elfrid gazed out of the pained tear-smudged eyes, submerging Gespry entirely. "Father loved him, for all his faults, it was that, that drove him mad, in the end. I had thought to serve Father's memory by killing Sedry—you're right, Fialla. It would have been wrong." Her eyes strayed across the bandage, harshly white against the blue velvet. "But he hurt you—*you*!"

"You could not have killed him," the Reader stated. Her voice was husky, she spoke as though her throat hurt. "It was not in you, to break your vow."

Elfrid shrugged. "For whatever reason, no." She smiled suddenly, a real smile. "You gave us quite a fright, my own. The poor Reader—I came back from Sevric's council to a darkened tent. She," the swordswoman gestured with her head, "was at the table, a crumpled paper in her hand, in such a state I could not get a sensible word from her—"

The Reader shook her head ruefully. "I was beyond sense. He shook me, more than once, before I could come to grips with the thing and tell him you had fallen into the King's trap." Accusing eyes met Fialla's. "You knew the risk, I warned you to avoid the man!"

"You *saw* this, and said nothing—." Elfrid broke in. Her voice was inflectionless, but her face was pale with sudden anger.

"I saw it," the Reader replied calmly, unmoved by her fury.

"There was no point to telling you of it, it was avoidable by more means than one. Nor was it a certainty." Her eyes held Fialla's, reproachfully. "The easiest of the ways to avoid it was for *you* to avoid him!"

"I—," Fialla started a shrug, abandoned it as her arm throbbed warningly. "I couldn't believe it, I suppose. That he would set a hand to harm me, risking the loss of such an ally as Gespry, the respect of those who served him. That anyone, let alone a King, would harm a woman so—." She swallowed tightly.

"You," Elfrid cut in pointedly, "and Fresgkel. He was capable of anything, you know that. I told you often enough, you saw him yourself. What he did—to Bal, if nothing else." Her fingers tightened on Fialla's. "Enough. I need not lecture you, we'd better to forget it. You would."

Fialla nodded. A warmth suddenly washed through her, forgotten, at least buried under pain, the events for the past hour. "Gespry," Fialla whispered. Her voice could not have carried to any of those remaining in the pavilion. "He is here. *He* is."

"He is—?" Elfrid half-rose. "He—Gespry?" Less than a whisper, a shaping of the lips. "No. In Rhames."

"Here. I swear it. Here, tonight."

"But . . ." Voices without. Several men, long shadows against the pavilion, were speaking with the guard. Fialla turned to face the flap, wincing as she jarred her arm. A long hand gripped her fingers reassuringly. Gelc jumped to his feet, muttering under his breath, "Soon send 'em off," and vanished outside. Silence. A murmur of voices. The armsman backed into sight again. Boresin followed, flattening himself against the flap. Both men looked as though they had seen a ghost. Four monks clad in the plain blue hooded traveling robe of the Rhamsean monastery stepped into the light: The tall monk led them.

The pavilion had been cleared with dispatch; only the armsmen—Zorec and his nephew now among them—remained. The Reader, exhausted, had retired to her blankets shortly thereafter. The four Rhamsean monks sat close together at the far end of the table, conversing now and again in low voices. Fialla lay back, eyes closed, against the monkishly garbed

Gespry; his arms were wrapped around her, carefully avoiding her bandaged arm. At his other side Elfrid leaned forward, elbows on her knees.

The resemblance between them was strong, unnervingly strong, if not what it had been: Gespry had gained weight over the past months, Elfrid's face wore the gaunt, pinched look of one acquainted with pain, and her dark eyes were haunted. Gespry's face was rough with beard.

"You succeeded." He added no praise, could find, at the moment and with that agonized face before him, no words for it.

Elfrid smiled, briefly and deprecatingly. "I wondered, often, whether we would. Luck was with us, more than we would have dared count upon."

"Your own skill—," Gespry began. Elfrid shook her head. The smile was gone.

"No. I—If I had known, if I had realized what it would be like, I would have never done it."

"No." Gespry dropped a kiss on his mistress's forehead. Fialla's fingers tightened on his forearm, relaxed again; she was more than half asleep. "That would not be like you. You have honor, and the strength of purpose of your father's line. You would not have gainsaid the task for its difficulty."

"I—you can't know that." Elfrid shook her head doggedly. "I scarcely know myself, even I don't know what I would do. How could I? And if I don't, how could you?" Silence. Gespry gazed at her in mild surprise. "Whatever I've been, whatever I am now, it was never myself, it was somebody, something of someone else: I was Father's favorite, his pet, his toy as Sedry called me. To Sedry, to his friends, I was the King's Bastard.

"Then Sedry took Arolet, and I was an exile, disgraced, a wanderer, guard and companion to a madman. Armsman, armswoman—And then, Gods help us, Gespry, Rhames's fighting Archbishop, beloved by all, the best fighting man and tactician in five kingdoms, wielder of the Holy Fire." She ran long hands through her hair. "I never was just Elfrid, and this *myself* you see, Gespry—I don't know her. I can't see her." She subsided back into the chair, a little embarrassed. "Sorry. I didn't mean to make such a matter of it."

"It's all right. It's over now—"

"No." She closed her eyes wearily. "Just this part of it. What I might be next . . ." Grey eyes met his again. "Sorry, I'm—I'm so tired. I'm babbling."

Tired. Exhausted, rather, near collapse. Gespry studied his companion, who had slipped further down into the chair. The blue veins were clearly visible across her eyelids, even from where he sat. She'd held to the part, longer than any of them had thought she'd have had to. For her to carry on much longer—"It's nearly over, Elfrid. Another five days, we'll be gone from Darion entirely."

"We'll—oh. Yes, of course." Elfrid stirred uneasily. Gespry eyed her with suspicion; something in her voice—what was she up to? Before he could follow it up, she sighed. "Gespry—I don't think I can keep it up any longer. I—"

"It's been hard on you, I know."

"Harder than anything else I've ever done. Not the way you thought, not the way I thought, either. I've spent too much of my life in man's clothes for that to be much difficulty. Though I'd never have done it without Fialla, or the men. The planning, the sending of men to likely death, that cost me, terribly. Though I know the loss of life always cost you, too. And I had good aid with the battle tactics, no one noticed—"

"They would not," Gespry broke in, mildly reproving. "You know enough of warfare to hold your own in such a situation, and give me no false modesty, we are both too tired for it."

That netted him another faint, tiredly amused smile. "To impersonate a man, just any, ordinary man, would have cost me no sleep. But you!—they love you," she waved an arm towards the Beldenian camp. "and with cause. Your warmth, your love for each of them—your trust and belief in the least of them! I never had any of that—love, trust—never knew or learned it. Except with Father," she added, her voice almost a whisper. "To share myself with a thousand men or more, to give of myself the way you do, that was the hardest thing I have ever had to do, Gespry."

It was Gespry's turn to be embarrassed. He shrugged it aside. "You did it well enough, however it fell out." He'd heard the men between Sedry's pavilion and this one, gazed at his exhausted companion with compassion. No mere acting on her part had produced such devotion in the commons of both

camps, any more than the family Trait had. She was too hard
on herself, but she'd always been that.

He reached, gripped her hand. "Sevric leaves on the morrow, After he is gone, we'll switch places. No," he forestalled
argument, "you must have rest, my dear cousin, a blind man
could see it, if we're to ride tomorrow night for the coast."
Again that flicker of—what?—across her pale, set face. Cold
certainly settled in his breast then: *She means not to return
with us.*

"Let me speak with this fair creature in private a moment or
so," he went on quietly. Later, when they'd all slept, he could
argue his hard-headed young cousin to sense. "And then you
had both better sleep. Fialla," he kissed her forehead again.
"I must go back to the King's camp shortly. Come and speak
with me first, beloved." He stood, bringing her up with him.
The heavy curtain to the bedchamber dropped into place.
Elfrid gazed after them, a growing determination in the set of
her mouth.

"My poor Fialla," Gespry murmured against her ear. "Of
all of us who might have been hurt—"

"No. I never thought it, either. But he—but Elfrid," she
corrected herself. Gespry smiled. "Habit," she smiled in
reply, but wanly. "It will be months before I can sort you
properly again. She—." She shook her head. "Later, I can tell
you all of it."

"Tomorrow night," Gespry promised. "Do not try now,
you are worn past bearing, and I would speak of pleasanter
things." He kissed her hair, his nose wrinkling involuntarily at
the scorched odor that clung to it. "We won through, though,
didn't we? Luck, as my young cousin said, though I suspect
some skill by you all. And the substitution was undiscovered
by any save the King." There was an urgent question in his
eyes. Fialla nodded.

"And his Steward. Both dead." She set her mouth in annoyance. Difficult to think, to remember. "No, two others."

"My new armsmen?" Gespry asked gently. "Old Zorec and
his nephew? That is no difficulty."

"No. They know nothing of it, not yet. No. I meant Fresgkel, Baron of Eavon."

"Fresgkel—oh. The Marcher, the one in charge of Sedry's

household guard when we arrived. He swore to the King before I'd a chance to start the prayers for Sedry's soul. And Elfrid swore by his loyalty." He closed his eyes, briefly. Better, far better, if no one had known of this. Unfortunate, to say the least, that any did. "And?" he prompted quietly.

"And? Oh." Fialla stirred, pressed her head against his shoulder. "Bal—Fresgkel's youngest son." She opened one eye. Gespry's face was impassive, thoughtful. He shook his head. "Baldyron, Baron of Korent?"

"Ah. Young Korent, of course." Something in his face puzzled her. Disapproval?

"He was once Sedry's man," she went on. What was wrong? "but he broke that oath a time since—a long time since," she added, "since it was he who aided her and Alster safely from Darion eight years ago."

Gespry tilted his head back and laughed. "Suddenly," he said finally, still chuckling, "the matter makes sense! She never gave me the name, indeed, she said very little of it ever. She told you that, did she?"

Fialla nodded, closed her eyes. "A while since. But, Gespry, it is all right, isn't it?" Anxiety pulled her upright. "He—Rolend didn't—I know he was Sedry's man, but after what Sedry did to him—"

"A thing you must tell me with the rest of it," Gespry said. "Since he would not speak of it himself. Save to say that he had been made exile by the King's wrath. As to your concern, my love, don't worry for the boy. There was a—a confusion, I suppose."

"But he swore fealty to Rolend—"

"No." Gespry chuckled again. "He would not. He said he had already sworn fealty to the Lady Elfrid, Princess of Darion, and that oath he would not break for any man." Fialla stared at him, wide eyed. Gespry nodded. "The new King accepted that, of course. He is actually rather pleased with Korent—"

"Korent no longer, Sedry took—"

"Oh. That." Gespry dismissed "that" airily. "The King has returned his lands to him. Baldyron refused them—he is a stubborn young man, isn't he? King Rolend has already told him, though, that his refusal is improper, possibly treasonous, and will not be taken under any circumstances." He traced the line of her jaw lightly with one finger. "Stubborn, both, though the King will win in the end, if I am any judge of men."

"I know you are, Gespry. Just as I know you can trust him with your secret. He carried Elfrid's almost from the first, he would as soon betray her as you."

"Indeed." A dry half-question.

"Truly. He loves her."

"Ah. He does?"

She shrugged, winced as her shoulder, forgotten for several minutes, announced its presence sharply. She brought a reassuring smile up from somewhere as Gespry leaned forward, distress in his dark eyes. "Of course he does. Anyone might see it, I did. The Reader saw it also. And," she added lightly, "after all, who are better matched than the Prince of Flames and the Princess?"

"No one," Gespry replied gravely, catching her chin in his fingers and kissing her upturned mouth, "save, perhaps, the Priest and the Lady of the Birds."

• PART THREE •
• ELFRID •

38

DAYLIGHT: THE AFTERNOON sun was warm enough for full summer, a light breeze taking the edge from the heat. There was a trampled rectangle of pale grass and tamped dirt where the Archbishop's pavilion had been; that had been packed before dawn and now jolted on one of the baggage carts in the Beldenian retinue towards Carlsport. On the far side of the River, no more than seventy-five men remained, Eavon's all. Old Marcham had departed not long before midday. On the near side of the water, there was only the Archbishop's party, which now included the twelve Rhamsean monks.

One of Sedry's couches sat incongruously in the short grass not far from the horse lines. A thin, wind- and sun-burned figure lay there, surrounded by, propped up on pillows. A chair from the same source held Darion's new King.

The two, though surrounded by furious activity as the remainder of the Archbishop's camp was broken, were effectively alone. Even Rolend's personal guard had been dismissed to help with the horses, with Fialla's packing, with various matters in Sedry's pavilion.

Mindful of the numbers of armsmen still present, they'd held to the fiction: Rolend dropped to one knee to receive the Archbishop's blessing; the light flared around his golden hair briefly. The King waved aside, in no uncertain terms, any attempts by the reputed Archbishop to rise and give him return honor. "No, your Grace." His voice, resonant like Sedry's if not so high, carried across the onlookers. "You are not well, I would have no part in preventing your riding tonight."

"As you choose, Sire." Elfrid smiled up at him wanly. Rolend dragged his chair forward until his knees touched the pillows, gripped her hand. She tensed in surprise, but hers tightened in reply.

"Alayya's ear, it is good to see you, kinswoman."

"And you, kinsman. You look no older than you did the last I saw you—when—." She faltered to a stop. Rolend's fingers gripped hers.

"I know. Do not think on it, Elfrid. I have repented that day more than anything else I ever did."

"Whyfor, Rolend? Do not, I beg you. Good came of it—if not for you, Father and I would have died—"

"That was not all my doing, from what I heard," Rolend broke in grimly. Elfrid shrugged.

"Oh. That. But we would not have made it so far as the road, without your intervention."

Oh. That. Rolend eyed her curiously. How oddly both of them spoke of the matter, as though embarrassed, ashamed for some reason. He dismissed it. "I—cannot think how to begin, Elfrid, to thank you for your aid—"

"It was gladly given, kinsman," she replied softly.

"Brother," he corrected her gently. A faint flush tinted her all too prominent cheekbones.

"Brother. We managed, somehow, didn't we? You are King. You will be a good one, too, I think."

"I hope to," he replied.

"As good as Father was. Better, really," she went on, her eyes focused beyond him. She spoke slowly, curiously, as though puzzling the matter out for the first time. "Better, because you are not so one-sided as he was."

"Father was a good King—"

"In some ways. In others—he had foresight, I grant him that. But he would have been much happier as a Marcher, like his friend Fresgkel. A farmer or herder, even. He had too much of the common in him to make a great King. I can see that, now."

Silence. "Were you surprised to see Gespry?" Rolend asked finally. Elfrid considered this, shook her head.

"A little, perhaps. Not really, though. I know how he fretted, not able to handle the matter himself, sending another, however willing, to take his place. And I knew that he was nearly well enough to attempt the journey, if not the fighting.''

"He was in the fore of those who took Orkry," Rolend said, grinning suddenly. His smile was all Alster's; Elfrid's heart constricted.

"How like him," she said, shaking her head.

"Though why he should have done this," Rolend went on, mostly to himself. "I sent the messages to him because he was the only hope I had, the only hope I could see for poor Darion. Though I knew he never interferes in internal matters—"

"No. He had good reasons, reasons he saw as good, anyway." Elfrid's eyes dropped to her hands. "I—"

"He told me." Rolend spared her the distress of continuing. "For love of a fool cousin, he said, who would otherwise have thrown herself at Sedry's headsman without chance of reaching Sedry first. For the honor," his eyes filled with tears, he blinked them away, "for the honor of a broken old man, kin of his—is he truly, Elfrid?"

She looked up, smiled at him. "You have seen it yourself. The resemblance. Astonishing, since the connection is so remote that records of it exist only in his family histories, nearly illegible records of ours. A son from his family, five generations ago, married the first daughter of Father's grandsire, five generations removed."

Rolend shook his head. Unnerving was more the word he'd have chosen for such a resemblance, though he could see in the harsh sunlight there were strong differences also. "It is a shame," he went on finally, "that the matter must be kept secret. His part in it—mostly yours, though. I see something of a way around that last, however, if you'll have it."

"If—." She frowned at her hands, transferred the gaze briefly to him.

"As I see it," Rolend continued as though he had not heard her, "you will return with Gespry to Rhames." She stirred, subsided again. "I, after I take residence at Arolet, will announce my intentions to find my lost sister. You would look less like Gespry," he went on, eyeing her critically, "with your hair grown out, without his clothing."

"Rolend, I—"

"Blast it, must every one of you argue with me when I seek

to reward you?'' He broke in with good-natured exasperation. ''You can return to Darion, after a year or so. I would give you lands of your own, you deserve them by blood—''

''No, Rolend!''

''Be quiet,'' he insisted, smiling widely. ''I am Darion's King, it is not manners to interrupt me, that much I already know. I *could*,'' he said, grinning slyly, ''let you have Merasma's holdings, but that she and the Earl were so helpful these past few days.'' Elfrid cast him a startled glance. ''It merely means I need continue to keep an eye on her, and make certain that she does not begin to see another main chance that would reward her better than I.'' He tipped her a grave wink. ''But to the matter of lands—besides that you deserve them by blood—you *are* aware, I hope, that your children are third in line for the Crown, until I marry?''

''My children. My—Rolend!'' Elfrid protested faintly. He went on, determinedly ignoring her interruption.

''Beyond that blood grants you holdings of your own, your aid to me and to Darion here—be quiet, I said, Sister!—grants them to you. No one,'' he added flatly, ''cares that much which side of the blankets you graced, really. I had better not hear of it, if they do.''

''Rolend.'' Her fingers tightened on his hand. ''I will keep warm the rest of my days on what you just said. But—no. No, I cannot.''

''But Gespry—''

''I cannot go with him, either. I am sorry,'' she added dryly, an urchin's grin momentarily erasing the drawn tiredness from her face, ''one does not interrupt the King. But listen to me. I cannot be seen with him, not now. We look enough alike that men would begin to wonder at it, and the riddle might be unraveled. None of us can afford that. Admit it!''

''Well—''

''You see? Of course, I could retire under a monk's hood, I suppose, darken my hair again, wait until it grew properly long, until he regains all the muscle and weight he lost three years ago. The resemblance was not so remarkable when I was his armswoman, you know. It was only there if you looked for it. Bone, mostly.

''But I cannot go to Rhames in the meantime. I dare less stay in Darion, you yourself realize that.''

"Gods, Elfrid—where will you go then?" Rolend protested. "You cannot simply disappear!"

"No. And I have not thought it out, properly. But—"

"Has Gespry heard of this?" The King eyed her suspiciously. She shook her head.

"I could not face it until I had more strength, he is harder to argue to a point than you are, Brother. But—look, you are being sought," she added softly. Her voice, a husky whisper, suddenly bore a lilt, her face was somehow different: She was, in that instant, again Gespry, Archbishop of Rhames. Rolend gazed at her in astonishment, turned as she freed her hands. Fresgkel stood a respectful several paces away; at his side, his Steward, Kanadry, a man only slightly older than himself but whose face wore a vexed, harassed expression that in a month would probably be set permanently. Rolend smote his forehead. "The Council! Seven Hells, I forgot, I was to meet with them—"

"Go, then." The Archbishop smiled warmly at him. Rolend returned the smile, but he was shaken at the change. It was difficult to remember that this was his kinswoman, his half-sister, and not the vigorous, if still convalescent, man who had freed him and helped him gain Darion's crown. "The Two willing, we shall meet at least once more, King Rolend, before we return to our separate duties." The Archbishop's voice; Elfrid's promise. He smiled, dropped to one knee before the couch again. The Blessing touched his hair, rippled warmth through him.

"The Two willing," he agreed as he stood. He turned away, moved to join his Steward, was surrounded by his personal guard; Kanadry began briefing him, swiftly and urgently, as they set out for the Darion camp.

"I came to see if thou'd'st ride with me this afternoon, but I see thou'rt not well." Elfrid came awake to find Fresgkel at her side; by the sun, she'd slept two hours at least.

"No." She maneuvered herself onto her elbows. "It was Fialla's idea, more than mine. They plan on reaching Carlsport in two days, you see, and—"

" 'They'. I see," Eavon said as she fell silent, "that thou need'st sense talked to thee. Can'st ride, then?" He glanced around, lips tightening in disapproval. "There are too many here, I would speak to thee without ears other than thine to hear.'' For reply, she stood up—she was steady again on her feet, the old Marcher noted critically, if slower than her wont —and started for the horse line. ''No, I brought one for thee.''

''Thank you, my friend. Fidric!'' The armsman brought his head up from a chest of odd goods he was repacking. ''I'm riding out with Fresgkel.''

''I won't keep him long, man,'' the Baron added.

''I'll tell Fialla—she worries,'' the armsman finished apologetically.

''I know. I'm fine, though. Enough to ride, anyway,'' Elfrid finished honestly. She turned back to Eavon, the two of them crossed the river, mounted, and rode out eastwards.

''What is this,'' the old man began fiercely when the last of the Darion tents were some distance behind, ''our new King tells me? He says thou'lt not return to Rhames!''

''Did he say why?''

''He said—''

''Can you find flaw in it?''

''Well—''

''Fresgkel.'' Elfrid reined her horse to a halt, gripped his forearm impulsively. ''What else can I do? To hide in the back corridors of Gespry's monastery for a year or so, until men no longer look at me and see him? Fearing that any do in the interval, and so find us out?''

''Thou could'st—''

''Or go with Rolend, and do the same at Arolet? I'd be found out either way. And what then for Rolend's chances of retaining the throne? Or Gespry's, of retaining his reputation?''

''And thou'd'st throw away thy life for both of them,'' Fresgkel replied resentfully. Elfrid gazed at him in surprise.

''It's not that, you know it isn't.''

''No? Where wilt thou go, then?'' Silence. Her eyes fell before his fierce glare. ''Hast not thought on it yet?'' She shook her head. ''Hast found nothing that will suit, or hast not thought?''

''I've thought, Fresgkel, I've thought of nothing—well, of little else. But—''

''Then come to Eavon. I'll keep thee safe there. And I own,'' he went on softly, ''I'd be glad to have thee there.''

"I don't know what to say to that, Fresgkel. But—"

"I look upon thee as I would a daughter," he began but caught his breath sharply, as though it hurt him. Elfrid leaned to grip his shoulders.

"Oh, Fresgkel, my poor friend. I—how can I say anything, that will not give you pain, or insult? But I cannot, word would get about—." She turned away, dropped to the ground.

"Wouldn't," he replied. He swung rather stiffly from his own saddle, gathered the reins over his shoulder. They walked slowly across the near silent, deserted valley: In the distance, red and grey meadowbirds cried out and took flight.

"And even if not—Fresgkel, I can't just *hide* for a year or two, I can't. If my life depended on it, if there were no other way, perhaps. But—"

"But?"

"But there must be. Another way. Someplace I can go."

"If not Eavon," the old man followed his own thought, "then Korent might suit thee. It's more distant, it's—"

"Surely," Elfrid replied, "it isn't yours to promise out?" A chill settled in her stomach. Was that why no one spoke his name? *Bal. My Bal. If I sent you to your death!*

Eavon scowled. For some reason, he seemed properly furious. "Well—perhaps not. Marchham, then. Cretony'd welcome thee."

"Fresgkel. If I could, I'd remain with you, and gladly. You're nearly as dear to me as Father was, you know that."

"But I cannot persuade thee, can I?" Silence. "I feared it. All right, then." He headed for a long tree, tied his mount to a low branch, dropped to the shaded ground. Elfrid joined him, leaned back gratefully against the trunk.

Tired, she was so tired that tears came all too easily these days. Reaction, she chided herself angrily, and swallowed them down. Nothing but reaction. That and the other thing that kept her from sleep the past nights, rode her waking thought: *Why don't they speak of him? Not even his own father, and why does Fresgkel look so, and why does Gespry eye me oddly when Bal's name is mentioned, why does Rolend?* What was wrong with them? And—what was wrong with her, that she could not bring herself to ask?

Eavon eyed her with a flat, frustrated anger. "Hast no sense in this world, riding off without friends at thy side. Hast not recovered properly from this fool's masquerade."

"Hardly a fool's, Fresgkel; we got away with it."

"Aye," he growled, "and it was nearly the death of thee.
Too many good lives were lost without thine added to them."
His face went bleak again; with a visible effort, he shook the
mood off. "I know thee all too well, thy mind's set and nothing I can say will change it for thee. I feared as much, but a
man tries."

"I appreciate it, Fresgkel, believe me, I do."

"Hah. Not enough, else thou'd'st listen to reason. However, I can tell thee something of the lands beyond the March,
if that would be of aid to thee. Places where Rhames has never
set foot, nor his shepherd mercenaries. Unsafe, all of them,
but what is that to thee?"

"I'm not intent on suicide, my friend. Go on, tell me."

The old Marcher hunched forward, pulled a bit of stick
from the dirt and began to draw. Elfrid watched him. "Now,
then," he began finally, "some of this thou know'st—Eavon
here, this valley here—." He made marks on the map. "Korent—so. Marchham. And—beyond them, east and north—,"
squiggly lines filled in these areas, "are Fegez lands. Thou'lt
not go there, I hope." He glared up at her with ferocity that
utterly failed to mask his concern. She shook her head gravely.
"And here, of course, Marga, but thou'lt say Marga is unsuit-
able, and so it is, by thy thinking. However, if thou'lt ride east
and a little south, so—." He drew a heavy line, just below the
edge of Fegez territory. "This way, thou'lt come, after a
number of days of forest and mountains and hills, upon a
range of astonishingly high peaks. Forest dries out less than
halfway up their flanks, they bear snow on Longest Day. I
know. Saw 'em several times—four or five—when we were
lads."

"We, Fresgkel?"

"Cretony, Alster and I. Before Alster had to take being
Crown Prince seriously. Now, there is—or was once—a road
through these peaks, though thou'd'st find it on no map I
know of. Through them, safely beyond, there's plain. Rivers.
Other lands."

"Oh." She'd never really thought much about the Eastern
Mountains. For at least fifty years, no one had crossed them,
either direction, that Darion knew.

"Chief of those lands is Gelborsedig."

"Oh!" Elfrid leaned forward, exhaustion momentarily forgotten. Gelborsedig!

Eavon nodded. "Know'st it. At least, the tales."

"Some of them." She eyed the rough-drawn dirt map with bright eyes. "We had trade with them, before Father was born. Caravans brought true silk, carved ivory, emeralds, and jade, returned with good Darion wool and—wool, anyway."

Eavon nodded again, approvingly. "They had civil troubles, wars one after another, and the Fegez raided the caravans. In the end, though, it was internal problems that stopped the trade. True silk," he mused. "And brocades. My first wife, Telborn's mother, wore cloth of silver brocade when I wed with her." He sighed, shook his head, and went back to the map. "Could I call myself my own man," he went on, blandly casual, "which I cannot, I would attempt Gelborsedig. The one who reopened trade with those folk would be rich indeed."

"Gelborsedig—"

"Not that the coin matters to thee, I know that. But, for the risk of it, the very unknown—and there, Gespry is less known than anywhere else might'st go. I would," he added sourly, "that thou would'st at least find company—no, I hear already the argument thou'lt make me," he waved a hand to silence her. "That hast no right to set others in danger—"

"Consider," Elfrid grinned at him abashedly, "it said, my friend. I would not argue with you, of all men I know, and you cannot change my mind on that point. I can," she added, "take care of myself, you know."

"I know it," he said gruffly. "Seen thee do it. Also saw thee take a barghest dart through no fault of thy own. Mind," he added fiercely, "that no such thing happens to thee again!"

"What I can do to prevent it, I shall do," she replied gravely. "I promise you, Fresgkel, I have as strong a desire to live, suddenly, as anyone you know."

"Hast thou? Mind that thou keep'st it!"

"I swear it, my friend. We'd better start back," Elfrid added, with a sigh. "I'm needed a while yet—and I need to talk the matter out with Gespry."

"Well, I wish thee joy of that." Eavon stood up, brushed dirt and leaves from his pants. They rode back to the camp in a companionable silence. As Elfrid dismounted and gave her mount's reins to him the old man leaned down to grip her shoulder. *"Promise* thou'lt see me before leaving."

"I swear it. If there is time, make a map, will you?"

"My duty," Fresgkel replied gloomily. "To keep thee from harm, as far as I can." He turned and cantered back to the Darion camp. Elfrid sighed and went in search of Fialla and Gespry. This, she knew unhappily, was going to be far from easy.

39

ELFRID REINED IN her horse, leaned over the saddle to gaze across the valley from the same cut on the south rim where she had first beheld it. It was nearly deserted: only fifteen tents on the Darion side, Eavon's surrounded by those of his armsmen. By midmorning, even those would be gone. On the near side, only the clutch of five that housed the Archbishop, his immediate household and his monks, the five Beldenians who had been left to bring the remaining baggage. These, also, would be gone long before sunset the next day, leaving the valley once more to deer, bear and the occasional Fegez hunting party.

The Archbishop's pavilion should, by now, be halfway to Carlsport, there to take ship for Belden, to wait for the next time Gespry rode with Sevric and his mercenaries. And that would not be long at all, Elfrid thought. Sevric's next contract, against the southern pirates, would likely be—like all such battles—brief and bloody. And already another contract loomed: Rolend's Steward had brought messages from Arolet, from the ambassador of the northern island kingdom of Zel Feq. The island, according to the messages, was again facing all-out war with its mainland neighbor, Belissa, a belligerent mountain land just north of Marga. The matter never varied: trade rights and rights of way through the narrow straits that divided the two countries.

Gespry, in fact, had already been approached by Sevric, and had tentatively agreed to lead the mercenary army against Belissa. Judging by the progress he'd made in the past three months, Elfrid thought, he'd take that contract with no difficulty at all. *Unlike me*, she added to herself, but without censure. It took more than semblance to make a Gespry, but no one, not even she, could be blamed for failure to measure to his length.

She turned away from the valley and set her horse to the narrow, well-worn path that continued up from the camps. As this forked she turned left and east, following a narrower trail into the trees. The packhorse Eavon had supplied her followed.

Gespry had been terribly unhappy that she was not returning to Rhames with them, though—she thought—not really surprised. And he had readily seen the sense of her reasoning. It was the armsmen—all five of them—who'd tried to argue her from her decision, and Fialla had openly wept. She'd managed a shaky laugh, though, when she'd opened the packet Elfrid had given her, referring to it, dryly, as "a thing to remember me by." Within the pale blue scarf lay the heavy bandage she'd worn to confine her breasts.

Not that it really made any visible difference, not in the sort of clothing she wore. But without it, she could breathe more easily, and she felt free.

Free. She dragged the horse to such a sudden stop the packhorse bumped into them. She drew a deep breath, let it out with a laugh that silenced the nearby birds. "I'm free." No man's armsman—no, nor armswoman, either. No longer bound by the terrible promise she'd made so many years ago over an old man's shrunken body, no longer bound to a tightrope course that hourly saw the possibility of her death. Bound by no man or woman, to nothing—held, by the Two, to no one else's notion of her. Elfrid again—Elfrid for the first time.

She let her head fall back, gazed at the darkening sky. Stars were pricking the velvety blue between the distant tops of pines. Eventually, she'd have to find a place to stop for the night; she was still too tired to cover much distance at a time, though she'd carefully concealed that from those who'd seen her off under cover of dusk. She'd not dared to remain until daybreak. Too much chance of comment among the remaining armsmen if anyone rode off at an odd tangent. And even though Fialla had steeped her hair in a horrid smelling mess that had left it near its own brown again, her size and shape could tell against her.

She patted the long, flat pouch that depended from her belt: a gift from Fresgkel, that. In one of its several inner pockets, the map he'd drawn her, his own careful work. She smiled as she urged the horse forward again. She could see him, the tip of his tongue peeking between his teeth, his forehead furrowed in concentration as he painstakingly traced out the lands and lettered the landmarks.

Poor man, he'd tried so hard. How she'd earned such unrestrained love—for herself, she knew, and wondered at it. Not because of anything she'd done, any thing or any aid she'd given—no. Just for herself, Elfrid. He'd tried once again, when he handed her the map, the fine leather case to carry it in. Realizing, finally, it was no use, he'd placed a kiss on her brow, as though he blessed his own child, and strode rapidly away before she could say anything at all.

If Bal lives—if he does, Rolend will not hold Sedry against him, surely he will not. Fresgkel will not notice I am gone, when he has his son again. A lie, she knew uncomfortably. You couldn't lie to yourself like that. There was only one reason why Fresgkel would not speak of his beloved youngest son. If, like the old Marcher, she didn't think of it, didn't speak of him—she swallowed, blinked furiously. Better that she went east. There was precious little in Darion for her at the moment.

She rode slowly for an hour, finally reached a wide clearing and slipped stiffly from the saddle. The trail, which had swung wide through the trees, inched near the rim here. The camp was some distance behind her now, invisible behind the trees save for a faint glow that might have been fires. From this vantage, she and Gelc had watched the sun rise over a Fegez camp a lifetime ago. As she watched now, stretching life into her tight muscles, a nearly full, blindingly blue-white hunter's moon topped the eastern ledges. Good. She could travel several more hours, making up for the slowness of her ride by the time she held to it. She'd be well on her way before morning.

She sighed, closed her eyes, leaned against her mount. Warm, roughly haired skin scratched agreeably against her cheek. Better start again, long enough here, and she'd sleep where she stood. The silence—without so much as a breeze to stir the statuelike blackness of the trees—was, for the moment, complete.

An owl uttered a long, twittering hoot; she started sharply as it sailed in near silence just over her head, casting a shadow across the horse's withers. She bent to check the saddle; stopped suddenly, one hand crawling across her belt to her sword hilts. Had there been wind, even the least of breezes, she'd never have caught it: Someone was riding up the trail behind her, hooves muffled on the needle-thick dust. Her heart lurched as the horse—its rider merely a dark shape—came into the glade.

Silence, save for the slow pad of the even-gaited horse. She fell back a step, had her sword half out of its sheath. The inner knowledge hit her just as the moon cleared the last of the trees on the northern ledges to shine full across the clearing.

"Bal?" The sword slipped, unnoticed, back into its sheath as her hand fell to her side. "Baldyron?"

It was, indeed, Baldyron. The horse closed the distance between them in silence. The Marcher dropped to the ground, walked slowly towards her, stopping only when he was in near reach of her.

He looked tired, tired to his bones; exhaustion pulled at his mouth, his eyes were dull with it. And since she had last seen him, he'd exchanged Korent's finely stitched green and black for the plain, rough brown of an unclaimed armsman. Stitched to the breast, however, was a small token, sewn on so roughly he might have done it himself, by firelight. She gazed at it blankly: Red and white: gules, a fret argent. Arms—but whose?

She might have spoken the word aloud. His eyes followed her gaze. "Alster's colors, thy arms."

"My—mine?" Astonished eyes caught his, dropped. "I have no arms."

"Hast them now. The King invested them."

"He said nothing to me—!"

"No. Knowing thou'd'st attempt to deny him the right—he has it, of course. And he is a very determined man, our new King. I advise thee to retain with grace what he has given thee already. And the other honors he plans thee, when we return."

"When—we—." She closed the step between them, gripped his shirt in a sudden fury. "Where *were* you these past days? *Where*? I was afraid—"

"Wast thou?" His eyes kindled, his hands covered hers. "I am sorry for that, I didn't know it. I thought—never mind. I stayed at Arolet one day behind Rolend, cleaning up a thing or two he had to leave in order to reach Sedry before too late." He hesitated. "I did not arrive until late this afternoon, and so exhausted at first I could scarcely crawl to Father's tents and sleep. Gespry's tent was gone when I arrived. I thought thou had'st gone with him." Silence. "Father told me tonight, all that chanced since I left. I was angered, then, and thought at first to leave thee alone to thy fate." He still, momentarily, sounded as furious as he must have felt. "Didst not even *ask* of me!"

"How could I?" She was no less furious than he: Her grip tightened on his shirt. "I thought you dead! Your father would not speak of you, Rolend would not speak of you, Gespry made odd noises but said nothing; what reason could I find for their behavior, save that?"

"Enough." His hands caught hers again. "We will be at each other's throats in a moment, and for no cause at all. The reason is more simple than thou'd'st think. They are displeased with me, that is all. No great matter, and no cause for concern." Silence. The owl burred its soft cry across the glade; far across the ledges came the faint squall of some kind of cat. "Do we ride further tonight, or do we stay here?"

"We?" The word registered this time. She shook her head fiercely. "No—oh, no! I do this for a reason—"

"And I do not? I know thy reason! To save Gespry's reputation, Rolend's standing with his precious Witan, would'st exile thyself—"

"Nothing of the sort," she began impatiently but subsided as he gripped her shoulders.

"We will not argue the matter, it will save thee the need of lying to me. Canst not ride alone—"

"No?" She scowled at him. "I can fend for myself."

"Hast a sworn vassal, it is only sense to take what is thine with thee." His face was grim. She opened her mouth, closed it again. "Good, that is settled. Do we ride further, or camp here tonight?"

"Korent," she protested faintly. "What of that? Your holdings? Gespry told me it was yours again—if you tell me," she added sharply, "that you refused it—!"

Bal threw back his head and laughed. "Art as bad as any of them! No. I would have. Sedry gave it to me, after all, I wanted to rid myself of the last of that. But they—"

"They?"

"King Rolend, my father, the Archbishop. Three of the most terrible men I have ever met, mind thou make'st no attempt to cross them in anything all three want! They argued until my head ached! Our new King would not listen, saying Korent was mine again for aiding him. Gespry backed him, adding that I had earned it by my aid to thee, and Father backed them both, allowing me no say of any kind. No, I did not refuse it, I had no chance at all."

"Well, then. You cannot leave it on a whim—," Elfrid began indignantly. Baldyron shook his head.

"Art not a whim, my Lady. Not," he added firmly, "to me. Korent will be well cared for in our absence. And Des—my brother Dessac—will gain valuable experience against the day Father hands him Eavon."

"You gave Korent to your brother," Elfrid said slowly. She could not piece the matter together. Her fingers wrapped tightly in his shirt, the rough cloth reassuringly real.

"No. Not as a gift. I tried *that* when I was still attempting to find a way past those three. Didn't work, of course. Dessac will hold her, but only until we return. And now," he added lightly, "for the third time, my Lady, do we ride further tonight?"

Elfrid laughed suddenly. "Bal. My Lord Baldyron. I call you by name, *mine* is Elfrid. Remember? I swear, do you call me 'my Lady' once more—!"

"A sworn vassal dare not call his sworn Lady anything else," he replied gravely, but his eyes were warm.

"No? Then I release you from that vow. Or shall I swear one to you in return? Because we ride to Gelborsedig as equals, you and I, or not at all."

The smile that lit his face erased years and fatigue alike. "Equals. Well, we have done that before, have we not? Now —that is settled, my Elfrid. Though—." Sudden doubt creased his brow. "Though—I would not force my company upon thee."

"Ah, no?" Sudden joy filled her, bubbling like laughter. "Well, then. Perhaps I had better admit that I will be most glad of it." They gazed at each other.

"Most—glad?" His hand reached, tentatively.

"Most glad." She caught his fingers hard in her own. His arms drew her close, tightened as his lips touched her brow.

She turned to her horse finally, gathered the leads from his hand. Baldyron went after his straying mount, urged it to her side. Moonlight caught them as they crossed the glade, so close together they might have touched, before they vanished into the silence and shadowed darkness of the Forest.

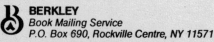